Praise for the Novels of Eli[n Hilderbrand]

The Love Season

"In a juicy peach of a summer tome, Hilderbrand again alchemizes her three favorite elements—food, love, and Nantucket—with eminently readable results. . . . *Season* is so gratifying." —*Entertainment Weekly* (Grade: A–)

"Summer fare that's a cut above the usual beach provisions . . . Hilderbrand, who wrote 2002's *Nantucket Nights*, serves up a mouthwatering menu, keeps the Veuve Clicquot flowing, and tops it all with a dollop of mystery that will have even drowsy sunbathers turning pages until the very satisfying end." —*People* (four stars)

"Hilderbrand's fifth book is a fulfilling tale of familial excavation and self-exploration. . . . It's a refreshing, resonant summertime treat."
—*Publishers Weekly*

"Hilderbrand's sensitive portrayal of a young motherless woman on a journey of self-discovery, and her guilt-ridden godmother's attempt to find the courage to confront the past, is very moving." —*Booklist*

"A good page-turner." —*Library Journal*

"As a storyteller, Hilderbrand ranks among the best, and she has ingeniously constructed this foray into the past around a meal. . . . This is a don't-miss novel." —*The Star-Ledger* (Newark)

Summer People

"Hilderbrand's third Nantucket-set novel effectively juxtaposes the surface calm of the season with the turbulence of the characters' lives. More entertaining beach reading from the author of *The Beach Club* and *Nantucket Nights*." —*Booklist*

"*Summer People* is striking not only for the ingenuity of its riveting plot, but also for the acute sense of character and the finely tuned craftsmanship with which Elin Hilderbrand brings its every nuance to life."
—Madison Smartt Bell, author of *Charm City*

"I find there is so much to admire in this book, from its crystalline prose to the deeply felt and finely rendered emotion of characters younger and older, male and female alike. By the end, the characters feel like good friends. Reading *Summer People* makes you feel like you've taken a long weekend in Nantucket. *Summer People* is simply a great read."

—Kathleen Hughes, author of *Dear Mrs. Lindbergh: A Novel*

Nantucket Nights

"Things get more twisted at every turn, with enough lies and betrayals to fuel a whole season of soap operas. . . . Readers will be hooked."

—*Publishers Weekly*

"What a perfect summer pleasure Elin Hilderbrand provides in *Nantucket Nights*, mixing the complexities of family life and friendship with suspense, romance, and moonlit Nantucket nights."

—Nancy Thayer, author of *Custody*

"Dips deep into *Peyton Place* country." —*Kirkus Reviews*

"Ms. Hilderbrand paints a picture of idyllic Nantucket life that slowly starts to unravel as the ugly underbelly is revealed. Hidden secrets, a mysterious disappearance, and the pain of betrayal form the basis for this haunting read." —*RT Book Reviews*

"The novel is fast paced and suspenseful enough to keep readers interested. A likely candidate for summer-vacation reading." —*Booklist*

The Beach Club

"Surprisingly touching . . . a work of fiction you're likely to think about long after you've put it down." —*People*

"A strong emotional pull . . . readers will remain absorbed until the surprising denouement." —*Publishers Weekly*

"A feisty novel . . . lively enough to keep a sunbather awake."

—*Kirkus Reviews*

"A charming, easygoing story about the tangled lives and loves of the summer crew and guests at a hotel and beach club." —*The Boston Globe*

"A steamy tale." —*Boston Herald*

THE
BLUE
BISTRO

Elin Hilderbrand

THE

BLUE

BISTRO

St. Martin's Griffin   New York

THE BLUE BISTRO. Copyright © 2005 by Elin Hilderbrand. All rights reserved. Printed in the United States of America. For information, address St. Martin's Press, 175 Fifth Avenue, New York, N.Y. 10010.

www.stmartins.com

Design by Kathryn Parise

The Library of Congress has cataloged the hardcover edition as follows:

Hilderbrand, Elin.
    The Blue Bistro / Elin Hilderbrand.—1st U.S. ed.
        p. cm.
    ISBN 978-0-312-31953-3
        1. Triangles (interpersonal relations)—Fiction. 2. Nantucket
Island (Mass.)—Fiction. 3. Restaurants—Employees—Fiction.
4. Restaurateurs—Fiction. 5. Restaurants—Fiction. 6. Cooks—
Fiction. I. Title.

    PS3558.I384355B55 2005
    813'6—dc22

                                                    2004065830

ISBN 978-0-312-62826-0 (trade paperback)

20 19 18 17 16 15 14

Finally, one for the kids.
To my sons, Maxwell and Dawson,
and to my goddaughter, Chloe.
Love, love, love.

Menu, Summer 2005

❦

Starters

Corn chowder with red peppers and smoked Gouda	$8
Shrimp bisque, classic Chinatown shrimp toast	$9
Blue Bistro Caesar	$6
Warm chevre over baby mixed greens with candy-striped beets	$8
Blue Bistro crab cake, Dijon cream sauce	$14
Seared foie gras, roasted figs, brioche	$16

Entrées

Steak frites	$27
Half duck with Bing cherry sauce, Boursin potato gratin, pearls of zucchini and summer squash	$32
Grilled herbed swordfish, avocado silk, Mrs. Peeke's corn spoon bread, roasted cherry tomatoes	$32
Lamb "lollipops," goat cheese bread pudding	$35

MENU, SUMMER 2005

Lobster club sandwich, green apple horseradish,
coleslaw $29

Grilled portobello and Camembert ravioli with
cilantro pesto sauce $21

Sushi plate: Seared rare tuna, wasabi aioli, sesame
sticky rice, cucumber salad with pickled ginger
and sake vinaigrette $28

Second Seating (9:00 P.M.) only

Shellfish fondue

Endless platter of shrimp, scallops,
clams. Hot oil for frying. Selection of
four sauces: classic cocktail, curry,
horseradish, green goddess $130

(4 people)

Desserts—All desserts $8

Butterscotch crème brûlée

Mr. Smith's individual blueberry pie à la mode

Fudge brownie, peanut butter ice cream

Lemon drop parfait: lemon vodka mousse layered with
whipped cream and vodka-macerated red berries

Coconut cream and roasted pineapple tart, macadamia
crust

Homemade candy plate: vanilla marshmallows, brown
sugar fudge, peanut brittle, chocolate peppermints

Executive Chef, Fiona Kemp
Pastry Chef, Mario Subiaco

Proprietor, Thatcher Smith

1

✤

Breakfast

Adrienne needed a job.

She arrived on Nantucket Island with two maxed-out credit cards, forty borrowed dollars, and three rules scribbled on an Amtrak cocktail napkin. She spent seven of the dollars on a dorm bed at the hostel in Surfside and slept with the cocktail napkin under her pillow. When she awoke the next morning in a room full of slumbering college students, she read the rules again. *Rule One: Become self-sufficient. Rule Two: Do not lie about past. Rule Three: Exercise good judgment about men.* The last thing Adrienne had done before leaving Aspen was to turn her boyfriend, Doug, in to the authorities. Doug had been living with Adrienne in the basement of the Little Nell, where Adrienne worked as a concierge; he had been stealing money from the hotel rooms to buy cocaine, and he had stolen more than two thousand dollars from Adrienne.

Adrienne quietly slipped into clothes and stashed her belongings in a locker, which was free until noon. She set out into the bright but chilly May morning with her money and the napkin, repeating a tip that a man had given her on the ferry the night before. A tip about a job.

The Blue Bistro, 27 North Beach Extension. The man who suggested this place was a freelance writer who had been coming to Nantucket for over twenty years. He came across as a normal guy, despite his square wire-rimmed glasses, thirty years out of style, and the way he licked his lips every five seconds, as though Adrienne were a T-bone steak. They had started chatting casually over the ketchup dispenser at the snack bar. He asked her if she was coming to Nantucket for a vacation. And Adrienne had laughed and said, *Hardly. I need a job. I need money.*

If it's money you want, the man had said, *the Blue Bistro is where you should go.*

I don't work in restaurants, Adrienne had said. *I work in hotels. At the front desk. I'm a hotel person.*

There's a hotel down the street from the bistro, the man had said. He paused, wet his lips. *But, like I said, if it's money you want . . .*

Adrienne walked to the North Beach Extension, stopping twice for directions. The road was quiet. There were a few houses along the way but most of them were still boarded up; one had a crew of painters working. Then, to the right, Adrienne saw a parking lot and a one-story cedar-shingled building with a green slate roof, all by itself on a stretch of windswept beach. Adrienne stopped in the road. This was the restaurant. The hotel, as the man on the ferry had described it, was down the street on the left. She should go to the hotel. But then she caught a scent of roasting meat and she thought about money. She decided it couldn't hurt to check the place out.

A sign taped to the front door read: THE BLUE BISTRO, OPENING FOR ITS FINAL SEASON JUNE 1ST. Adrienne perused the menu. The food was expensive, it sounded delicious, and her stomach complained. She'd trekked halfway across the island without any breakfast.

She peered in the dark window, wondering what she might say. She had never worked in a restaurant before; she knew nothing about the business except that it was, prostitution aside, the quickest way to make money. She supposed she could lie and say that she'd waited tables in college. She could pick up the skills once she started. Kyra, her desk manager at the Little Nell, had told her that waiting tables was a piece of cake. Nantucket had been Kyra's idea. After the whole disaster with Doug, Kyra suggested that Adrienne get as far away from the Rocky Mountains as possible. *If it's money you want, Nantucket is where you should go.*

Adrienne tried the door. Locked. She tapped on a windowpane. *Hello?*

She felt like the Little Match Girl, hungry and tired, bereft and friendless. *Can you save me?*

She thought of her father, at that minute probably elbow deep in a root canal. Since Adrienne's mother died, his concern for Adrienne's well-being seemed so heavy as to actually pull the corners of his mouth into a frown. He worried about her all the time. He worried that she was too adventurous, working in all these exotic locales where the men weren't necessarily principled. And he was right to worry. He was so right that Adrienne hadn't been able to tell him how guests of the Little Nell had been complaining about cash missing from their rooms and about how Kyra had interrogated the battalion of Mexican chambermaids. When the chambermaids proved a dead end, Kyra had come to Adrienne and asked if she had any idea who might be taking the money. Adrienne was confused about why Kyra was asking *her* but then, somehow, she realized that Kyra meant Doug. Doug, who had lost his job in February and whose behavior was becoming increasingly erratic. Doug, who traveled down-valley several times a week to visit a "friend" in Carbondale. Adrienne had snuck down to their basement apartment while she was supposed to be at work. She found her hotel master key card in the pocket of Doug's ski jacket. And then, on a second dreadful hunch, she checked the tampon box where she saved her tips, the money for her Future, which she had always thought of with a capital "F"—money for something bigger and better down the road, a house, a wedding, a business. The box was empty. He had stolen her Future; he had snorted it. Instead of killing Doug herself, Adrienne followed Kyra's advice and called the Pitkin County police. They caught him robbing the Alpine Suite in the middle of the day. He was arrested for larceny and possession, and Adrienne left town in the midst of his court proceedings, flat broke.

She had only asked her father for a small loan—two hundred dollars—enough to get her back east on the train and set up someplace else. But he must have sensed something in her voice, because he sent her three hundred, no questions asked.

Adrienne heard someone shout, "Hey!" She whipped around. A man was striding toward her from a silver pickup truck in the parking lot. She smiled at him, squinting in a way that she hoped conveyed her innocence. *I'm not trying to rob you. I just want . . . a job?* When he got closer, she saw he had red-gold hair and freckles—he was a man who looked like a twelve-year-old boy. His hand shot out as though he'd been expecting her.

"Thatcher Smith," he said. "Thatch."

"Oh. Uh." Adrienne was so nervous, she couldn't remember her name. The man raised his pale eyebrows expectantly, waiting for her to identify herself. "Adrienne."

"Adrienne?"

"Dealey."

"Adrienne Dealey." His tone of voice said, *Of course, Adrienne Dealey,* like they had an appointment. "Can I help you, Adrienne?"

Adrienne opened her mouth but no sound came out. So much for knocking them dead with her confidence and charm.

Thatcher Smith laughed. A short, one-syllable "ha!" Loud and spontaneous, as if she had karate-chopped his funny bone. "Cat got your tongue?"

"I guess," she said. "Sorry. I came for a job. Is there an application or something I can fill out?"

"Application?" He looked at her in a strange but pleasant way, as though he'd never heard the word before.

"Don't you work here?" Adrienne asked.

"I own here."

"Oh." The *owner*? Adrienne took another look at this guy. He was about six feet tall with sloping shoulders, strawberry blond hair, green eyes, freckles. He wore jeans, running shoes, a red fleece jacket that was almost too bright to look at in the morning sun. She couldn't tell if he resembled Huckleberry Finn or if it was just the name, Thatcher—like Becky Thatcher—that summoned the image. He had a clean, friendly Midwestern vibe about him. He wasn't handsome so much as wholesome looking. Adrienne corrected her posture and cleared her throat. She was so destitute it was hard to feel impressive. "Would it be okay if I filled out an application, then?"

"We don't have any applications. It's not that kind of place. I do all the hiring face-to-face. What kind of job are you after? Front of the house? Back of the house? Because I can tell you right now, we're not hiring any back of the house."

Adrienne had no idea what he was talking about. She was after money, a thick wad of twenties she could roll out like a Mafia boss.

"I thought maybe I could wait tables?"

"Do you have any experience?" Thatcher asked.

I waited tables in college, she thought. But she couldn't make herself say it.

"None," she said. "But I'm willing to learn. Someone told me it's a piece of cake."

Thatcher laughed again—"ha!" He moved past her to the door of the restaurant and took a giant ring of keys from his jacket pocket. Adrienne noticed a wooden dory by the front of the restaurant filled with fresh soil. They probably grew flowers in the dory all summer. That was a nice touch. This was a nice restaurant. Too nice for Adrienne. If she wanted to be self-sufficient, she would have to sell her laptop.

"Never mind," Adrienne said. "Thanks for your time."

She turned to leave, making an alternate plan of attack. Back to the road, down the street to the hotel. After she filled out an application there, she would have to surrender some of her money for breakfast.

"You understand?" Thatcher said. "I can't exactly hire you to wait tables when you've had no experience."

"I understand," Adrienne said. "I was just checking. Someone I met on the boat told me how great your restaurant was. He also said there's a hotel down here?"

"The Nantucket Beach Club and Hotel," Thatcher said. "But Mack won't hire you without experience either."

"I have hotel experience," Adrienne said. "I just came from Aspen. I worked at the Little Nell."

Thatcher's pale eyebrows shot up. "The Little Nell?"

She nodded. "You've heard of it?"

"Of course, yeah. What did you do there?"

"Front desk," she said. "Concierge."

Thatcher pointed his head at the open door. "Are you hungry?" The door of the restaurant swung open. "I was going to have an omelet. Would you like to join me?"

Adrienne glanced back at the sandy road. She should go. An omelet, though, sounded tempting. "I don't know," she said.

"Oh, come on," Thatcher said. "I hate to eat alone." He ushered Adrienne in. The roasting meat and garlic smell was so overpowering that Adrienne nearly fell to her knees in hunger. What had she had for dinner last night on the ferry? A hotdog that had spent seven hours spinning on a rack and a cup of gluey clam chowder.

"Someone's cooking?" she said.

"My partner," Thatcher said. "She never sleeps. Follow me. I'll give you the grand tour."

When they stepped inside the front door, Adrienne was overcome with anxiety. She checked her watch, a jogging watch with an altimeter. It was just after ten o'clock; she was three feet above sea level. What was she doing? She had to find a job today. Still, she trailed Thatcher, trying to seem polite and interested. *Free food,* she thought. *Omelet.*

Thatcher stopped at an oak podium. "This is the host station, where we greet guests and make reservations. We have two public phone lines and a private line. The private line is very private, but sometimes guests get ahold of it. Don't ask me how."

He led her past a bar topped with a shiny slab of blue-gray stone. "Now here," he said proudly, "is our blue granite bar. We found the stone in a quarry in northern Vermont." The wall behind the bar was stocked with bottles on oak shelves. "We only sell call and top shelf. I don't ever want to drink Popov and I don't want my guests drinking it. Not in here," Thatcher said. There were two small tables in the bar area and a black baby grand piano. "We have live music six nights a week. My guy knows everything from Rogers and Hart to Nirvana." Down two steps was the dining room, maybe twenty tables, all with views of the ocean. The restaurant had no walls—it was open from the waist up. In winter, Adrienne could see, they hung plastic sheeting to keep the wind and sand out. There was an awning skeleton off the back. They placed six tables under the awning on a deck, Thatcher said, and four four-tops out in the sand under the stars.

"Those are the fondue tables," he said. "It makes a royal mess."

They returned to the bar, where the tables were set with white tablecloths, china, silver, wineglasses. Thatcher indicated Adrienne should sit.

"Let me take your jacket," he said.

"I'll keep it on," Adrienne said.

"You're going to eat with your *jacket* on?" he said.

She handed him her purple Patagonia Gore-tex that she'd bought with an employee discount from the ski shop at the Little Nell, and lowered herself daintily into a white wicker chair, as though she were accustomed to having breakfast in glamorous bistros like this all the time. Thatcher hung up her jacket then disappeared into the back, leaving Adrienne alone.

"The Blue Bistro," she said to herself. This was the kind of place that Doug would have called, disparagingly, "gourmet"; if it wasn't deep-fried or residing between two pieces of bread, Doug didn't want to eat it. Prison food would suit him fine.

Adrienne took a white napkin off her plate and unfolded it on her lap. She lifted the fork; it was heavy, beautiful silver. And the charger—she flipped it over. Limoges. She replaced the plate quickly—this was the restaurant equivalent of checking someone's medicine cabinet. Before she could inspect the pedigree of the stemware, Thatcher was back with two glasses of juice.

"Fresh-squeezed," he said. "The last of the blood oranges." He set the glasses down then disappeared again.

Adrienne eyed her glass. "The last of the blood oranges," she whispered. The juice was the fiery pink of some rare jewel. Was it okay to take a sip before he got back? Adrienne listened for noises from the kitchen. It was silent. She took a deep breath. The air smelled like something else now: toast. *Hunger and thirst,* she thought. *They'd get you every time.* Thatcher hurried out of the kitchen with two plates and set one in front of Adrienne with a flourish, as though she were someone very important.

It was the best omelet Adrienne had ever eaten. Perfectly cooked so that the eggs were soft and buttery. Filled with sautéed onions and mushrooms and melted Camembert cheese. There were three roasted cherry tomatoes on the plate, skins splitting, oozing juice. Nutty wheat toast. Thatch had brought butter and jam to the table. The butter was served like a tiny cheesecake on a small pedestal under a glass dome. The jam was apricot, homemade, served from a Ball jar.

Adrienne dug in, wondering where to start in the way of conversation. She decided the only safe thing was to talk about the food.

"This jam reminds me of when I was little," Adrienne said, spreading a thick layer on her toast. "My mother made jam."

"Is she a good cook?" Thatcher said.

"Who?"

"Your mother."

Adrienne paused. *Rule Two: Do not lie about past!* But it was hard when someone hurled a question at her like a pitch she couldn't hit.

"Yes."

For Adrienne, the silence that followed was studded with guilt. She should have just said, "She was," but then, by necessity, there would be tedious personal explanations about ovarian cancer and a motherless twelve-year-old that she was never in the mood for. She would rather talk about her felonious ex-boyfriend and her empty Future. *It's okay,* she thought. She would never see this guy again after today and she vowed she would tell the truth to the next person she met. Her mother was dead.

"Well," Adrienne said. "This is the most delicious breakfast I've ever had in my life."

"I'll tell Fee," he said. "She likes to feed people."

Adrienne ate every bite of her eggs and mopped up the tomato juices with her bread crust and drained her juice glass, thinking to herself—*Manners, manners! Turn the fork upside down on the plate when you're finished, very European.* If nothing else, this would make a great e-mail to her father. Her first morning on Nantucket she ends up eating a breakfast of champions in a restaurant that wasn't even *open.*

She collapsed in her chair, drunk with food, in love with this restaurant. If she ever caught up enough to pay off her credit cards and refund her father with interest, she'd come here for dinner and order the foie gras. "Why is it your last season?" she asked.

"Ahhh," Thatcher said. He pushed away his plate—half his omelet remained and Adrienne stared at it, wondering how audacious it would be to ask if she might finish it. Thatcher propped his elbows on the table and tented his fingers. Even his fingers, Adrienne noticed, were freckled. "The time has come."

The time has come? That was a noncommittal answer, an art form Adrienne wished she could perfect. So she, too, had asked a tricky question. In the interest of changing the subject, Adrienne offered up something else.

"I just got here last night."

"You've never been to the island before?"

"Never."

"You came straight from Aspen?"

"I did."

"I'm intrigued by the Little Nell. They say it's the best."

"One of. Relais and Chateaux and all that. They gave me housing."

"In the hotel?"

"Yes."

"That must have been sweet."

"It was okay," Adrienne said. She and Doug had lived in a studio apartment with his retriever, Jax, even though pets weren't allowed. No pets, no drugs, no stealing from the rooms!

"Did you go out at night?" Thatcher asked.

"Sometimes."

"My bartender here, Duncan, works at the Board Room in Aspen all winter. You ever go there?"

"Sometimes."

"So you know Duncan?"

Adrienne tried not to smile. She knew Duncan. Every single woman between the ages of twenty-one and thirty-nine who had been in Aspen for more than five minutes knew Duncan from the Board Room. There had actually been a picture of him in *Aspen* magazine making an espresso martini. Kyra had been *dying* to sleep with him, and so she dragged Adrienne to the Board Room during the week when she guessed the bar would be less crowded—but it was three deep from après ski until close. It drove Doug crazy. He not only disliked gourmet, he disliked *popular*. Still, Adrienne and Kyra went so often that Duncan began to remember their drinks—a cosmo for Kyra and a glass of champagne for Adrienne. He knew everyone's drinks.

"He works *here*?"

"He's the best bartender on the island," Thatcher said. "Maybe in the whole country. All the men want to get him for golf and all the women want to get him into bed."

"That sounds right," said Adrienne.

"Where else have you worked?" Thatcher asked.

"All over," she said. "The Princeville in Kauai, the Mar-a-Lago in

Palm Beach. The Chatham Bars Inn. And I spent a year in Thailand."

"Thailand?"

"Koh Samui," she said, thinking of Kip Turnbull, another one of her poor companionship choices. "Chaweng Beach. Have you ever been there?"

"I haven't been anywhere," he said. "But that will change. As soon as we close this place, I'm taking Fee to the Galápagos. She wants to see the funny birds."

"Is she your wife?"

Thatcher drained his juice glass then spun it absentmindedly on the table. Maybe he hadn't heard her. Maybe it was another trick question. Or maybe it was like when her father's patients asked Adrienne if Mavis, the hygienist, was her *mother*. Not worth answering. Adrienne noticed Thatcher wasn't wearing a wedding ring.

"So you came here for a job," he said. "But you have no restaurant experience. None? Not even Pizza Hut?"

"Not even Pizza Hut," she said. She envisioned herself with a tray piled high with dishes and food, glasses and drinks. She would drop it. "I don't know what I was thinking." She had been thinking of money, of Rule One: *Become self-sufficient*. But she didn't belong here; she belonged down the street, at the hotel. The hotel front desk was the right place for Adrienne. The pay wasn't great, but housing was almost always included. It wasn't loud or messy or hot. And the transience of a hotel suited her. All through high school she had worked as a receptionist in her father's dental offices (three offices in ten years and now he was somewhere new again—the eastern shore of Maryland). She had attended two high schools and three colleges. Since her mother died, Adrienne's life had been like a hotel. She checked in, she stayed for a while, she checked out. "I mean, don't get me wrong. This place is lovely and the food is amazing. I'll come back for dinner once I have some . . ."

"Money?" Thatcher said.

"Friends," she said.

Thatcher poked the uneaten portion of his omelet with his fork. "We open next week," he said. "We'll be booked solid for two seatings every night in July and August. Maybe, *maybe*, on a Monday night in June you can get a table without a reservation. By eleven o'clock every night the bar is full and I have to put someone at the door. I have to hire a bouncer, *here*, at a high-end *bistro* because there is always a line out into the parking lot. People get in fistfights over cutting in line, like they're in fifth grade. I try to tell the people, 'It's just a cocktail.' Ditto for dinner reservations. 'It's just a dinner. Just one night in the landscape of your *whole life*.' But what I have grown to realize is that it's more than just a cocktail and more than just dinner. They want to be a part of the scene. And how can I deny them that? This place . . ." He swept his arm in a circle. "Has magic."

Adrienne might have laughed. She might have thought Thatcher Smith was full of himself, but she had been here for thirty minutes. She had eaten the best breakfast of her life and now she couldn't even sit up, much less bring herself to leave.

"You must be good at what you do," Adrienne said.

"Fee is good at what she does," Thatcher said. "She's the best. The best, best, best. And we got lucky." He pressed his eyes closed for a long second, like he was praying. Then he collected their plates. "Fee will want these."

"I should go," Adrienne said. She grabbed the armrests of the wicker chair; she was positively slouching. "I have to find something today."

Thatcher held up a palm. "Wait, please. Please wait . . . thirty seconds. I have an idea. Will you wait?"

She didn't have to move just yet. She would wait.

"Back in thirty seconds." He gathered every dirty dish and utensil from the table, as well as the cake of butter and the jam that had caused Adrienne to break Rule Two, and balanced them on an outstretched arm. He vanished into the kitchen. Adrienne listened. If he was talking to this Fee person, she wanted to know what he was saying. It was silent, except for the sound of the ocean. She closed her eyes. She could hear the ocean. And then Thatcher's voice.

"This is the most popular restaurant on Nantucket. It has been for ten years. The food is delicious, the food is fun. It's a fun place to eat. It is see and be seen. It is laugh and talk and sing in here every night of the summer. The Blue Bistro is what a summer night on this island is all about, okay?" He was standing in front of the table.

"I can tell it's a special place," Adrienne said. "Really, I can."

"It just so happens, I got a phone call this morning from my assistant manager who spent the winter in Manhattan. He told me he's not coming back," Thatcher said. "And so now I have a gaping hole in the front of the house. I need someone to answer the phone, work the book, arrange a seating chart, learn the guests, make everyone feel not just welcome, you know, but *loved.* Keep track of the waitstaff, the wine, the requests for the piano player. Stroke the VIP tables—birthdays, anniversaries, the whole shebang. I need someone to be me. I need . . . another . . . me." He laughed again—"ha!" Like he knew what he'd just said was ludicrous. "And when you first asked, I thought, *Who in their right mind would give a* manager's *position to someone without a day of restaurant experience?* That would be foolish. Bad business! But now I'm thinking that what I need is someone with concierge skills. I need someone who understands old-fashioned service."

"I do understand old-fashioned service," Adrienne said. Hadn't she warmed towels in the dryer for guests with a newborn baby at the Princeville? Hadn't she finagled a veterinarian appointment for a couple with a sick parrot at the Mar-a-Lago? Hadn't she arranged for private lighthouse tours while at the Chatham Bars Inn?

"Most of my staff has been here since we opened twelve years ago. They love it here. They love it because Fee puts out the best family meal on the is-land and at midnight she sends out homemade crackers. Ninety-nine percent of the world think that crackers only come out of a box, and then here's Fee sending out baskets of hot, crisp cheese crackers and after eight hours of busting their asses and raking in three, four hundred bucks, the staff gets first dibs—and that's why they want to work here. Because of the crackers. And the money, of course." He grinned at Adrienne. "This is our last hurrah. The end of an era. I need someone *good.* I've never hired a woman for this position before. I've never hired someone without any restaurant back-ground. But I'm not afraid to try. Well, to be honest, I am a little afraid."

"Wait a second," Adrienne said. She was confused. What was happening here? Was he offering her a job?

She glanced around the restaurant. Even through the plastic sheeting the ocean was brilliant blue. It made her head spin. That and the food smells and this man who was like nobody she'd ever met before. He was as honest and as nutty as the toast.

"Your second is up," Thatcher said. "Do you want the job?"

Did she want the job? It would be a huge risk, but something about that appealed to her. Not a single decision she had made in the past six years had worked out all that well, and she had promised herself on the train east that Nantucket would be different. Working here would be really different. She was so busy thinking, *Should I say yes, should I say no,* that she never actually gave Thatcher Smith an answer, but he didn't seem to notice.

"Good," he said. His face came alive; it looked like his freckles were dancing. "You're hired."

TO: DrDon@toothache.com
FROM: Ade12177@hotmail.com
DATE: May 24, 2005, 3:54 P.M.
SUBJECT: The Blue Bistro

Found a job. You're going to freak out so close the door to your office and sit down, okay? I took a job in a restaurant. Not waiting tables! Not cooking (obviously)! I am going to be the assistant manager at a place called the Blue Bistro. It's a French-American menu, four dollar signs, right on the beach. Owned by a very nice guy named Thatcher Smith. His partner, Fiona, is the chef and she's famous, but she's a recluse. Never comes out of the kitchen. I haven't even met her—though I will, I guess, soon enough.

I'm making twenty-five an hour—can you believe *that*? But I don't start for another week and I need to buy some clothes and pay my first month's rent. Is there any chance you might wire me a thousand dollars, please, sweet Dad? I am trying to put some structure in my life, and this time I will pay you back with interest, I promise!

I rented a room in a cottage from one of the women who waits tables at the restaurant. Her name is Caren. She's waited tables since the place opened and she makes so much money in the summer that after Christmas she goes down to St. Bart's for the winter and she doesn't have to work. She said the job I have is harder to get than a seat on the space shuttle.

How do you like the eastern shore? Eaten any crab cakes? Love.

TO: Ade12177@hotmail.com
FROM: DrDon@toothache.com
DATE: May 24, 2005, 5:09 P.M.
SUBJECT: You Blue Me Away

No crab cakes yet. We're still getting settled in. The schmo in here before me made a mess of his records and the bookkeeper said she can't untangle his billing. But we'll figure it out. We always do.

About your new job. Mavis says restaurants are dangerous places to work. Sexual harassment and the like. Foul language in the kitchen. Alcohol. Drugs. Everybody suffering from too much cash money. These are not people who floss, honey. (And that's a joke, but you know what I mean.) Be careful! You're an adult and I know you like the way you live but I am growing older by the day fretting about the situations you get yourself into. Which brings me to the question of money. I won't go on about how you're twenty-eight years old or about how I'm not your personal bank. I will just wire you the thousand dollars as long as you promise me that one of these days you'll pick a place and settle down. Love, love.

TO: DrDon@toothache.com
FROM: Ade12177@hotmail.com
DATE: May 24, 2005, 7:22 P.M.
SUBJECT: none

You're one to talk!!!

TO: Ade12177@hotmail.com
FROM: DrDon@toothache.com
DATE: May 25, 2005, 8:15 A.M.
SUBJECT: I'm Blue without you

Just please, please be careful. Love, love, love.

Adrienne felt like one of the born-again Christians on early Sunday morning TV. She had been saved! New job, decent, affordable housing, complete with Internet and a used ten-speed bike. The first morning in her new bed she lay with her eyes closed and banished Doug Riedel from her mind once and for all. In the six months of their dating, he had lied to her about his drug use and stolen all her money. But it hadn't been all bad. At the bottom of her trunk rested a lovely pair of shearling gloves that Doug had given her when they first started dating, and there had been some nice walks, the two of them throwing Jax sticks along the snowy banks of the Frying Pan River. Adrienne felt some white noise coming from her heart, but she sensed it was because she missed Jax. She loved that dog.

So it was good-bye and good riddance to another man, another town, another phase of her life. Nantucket would be the start of sound decision-making, a healthy lifestyle, the straight and narrow. Adrienne loved the island already—the historic downtown homes with their lilac bushes and their snapping flags; the wild, pristine beaches. It was so easy to breathe here.

Adrienne's new housemate, Caren Friar, had been a waiter at the Blue Bistro since the beginning. (When they first met, Adrienne made the mistake of calling her a waitress and Caren curtly corrected her—*Waitresses worked at diners in the 1950s, okay? This is fine dining and I bust my ass as hard as any man out there. . . .*) Caren was tall and extremely thin. She had been with a ballet company in New York City for three years before she accepted that she was never going to make a living at it. That's when she got sucked into what she called the life of hash and cash. Caren had a long, graceful neck, regal posture, a way of floating from place to place rather than walking. She wore her dark auburn hair in a bun so tight it made Adrienne's head ache just to look at it. Caren knew the ropes at the bistro—she knew the dirt on every person who ate there and every person who worked there—and although Adrienne was dying to mine the woman for information, most pressingly about the chef, Fiona, she intuited that she should proceed with caution.

Adrienne had already done a little bit of research on her own. The day she was hired, she dug up three articles about the Blue Bistro from the magazine archives of the public library: one in *Cape Cod Life* (August 1997), one in *Bon Appétit* (June 2000), and one in *Travel & Leisure* (May 2003). The articles offered variations on the same information: The Blue Bistro was wildly popular because it was the only restaurant on the beach on Nantucket and because of the food. *T & L* called the food "consistently delightful . . . Fiona Kemp is one of the most talented chefs in New England today." *Cape Cod Life* said, "Fiona Kemp never does interviews but her plates speak volumes. . . . She is a master at giving every diner an unforgettable taste experience." Each article referred to Thatcher and Fiona as partners and *Bon Appétit* mentioned that they had grown up together in South Bend, Indiana. Fiona attended the Culinary Institute of America in Hyde Park, New York, and she landed her first job as a line cook at the Wauwinet Inn on Nantucket. Thatcher was quoted as saying, "She convinced me to come out to the island for a visit in 1992. She had found a great spot for a restaurant. Once I saw it, I decided to leave the family business in South Bend behind. We were up and running the following year." Thatcher went on to explain how, the first two summers, they struggled to get the menu right. "We were trying to make the food really grand. It took us a while to figure out that fancy French food wasn't the answer. The answer was simple, fresh, fun. Food you'd want to eat on the beach." A photograph of Thatcher appeared in each article—Thatcher holding up a bowl of coral-colored soup, Thatcher in a white wicker chair grinning in a Notre Dame baseball cap. And the most surprising was a photo of Thatcher in a navy blazer and red paisley tie standing behind the oak podium. It was Huck Finn, all gussied up. There were no pictures of Fiona.

Caren had rented the same two-bedroom cottage on Hooper Farm Road for as many years as she'd worked at the restaurant and she took a roommate every year. Thatcher had asked Caren—as a favor to him—to rent the spare bedroom to Adrienne. Adrienne had been forced upon her, basically, because nobody turned Thatcher down and certainly not in the final year, when there might be a farewell bonus for loyal employees to consider. Adrienne was just happy for housing, and not only housing, but company. In the morning, Adrienne and Caren sat at the kitchen table drinking espresso. The following night was the first night of work, the soft opening. Adrienne was unsure of what to wear. She had two trunks of clothes from her days on the front desk, but somehow looking nice-at-a-day-job clothing didn't seem suitable for representing the front of the house at the hottest restaurant on Nantucket. She asked Caren.

"The other assistant managers have all been men," Caren said. "They dressed like Thatch."

"He wears a coat and tie?" Adrienne said.

"A tie if there's somebody big on the books. Otherwise he wears blazers and shirts from Thomas Pink. And Gucci loafers, a new pair every year. At first, he couldn't stand the idea of spending three hundred bucks on shoes, coming from Indiana and all, but he grew into it, and now his loafers are a part of the whole show. They're as much of an institution as the blue granite and the crackers."

"I heard about the crackers," Adrienne said.

"Let's look in your closet," Caren said. "Another espresso?"

"No, thanks," Adrienne said. The espresso machine was Caren's. She hauled it between Nantucket and St. Bart's the same way Adrienne schlepped her laptop. Caren even owned a set of demitasse cups and saucers. It was a very sophisticated setup except Adrienne discovered she didn't like espresso. It tasted like a cross between gasoline and tree bark, but she'd accepted a cup to be polite and now that the caffeine was coursing through her blood, she was ready to leap out of her skin. Soft opening tomorrow night! She needed to find something to wear!

As she feared, Caren deemed every item of clothing Adrienne owned too frumpy, too corporate, too Banana Republic. "You've worked in resorts for six years," Caren said, "and you haven't learned how to *shop*?"

Caren took her to Gypsy on Main Street where Adrienne's pulse reached an unsafe speed. The clothes were so gorgeous, and so expensive, that Adrienne thought she was going to pass out.

"We have to go someplace else," Adrienne said. "I can't afford any of this."

"Oh, come on," Caren said. "You're going to be making more money than you know what to do with."

"I doubt that," Adrienne said. Still, she mustered enough courage to browse the sale rack, and there she found two pairs of silk pants and a stunning Chloe dress that was marked down 70 percent. Adrienne put the dress back but bought both pairs of pants; then, at the last minute, she decided to try the dress on.

Caren whistled. "You can't pass that one up."

Adrienne scowled at herself in the mirror. Becoming self-sufficient did not mean spending exorbitant amounts of money on last year's designer clothing. She would probably get fired her first week and end up living in the back of a junkyard car . . . but no, she couldn't pass the dress up.

Adrienne bought the dress, her hand trembling as she signed the credit card slip, a combination of the price and the espresso. Once she had enough clothes to get her through the weekend, she felt better about starting this new life. This, after all, was what she had needed. A clean slate. A chance to get it just right.

2

❧

Menu Meeting

"Let's pretend for twenty minutes of every day that the restaurant business is about food," Thatcher said.

Adrienne wrote on a yellow legal pad: "Restaurant = food." She sat at one end of a very long table, a twelve-top, in the dining room with the rest of the staff—five waiters; three bussers; the bartender, Duncan; and a young female bar back. Thatcher was the professor. Adrienne was the nerdy kid who took too many notes—but Thatcher had asked her to *Please absorb every word I say*, so that this, the soft opening, might go as smoothly as possible.

The dining room had been completely transformed since the morning of her breakfast. The wood floors had been polished, the wicker chairs had been cleaned, the plastic sheeting was rolled up so that every table had an unimpeded view of the gold sand beach and Nantucket Sound. Landscapers had planted red and pink geraniums in the window boxes that lined the outer walls of the restaurant and in the wooden dory out front. All of the tables were set for service and the waiters (three veterans, two newcomers) had arrived early to polish the glasses. The waiters wore black pants, crisp white shirts, and long white aprons. The busboys and the bar back wore black pants and white oxfords. Duncan wore khakis, a blue silk shirt, a sailboat-print tie, and black soccer sneakers. Adrienne had decided on her new pink silk pants with a gauzy white top and a pair of Kate Spade slides that she bought off the sale rack at Neiman's in Denver. Her black hair was short enough that she only had to blow it dry and fluff it. She would have looked okay except that morning had been so sunny and warm that she had headed off to the beach. She came home sunburned, and when she applied her fuchsia lipstick it matched not only her toenail polish and her new pants, but the stripe across her cheeks and the bridge of her nose. Ten minutes ago, when she'd arrived, Thatcher had narrowed his eyes at her (just the way her father would if he could see her). She was certain she was going to get a word about sunscreen.

"Diaphanous top on the first night," he said. "Gutsy. I like it. What size are you?"

Was this any of his business? "A six."

He nodded. "The shoes won't work, though." He checked his watch—she thought it was a Patek Philippe. "But you don't have time to go home and change. Sorry. Menu meeting at table nine, right now." He handed her the yellow legal pad. "Please absorb every word I say. You're trailing me tonight. Soft opening. That means friends of the house. Nobody gets a bill for anything but alcohol, and everything has to be as close to perfect as possible. Then, tomorrow night, close isn't going to cut it."

Now he was lecturing. The professor in his Gucci loafers and twenty-thousand-dollar watch. Everyone around the table sat in rapt attention. This was the big time. The Harvard Business School of resort dining.

"I thought Fee might come out and tell you about the food, but she's in the weeds back there. No additions tonight. There are a lot of our standards on this year's menu but there's some new stuff, too, and since we have two new waitpeople, two new bussers, and a new assistant manager, and since the rest of you spent all winter skiing bumps or sizzling in the equatorial sun, I'm going to run through the menu with you now. Everyone's met Adrienne Dealey, right?" Thatcher held out his arm to introduce Adrienne and the staff turned to look at her. She blushed on top of her sunburn. "On the floor, Adrienne is going to be my second in command, taking over for Kevin who conned his way into the maître d' job at Craft in New York. As some of you know, Fee and I might be gone more often this summer than we've been in years past. And Adrienne is going to run the floor in my stead and alongside of me. But let's give her a week or two to learn what it is we do here. She has never worked in a restaurant before. Not even Pizza Hut."

Adrienne was sure she heard groans. But then one of the waiters, shiny-bald, black square glasses, said, "Let's welcome, Adrienne."

"Welcome, Adrienne," the rest of the staff echoed.

Adrienne smiled at her yellow legal pad. She heard someone say, "You drink champagne." She looked up. Duncan was pointing at her.

She nodded, overcome with a bizarre shyness. He remembered her. Hopefully, he didn't remember her as the woman whose boyfriend had been ripping off the esteemed patrons of the Little Nell.

"You drink champagne?" Thatcher said. "That gives me an idea. Make a note to ask me about champagne. Now, let's pretend for *eighteen* minutes that the restaurant business is about food."

Adrienne never worked in restaurants, but she loved to eat in them. Until her mother died of ovarian cancer when Adrienne was twelve, her family had lived in Valley Forge, Pennsylvania, and her father ran a successful dental practice in King of Prussia. They used to eat out all the time—at the original Bookbinders in downtown Philadelphia, the City Tavern, and her mother was a sucker for all of the new, funky cafés on South Street. What was it Adrienne loved about restaurants? The napkins folded like flowers, the Shirley Temples with maraschino cherries speared on a plastic sword, seeing her endless reflection in the mirrors of the ladies' room. The pastel mints in a bowl by the front door.

After her mother died and Adrienne and her father took up with wander-lust, Adrienne became exposed to new foods. For two years they lived in Maine, where in the summertime they ate lobster and white corn and small wild blueberries. They moved to Iowa for Adrienne's senior year of high school and they ate pork tenderloin fixed seventeen different ways. Adrienne did her first two years of college at Indiana University in Blooming-ton, where she lived above a Mexican cantina, which inspired a love of tamales and anything doused with habanero sauce. Then she transferred to Vanderbilt in Nashville, where she ate the best fried chicken she'd ever had in her life. And so on, and so on. Pad thai in Bangkok, stone crabs in Palm Beach, buffalo meat in Aspen. As she sat listening to Thatcher, she realized that though she knew nothing about restaurants, at least she knew some-thing about food.

"This year, as every year, the first thing that hits the table—after the cocktails—is the bread basket." There was an appreciative moan, and Caren arched her eyebrows at Adrienne from across the table. "The bread basket is one of two things. Bruno! Go into the kitchen and get me two baskets, one of each, please." The bald waiter zipped into the kitchen. *Bruno*. Adrienne mentally pinned the name to him. Bald Bruno, who had welcomed her earlier. His voice had a little bit of a sashay to it, like he was from the south or was gay. She would ask Caren later.

Bruno reappeared with two baskets swathed in white linen napkins and a ramekin of something bright yellow.

Thatcher unveiled one basket. "Pretzel bread," he said. He held up a thick braid of what looked to be soft pretzel, nicely tanned, sprinkled with coarse salt. "This is served with Fee's homemade mustard. So right away the guest knows this isn't a run-of-the-mill restaurant. They're not getting half a cold baguette, here, folks, with butter in the gold foil wrapper. This is warm pretzel bread made on the premises, and the mustard ditto. Nine out of ten tables are licking the ramekin clean." He handed the bread basket to a waiter with a blond ponytail (male—everyone at the table was male except for Adrienne, Caren, and the young bar back who was hanging on to Duncan's arm). The ponytailed waiter—name?—tore off a hunk of bread and dipped it in the mustard. He rolled his eyes like he was having an orgasm. *The appropriate response*, Adrienne thought. But remembering her breakfast she guessed he wasn't faking it.

"The other basket contains our world-famous savory doughnuts," Thatcher said. He whipped the cloth off like a magician, revealing six golden-brown doughnuts. Doughnuts? Adrienne had been too nervous to think about eating all day, but now her appetite was roused. After the menu meeting, they were going to have family meal.

The doughnuts were deep-fried rings of a light, yeasty, herb-flecked dough. Chive, basil, rosemary. Crisp on the outside, soft on the inside. Savory doughnuts. Who wouldn't stand in line for these? Who wouldn't beg or steal to access the private phone line so that they could make a date with these doughnuts?

"If someone wants bread and butter—and it happens every night—we also offer warm Portuguese rolls. But the guest has to ask for it. Most people will be eating out of your hand after these goodies."

Thatcher disappeared into the kitchen. Seconds later, he was out, carrying another plate. "All VIPs get the same canapé," he said. "Years ago, Fee knocked herself out dreaming up precious little *amuses-bouches,* but then we came up with the winner. Chips and dip." He set the plate on the table next to Adrienne and she nearly wept with gratitude. He was standing beside her now, so she could study his watch. Her suspicions were confirmed: It was a Patek Philippe, silver, rectangular face, black leather band. The watch matched Thatcher's shoes, the Gucci loafers, black with sleek silver buckles. Adrienne had to admit, when he was dressed up, the man had a certain elegance. "You're getting the idea, now, right? We have pretzels and mustard. We have doughnuts. And if we really, really like you, we have chips and dip. This is fun food. It isn't stuffy. It isn't going to make anyone nervous. The days of the waiter as a snob, the days of the menu as an *exam* the guest has to *pass* are over. But at the same time, we're not talking about cellophane bags here, are we? These are hand-cut potato chips with crème fraîche and a dollop of beluga caviar. This is the gift we send out. It's better than Christmas."

He offered the plate to Adrienne and she helped herself to a long, golden chip. She scooped up a tiny amount of the glistening black caviar. Just tasting it made her feel like a person of distinction.

Adrienne hoped the menu meeting might continue in this vein—with the staff tasting each ambrosial dish. But there wasn't time; service started in thirty minutes. Thatcher wanted to get through the menu.

"The corn chowder and the shrimp bisque are cream soups, but neither of these soups is heavy. The Caesar is served with pumpernickel croutons and white anchovies. The chevre salad is your basic mixed baby greens with a round of breaded goat cheese, and the candy-striped beets are grown locally at Bartlett Farm. Ditto the rest of the vegetables, except for the portobello mushrooms that go into the ravioli—those are flown in from Kennett Square, Pennsylvania. So when you're talking about vegetables, you're talking about produce that's grown in Nantucket soil, okay? It's not sitting for thirty-six hours on the back of a truck. Fee selects them herself before any of you people are even *awake* in the morning. It's all very Alice Waters, what we do here with our vegetables." Thatcher clapped his hands. He was revving up, getting ready for the big game. In the article in *Bon Appétit,* Thatcher had mentioned that the only thing he loved more than his restaurant was college football.

"Okay, okay!" he shouted. It wasn't a menu meeting; it was a pep rally! "The most popular item on the menu is the steak frites. It is twelve ounces of aged New York strip grilled to order—and please note you need a *temperature* on that—served with a mound of garlic fries. The duck, the sword, the lamb lollipops—see, we're having *fun* here—are all served at the chef's temperature. If you have a guest who wants the lamb killed—by which I mean *well done*—you're going to have to take it up with Fiona. The sushi plate is all spelled out for you—it's bluefin tuna caught forty miles off the shore, and the sword *is* harpooned in case you get a guest who has just seen a *Nova* special about how the Canadian coast is being overfished."

Just then the door to the kitchen opened and a short, olive-skinned man carried out a stack of plates, followed by his identical twin, who carried a hotel pan filled with grilled steaks. The smell was unbelievable.

"That's your dinner," Thatcher said. "I just have a few more things."

A third guy, taller, with longer hair, but the same look of Gibraltar as the other two men, emerged with a hotel pan of French fries, and two bottles of ketchup dangling from his fingers. The staff shifted in their chairs. Adrienne wiggled her feet in her slides. *What*, she wondered, *is wrong with my shoes?*

"The last thing I want to talk about is the fondue. Second seating only, four-tops only, otherwise it's a logistical nightmare. You all know what fondue is, I assume, remembering it from your parents' dinner parties when you were kids? We put out a fondue pot with hot peanut oil and we keep it hot with Sterno. So already, servers, visualize moving through the crowded dining room holding a pot of boiling oil. Visualize lighting the Sterno without setting the tablecloth on fire. Adding this to the menu tacked *thousands* of dollars to our insurance policy. But it's our signature dish. The table gets a huge platter of shrimp, scallops, and clams dredged in seasoned flour. They get nifty fondue forks. What they're doing, basically, is deep-frying their own shellfish. Then we provide sauces for dipping. So imagine it's a balmy night, you've spent all day on the beach, you've napped, you've showered, you've indulged in a cocktail or two. Then you're led to a table in the sand for the best all-you-can-eat fried shrimp in the world while sitting under the stars. It's one of those life-is-good moments." Thatcher smiled at the staff. "This is our last year. Everything we do this year is going to reflect our generosity of spirit. You will notice I never use the word 'customer' or 'client.' The people who eat at this restaurant are our *guests*. And like good hosts, we want to make our guests happy. Now go eat. And for those of you who are new—all wine questions go to me—and familiarize yourself with the dessert menu while you chow."

Everyone charged for the food. A few more cooks in spiffy white coats materialized from the kitchen. They were all lean and muscular with skin like gold leaf and dark hair. Latino? They looked alike to Adrienne—maybe they were brothers?—but this, surely, was just an example of her ignorance. The most handsome of the bunch stood in front of Adrienne in line. He looked her up and down—checking her out? Her diaphanous top? Then he grinned.

"Man," he said. "Everyone's in the shit back there. Except for me, of course, but I have the easy job."

Adrienne peered over his shoulder at the hotel pan filled with steaks. And a vat of béarnaise—how had she missed that? "What's the easy job?" she asked.

"I'm the pastry chef," he said. "You're new?"

"Adrienne." She offered him her hand.

"Mario. How're you doing? I heard about you. Fiona's been making a big deal all week because you're a woman."

Adrienne studied him. Although he looked like he hailed from the Mediterranean, his accent said Chicago. He was several inches taller than she was, his hair was buzzed down to his scalp, and he had very round black eyes. Beautiful eyes, really. His skin was shiny with sweat and inside the collar of his chef's jacket at the base of his neck she saw a scar, a raised purple welt.

"I'm sorry? Fiona's making a big deal about *me*?" Adrienne said. "I don't even know her. I've never met her."

"I know," he said cheerfully. He helped himself to a steak, gave it a generous ladle of béarnaise, plopped a handful of golden fries right on top.

Adrienne followed suit. There was salad, too, a gorgeous crisp-looking salad that had already been lightly dressed with something. Adrienne mounded her crowded plate with salad, thinking about what Thatcher had said about the vegetables. Fiona picked them out before the sun was up.

Fiona! Fiona, whom Adrienne could not pick out of a crowd of two, was making a *big deal* about her. Adrienne needed to question this Mario person further to find out what was being said. Fiona Kemp, the reclusive genius chef, had been making a big deal all week because Adrienne was a woman. What had Thatcher said? He'd never hired a woman for the job before.

Adrienne poured herself a tall glass of water then sat down next to the waiter with the blond ponytail. Mario took his dinner back to the kitchen. Adrienne felt weak, like her legs were made of baby greens. Before she got here she had been nervous to meet Fiona; now she was afraid.

No one was talking. The only sounds were knives and forks on plates, the occasional palm tapping the bottom of the ketchup bottle. Two waiters were studying the menus. The new guys. One pale and thin with a bushy head of loose curls and a weak chin, and one handsome dark-haired guy wearing two gold hoop earrings. The guy with the earrings was reading the menu so intently that he shot food off his plate when he cut his steak. Adrienne concentrated on eating carefully—one drop of ketchup on the diaphanous white blouse and . . . well, there was no time to go home and change and nothing at home to change into. Adrienne ate her steak, the béarnaise, the garlicky fries—did she even need to say it? It was steak frites from a rainy-day-in-Paris dream. The steak was perfectly seasoned, perfectly cooked, pink in the middle, juicy, tender. The salad was tossed in a lemony vinaigrette but it tasted so green, so young and fresh, that Adrienne began to worry. This person Fiona had a *way*. If the staff meal tasted this good then the woman was possessed, and Adrienne didn't want a possessed woman on her case.

The whole thing had been too easy, she saw now. She shouldn't be here, she didn't belong here, but she had been swept along by her own greed and by Thatcher, who had been described in a major food magazine as "charismatic, compelling . . . he could talk a teetotaler into a bottle of Chateau Lafite." He had convinced her, somehow, to take this leap. Adrienne thought it was weird that she hadn't even *met* Fiona, but she'd chalked it up to the fact that Fiona was a recluse. A culinary Greta Garbo, or J. D. Salinger. Were Thatcher and Fiona married, engaged, committed, together, dating—or, worst of all, *exes*? She had to ask Caren. Caren who was three seats down eating a plate of only salad. Drinking, yes, espresso. Caren had advised Adrienne to keep a toothbrush and toothpaste at the restaurant. Caren knew everything.

There was soft female laughter, as jarring to Adrienne as a tray of stemware crashing to the floor. She looked around to see Duncan and the bar back engaged in quiet conversation. They looked so familiar, so at ease—the girl grabbed Duncan's forearm when she talked. Adrienne wondered if something was going on between them. The girl was young—in college still, Adrienne guessed—she had curly light brown hair and big brown eyes. Big boobs, too, and her oxford was unbuttoned one too far.

Adrienne was one to talk. *Diaphanous top . . . gutsy . . . I like it.* "Diaphanous" didn't mean transparent. You certainly couldn't see anything. Besides, she was wearing a very sturdy, very modest beige bra. And her shoes—what, exactly, was wrong with her shoes?

Adrienne did *not* like the idea that while she was getting moved into the cottage, setting up her bank account, and strictly adhering to all three of her rules, someone she'd never laid eyes on was down here talking about her. News of the diaphanous top and the inappropriate shoes had probably already made it back into the kitchen. What would Fiona say to *that*?

Thatcher appeared, holding a flute of pink champagne. "You're all done."

It wasn't a question, though Adrienne still had food on her plate, and she didn't want to be separated from it. He nodded toward the front door. "Service starts in ten minutes. Mr. and Mrs. Parrish will be here *at* six. There are some other things I have to explain."

Adrienne cleared her plate into three bins the way she'd seen others doing, though it killed her to throw food away. She followed Thatcher, who was holding the champagne out in front of him. "You liked dinner?" he asked.

"It was delicious." This felt like a gross understatement and she wondered what words might convey the physical pain she felt at scraping her plate. "Did you eat?"

He laughed, the old karate-chop "ha!" It was a noise he made not when something was funny, she realized, but when something was preposterous. "No. I eat with Fee after service."

Is she your wife? Girlfriend? Can someone please turn on the lights so I can see? Is this the restaurant's last year because you've split up? Is the fact that I'm a woman going to be a bigger problem than you initially anticipated? Adrienne followed him silently, but not silently at all. Her shoes were making a tremendous racket against the wooden floors.

"I'm clomping," she said.

Thatcher turned to her. "Yes. The shoes. I told you. You have to watch the way you walk. Tomorrow night, different shoes. A soft sole. Slippers or something, but elegant, okay?"

Adrienne deducted another hundred dollars from her rapidly diminishing savings for elegant slipper shoes. Fine for pants, but the dress she'd bought would look funny without heels.

"Taking this job was a mistake," she said. "Behind the front desk of a hotel, no one could even see my shoes."

They reached the oak podium, home to the phone, the reservation book, a Tiffany vase with a couple dozen blue irises. A shallow bowl of Blue Bistro matches. A leather cup containing three sharpened pencils and a funny-looking wine key. Thatcher held up the champagne flute.

"This is a glass of Laurent-Perrier rosé," he said. "We sell it at the bar for sixteen dollars a glass, ninety-five dollars a bottle. This is what you're going to drink on the floor."

"I *said*, taking this job was a mistake."

"We both took a gamble," he said. "Please give it one night. I promise you will love it so much you will be counting the minutes until you can come back. If you don't feel that way, then we'll talk. But we can't talk now. Right now, I'm going to talk and you're going to listen, okay?"

His okays were purely rhetorical.

"I want to brush my teeth," she said.

Before she knew what was happening, Thatcher leaned over and kissed her. Very quickly, very softly. "You're fine," he said. "I detect a trace of vinaigrette, but it's really very pleasant." He held the flute out to her, and as it gave her something to do other than fall over backward, she accepted it.

"My father is a dentist," she said. If her father had seen what just happened—well, she could hear him now. *These are not people who floss, honey.* Adrienne looked at Huck Finn, the professor, resplendent in his watch and shoes, a yellow linen shirt and navy blazer. He did not seem at all fazed by what had just happened. *The professor kissed me! It was really very pleasant, the kiss. This champagne is what I drink on the floor. I wear diaphanous tops and clompy shoes. He kissed me! No wonder they talk about me back in the kitchen!*

"Pretend you're hosting a cocktail party," he said. "You greet people at the door holding your glass of Laurent-Perrier rosé. The first thing they'll notice is your pretty face, then your clothes. Then what you've got in your hand. They will want to drink pink champagne just like the beautiful hostess. Sixteen dollars a glass, you see? When you're working the room, you should always have your flute of pink champagne. Right away, it gives you an identity, it gives you style. Your champagne is an accessory. You don't have to get tanked. In fact, I'd appreciate it if you didn't. But a glass or two—three on a busy night, sure. Duncan will fill you up." He watched her while she took a sip. "This is great," he said. "Kevin drank bourbon—nothing sexy about that—and occasionally he deigned to walk around with a glass of merlot, but he didn't enjoy it and the guests could tell."

"Do you drink while you work?" Adrienne asked.

"I'm an alcoholic," he said. He gazed at her so intently she thought he might kiss her again. What was going *on* here? It felt like she was breaking one of her rules, though she was so flustered she couldn't remember what her rules were. Was there a rule about not kissing her boss?

"Oh."

"There's something else you have to know," Thatcher said. "Something I should have mentioned when I hired you."

Adrienne's dinner shifted in her stomach. Something else?

He lowered his voice. "There's no press allowed in the kitchen."

"Okay."

"I don't care if it's the *New York Times Magazine*. I don't care if it's the *Christian Science Monitor*."

"Okay."

"I don't care if they tell you they have an appointment. They don't. There is no press allowed in the kitchen. And no guests, of course. I mention the press because they come here all the time trying to get a story about Fiona. Word has gotten out that it's our last year, therefore it's crucial you understand."

"No press in the kitchen," Adrienne said.

"Very good. I'm sorry to be so strict."

"You don't have to be sorry."

"Tonight, it's friends of the house," Thatcher said. "I want you to shadow me around the dining room so you learn the faces. I want you to man the host station if I'm back in the kitchen."

"Am I allowed in the kitchen?" Adrienne asked.

Thatcher looked at her strangely.

"Thatcher!" Bruno was calling from the dining room. Both Thatcher and Adrienne spun around to find the dining room transformed. All of the candles had been lit and the waiters stood in a line, hands behind their backs, military-style, among the impeccably dressed tables with their starched tablecloths, the sparkling stemware, a single blue iris in a silver bud vase. Behind the restaurant, the sun was dropping in the sky. Just then a few notes came from the piano, like peals of a glass bell. A tall mop-haired man in a black turtleneck had started to play.

"It's beautiful," Adrienne whispered. It was like a theater set before the opening performance and she found herself wanting it to stay like this. She didn't want anything to ruin it, but no sooner did Adrienne wish for this than a white Mercedes pulled into the parking lot.

"This is it," Thatcher said. "The beginning of the end."

At the Blue Bistro, the service wasn't the only thing that was old-fashioned. There was no computer. Tickets were written by hand and delivered to the kitchen by the server, a system that was as outdated as the pony express. Reservations were made in pencil, in a big old book with a tattered binding. Most tables were marked with the party's last name; VIP tables had the first and last name.

"Some restaurants actually write 'VIP' next to a name," Thatcher said. "Or, if they're trying to be tricky, they'll use other initials, like 'PPX.' But too many people today are tuned into that kind of thing. It causes problems."

"What makes someone a VIP?" Adrienne asked. "Does it have to do with money?"

"Money?" Thatcher said. "No. It has to do with how often someone dines with us. The Parrishes, for example. The ultimate VIPs." Thatcher checked his watch. "You see, it's the stroke of six."

At that second, a couple Adrienne took to be the Parrishes stepped in the door. They were an older couple who exuded an air of gracious retirement: golf, grandchildren, travel on European ships. Mr. Parrish wore kelly green pants and a green-and-white striped shirt, a navy blazer. He had silver hair, he was sunburned and he shook ever so slightly when he leaned over to kiss Adrienne. Another kiss—this time from a complete stranger.

Adrienne stole a glance at Thatcher. Was kissing a part of the job description that she had missed? Mrs. Parrish gave Thatcher a hug. On her right hand, which rested on the front of Thatcher's butter-yellow shirt, she wore one enormous emerald-cut diamond ring and a platinum band with sapphires and diamonds. She had dark hair styled like Jackie Onassis, and clear blue eyes that took Adrienne in and immediately understood that she was motherless. Adrienne had met other women with this power—mothers of friends and boyfriends who wanted to adopt Adrienne, like a nine-year-old with a stray kitten, and Adrienne had never been able to resist their kind words or fluttering of attention (except in the case of Mavis—Mavis was not her mother!). Mrs. Parrish released her hold on Thatcher and reached out to Adrienne with both hands. Adrienne set her champagne down on the podium.

"Thatcher," Mrs. Parrish said. "Where did you find such a lovely girl?"

"Darla, Grayson, may I introduce Adrienne Dealey," Thatcher said. "She's never worked in a restaurant before."

"Good for you," Mrs. Parrish whispered. She leaned over and kissed Adrienne: Adrienne felt the lipstick, a cool spot of paint on her cheek. Was that *good for you* for never working in a restaurant? Or *good for you* for landing a job here, alongside the world's most charismatic restaurateur? Since Adrienne didn't know how to respond, she smiled. Her sunburn made her face feel funny, like her skin was too tight. She hoped there wasn't anything stuck in her teeth.

Thatcher led the Parrishes into the dining room and although he said Adrienne should shadow him, she felt foolish doing so. She popped into the ladies' room, a mere four feet from the oak podium, to wipe the lipstick from her face and check her teeth. Regrettably, no time to brush. She could hear Thatcher's voice asking about someone named Wolf; she could hear Mr. Parrish offer up a round of golf at Sankaty. And then she heard the phone.

She rushed back to the hostess station. It was, of all things, the private line. Thatcher hadn't said anything about how he wanted her to answer the phone and especially not the private line. But hey—six years of resorts, five front desks including one in which she had to answer in Thai. One thing she could do correctly in this restaurant was answer the phone.

"Good evening," she said. "The Blue Bistro."

"Yeah." There was a telltale crackle. Cell phone, bad signal. "We're running late. Ten minutes. Make that twenty to be safe."

"No problem, sir," Adrienne said, though she had no idea if this were a problem or not. She tried to catch Thatcher's eye. He was across the room, seating the Parrishes at table twenty, which Adrienne knew to be the best table. The dining room was shaped like a triangle, and table twenty was the top, the focus of everybody else in the restaurant. Thatcher was up to his neck in schmooze; he was unreachable. "We'll see you when you get here," Adrienne said into the phone. "Thank you for calling." But the man had already hung up. And then Adrienne realized she hadn't gotten his name.

She tried to explain this enormous gaffe to Thatcher when he returned—the first task she tackled on her own a complete failure—but he didn't seem interested. "If the call came in on the private line, it was probably Ernie Otemeyer," he said, making a note by the name "Ernie Otemeyer" in the book, table sixteen for two people at six fifteen. "He's our plumber. He comes twice a year—soft opening and his birthday in August. He's always late because he has to stop on the way and buy his own beer. He drinks Bud Light."

Adrienne wondered about her legal pad—what had she done with it? Here was the kind of thing she needed to write down. *Plumber Ernie comes twice a year and brings his own Bud Light.*

"I don't know what I did with my legal pad," Adrienne confessed. Through the open door, she saw more cars pulling in. The piano man was playing "What I Did for Love."

"I have good news," Thatcher said.

"What?"

"The Parrishes want you to bring them their bread."

"Why is that good news?"

"It means they like you. They want to see you at their table. Please wait until Bruno gets their cocktails. You have to be watching. And don't think you have plenty of time because Duncan knows their drinks—heck, the whole staff knows their drinks—Stoli tonic with lime for Grayson and a Southern Comfort old-fashioned for Darla. See that? The drinks are up. Now, as soon as Bruno delivers them, you get the bread. They like bread and butter—always."

"Where do I get the bread?" Adrienne asked.

"In the kitchen."

"So it's okay if I . . ."

A party of six stepped in the door—four men, rugby-playing types, and two teenaged boys who looked like Abercrombie & Fitch models with mussed hair and striped ties loose at the neck. "Thatcher!" one of the men boomed like he was yelling across a playing field.

"Get the bread," Thatcher whispered, nudging Adrienne toward the kitchen. He moved to the front of the podium and started slapping backs.

Adrienne eyeballed the kitchen door. Well, she worked here now. And for some reason the Parrishes wanted her to deliver their bread. She felt singled out. Special. The Parrishes wanted her. They were not offended by her diaphanous top. They weren't put off because she was a *woman*.

Adrienne pushed open the door.

The kitchen was brightly lit. And very, very hot. And quiet except for the sounds of knives—*rat-tat-tat-scrape*—against cutting boards and the hiss of the deep fryers. Adrienne saw a line of bodies in white coats, but nobody's face. There were two six-burner ranges side by side, there was a grill shooting flames, and up above, blocking everyone's face, was a shelf stacked with what must have been fifty blackened sauté pans. Adrienne watched a pair of hands preparing the doughnuts. She watched another pair of hands filling ramekins with mustard. She noticed a cappuccino machine, big brother to the one that Caren owned, and next to it, a huge refrigerator, a cold stainless-steel wall. Where, exactly, was the bread? The kitchen was filled with people, yet there was no one to ask.

"Yes?"

A woman's voice. Adrienne's eyes adjusted to this alternate universe that was the restaurant kitchen and she saw Fiona Kemp. She knew it was Fiona Kemp because it said so in cobalt blue script on her white chef's jacket. Fiona Kemp who, contrary to every vision Adrienne held in her mind's eye, was only five feet tall and may have weighed a hundred pounds with a pocket full of change. She was small. And adorable. She had long honey-blond hair in a braid and huge blue eyes. She wore diamond stud earrings. Adrienne had expected a hunchback, a hermit; she had expected the old woman who lived in a shoe.

"You're Fiona?"

"Yes."

"I'm Adrienne."

"I know."

Should they shake hands? Fiona made no move to do so and Adrienne was too intimidated. She had never been clear on when women should shake hands, anyway.

"I came for the bread."

"For whom?"

Adrienne watched a batch of doughnuts descend into the deep fryer. Her brain was deep-frying. "The Parrishes."

"Thatcher takes them their bread."

"Okay," Adrienne said. "Is there a special place the bread is kept?"

"Yes."

"Where is that?"

Fiona nodded at the stainless-steel counter to Adrienne's left. "The Parrishes' bread is right there. You're running for Thatcher?"

Adrienne stared at the basket of rolls and the cake of butter covered by a glass dome. "He told me I'm supposed to take the Parrishes their bread."

"Thatcher takes the Parrishes their bread," Fiona said. "That's the way it works around here. Especially on the first night."

"He said they asked for me."

Fiona stared at Adrienne as though she was trying to figure out what had prompted Thatcher to offer her a job. Adrienne didn't look like Heidi Klum, and she didn't have enormous breasts. So why else would he cajole her into taking a job that she wasn't qualified to do? *I have no idea!* Adrienne wanted to shout.

"Thatcher was right about you, then," Fiona said.

"Right about me how?" Adrienne asked. "What did he say?"

Fiona pinched her lips together. She had freckles across her nose, like someone had sprinkled it with cinnamon.

"You're not going to tell me?"

"No."

"Is my working here going to be a problem?" Adrienne asked. She felt like in the bright lights her top was positively sheer.

"Since it's only the first hour of the first night, that remains to be seen," Fiona said. "But I can tell you one thing."

"What's that?"

"The Parrishes are very important to us. They shouldn't have to wait for their bread." She pointed at the door. "Go."

Adrienne was shaking when she reached the Parrishes' table. Normally when she felt uncomfortable, she sent a mental e-mail to her father. But now Adrienne was facing a blank screen. What had happened in there? No time to wonder because the Parrishes wanted to chat about Aspen. They had vacationed in Aspen long ago, before it was fashionable, and they stayed at the Hotel Jerome. Adrienne learned that Grayson's business was importing custom tile and stone from Italy, a business his sons now ran that was doing better than ever due to the home-improvement boom. The Parrishes had three sons, the oldest was thirty-six, and none of the sons was currently married. They had one grandchild, a little boy named Wolf who "lived with his mother." Adrienne managed to keep up the conversation until she felt Bruno breathing on the back of her neck, and she excused herself.

She returned to the hostess station and drank down her pink bubbly. The exchange with Fiona nagged at her. She had to talk to Caren. There wasn't time now, of course. No sooner had Adrienne set her empty glass on the blue granite for Duncan to refill than the front door became inundated with three six-thirty reservations and the late arriving Ernie Otemeyer carrying a paper bag. The place was hopping. Busboys presented baskets of pretzel bread and doughnuts. The piano man launched into "Some Enchanted Evening." Caren floated by, taking Adrienne by the elbow.

"I have apps up on table seven. Can you run some food for me?"

Adrienne glanced at the clot of people by the front door. Thatcher was in the thick of it.

"Run some food?" This sounded suspiciously out of bounds. "I'm not trained for that. And what about Thatcher? Can he seat all those tables by himself?"

"It'll take two seconds," Caren said. She vanished into the kitchen and came back balancing a tray of plates on the palm of one hand and carrying a stand in the other. Adrienne followed her out into the dining room. Caren snapped open the stand and lowered the tray. Adrienne felt a bloom of optimism from the champagne. Fiona was an ogre trapped in a doll's body, like some screwed-up fairy tale, but just look at the food: two salads with the red-and-white striped beets, a foie gras, a crab cake, and two corn chowders. Absolutely beautiful.

"The salads go to the two ladies closest to you," Caren whispered. "Serve from their right."

Adrienne watched Caren's graceful movements. She tried to imitate her. She slid the salads in for a landing on top of the Limoges chargers. Caren served the last two plates, then asked if anyone cared for freshly ground pepper. A burst of laughter came from the rugby players' table. The piano man segued into "The Entertainer." It jangled in Adrienne's head. She had served the two plates without incident. Piece of cake! And now . . . what? Thatcher was leading the plumber to his table, two down from the Parrishes. He held out the paper bag.

"Would you ask Duncan to put this on ice?" Thatcher said. "And get a cold one in a pilsner for Ernie and a glass of the merlot for his wife, Isadora, please." Under his breath, he said, "Champagne, champagne."

"It's at the bar," Adrienne said. "I'll get it right now." There were still people waiting at the podium. She had to hurry! She carried the paper bag through the dining room to the bar. Even over the conversation, the clink of glasses and silver and china, and the piano, Adrienne could hear her shoes. She sounded like a Clydesdale.

"Adrienne!"

Thatcher was at her back. "The Parrishes want you to serve their wine."

"I don't know how to do that," she said. She pictured snapping the cork in half, or spilling cabernet down the front of her diaphanous blouse. "Don't make me do that."

"I told them you haven't been trained with the wine key yet," he said. "I told them you would do it next time. But you can deliver their chips and dip. They just want your face at their table. Where's your champagne?"

"I told you, I'm getting it." She wanted to give the beer to Duncan and order the merlot before she forgot. Thatcher set off to deal with the people at the podium.

Adrienne paid close attention to where she placed her feet. It forced her to slow down. Confrontation with Fiona aside, the first hour wasn't going badly. She had answered the phone, she had conducted a pleasant conversation with two VIPs, she had served two plates of salad without dumping them in the guests' laps. Now, at the bar, she delivered the plumber's beer and ordered the merlot, and without even having to ask, Duncan slid a flute of champagne across the blue bar. She took a sip, then put it down. She had to go back into the kitchen for the chips and dip. The piano man played "Somewhere, Beyond the Sea." This had been Adrienne's parents' favorite song; she was never able to listen to it without getting weepy. But what was nice about the restaurant business, Adrienne realized, was that there was no time to reflect on the way her parents used to dance together at weddings. There wasn't time to worry if her father was now dancing with Mavis. There wasn't time to muse over Doug or Kip or Sully or any of the men she'd sat at a table for two with over the last six years and question her own good sense. There wasn't even time to wonder about the kiss from Thatcher. The restaurant business was doing her a favor. It locked her into the moment: her glass of pink champagne, the trip back into Fiona's lair. Locating her yellow legal pad. Learning the table numbers and the wine key. Getting a look—just a look—at all the beautiful food. History in the making. The last soft opening of the Blue Bistro.

By the end of the first seating, Adrienne's legs ached. And her lower back. In three hours of work she had walked at least five miles. So that was it, absolutely, for the fucking slides. She would never wear them again.

There were seventy reservations on the books and forty-two of those were sitting at nine o'clock.

"First seating was *nothing*," Thatcher said. "It was a *warm-up*."

At eighty thirty there was a nice lull—most of the tables had finished their dinners and were lingering over dessert. Thatcher snatched a piece of the brown sugar fudge from one of the candy plates headed back into the kitchen and handed it to Adrienne.

"I always wondered if you ate off the plates," she said.

"Taste it," he said.

The fudge was an explosion of vanilla and caramel, and it gave her a much-needed sugar kick. She checked in on the Parrishes. They were one of those couples who didn't speak to each other during dinner; only when Adrienne approached did they brighten. When she had delivered their caviar, they chatted with her about their home on Cliff Road. Between courses, at Thatcher's prompting, Adrienne checked in with them again. They were both staring out at the water, each seemingly lost in thought. But when Adrienne appeared, Darla raved about the crab cake, and Grayson swirled his white burgundy in his glass. They asked Adrienne if she cooked at home and the expression on her face—which was horror and quite genuine—gave them all a good laugh. At a little after eight, Adrienne delivered a cup of decaf cappuccino to Darla and a glass of tawny port to Grayson. She placed the check (which consisted only of the bar tab and the two-hundred-dollar bottle of wine) on the table in what she hoped was a discreet way, and informed them that they were welcome to stay and enjoy the sea air for as long as they wished. This was not, of course, true—the entire restaurant was being reseated at nine. When Darla and Grayson made their move to stand, Adrienne floated—this was her goal, to float like Caren—to their table and held Grayson's arm all the way to the front door. Before they left, Darla kissed Adrienne again—more lipstick—and Grayson pressed money into her hand, which took her so by surprise that she nearly dropped it. The Parrishes then lavished Thatcher with attention and sent their love "to darling Fiona. Tell her everything was superb. We'll see you Friday at six." And they set off into the night. Thatcher winked at Adrienne; she felt sorry to see them go. It was like visiting with her grandparents when she was young, complete with the gift of money. Adrienne checked her palm. Grayson had given her a hundred dollars.

She showed the bill to Thatcher. "What should I do with it?"

"Keep it."

"What about Bruno?" she asked. "What about Tyler?" Tyler was a busboy who was a senior at Nantucket High School. In the thirty seconds Adrienne had conversed with him, she could tell he was precocious. He had, he informed her, twelve days until graduation when he planned to get shit-faced at a bonfire on the beach just down the way from the restaurant. The only reason he got this job in the first place, he said, was because his father was the island's health inspector.

"There was a tip added to the bill for them," Thatcher said. "If anybody puts money in your hand—unless he tells you it's for someone else—then it's yours to keep."

An electric thrill ran up Adrienne's spine, the singular pleasure of windfall. The start of her new Future! She tucked the money into her pocket.

"The Parrishes didn't speak to one another during dinner," she said.

"They never do," Thatcher said. "That's why they like to have someone visit their table, three, four times a night. It peps things up."

The rest of the tables were slowly rising and moving around. Some people headed for the door, some walked to the edge of the restaurant to peer at the water. The busboys worked like crazy to strip the tables. The piano man took a break and the CD player kicked in with Billie Holiday. Adrienne's sunburn throbbed like a red alarm; she was tired. She could easily go home and sleep with the hundred dollar bill under her pillow until morning.

"Now," said Thatcher. "Now you're going to earn your money."

Adrienne wanted to tell Thatcher about her exchange with Fiona. She wanted to ask what he'd said about her but there wasn't time. Between seatings, Thatcher reviewed the book with Adrienne.

"You're going to have to learn our guest list night by night," he said. "Some of our favorite guests only stay on Nantucket for one week of the summer, but they eat here three times during that week. They've been doing so for twelve years."

Adrienne had found her yellow notepad. It was handed to her by the young bar back whose name was Delilah. Delilah was not Duncan's paramour, but rather, his kid sister. She had just finished her junior year at Bennington, she said, and all her life she'd been waiting for her parents to give her the okay to work with Duncan.

"I have two other brothers," she said. "David and Dennis. And they are such sticks-in-the-mud. They have kids." As if that explained it. "Duncan is the only person in our family who leads an exciting life, and so I said to the parents, 'As soon as I turn twenty-one, I go where he goes.'" She gave Adrienne a toothy smile with her eyes all scrunched, and headed, butt-first, into the kitchen, bracing a crate of dirty bar glasses against her midsection.

Adrienne was glad for the return of her notepad. She studied the diagram of circles and squares and rectangles that was the seating chart—it might have seemed as easy as nursery school but it was more like plane geometry. She looked expectantly at Thatcher. Nerdy student a hundred dollars richer at the ready!

While some of the guests of the soft opening were summer people who had arrived early, most were year-round Nantucketers. Mack Peterson, the manager of the Nantucket Beach Club and Hotel, was coming with Cecily Elliott, the hotel owners' daughter.

"Great guy," Thatcher said. "He sends us *tons* of business. Good business, too—people who show up on time, drink a lot of expensive wine, et cetera."

Adrienne wrote down their names. "Are they married?" she asked. "Mack and Cecily?"

"No," Thatcher said. He furrowed his brow. It was funny, Adrienne thought, how Thatcher's hair was red but his eyebrows were the palest blond. "What is your obsession with whether people are married?"

Adrienne wanted to inform him that asking if one couple was married could hardly be classified as an *obsession*, but then she remembered that she had also asked about him and Fiona. "I'm sorry," she said, with as much poison in her voice as she could muster in her state of weariness.

Thatcher held up his pen. "Never mind."

She recalled Fiona's words. *Thatcher was right about you, then.* "You don't know the first thing about me," Adrienne said.

"Well, I know that your father is a dentist," he said. "Your mother is a good cook. You worked in Aspen at the Little Nell, and in Thailand, Palm Beach, Hawaii, and on the Cape. You have black hair and green eyes. You're a size six. You go to the beach without sun protection. You don't know how to walk in slides. And"—he pointed his pen at her—"tonight is your first night of restaurant work." He smiled. "How'd I do?"

Adrienne stared at the faint blue lines of her legal pad. She desperately wanted to set the record straight about her mother—although her mother *had been* a good cook, she had also been dead for sixteen years. But Adrienne didn't have the energy. She was tired. And he was right that she went to the beach without lotion and didn't know how to walk in these shoes. Her legs hurt, her face hurt. She wanted to sit down.

"Let's just do this," she said.

"We have a lot of Realtors coming in tonight," he said. "Hopefully one of them will help me sell this place. The president of the bank is coming. The electrician is coming with her husband, her sister and brother-in-law. I don't need to tell you how important the contractors are, right? Ernie the plumber and Cat the electrician. They are the *most* important. Because if one of the toilets overflows or an oven quits in the middle of service on a

Saturday night, we need to be able to call that person's cell phone and have them show up in *minutes*. Let's see . . . we have a famous CEO coming with a party of ten—I'll let you be surprised. No other celebrities, really—a couple of local painters and writers. They drink a lot. Where is your champagne? We didn't sell a single glass of Laurent-Perrier first seating."

"Sorry," Adrienne said. She felt oddly culpable, like maybe she wasn't enticing enough, or worthy of emulation. She headed over to the bar and when Duncan saw her he whipped a clean flute off the shelf.

"This is your third glass," Duncan said. "How many did Thatch say you could have?"

"Three, if it's busy."

"It's going to be busy in a few minutes," he said. He poured a glass and slid it across the bar. "You'd better nurse this, though. I'll pour you however much you want after service."

"Thanks," Adrienne said. "But after service, I'm going home to bed."

"Maybe you should have an espresso," Duncan said. "Do you want me to order you an espresso?"

"No, thanks." But since it was nice of him to offer, she said, "I met your sister. She's cute."

Duncan rolled his eyes, wiped down the blue granite with a rag, and checked the level of his cranberry juice. "She doesn't know what the fuck she's doing."

Adrienne twirled her flute by the stem. "That makes two of us."

Caren appeared with two espressos. "Let's do a shot," she said to Duncan. They both threw back the coffee. Caren pointed at Adrienne's champagne. "Better watch it. That stuff will kill you."

Adrienne wandered back toward the front door as headlights started to pull into the parking lot. The piano player returned, smelling like cigarettes. The two new waiters had also been out on the beach smoking. The guy with the hoop earrings—name?—offered bushy hair—name?—an Altoid. The piano player—name?—glissando-ed into "We've Only Just Begun."

Somehow Adrienne caught a second wind. The people who arrived for second seating were younger and better looking. In fact, they all looked like models. Cat, the electrician, was a six-foot blonde in a pair of Manolo Blahniks. She was one of the most attractive women Adrienne had ever seen and she was the electrician. Welcome to Nantucket! When Thatcher introduced Adrienne, Cat's eyes went first to Adrienne's shoes, then to her glass.

"You're drinking pink champagne," she said. "That's what I want. Pink champagne. Let's get a bottle. No, a magnum."

Adrienne smirked at Thatcher. Redeemed! Thatcher led Cat's party to table twenty while Adrienne sat a husband and wife Realtor team with a party of six. When she returned to the podium, Holt Millman—a CEO who was famous for being not only obscenely rich but legitimately so—was heading up a party of ten.

In her mind, Adrienne dashed a one-line e-mail to her father. *Holt Millman looks just like his picture on the cover of* Fortune*!* Thatcher sat the Millman party and left Adrienne to handle a party of six women, wives of the owners of other restaurants in town. Thatcher had told Adrienne that this table was super-VIP. "Because we want them to return the favor when we go out on the town."

One of these women—again, gorgeous, red hair, fabulous shoes—said, "You're new."

"I'm Adrienne Dealey."

The redhead shook Adrienne's hand and squeezed it. "I've been telling Thatcher for years that he should have a woman up front. Don't let Fiona give you a hard time."

This caught Adrienne off-guard. *How did you know Fiona would give me a hard time?* she wanted to ask. *What does everybody on this island know about Fiona that I don't?*

"I won't," Adrienne assured her. She felt not only redeemed, but validated. Fiona was famous for giving people a hard time. So there. Adrienne handed out menus to the women and summoned enough courage to say, "I've been drinking Laurent-Perrier rosé champagne. Can I interest you ladies in a bottle?"

"Sure," the redhead said. "Sounds great."

Adrienne was afraid that if she stopped moving, she would keel over. She led the good citizens of Nantucket to their tables, handed out menus, and delivered drinks for Caren and Bruno who she could see were getting slammed. A local author came in with a party of eight. They had been barhopping in town and as soon as the author stepped in the door, she started singing along with the piano. Another party of four stepped in, among them a woman with a luscious pink pashmina who pointed at Adrienne's shoes.

"Great shoes!" she cried.

You can have them, Adrienne thought.

Thatcher approached the podium. "I don't want you to look right now," he said. "But in a second, casually, study the man to Holt Millman's left. He is Public Enemy Number One."

Instinctively, Adrienne turned.

"Don't look," Thatcher said. "Because he's watching us."

"Who is it?" Adrienne said.

"Drew Amman-Keller. Freelance journalist. He's basically on Holt's payroll writing pieces for *Town & Country* and *Forbes* about Holt and Holt's friends. He's been so aggressive in pursuing a story about Fiona that we had to ban him from the restaurant. But he's not stupid. He comes with Holt."

"Can I look now?"

"In a second. Let me walk away. I see table seven is drinking Laurent-Perrier."

"I suggested it."

"I want you to deliver the VIP order to Holt's table," Thatcher said. "In fact, I want you to deliver the VIP orders from now on. All summer. That will be your job."

"But . . ."

"Go to the kitchen right now," Thatcher said. "Don't turn around."

Adrienne learned that the person making the chips and dip was a kid named Paco, the assistant to the garde-manger. Paco was gangly, pimply, wearing a Chicago White Sox hat. Adrienne went right to him for pickup, sidestepping the frenetic scene that was going on between the waitstaff and Fiona and the line cooks and Fiona.

The kitchen, which had been so peaceful when Adrienne had first entered it, was now a house on fire. Fiona wasn't actually cooking; she was standing in front of what Paco referred to as the pass, yelling out orders from the tickets.

"Ordering table eight: one crab cake, two beets, one Caesar."

From the other side of the stoves, a cook called out, "Ordering one crab cake, chef."

The garde-manger, whose name was Eddie, called out, "Two beets and one Caesar, chef." Adrienne watched Eddie reach into two giant bowls of greens to plate the salads. She was entranced by the speed and the grace of this kind of cooking. It was as amazing as watching someone blow glass or weave on a loom, and it was all the more impressive because these men were barely men. Eddie might have been legal to drink, but Paco looked about nineteen. Adrienne watched him slice potatoes on a mandolin—*pfft, pfft, pfft*—until he had a pile of potatoes in perfect coins.

"Ordering table seven: one crab cake, one chowder, one bisque, two beets, one foie gras," Fiona said. For such a small individual, her voice was very forceful. "And where is table twenty's chowder? That's Cat, people, *vamos!*"

"You know," Adrienne said to Paco, "this is going to a party of ten. Maybe we should give them extra?"

"Party of ten?" Paco said. He, too, had a Chicago accent. "Why the fuck didn't you tell me?" He dropped another batch of sliced potatoes into the oil. It hissed like a snake.

"Ordering table twenty-five: two foie gras, two bisque, two crab cake, one SOS," Fiona said. A crab cake appeared in front of her and she studied it, tasted the sauce with a spoon, then wiped the edge of the plates with a towel. She tasted a bowl of shrimp bisque and sprinkled it with chives. "Where is Spillman?" she said. "Table thirty is up." She glanced over at Adrienne, who shifted her eyes to the slabs of foie gras sizzling in the sauté pans. "Are you running for Spillman?"

"Who's Spillman?" Adrienne asked.

Fiona huffed in a way that meant nothing good. Adrienne wanted to ride her second wind right out of the kitchen. As soon as Paco supplemented her chip plate for Holt Millman's table, she bolted. The dining room, with its open walls, was much cooler than the kitchen. It was sparkling with candlelight and was alive with music and conversation.

"Compliments of the chef," Adrienne said to the table at large, though her eyes landed, light as a butterfly, on the man to Holt Millman's left.

"Ooohrrg," she said. "Hi." The man whom Thatcher had identified as

Public Enemy Number One, Drew Amman-Keller, was the same man Adrienne had met on the ferry, the man who was responsible for her being here in the first place. He was staring at her over the top of his Bordeaux glass, but he said nothing. Maybe he didn't recognize her. Was that too much to hope for?

Adrienne set the plate down in front of Mr. Millman. "Hand-cut russet potato chips with crème fraîche and beluga caviar." Holt Millman beamed. A woman in a gray toile pillbox hat clapped her hands. Thatcher was right; even if you had all the money in the world, it was better than Christmas.

The night kept going and going. People ordered wine—and five tables ordered champagne—and Thatcher made Adrienne follow him into the wine cave, which was a room next to the bathroom that was cool and dry and filled with wine.

"This used to be a utility closet," he said. "We had it totally reoutfitted." The red wine rested on redwood racks and the white wine and champagne were kept in a refrigerated unit that took up a whole wall. Thatcher showed Adrienne how to identify a wine by its bin number from the wine list.

"We're selling a lot of the Laurent-Perrier," he said. "Get yourself another glass."

Adrienne's head was so loose that she was afraid it was going to unscrew completely and go flying through the dining room.

"I don't need another glass," she said.

"Get another glass," he said.

She informed Duncan that this was an order from Thatcher and she was given another glass. Duncan was moving fluidly behind the bar. Everyone wanted cocktails replenished; everybody wanted wine by the glass. A handful of men had actually left their tables to talk to Duncan at the bar, so the whole time he was wiping and pouring and shooting mixers out of the gun, he was talking about his winter in Aspen and the people who were regulars at the Board Room. Elle McPherson, Ed Bradley, Kofi Annan.

Adrienne scoffed. "Kofi Annan was a regular at the Board Room?"

A bead of sweat threatened to drop into Duncan's eye. "He drinks Cutty Sark."

"Okay," Adrienne said. She had no interest in busting Duncan's rap;

she'd had so much to drink that she should really keep her mouth shut. She picked up her fourth glass of champagne and was about to walk away when he said, "Listen, I'm out of limes. Can you find my sister and ask her to get me more limes, pronto?"

"Sure." Adrienne feared Delilah was in the kitchen, but then she saw her pop out of the ladies' room. "Your brother needs limes," Adrienne said to her. "Right away, I guess."

Delilah flashed her a toothy smile. Her eyes were bright. "Okay!" she said. "I love this job, don't you?"

"Hot oil!" someone called. The weak-chinned waiter. Adrienne still didn't know anyone's name. "Out of the way!" He had a fondue pot by the handle and the heating rack and the sterno in the other hand. A second waiter who had definitely not been at the menu meeting or family meal, a tall, heavyset black man, followed with a huge platter of seafood. He caught Adrienne's eye. "My name is Joe," he said. "This is going to table twenty. Would you mind running the sauces for me? They're on the counter."

Since he had so politely identified himself, Adrienne could hardly say no, even though his request put her back in the kitchen. She pushed through the door, narrowly missing Bruno with another fondue pot. Adrienne shrieked—to have splattered Bruno with hot oil on her first night! Fiona shot Adrienne a look of blue fire, then called out, "Ordering table fourteen: one sword, three frites—rare, medium rare, medium well, two clubs, one duck SOS, two sushi, and a lamb killed for Mr. Amman-Keller. It appears he didn't learn anything about food over the winter. Can I help you, *Adrienne?*"

The use of her name threw her. "Sauces?" she squeaked.

"Who has time to get the girl some sauces?" Fiona said. "Eddie?"

A wicked laugh came from the garde-manger station. The rest of the cooks didn't even deign to answer. There were six sauté pans on the range and Adrienne watched a piece of marinated swordfish hit the grill. One of the cooks pulled a pan of steaks from the oven. Paco lowered a batch of fries into the oil.

Fiona checked the tickets hanging like they were pieces of laundry she wanted to dry. "I don't have time for this," she said.

"Joe said they'd be out on the counter," Adrienne said.

"Someone else took those."

"Can you tell me where to look?"

Fiona stormed away. Adrienne watched Eddie construct the lobster club sandwich; she was hungry again. Someone spoke up from behind the pass. "You'd better go with her, girlfriend."

Adrienne hurried after Fiona's braid, her slides clomping even worse in here with the cement floor. Fiona, Adrienne noticed, was wearing black clogs. They stepped into a huge refrigerator. "This is the walk-in," Fiona said. She used the overly patient, patronizing voice of a teacher speaking to a very stupid pupil. "The sauces are parceled out and kept in here." She handed Adrienne four bowls that comprised a lazy Susan that went around the fondue pot. "Cocktail, goddess, curry, horseradish. Please identify the sauces when you put them on the table."

"Yes, chef," Adrienne said. Then wondered if that sounded snide. She took the bowls from Fiona. "Thank you for your help." She wanted to say something to save herself. "Your cooking is the best I've ever tasted. You probably hear that all the time."

Fiona shook her head, said nothing.

On the way back to the hot line, Adrienne spied Mario standing at a marble-topped table in a back enclave of the kitchen. He wore surgical gloves and was blasting the top of a crème brûlée with a blowtorch. He was listening to something on a Walkman that was making him dance. When Adrienne and Fiona walked by, he whistled.

"That's enough, Romeo," Fiona called out. "I know you're not whistling at me."

"You got that right, chef," he said.

Adrienne was too embarrassed to breathe.

Back at the pass, the tickets had multiplied in the thirty seconds that they'd been gone. Adrienne had belly flopped with Fiona, and now she had to worry about how to lift the fondue pot to get the sauces in place.

Someone from the line called out, "Eighty-six the sword."

"Damn it!" Fiona shouted, so loudly and angrily that Adrienne nearly dropped the sauces. "How did that happen?"

"We're out of ripe avocados," the cook said. "I thought there was a whole other crate, but I just checked them and they're hard as rocks. You want to put a different sauce on the fish?"

"No," Fiona said. She yanked a ticket down and studied it. "Hey, Adrienne! You want to fly to California and get us some ripe avocados? If you need an escort, Mario will happily join you."

The guys on the hot line hooted. Adrienne smiled weakly. She was being teased. Adrienne took it as a possible sign of improvement.

She ran the sauces to Cat at table twenty, she fetched a bottle of Laurent-Perrier from the wine cave for Bruno, she checked in with the table of women—all enjoying their appetizers. The local author's table was on their third round of cocktails; they'd decimated two baskets of pretzel bread and one of the doughnuts, but hadn't ordered a thing. Caren was growing frustrated. "They're not getting their fucking chips until they order," she growled in Adrienne's ear. "And if the kitchen runs out of beluga, it will serve them right."

As Adrienne walked by Holt Millman's table, Drew Amman-Keller flagged her down. She stopped, confused. He indicated that she should bow to him.

"Can I help you?" she asked.

"I'm glad everything worked out," he said.

"Excuse me?"

"For you. With the job."

Drew Amman-Keller's voice was melodious, like a radio announcer's. She didn't remember that from the ferry ride.

"Yes," she said. "Thank you for suggesting it. It's only my first night, but . . ." Okay, wait. She wasn't supposed to be talking to this guy. If Thatcher found out she already knew him, he might fire her. Before Adrienne could escape, Drew Amman-Keller pressed some money into her hand.

"One is for you," he said. "And one is for Rex."

"Rex?"

"The piano player. Would you ask him to play 'The Girl from Ipanema'?"

Adrienne nodded and turned away. She hid behind a pillar and checked the bills. Two hundreds. Adrienne stared at the money for a few silly seconds. What to do? She clomped over to Rex.

" 'The Girl from Ipanema,' please," she said. "For Holt Millman's table."

"As ever," he said wearily.

Since he didn't have a cup out, Adrienne left one of the hundreds on the ledge above the piano keys. Rex eyed her quizzically. Was there another place she was supposed to put it? It did look crass, a hundred dollar bill laid out on the piano. She picked it back up. "I'll give it to you on your break?" she said. He nodded. She put the two bills from Public Enemy Number One in her pocket. Rex played "The Girl from Ipanema."

By the time desserts went out, coffee, and after-dinner drinks, it was midnight. Adrienne went to the ladies' room and nearly fell asleep on the toilet. How would she keep this up all summer? It felt like she'd been here seven days, not seven hours. And even worse—she was starving! The steak frites at family meal was another lifetime ago. Back when she was young, naïve, and . . . poor. She had two hundred dollars in tips now and eight hours of work would bring two hundred more. It was all going right into the bank. At this rate, she could pay her father back by the end of the week.

She emerged from the ladies' room as some tables were leaving. Thatcher bid everyone good-bye and Adrienne took her place next to him at the podium, the two of them waving like Captain Stubing and Julie McCoy from *The Love Boat*.

"We're lucky tonight because there isn't any bar business," Thatcher said. "Tomorrow night the bar will be mobbed."

"Great," Adrienne said.

"I'm going to do a sweep," Thatcher said. "See if I can get table eighteen to move things along." That was the author's table. They had only now received their entrées. "You stay here."

The author's table were just cutting into steaks and two tables out in the sand were still eating fondue. If these tables ordered dessert, they had a good forty minutes left. Everybody else was paying the bill or close to it.

Holt Millman's party stood up to leave. Adrienne kept her eyes on Drew Amman-Keller. Thatcher had made it sound like he might try to sneak into the kitchen, but he simply slid on his blazer and meandered toward the door with the rest of Holt's contingency. Adrienne murmured good-byes. Drew Amman-Keller ushered everybody out the door ahead of him in a way that seemed very polite. Then he turned to Adrienne and handed her a business card.

"Good to see you again," he said. "Call me if you ever want to talk."

Adrienne was so startled that she laughed—"ha!"—sounding just like Thatcher.

Drew Amman-Keller disappeared out the door.

Adrienne checked out his card, but then the husband–wife Realtor team was on top of her, and so Adrienne slipped the card into her pocket with her tips. Cat and her husband followed on the Realtors' heels.

"The fondue was phenomenal," Cat said. "Is Fiona coming out to take a bow?"

Adrienne laughed, like this was a joke. "I'll tell her you said hello."

A second later, Thatcher reappeared. "Where's your champagne?"

"You're kidding, right?"

"Go to the bar," he said. "Right now. That's an order."

Huck Finn, fascist dictator, she thought as she limped toward the bar. She wanted a blue granite gravestone. The entire waitstaff was crowded around the bar and she could barely wedge her way in. They were eating from two baskets. The crackers. They were eating the crackers. Adrienne had no hope of getting even a crumb; she was the runt at the trough. But then Joe, whom she barely remembered in the blur of new faces, turned around and gave her a handful.

"Thanks for running those sauces."

Adrienne accepted the crackers like a hungry beggar. She gobbled the first cracker and it was so delicious that she let the second one sit on her tongue until it melted in a burst of flavor. It tasted like the crisped cheese on top of onion soup that she used to devour after a day of skiing. But better, of course, because everything that came out of this kitchen was better.

Two more baskets of crackers were delivered to the bar and Adrienne was able to procure another handful. Thatcher waved at her from the podium. More tables were leaving. Rex played "If." Adrienne put her crackers on a napkin, and went to help Thatcher send the guests on their way. The bank president palmed Adrienne some money. The redhead from the all-women table touched the sleeve of Adrienne's blouse.

"I own a women's clothing store in town called Dessert," she said. "If you come in, I'd love to dress you, free of charge."

Mack Peterson, manager of the Beach Club, who was another sandy-haired Midwesterner, shook Adrienne's hand and assured her he would only send her his best clients.

"You know, Mack," Thatcher said. "This girl used to work at the Little Nell in Aspen. She's a hotel person."

"Well, if you ever want to come back from the dark side," Mack said, "we'd love to have you."

"I'll keep that in mind," Adrienne said, though she had to admit, after only one night she was hooked on the restaurant business. Yes, she was in pain and she was exhausted. But she wasn't trading in this job. She loved it and it wasn't just because of the money—it was because of the crackers.

Hunger and thirst, she thought. *They'd get you every time.*

3

❧

See and Be Scene

Andrew Amman-Keller
Journalist

P.O. Box 383   P.O. Box 3777
Providence, RI 05271   Nantucket, MA 02584
Cell: 917-555-5172
aakack@metronet.net

When Caren emerged from her bedroom the next morning, her hair was down. It was a good look for her, Adrienne thought. She looked softer, sexier, more approachable, which was handy since Adrienne wanted to approach her, first thing, on the subject of Fiona. Caren was wearing a white T-shirt that had the words LE TOINY stitched in red on the left breast. The T-shirt was just long enough to cover Caren's ass in what looked to be thong underwear. She beelined for her espresso machine.

"You want?" she asked Adrienne.

"No, thanks. I have tea." Ginger-lemon herbal tea that Adrienne drank for a hangover, which she was nursing right now. There had been six glasses of champagne before the night was over because after the last guests left (as it happened, the author's table) Duncan poured a drink for everyone on the staff and he had poured two glasses for Adrienne in the interest of finishing off the bottle of Laurent-Perrier. So that was a whole bottle over the course of one evening, probably four glasses too many. Adrienne had taken three Advil and chugged a glass of ice water when she got home, but she still felt dull and flannel-mouthed this morning. It was such a gorgeous day—so sunny and crystalline—that Adrienne had entertained thoughts of going for a jog. But her legs ached too much. She was excited to have the whole day to herself—well, until five o'clock—and she wished she could just shrug off the pain and enjoy it.

So the tea. And three more Advil. She wanted to go to the beach again, with sunscreen. She wanted to buy a pair of quiet shoes and send the first installment of payback to her father. But mostly she wanted to figure out what was going on at that restaurant. The place had mystique that seemed to come from a flurry of secrets, some of them just below the surface and some of them deeper-seated. And Adrienne had her own secret, which now that she wasn't working, she had the luxury of thinking about: Thatcher had kissed her.

Last night after service, Duncan poured every member of the staff a drink except for Thatcher and Fiona. They were back in the kitchen counting money and eating dinner. Eating dinner at one o'clock in the morning! This information was served up by Bruno. Fiona and Thatcher ate in the small office that had a back door that opened to the beach. Adrienne had had enough to drink to accept this tidbit from Bruno then ask for more. "So what's the deal with those two, anyway? Are they an item?" And Bruno, who was drinking a vodka martini, laughed so shrilly that there was no room for speculation: The man was gay. When Adrienne asked why he was laughing, Bruno only laughed harder. He was turning heads; Duncan popped him in the eye with a lime wedge. Adrienne judged that the moment had come to either leave or make an ass of herself. She called a cab from the podium and waited for the cab outside, hoping Bruno didn't share the nature of their conversation with anyone.

The espresso machine geared up; it was as loud as an airplane ready for takeoff. Adrienne tried to select the least intrusive and obvious words to broach the subject of Fiona. When the espresso was done, Caren poured herself a tiny cup, threw it back like a dose of cough medicine, and poured herself another. Adrienne shuddered. At least she hadn't vomited; those crackers at the bar had saved her life.

"So what did you think of last night?" Adrienne asked.

Caren shrugged. "What did *you* think?"

"It was fun," Adrienne said. In retrospect, the night seemed like a manic blur, as if she had been backstage at a rock concert, blinded by the lights, deafened by the music—and yes, pursued by journalists. "My feet hurt. It was a lot of standing up. My shoes were all wrong."

Caren tossed back the second espresso. "Well, yeah."

"I'm going to buy some new shoes today."

"Go to David Chase," Caren said. "Main Street."

"Okay."

Caren smiled in a knowing way. "Did you make money last night?"

"Yeah. A lot."

"Me, too. As a rule, though, never tell how much you bring in. Everyone is so damn greedy. And something else you might not know is that if you have someone helping you out in the kitchen, you should slide him money every once in a while."

"Like Mario?" Adrienne said.

"Mario?" Caren said. A mischievous smile spread across her face. "Mario might help you out, but it's nothing you should pay him for. Did he come on to you *already*?"

"No," Adrienne said. Why had she said Mario? She hadn't meant Mario, she'd meant Paco, the chip kid.

"Don't be surprised if he does," Caren said. "He's a ladies' man. As charming as they come and a great dancer, but *truh-bull*. Anyway, I was talking about one of the guys on the line. Hector, Louis, Henry . . ."

"Paco?"

"Exactly," Caren said. "Some time this weekend, give Paco fifty bucks. He'll be on your team for the rest of the summer. I always tip out the guys in the kitchen and they time my food perfectly. They slide me snacks. And Fiona likes it. She thinks the money we make on the floor is a cardinal sin."

Fiona's name was as bright as an open door. All Adrienne had to do was step through.

"I wanted to ask you about Fiona," Adrienne said.

Caren turned away. She opened a cabinet and brought down another espresso cup, which she filled. Adrienne was confused, and worried that the espresso was meant for her. Then she became even more confused because she heard the toilet flush in the hall bathroom. Was there someone else in the house? A few seconds later, a half-naked man sauntered into their kitchen. Adrienne tried to keep her composure. Never mind that her vague but very important overture was floating away like a released balloon. Never mind that because the shirtless man in their kitchen was Duncan. He was wearing his khaki pants from the night before. Adrienne could see one inch of the top of his boxers—they were white with black martini glasses. His brown hair was mussed and Adrienne was temporarily mesmerized by his bare torso. His beautiful chest and arms, a black cord choker around his neck with a silver key on it. He must have noticed her staring because the first thing he did was hold the key out to show it to her. "This opens my ski locker at the Aspen Club Lodge," he said. "Where did you work?"

Adrienne was reminded of her ex-boyfriend Michael Sullivan. Sully was a golfer and he loved golf lingo. In this instance, he would have suggested Adrienne *play through*.

"The Little Nell."

"And your friend? She worked there, too?"

"Kyra. Yep."

"You got a pass with the job?"

"Of course."

"How many days did you ski?"

"I didn't keep track."

Duncan nodded thoughtfully, and Adrienne could tell he was swallowing the urge to brag about how many days he'd skied. Men were like that—Doug, for example, had marked the days on his calendar when he got six runs in. Duncan accepted the espresso from Caren. He threw it back and Caren poured him another.

The kitchen, like the rest of the rental cottage, was unremarkable. The appliances were all about fifteen years old and barely functional. There was a white Formica counter, three ceramic canisters decorated with sunflowers, two magnets hanging on the fridge from a liquor store on Main Street called Murray's. Adrienne sat drinking her tea at a round wooden table that had been sawed in half so it would sit flush against the wall. And yet, in this humdrum room, a drama unfolded—well, maybe not a drama, but a situation that Adrienne never would have guessed on her own.

Duncan and Caren were sleeping together. Or had slept together last night.

The sight of Caren's hair down and the knowledge of her thong underwear and the smooth, tan skin of Duncan's chest and the flushing toilet—had he even *closed the door?*—only served to make Adrienne hot and uncomfortable. So, too, the way they stood at the counter with their tiny cups of poison like two strangers at a bar in Milan.

Adrienne moved to the microwave and heated her tea, which had grown cold. Thirty seconds—with her back to them, they felt free to touch. Adrienne heard the sucking noises of kisses. The microwave beeped and Adrienne took her tea, retreated down the hall.

"You don't have to leave," Caren said.

"Oh, I know," Adrienne said quickly, though there was no way she was going to be part of their postcoital espresso ritual. "I have to send some e-mail."

She would write to her father with the news of Holt Millman, the six hundred dollars in tips and a basic celebration that she had survived an entire night in the restaurant business. The e-mail to Kyra in Carmel would detail the first scoop of the summer—Adrienne working at the same restaurant as Duncan and Duncan sleeping with Adrienne's roommate. But before Adrienne turned on her computer, she studied the business card from Drew Amman-Keller. Something was going on at the restaurant that he wanted to know about, and Adrienne intended to find out what it was. She would not stand by, blissfully unaware, while the person closest to her robbed her blind. Not this time.

Adrienne's second night at the restaurant was called "first night of bar," and the place had a different feel. The nervous anticipation of soft opening had vanished and in its place was "we mean business." Everyone was paying tonight.

We mean business. When Adrienne arrived, Thatcher inspected her outfit: tonight, the sensational Chloe dress and a new pair of shoes.

"I know you suggested slippers," Adrienne said. "But a dress needs heels."

"It's okay," Thatcher said. "I like the shoes."

"Do you?" Adrienne said. They were Dolce & Gabbana thong sandals with a modest heel, in pink leather with black whipstitching. The pink of the leather matched the trim of the Chloe dress as well as her pink pants, and the salesperson at David Chase assured her that a thong sandal would be more comfortable, not to mention quieter, than a slide. They had cost Adrienne more than half of her cash earnings of the night before, but as soon as she tried the shoes on, she'd been hooked. She never imagined owning such gorgeous shoes, especially since she was in such dire straits. However, she felt that after the rigors of her first night, she deserved a treat.

"I like the dress, too," Thatcher said. "It suits you better than the pants did. But I don't know—we have to work on defining a look for you."

"I don't want a look," Adrienne said.

"You will when we find the right one."

Thatcher was both charming and annoying her. Or annoying her because he was charming. She wanted to whipstitch his mouth shut. Thatcher had his own look: the Patek Philippe, the Gucci loafers, and tonight a gorgeous blue shirt with pink pinstripes and pants that were halfway between khaki and white. The navy blazer. He looked wonderful but that, too, irritated her. She liked him better as she had first seen him—in jeans and sneakers. The dress-up clothes and the watch made it seem like he was trying too hard. But she was being mean. He smiled at her in a warm, genuine way then offered his arm and escorted her to the twelve-top for menu meeting.

After menu meeting came a delicious family meal: fried chicken with honey pecan butter, mashed potatoes, coleslaw. As Adrienne slathered her fried chicken with butter she thought happily of all the money she would save on food this summer. She ate without looking left, right, or toward the water. She would not be cheated out of one bite of this meal! When all that remained on her plate were chicken bones and a film of gravy, she raised her eyes to the rest of the staff. Caren sat across from her with her hair back in its usual tight bun. Duncan ate at the other end of the table with his sister.

That morning, after Duncan had driven off in his black Jeep Wrangler, Caren tapped on Adrienne's door. Adrienne was standing in front of her mirror diligently applying sunscreen to her face and chest. Caren was still in just the T-shirt, but now that Duncan had left, her face had changed; instead of glowing, she looked tired, artificially revved up on jet fuel.

"I'm sorry if Duncan freaked you out," Caren said.

"He didn't freak me out."

"I wasn't planning on bringing him back here. It just sort of happened."

"Believe me, I understand," Adrienne said.

"I've known him a long time," Caren said. "I guess with this being the last year and all, we both felt a little funny. Like it's now or never."

"You don't have to explain," Adrienne said. "I don't care who sleeps over."

"Nobody else knows about this," Caren said.

"I'm not going to tell," Adrienne said. "I don't even know anyone's name."

Adrienne cleared her plate and silverware into the bins and collected her yellow pad from the podium. Thatcher gnawed on a pencil as he went over the reservations.

"Are you ready for a briefing?" he asked.

She held up her pad. "I'm supposed to be managing these people," she said. "And I don't even know who they are." She headed back to the table.

Adrienne assured each member of the staff that this reconnaissance mission was for names only—she wasn't a cub reporter for the tabloids and she didn't work for the IRS. Still, she found that no one was content to state only his name, and so she learned other things as well. The new waiter with the bushy hair and weak chin was named Elliott Gray. He was getting his doctorate in Eastern religions at Tufts. The good-looking waiter with the gold earrings was Christo. He had been a waiter at the Club Car for seven years, the whole time waiting for a job to open up at the Bistro. The blond ponytail was Spillman—this was actually his last name, his first name was John. Spillman, along with Caren and Bruno, had worked at the bistro since the beginning. Spillman was married to a woman named Red Mare who was part Native American; she worked as a hostess at the Pearl. Then there was Joe, the black waiter, who in addition to being a waiter, worked in the kitchen. He wanted to be a chef, but he earned too much money waiting tables to make the switch. Fiona paid him to do prep work in the morning. That morning, he told Adrienne, he had been in charge of making the "pearls" of zucchini and summer squash that accompanied the duck. He made the pearls with a parisienne scoop, something the French invented to make lives like his miserable. "Now that," Joe said, "was hard work."

The busboys were Tyler, son of the health inspector, whom Adrienne had already met, and Roy and Gage. Roy had just finished his junior year at Notre Dame. He called Thatcher for a job after reading about the restaurant in *Notre Dame* magazine, an article Adrienne had missed at the public library. She made a mental note to go back and read it. Gage was older, with long hair in a ponytail and a face that looked like it had been stamped by too much loud music, too many cigarettes, and too little sleep. He said he'd met Thatcher at an AA meeting.

It was a lot of names but Adrienne was good with names. And although she was mostly worried about the front of the house, she decided to ask Joe about the kitchen staff.

"Eight guys work back there," he said. "They're all cousins. Last name Subiaco, they're from Chicago, they're Cuban-Italian and proud of it. Most importantly, they're White Sox fans. Mario brought the whole gang here in 'ninety-three when the place opened. He knew Fee from culinary school."

"Mario, the pastry chef?"

"He's a lady slayer," Joe said. "He calls himself King of the Sweet Ending and he doesn't mean desserts."

Adrienne blushed. "Well, I'm not writing that down."

"You asked," Joe said.

It was ten minutes before service, and Adrienne returned to the podium. Her notebook had some actual information in it now.

"Champagne," Thatcher said.

Adrienne sighed. Duncan was wiping down the bar. She felt strange knowing that under his seersucker shirt and Liberty of London tie was the black cord and the key. She walked over. He saw her, and with a quick flourish of his wrist, Adrienne heard the new sound of *we mean business*: a cork popping.

We mean business. The tablecloths were white and crisp, the irises fresh, the glasses polished, the candles lit. The waiters lined up for inspection, a band of angels. Rex played "Someone to Watch Over Me." Cars pulled into the parking lot. The well-dressed, sweet-smelling guests cooed at Thatcher and some of them at Adrienne. She received four compliments on her shoes. Cocktails were ordered and two glasses of Laurent-Perrier and then a bottle. The pretzel bread went out. The doughnuts. The sun began its descent toward the water, and the guests watched it with the anticipation of the ball dropping in Times Square. It was New Year's Eve here every night.

A man at table twelve beckoned Adrienne over with an impatient finger wagging in the air, and immediately the spell was broken. Didn't he notice her dress, her shoes, her champagne? She was the hostess here, not his bitch.

"Yes, sir, can I help you?"

He held up the basket of doughnuts. "What are *these*? If I'd wanted to eat at Krispy Kreme, I would have stayed in New York."

Adrienne stepped back. The man had very close cut ginger-colored hair and so many freckles that they gave him patches of disconcertingly brown skin. He wore strange yellow-lensed glasses.

Adrienne glanced at the basket but did not take it from the man. Table twelve: she tried to remember if he was a VIP.

"Have you tasted the doughnuts?" she asked. "They're not sweet—they're onion and herb doughnuts. If I do say so, they're delicious."

The woman to the man's left had very short black hair and the same funny glasses with lavender lenses. "I'll try one, Dana."

The man named Dana thrust the basket at Adrienne's nose. "We don't want doughnuts."

"But you haven't tried them. I assure you, if . . ."

"We don't want doughnuts."

Adrienne took the basket, but the man, Dana, was holding on tighter than she expected so the exchange took on the appearance of a struggle. The basket zinged into Adrienne's chest. There was a smattering of applause and both Adrienne and the man named Dana pivoted to face the rest of the room. The applause was for the sun, which had just set.

"Would you like bread and butter, sir?" Adrienne asked. "Or we have pretzel bread. That's served with the chef's homemade mustard."

"You have *got* to be kidding me."

"I'll get you bread and butter, then."

"Yes," Dana said. "Do that."

Adrienne walked away thinking *Asshole, asshole, asshole!* What could she do to get back at him? Order the chips and dip for all the tables surrounding his? Run her tongue across the top of his perfect cake of sweet butter?

She searched for a busboy, but they were all humping—pouring water, delivering doughnuts—so that now the worst thing about the ugly freckled man who looked at the world through urine-colored glasses was that he was forcing Adrienne into the kitchen.

She pushed through the door. Hot, bright, quiet. Eddie wolf-whistled and Adrienne felt all eyes on her. Including Fiona's.

"Did you get those avocados?" Fiona asked.

Adrienne had spent a good part of her day at the beach wondering how to get Fiona to like her. But now, thanks to a man named *Dana*, she was in no mood to be joked to or about. "No, chef."

"What are you doing in here, then? It will be at least another six minutes for the chips. Right, Paco?"

Pfft, pfft, pfft. "Right, chef."

Adrienne put the doughnuts on the counter in a way that indicated slamming without actually slamming.

"If table twelve wanted to eat at Krispy Kreme, he would have stayed in New York."

"The salient phrase there is 'stayed in New York,'" Fiona said. "And people wonder why I don't come out of the kitchen."

"Is there bread, chef?"

"Of course."

"Where?"

"We went over this last night, did we not? The bread is where the bread is kept."

"I don't know where that is," Adrienne said. "You never told me. So, please. Chef."

Fiona eyeballed her for a long time, long enough to indicate a showdown. *Fire me,* Adrienne thought. Fire me for asking for bread for a man who looks like one of the villains in a Batman comic. But instead of yelling, Fiona smiled and she became someone else completely. She went from being a little fucking Napoleon to a china doll. She reminded Adrienne of her favorite friend from Camp Hideaway, where she had been shipped the summer her mother was dying. In the second that Adrienne was thinking of this other girl—her name was Pammy Ipp; she was the only girl at camp that Adrienne had told the truth—Fiona left and reappeared with a basket of rolls and the butter. So Adrienne still had not learned where the bread was kept.

"I told him how good the doughnuts were," Adrienne said.

Fiona rolled her blue eyes. "Get out of here," she said.

Table twelve was turning out to be a real problem. Adrienne delivered the bread and butter with a smile, but a few minutes later she saw Spillman engaged in a heated conversation with the man named Dana over what appeared to be his bottle of wine. Spillman tasted the wine himself then carried the bottle, gingerly, like it was an infant, over to Thatcher at the podium. Adrienne was chatting with an older couple at table five—neighbors of the Parrishes as it turned out—but when she saw this happening, she excused herself. She wanted to know what was going on.

"What's going on?" she asked Spillman.

"The guy's a menace," Spillman whispered. "He ordered a 1983 Chevalier-Montrachet at four hundred dollars a bottle and he claims it's bad. I tasted it and it tastes like fucking heaven in a glass. But Menace says he has a cellar full of this wine at home and he knows how it's supposed to taste, which is not like this. I asked him if he wanted me to decant it because the wine's been in that bottle for over twenty years, it could probably do with a little elbow room, and he just said, 'Take it away.' He said they're going to stick with cocktails. He orders the most expensive bottle on the list and now suddenly he wants vodka. Plus, he harassed me about the apps. He insisted he wanted the foie gras *cooked through*. Fiona said it would taste like a rubber tire. I hope it does."

Adrienne looked at Thatcher. He seemed on the verge of a smile.

"It's not funny," she said. "The guy gave me a hard time about the doughnuts. He said if he wanted to eat at Krispy Kreme he would have stayed in New York."

"That's an old one," Spillman said. "I hear that one every year."

Thatcher checked the reservation book. "The reservation was made four weeks ago by his secretary." He scribbled a note in the book then pointed the eraser end of his pencil at Adrienne. "Okay, that's the last time we take a reservation from a secretary. Except for Holt Millman. His secretary is a great lady named Dottie Shore. Not only did I give her the private number, I gave her my home number. But nobody else makes a reservation through a secretary. If they want to eat here, they have to call us themselves. It's a little late in the game to be making up new rules. However"—Thatcher turned to Spillman—"we'll offer the wine by the glass as a special. Twenty dollars a glass, only six glasses available and that's a bargain. We'll take a hit on the bottle. Adrienne, I want you to offer table twelve a round of cocktails on the house."

Adrienne gasped. "Why?"

"The guy obviously had an unhappy childhood. He's angry for whatever reason, he wants something from us. We could send him out the caviar, but we don't like him. So we'll give him drinks. And I'm going to let you be the hero."

"I'd rather not go over there again," Adrienne said. "Spillman can do it."

Spillman had already walked away; Adrienne watched him present the bottle to Duncan at the bar.

Thatcher took Adrienne's shoulder and wheeled her toward the dining room. "I'm going to let you be the hero," he said. "Old-fashioned service. You said you knew all about it."

Adrienne straightened the seams of her dress and tried to straighten out her frame of mind as she headed to table twelve. She put her hand on the back of Dana's wicker chair; she couldn't bring herself to touch him and she wasn't sure she was supposed to. "We're sorry about the bottle of wine," she said. "We'd like to buy you a round of drinks on the house."

"Lovely," the woman in lavender glasses murmured. For the first time, Adrienne noticed the other couple at the table. They were in their fifties, distinguished-looking, Asian.

"Thank you," the Asian man said, dipping his head at Adrienne.

But Adrienne was waiting to hear from the man named Dana. She was the hero and she wanted him to acknowledge as much. He said nothing, and after a second Adrienne realized that he was one of those people who didn't have anything to offer unless he was angry or upset. He deserved an old-fashioned kick in the balls.

In two seatings, only one person ate at the bar—a man in his midthirties who wore a red sailcloth shirt over a white T-shirt. He smiled at Adrienne every time she passed by. Red Shirt chatted with Duncan and drank a glass of Whale's Tale Pale Ale. Then a huge portion of chips and dip came out. So the guy was a VIP. He was wearing jeans and driving moccasins. He had brown hair receding a very little bit and nice brown eyes. He looked kind and responsible, no flashy good looks, no whiff of creepy lying bastard. *Rule Three: Exercise good judgment about men!*

Red Shirt's appetizer was the beet salad. Adrienne liked men who weren't afraid to order a salad. When she wandered up to the bar to have her champagne glass refilled she actually bent her leg at the knee to show off her new shoes. Rex played "Waltzing Matilda," and Adrienne said, to no one in particular, "Oh, I love this song." Duncan introduced Red Shirt to Delilah, but Adrienne didn't catch his name. *Introduce me!* she thought.

Adrienne ran appetizers for Joe, she retrieved three bottles of wine from the wine cave, she replaced the toilet paper in the ladies' room, she delivered two checks and got a lesson on the credit card machine from Thatcher. When she found a second to float by the bar again, Red Shirt was eating the lobster club, the entrée Adrienne herself most wanted to try. She approached Thatcher at the podium.

"Nine bottles of Laurent-Perrier tonight," he said. "Our experiment is really working. I still have to teach you how to use the wine key. When you can open wine, that will free me up. And champagne. There's a nice quiet way to open champagne. I'll show you."

"Who's that sitting at the bar?" she asked.

Thatcher didn't even look up. "Jasper Zodl."

"Jasper Zodl?"

"JZ. He drives the delivery truck. He comes every morning at ten."

"Will you introduce me?"

"No."

"Why not?"

Conveniently, the phone rang.

The phone had been ringing all night. Half were reservation calls, half were inquiries about the bar. Was tonight, as rumor had it, first night of bar? This call was about the bar.

"The bar is open tonight until one," Thatcher said.

When he hung up, Adrienne said, "I heard about this huge bar scene, I heard about you hiring a bouncer and a line out into the parking lot, and yet, the only person at the bar is the delivery driver who is so undesirable you won't even introduce me."

"He's not undesirable," Thatcher said. "He's a very nice guy. As for the bar, you just wait. Wait and see."

Adrienne would have been just as happy if nobody had shown up. At the end of second seating, there was a problem with one of the guest's credit cards. She ran it and ran it and each time the machine informed her that the card was unacceptable but Adrienne wasn't about to tell the guest this when she had only learned the credit card machine that night and it could just as easily have been she who was unacceptable. So she kept Joe waiting, as well as the guests, who had told Adrienne that they wanted to get home and pay the babysitter. She didn't take the problem to Thatcher primarily because she thought it was time she worked through a crisis by herself but also because he had refused to introduce her to JZ.

Joe, whom Adrienne had initially characterized as heavyset now just seemed big and soft and rather handsome—his skin a chocolaty brown, distinct from the deep-fried russet color of the Subiacos. But even Joe, so polite and gentlemanly, had his limits. He glared at her as she ran the card again, punching the numbers in one by one.

"What the fuck is taking so long?" he said.

Adrienne brandished the card. "It's no good. I've run the card six times, three times manually, and I can't get a bite. You're going to have to tell them."

"And jeopardize my tip? No way, sister. You tell them."

Adrienne peered over Joe's shoulder at the table. The lovely dark-haired wife was sitting sideways in her chair; she was all wrapped up in her pashmina like a present, her Louis Vuitton clutch purse in her lap. The husband had his pen poised. There would be no lengthy calculations with the tip, forty, fifty, a nice round number on the generous side, a dashed off signature, and these people were *out the door.*

"Okay, I'll tell them," she said.

Joe studied the card, "Tell them it's expired," he said. "This card expired in May. Today is the second of June. Didn't Thatch tell you to check the expiration first thing?"

Of course he had. Adrienne hurried the card back over to the couple, explained the problem, and the man, with apologies, offered her an identical card with a different expiration, and Adrienne ran it without incident. Sixty seconds later the couple was breezing past her with a happy, rushed wave.

Thatcher in the meantime had asked Joe what the problem was—he had seen Joe and Adrienne conferring by the credit card machine as he chatted with one of the fondue tables out in the sand—and Joe had tattled.

Thatcher handed Adrienne another leather folder. "Run this. And always remember to check the expiration. I'm surprised you didn't learn that on your five front desks."

She wanted to tell him to go to hell, but she would be satisfied if nobody showed up for first night of bar, if the place didn't turn out to be as "wildly popular" as Thatcher and Duncan and *Bon Appétit* thought it was. Plus, she was tired again tonight. She'd had two glasses of champagne, two glasses of water, and a regular coffee loaded with cream and sugar. As the guests from second seating finished up and wandered toward the door, Adrienne stood at the podium and bid them good-bye, hoping nobody could tell that the podium was holding her up.

JZ rose from the bar—he had finished his meal with Mario's ethereal candy plate—and Adrienne thought he, too, was leaving. But he walked wide of the podium like he was headed for the men's room. Except he bypassed the men's room and pushed open the door of the kitchen.

The kitchen. Adrienne stared at the swinging door with dread. What had Thatcher said? *No guests allowed in the kitchen.* Adrienne waited a second to see if JZ would come flying out on his butt. She stopped Caren.

"That guy who was sitting at the bar—did you see him?—he went into the kitchen. He just . . . I didn't realize that's where . . . is that okay?"

"Who, JZ?" Caren said.

"Yeah."

"Well, you know who he is, right?"

"The delivery driver?" Adrienne said.

Caren laughed and pushed into the kitchen behind him.

And then, just when the restaurant was beginning to take on a sense of calm—Tyler, Roy, and Gage the only flurry of activity as they cleared tables and stripped them—the headlights started pulling into the parking lot. The first people to reach the door were four large college boys wearing oxford shirts over tie-dye and loafers from L.L. Bean. One of them had a black cord at the neck like Duncan's only this cord had a purplish bead on it. From Connecticut, Adrienne thought. Listened to Phish.

"Bar open?" the one with the necklace asked, and Adrienne surveyed the bar. Its four bar stools were deserted and Duncan was checking over his bottles while Delilah worked around him, replacing glasses. Adrienne held up a finger. Boys like this—boys like the ones she used to date at the three colleges she attended (Perry Russell, junior year at Vanderbilt, from Connecticut, listened to Phish)—now made her feel old and prim. Like a librarian.

She went over to check with Duncan; Thatcher was MIA. "Is the bar open?"

This was possibly the dumbest question of all time—why would to-night be called first night of bar if the bar wasn't open? But Duncan simply straightened his tie, squared his shoulders, punched a button on the CD player—R.E.M.'s "I Am Superman"—and said, "I'm as ready as I'll never be."

It was nearing eleven o'clock. The four boys shook hands with Duncan, claimed the bar stools with a whoop, and ordered Triple 8 and tonics. Adrienne returned to the podium. A couple on a date came in followed by a group of six women who called themselves the Winers, followed by two older men who informed Adrienne of her loveliness and told her they'd just finished an exquisite meal at Company of the Cauldron and wanted a nightcap. More women—a bachelorette party. The return of the local author and her entourage. By ten after eleven, Adrienne couldn't even see Duncan through the throng of people. He'd turned up the stereo and the floorboards vibrated under Adrienne's shoes. Headlights continued to pull into the parking lot.

Where, exactly, was Thatcher?

Caren and Spillman still had tables out in the sand finishing dessert, but the other waiters would be cashing out. Adrienne found Thatcher doling out tips from the cash box at a small deuce in the far corner of the restaurant.

"People keep pulling in," Adrienne said. "Where's the bouncer?"

"I was kidding about the bouncer," Thatcher said. "Go back up front. When Duncan gives you the 'cutthroat' sign, start your line. And then it's one for one. One person goes out, one person comes in."

Adrienne rubbed her forehead—really, could the man irritate her more?—and headed back by the bar.

"Adrienne!"

It was Duncan, holding aloft a glass of Laurent-Perrier. Only two days earlier, good French champagne had been her favorite indulgence, but now it held all the appeal of a glass of hemlock. Still, the guests at the bar parted for her like she was someone important, thus she felt compelled to take the glass and shout, "Thank you!" over the strains of an old Yaz tune.

Duncan smiled and gave her the "cutthroat" sign.

She carried her champagne to the podium just as two women stepped through the door. They were wearing black dresses and high heels, one woman was blond, the other brunette. They looked to be in their forties. Divorced, Adrienne guessed. Out on the prowl.

"I'm sorry?" Adrienne said.

The brunette flicked her eyes at Adrienne but didn't acknowledge her. The women kept walking.

"Excuse me!" Adrienne called. She put her glass down and took a few strides toward the women until she was able to reach out and touch the middle of the brunette's bare back. That did it—the brunette spun around.

"What?"

How predictable was this? *I was kidding about the bouncer.* What Thatcher meant was, *You, Adrienne, are the bouncer.*

"The bar's full," Adrienne said. "You'll have to wait by the door until someone leaves."

The brunette might have been beautiful at one time but it looked like she'd gotten in a lot of afternoons at the beach over the years without sunscreen—that and something else. When her brow creased at Adrienne's words, she looked like a witch. It was probably the face she used to scare her children.

"We're friends of Cat," she said.

Friends of Cat, the electrician. Cat, who was the most important VIP in the unlikely event of a blackout.

"Okay," Adrienne said, but she didn't smile because she wasn't that much of a pushover.

A minute later, Caren appeared. "Duncan's pissed."

Adrienne blinked. Duncan had every right to be pissed—he'd given her the "cutthroat" sign and not thirty seconds later she let in more people—but

Adrienne did not like being confronted by Caren in her new capacity as Duncan's girlfriend.

"They said they were friends of Cat's."

"Everyone on the island is friends with Cat," Caren said. "If that bar gets any heavier, it's going to sink into the sand. But more importantly, if you let any more people in, you're going to ruin it for the people who are already here."

"I understand that," Adrienne said tersely. "Thatcher just *left* me here to bounce."

Caren shrugged and reached for her hair. With the release of one pin, it all came tumbling down.

"Are you going home?" Adrienne asked.

"And miss first night of bar?" Caren said. "No way."

"Do you want to help me keep the masses at bay?"

"No," Caren said, "I'm going to change."

As she left, more headlights materialized. Adrienne tightened the muscles in her face. Nobody else was getting past.

The next people to approach were another couple on a date. The girl wore a cute sequined dress that Adrienne had seen at Gypsy but couldn't afford. "Sorry," Adrienne told them, and she did, to her own ears, sound genuinely sorry. "You'll have to wait." Like magic, they obeyed, staying right in front of the podium. Turned out, the couple was used to standing in line here. And once this couple formed a willing start to the line, everyone who came after had no choice but to follow suit. In ten minutes, Adrienne had a line a dozen people long. She felt a brand-new emotion: the surge of pure power. She was the gatekeeper.

At one point, a man with wet-looking black hair and a chain with a gold marijuana leaf dangling from it swaggered toward her, nudging aside the couple on a date.

"I'm a friend of Duncan's," he said.

"Everyone's a friend of Duncan's," she said, and she sent him to the end of the line.

Finally, Thatcher came sauntering up with the cash box under his arm and a wad of paper-clipped receipts.

"How's everything going?" he asked.

"Fine," Adrienne said.

"Is the line moving?"

"No."

"No," he said. "It never does."

"So some people stay in this line until closing?"

"Oh, sure," he said. He smiled at the adorable couple on their date and Adrienne could tell he recognized them but didn't remember their names.

"Eat," she said. She felt wonderful saying this. She knew better than to count on him!

It was midnight; only one hour left of this madness. As Thatcher walked into the kitchen, JZ emerged. They exchanged a few quiet words. Adrienne was so keenly interested in what they were saying that it took her a moment to notice the author and her entourage on their way out.

"We're going to the Chicken Box," the author said. "Want me to count off eight heads for you?"

"Please," Adrienne said.

So her line was less by eight—Adrienne was happy to see the young couple make it in—but there were still a dozen people in her line and now the person at the front was the wet-haired "friend" of Duncan. He glared at Adrienne in such an overtly malicious way that she considered asking him why he was wearing a marijuana leaf around his neck. Did he want people to know he smoked pot? Did he think it would encourage interest from the right kind of women? Her thoughts were interrupted when JZ handed her a basket of crackers.

"Thank you," Adrienne said. "Thank you, thank you."

"I'm JZ," he said.

Adrienne held out her hand. "Adrienne Dealey. The new assistant manager."

"I know. Fiona told me."

Adrienne tasted a cracker. They were a different kind tonight—cheddar with sesame seeds. Scrumptious. Wet Hair watched her eat the cracker with envy and Adrienne hoped he was hungry. She hoped that all he'd had for dinner were fries from Stubby's on the strip by Steamship Wharf.

"What did Fiona say?" Adrienne asked JZ.

"That the gorgeous brunette by the front door was Adrienne Dealey, the new assistant manager."

At this point, Wet Hair, who had been eavesdropping, felt entitled to join the conversation. "I had a feeling you were new," he said. "Otherwise you would have let me in."

Adrienne ignored him. "Did Fiona actually call me a gorgeous brunette?"

"No," JZ said. "I did." He pointed to the basket of crackers. "Please, help yourself. I have to make the rounds with these, then get out of here. I have a buddy at the airport waiting to fly me home."

"Fly you home?"

"I live on the Cape. Normally I take the boat back and forth every day."

"That's quite a commute."

"Lots of people do it," he said. "I sleep on the boat. And it pays the bills. Listen, it was nice meeting you."

Adrienne was so crestfallen he was leaving that even the pile of crackers didn't cheer her. She stacked them on the podium like so many gold coins. She watched JZ pass the basket to Delilah, the busboys, and Joe, who was left with a single cracker. Then JZ said good-bye to a bunch of people at the bar and headed for the door.

He waved to Adrienne on his way out.

"Bye," she said.

Wet Hair roused Adrienne from her reverie by tapping her arm. "He left, right? So I can go in?"

"No," she said.

Somehow, she got drunk. To avoid further conversation with Wet Hair, Adrienne concentrated on her crackers and her crackers made her thirsty so she drank her champagne. Someone in the bachelorette party decided to buy every woman in the restaurant a shot called prairie fire, which was a lethal combination of tequila and Tabasco. This same woman convinced Duncan to play "It's Raining Men" at top decibel and further convinced him to allow the bride-to-be to dance on the blue granite in her bare feet. Adrienne watched all this from the safety of the podium, thinking about how much more she would enjoy these shenanigans if she didn't have Wet Hair breathing into the side of her face. Then Caren appeared, wearing a black halter top that showed off her perfectly flat, perfectly tanned stomach, and a pair of low-slung white jeans. She was dressed like a twenty-year-old but she looked better than any twenty-year-old could ever hope to. Adrienne suddenly felt dowdy; here she was in Chloe and Dolce & Gabbana in an attempt to get away from the kid stuff.

Caren held out a shot glass, Adrienne's prairie fire, because she did, after all, qualify as a woman in the restaurant.

"Come on," Caren said. "Let's do them together."

Adrienne accepted the shot glass. Well, it was better than espresso.

They did the shots and Caren offered Adrienne a swig from her beer as a chaser. Adrienne's throat burned, her eyes watered. The bride-to-be was doing the twist on the bar, every man in the place looking up her Lilly Pulitzer skirt.

Then Caren screamed, "Charlie!"

She hugged the man with the wet hair. He threw Adrienne a look of enormous satisfaction and contempt over Caren's shoulder. Adrienne felt no remorse, only distaste that Caren should actually know this person.

"This is Charlie," Caren explained. "A friend of Duncan's. He doesn't have to wait."

Adrienne was just as happy to have Wet Hair leave her proximity. "Go," she said. The tequila and Tabasco had warmed her mood. "Enjoy."

The new head of the line was a kid who looked about twelve. He was short and had acne around his nose. *Do I have to card?* Adrienne wondered. She wasn't going to card. Her job was pure mathematics—one out, one in. She heard a deep, metallic thrum; it sounded like a gong. Adrienne looked to the bar to see Duncan holding an enormous hand bell, the kind used in church choirs. "Last call!" he shouted. Last call, music to her ears. Paco wandered past the podium still in his chef's whites, and Adrienne yelled out to him. She pulled a fifty-dollar bill out of her change purse, which was stashed inside the podium.

"You've been a big help," she said. "Thank you." She pressed the bill into Paco's hand.

"Thank *you!*" Paco said. "You want me to get you a drink?"

"Yes," Adrienne said, surveying the dancing, pulsing crowd. "Two."

She should have gone home when the restaurant closed—it was very late—but Caren told her about a party at the Subiaco house in Surfside. Practically the whole staff was going and Caren felt that Adrienne should go, too.

"To prove you're one of the gang," she said.

Adrienne agreed to go with Caren and Duncan in Caren's Jetta. She would stay for one drink then call a cab and be home in bed by three o'clock at the very latest. It wasn't until Adrienne was already ensconced in the backseat of the car that she realized Wet Hair Charlie was coming with them. The opposite door opened and he climbed in. Adrienne's enthusiasm flagged.

"I don't know about this," Adrienne said. "It's getting late."

"I figured you for a stick-in-the-mud," Charlie said.

"Come on," Caren said. "It'll be fun."

During the ride, Charlie pulled out a joint, lit up, and passed it around. Adrienne refused, then cracked her window. This was what she'd always thought the restaurant life would be like: two o'clock in the morning doing drugs on her way to a party where she would proceed to drink even more than she had drunk during her eight-hour shift. She laughed and then Charlie laughed, though he had no idea what was funny.

The Subiaco house was huge and funky. It had curved steps that led up to a grand front porch with a swing. The house had diamond-shaped windows, some panes of stained glass, and a turret. Inside, though, it was a bad marriage of down-at-the-heels beach cottage and urban bachelor pad. In the first living room Adrienne entered, the furniture was upholstered in faded, demure prints, there was a rocking chair and a few dinged tables. There was a second living room with a cracked leather sofa and a state-of-the-art entertainment system: flat-screen TV on the wall, surround sound, stereo thumping with ten-year-old rap. Adrienne couldn't stand the noise. She headed out to the sun porch, where there was wicker furniture and an old piano. She took a seat on the piano bench. Caren appeared, bearing two bright red drinks, and she handed one to Adrienne.

"What's this?" Adrienne asked.

"I don't know," Caren admitted.

Adrienne took a sip. It tasted like a mixture of Kool-Aid and lighter fluid. She put the drink down on the piano.

"Duncan didn't make this?"

"No," Caren said. "It was in a punch bowl on the kitchen table."

"They're trying to poison us so they can take our money," Adrienne said. She had left her change purse, with three hundred dollars in it, in Caren's car.

Duncan came onto the sun porch and he and Caren settled down on the wicker sofa. Then Charlie walked in and after looking around the room— no doubt hoping for better company—he plopped down on the piano bench next to Adrienne. That was all she needed.

"I'm getting out of here," she said.

"Stay," Caren said. "It's fun."

"Stick-in-the-mud," Charlie said.

Adrienne peeked into the next room. Elliott, Christo, and a few of the unidentified Subiacos were smoking cigarettes watching *Apocalypse Now* to a soundtrack of Dr. Dre. Fun? In the kitchen, Tyler and Roy, the most definitely underage busboys, were doing shots of Jägermeister. Adrienne thought she might get sick just watching them.

"Phone?" she said.

They pointed down the hall. She located a wobbly pie crust table where the last rotary phone in America rested on a crocheted doily.

Adrienne called A-1 Taxi but was unable to give them her exact location. "Out by the airport?" she said. "Surfside? It's a big house at the end of a dirt road? The Subiaco house?"

"Subiaco?" the cab driver said. "I'll be there in twenty minutes."

"Okay," Adrienne said. She went outside to retrieve her change purse from Caren's car and decided to wait for the cab on the bottom step of the porch. Then she heard someone whisper her name. She turned around. Mario was lying on the porch swing, drinking a beer. "What are you doing here?" he asked.

"I came to the party," she said, wondering if because she was a manager this would sound weird. She climbed the steps to the porch and leaned back against the railing, checking it first to make sure it wouldn't give way, dumping her into the bushes. "But I have to go home. I'm tired."

"You can sleep upstairs with me," he said.

"No, thanks," she said. "I've been warned about you."

"Oh, really?"

"The King of the Sweet Ending?"

Mario laughed. "Please," he said. "Just call me King." He drained his beer then sat up. He wore jeans and a black T-shirt. *There was something about him*, Adrienne thought. He emanated heat. Smoldered, like all the other womanizers she had ever known.

"How'd you get that scar on your neck?" Adrienne asked.

"Pulling a cookie sheet out of a high oven," he said. "A million years ago, in culinary school."

"You went to school with Fiona?"

"Met her in Skills One," he said. "It was a very tough class. We bonded." He laughed. "She's a big hotshot now but when I first met her she couldn't even carry a tray of veal bones, okay? We had to roast fifty pounds a day for stock and that's more than half Fee's body weight. Our instructor did a double-take when he saw her. He was like, 'How did a fourth grader get into our classroom?'"

Adrienne turned around to search the darkness for the lights of her cab. It felt dangerous to be talking about Fiona like this, though of course Adrienne was enthralled. "Was cooking school tough?"

"A killer," he said. He patted the spot next to him on the swing. "Sit here, I'll tell you all about it."

"I'm fine," Adrienne said.

"You got that right," Mario said. "If you're wondering how an inner city Cuban schlub like me got into the CIA, the answer is, I'm a minority." He laughed again. "And a fucking genius, of course."

Adrienne tried to smile but she was too tired. She checked behind her. Nothing.

"I'm only kid-ding," Mario sang out. "My whole family works in kitchens. My old man and his three brothers worked the line at the Palmer House in Chicago, and all the brothers had sons. There are eleven of us altogether and we all work in kitchens. My brother Louis was a prep cook at Charlie Trotter, Hector worked at Mango, Eddie flipped eggs at the North Side. I worked at so many places I can't even remember them all, but after high school I got tired of making five bucks an hour. I wanted to learn technique. So off I go to the best cooking school in the country and it kicked my ass. I nearly quit."

"Really?"

"I hated the hot line. Hated it. Now Fiona, she loved the hot line. The hotter and the busier it was, the more she liked it. The other guys worshipped her. Tiny little thing like that couldn't even get the veal bones from the oven to the counter and here she is doing eighty plates an hour, swearing like a sailor. She was the one who told me I belonged in pastry, but you know what I thought? Pastry is for chicks. So I got a big, brawny externship at the Pump Room back home and that made school look like *Sesame Street*. When I went back to the CIA and tried pastry, I realized there's worse things in life than being in a room full of chicks."

"I guess so."

"You like dessert?"

"Of course I like dessert."

"Everybody likes dessert," Mario said. "And pastry is cool, okay? It's quiet. It's solitary. It's a place where you have the time and space to lavish the ingredients with love. I'm all about the love."

He made the word "love" sound like a big soft bed she could fall into. Adrienne gripped the railing. *Rule Three!* She took a big drink of night air. It was absurdly late. She checked the gravel driveway and the dirt road again. She couldn't tell if the glow in the distance were headlights or lights from the airport.

"So you brought everybody here?" Adrienne said. "All your cousins."

"Three stayed back home," Mario said. "My brother Mikey is a lawyer. And Hector's twin brothers, Phil and Petey, didn't want to leave Chicago. They work together at the hottest sushi place in the city and have season tickets to the Bulls. So."

"So," Adrienne said. "What will you do next year, when the restaurant is closed?"

"Cry my eyes out," Mario said. "But it's far from over. We have a long summer ahead."

"Yeah," Adrienne said. It was going to be a very long summer if she didn't get any sleep. Her head felt like it was filled with dried beans. But then she saw headlights, actual true headlights and even better, the bright top hat of a taxi. The cab stopped in front of the house and the door popped open.

"Hey, everybody!" a voice called out. It was Delilah. She was, inexplicably, wearing a belly dancer costume—a red satin bra and transparent harem pants. She ran up the steps, dinging finger cymbals. Adrienne hurried past her, before the cab drove off. As she pulled away, Adrienne gazed back at the house in time to see Mario, ever the gentleman, leading Delilah inside.

TO: DrDon@toothache.com
FROM: Ade12177@hotmail.com
DATE: June 7, 2005, 8:37 A.M.
SUBJECT: See and be scene

At first I thought the Bistro was all about the food but after a week of work I can tell you, it's all about the drinks. It's a huge scene. Some nights it's like a fraternity party and some nights it's something else entirely (think of a dozen women in for a fiftieth birthday party belting out "New York, New York" while doing chorus line kicks). Last night, I let a man into the bar and he tipped me five hundred dollars. I told him I couldn't possibly accept it and he said, 'You want me to give it to the bartender instead?' So I put it in an envelope and mailed it off to you this morning. Only five hundred to go!

I never considered myself a night owl but since I started work I haven't gotten to bed before two. I sleep until at least eight then take a nap on the beach. I haven't gone jogging even once! But I am brushing and flossing and doing my best to stay away from the candy plate. How are the smiles in Maryland? Love.

TO: Ade12177@hotmail.com
FROM: DrDon@toothache.com
DATE: June 7, 2005, 8:45 A.M.
SUBJECT: Nobody knows the troubles I've scene

I'm not sure how I'm supposed to handle being the father of the doyenne of Nantucket nightlife. Should I be worried or proud? Or both? Mavis says she wants to visit Nantucket—I know I always promise and never come, but this time I think we might. Can you research some B & Bs? And book us a night at your restaurant, of course. I'd love to see my little girl in action. Love, love.

TO: DrDon@toothache.com
FROM: Ade12177@hotmail.com
DATE: June 7 2005, 8:52 A.M.
SUBJECT: Don't book 'em yet, Don-o

Let me get my sea legs before you show up, okay? Promise me you won't book anything without double-triple-checking with me first?

TO: Ade12177@hotmail.com
FROM: DrDon@toothache.com
DATE: June 7, 2005, 8:59 A.M.
SUBJECT: I promise

Love, love, love.

TO: kyracrenshaw@mindspring.com
FROM: Ade12177@hotmail.com
DATE: June 7, 2005, 9:04 A.M.
SUBJECT: sex, drugs, and lobster roll

Duncan has spent every night here for the past nine nights. They always look so tuckered out in the morning—thank God the walls are thick! Caren thinks it's this big secret, but one of the other waiters at work said he was pretty sure the only reason Duncan shacked up here was because he doesn't want to sleep in the same apartment with his sister. I, of course, pretended like I didn't know what he was talking about.

Aspen seems like a million years ago. I haven't thought about Doug in weeks. I miss you, though. How's Carmel? Seen Clint Eastwood?

4

❦

Reservations

Adrienne wasn't sure how long her father's affair with Mavis had been going on. When he set up his dental practice in 1984, the office had three employees: Adrienne's father, whom everyone called Dr. Don, Adrienne's mother, Rosalie, who worked the reception desk, booked appointments, and did all the billing, and Mavis, the hygienist. Five years later, when Adrienne's mother got sick, Adrienne was old enough to fill in for her mother after school and on Saturdays—and to work during the week they had hired a retired woman named Mrs. Leech.

But there had always been Mavis with her blond Dorothy Hamill haircut, her smell of antiseptic soap, and the Juicy Fruit gum that she chewed to freshen her breath after lunch (despite Dr. Don's fatwa on chewing gum of any kind). When she was first hired, Mavis was a single mother with three-year-old twin boys named Coleman and Graham, who was deaf. Mavis's husband had left her and Mavis's family lived in the French part of Louisiana, which she described as a "stinking swamp." She had no desire to return. Adrienne's parents took pity on Mavis, especially Adrienne's mother, who was prone to fits of do-gooding. As a happy coincidence, it turned out that Mavis was a talented hygienist. She had a light touch, a Southern accent, and because she dealt on a daily basis with her deaf son, she took great pains to make her communications with children gentle and clear. How many times had Adrienne heard her go through the brushing spiel? *Now I'm just gonna put a little bit of paste on the brush—see, it tastes like bubble gum. Don't tell the doctor! The brush is gonna move in really fast circles so it might tickle a bit. You're laughing already, I can't bee-leeve it!*

It was impossible to think of Mavis without thinking of Rosalie, not only because Rosalie and Mavis were best friends, but also because as Rosalie's presence in Adrienne's life waned, Mavis's increased. Rosalie's illness came on very strong and suddenly. There might have been a clue in the fact that Rosalie had lost her first child in a hard labor, and after Adrienne, Dr. Don and Rosalie had not been able to conceive another child. But Rosalie's outlook was that some people were blessed with many children and some with only one, and she reveled in the fact that her one child was as well-adjusted and delightful as Adrienne. Then when Adrienne was eleven going on twelve (and was, at that age, neither well-adjusted nor delightful) Rosalie started having pains. She went to her gynecologist and came home looking like she had seen a ghost. A biopsy a week later at the Hospital of the University of Pennsylvania had diagnosed her with inoperable ovarian cancer and four to six months to live.

Adrienne knew these details now, as an adult, but at the time she had not been well-informed. Her father, a graduate of the dental school at Penn, was friends with the head of internal medicine at HUP and Adrienne was aware of her father's conversations with him and other doctors at the hospital. Initially, she thought it was Dr. Don who was sick because it was he who looked like he might die. Eventually both her parents sat her down and told her that Rosalie had cancer.

It was Mavis's idea to send Adrienne to Camp Hideaway in the Pocono Mountains. Adrienne didn't want to go. She claimed she wanted to help take care of her mother, but really she didn't want to leave her friends and she was addicted to *General Hospital* and she knew from reading the brochure that Camp Hideaway didn't have a single TV. She begged her father to let her stay home and when begging didn't work, she threatened him. She would run away. She would hitchhike. She would accept a ride with any stranger, even if it was a man with yellow teeth. Finally, Adrienne appealed to her mother. Adrienne knew her mother loved her to the point of distraction. Once she had snooped through Rosalie's desk, where she found a tablet on which Rosalie had written Adrienne's name a hundred times, and in the middle of the page, it said, "Unconditional love." When Adrienne spoke to Rosalie about camp, Rosalie said, "Please do as your father says. He and Mavis think it's for the best." Rosalie's tone of voice was distant; it was as if she were already gone.

Adrienne went to Camp Hideaway for six weeks, and when Adrienne looked back on her life, she could say that she went to Camp Hideaway as one kind of person and left as another. Her first day at camp was up and down. The cabin was musty, her top bunk stared right into the cobwebby rafters, her cabin mates were all scrawny and knew nothing about puberty, the bathhouse smelled like a chemical toilet, the water at the fountain tasted like rust, and the dining hall served stale potato chips. However, things improved during taps, the flag lowering, and the campfire where one very cute male counselor played the guitar. There was the promise of swimming the next day, and canoeing and a scavenger hunt. After lights out, in the dark musty cabin, where some of her cabin mates were actually *crying*, Adrienne started telling lies. She told the twelve girls she had just met that she had been sent to camp because her brother was dying. Maybe she had meant to say "mother," but she didn't. She said, very distinctly, "brother," and the girls were hooked. Adrienne felt bad almost immediately and wished that she could retract the claim or amend it, but there was no way to do so without being labeled a fake, a liar, a person to be gossiped about for the next six weeks. She told herself it wasn't a complete lie because Adrienne had had a brother once upon a time—her mother had delivered a stillborn baby three years before Adrienne, a baby named Jonathan. Adrienne had wondered for years about Jonathan and what he had looked like and whether or not he was technically her brother if he had died before she was even born. She wondered why Jonathan's name hadn't been on her mother's tablet with the words "Unconditional love." When the girls in her cabin asked her what her dying brother's name was, she told them, and saying it out loud had made him seem real.

On the last night of camp, Adrienne confessed the truth to Pammy Ipp. By this time, Adrienne and Pammy were such good friends that Adrienne wanted to set the record straight: It wasn't her brother who was dying, in fact, she had no brother. It was her mother who was dying.

Pammy Ipp had looked nonplussed. "Why didn't you just tell us that in the first place?" she said.

When Adrienne walked into her mother's hospital room upon her return home, she gagged. All of Rosalie's hair was gone; she looked like a health class skeleton, a space alien. The worst thing was that Rosalie seemed to know how hideous she looked and she told Adrienne that she didn't have to visit the hospital again if she didn't want to. Didn't have to visit her own sick mother!

Adrienne went home and cried. She was plagued by confusion and guilt. Why had she lied to her camp friends? Why had she bothered telling Pammy Ipp the truth at the last minute? Pammy hadn't said a proper goodbye that final morning and Adrienne had seen her whispering with the other girls. Telling them, probably. Adrienne had lied and her mother was getting worse, not better, and Adrienne felt responsible.

She begged her father to take her to the hospital every day. Rosalie wore head scarves or an old Phillies baseball cap. She and Adrienne drank Pepsi and watched *General Hospital* and they talked about Adrienne's friends at school. They did not talk about death, or even love, until the very end. Rosalie made it clear that the worst thing about dying would be leaving Adrienne behind without a mother. Adrienne wanted to ask her mother about the tablet she had found, she wanted to ask about Jonathan, and most of all, she wanted to confess to the insidious lies of the summer, but she didn't want to upset her mother or make her sicker. And then, the night before Adrienne was supposed to start seventh grade, Rosalie fell into a coma and died.

It was at the reception following the funeral that Adrienne decided to hate Mavis. Mavis called the school to say Adrienne wouldn't be starting for two weeks. Mavis made the tea sandwiches and her mother's favorite asparagus roll-ups; Mavis kept her arm around Adrienne's shoulders and steered her toward this person and that person who wanted to express their condolences. In the days following, Mavis prodded Adrienne to write thank-you notes for flowers and food. Despite these things, or perhaps because of these things, Mavis became the enemy. Adrienne was relieved—happy, even—when, a few weeks later, her father told her they were moving to Maine. Adrienne wanted to leave. The town where she lived had become a minefield—here was the road where Rosalie once got a speeding ticket, here was the expressway that led to the hospital, here was the cemetery where Rosalie was now buried. Adrienne wanted to leave her friends who barely understood what had happened and her teachers who fully understood and treated Adrienne so gingerly it was as though she was the one with the disease. But most of all, Adrienne wanted to leave Mavis.

They sold their house and moved to Maine at the beginning of November. By Christmas, Adrienne's father still hadn't hired a hygienist. He was doing every single cleaning himself and it was too much. Finally, he hired a young girl named Curry Jones who had just finished her hygiene courses. Because she was brand-new, Dr. Don figured he could train her to work just like Mavis. Curry Jones was a pretty girl with a permanent scowl. During every cleaning, she dug the probe into the patient's soft pink gums until blood sprang to the surface. Don fired her after two weeks.

He called Mavis in Philadelphia, he helped her find a school that would take Graham, and she relocated. The first thing she said to Adrienne upon arriving in the new office was, "I couldn't stand to think of your father working with that *sadist.*" That, Adrienne later realized, was probably when the affair started, less than six months after Rosalie's death. Adrienne was thirteen and the twins were eight. Adrienne was called on time and time again to babysit for them while her father and Mavis worked late. Adrienne had actually learned the alphabet in sign language.

Mavis followed them three years later to Iowa and eighteen months after that to Louisville, Kentucky. Dr. Don was a good dentist and he was respected and well-loved in each of his practices, but he didn't have staying power. Before this last move, to the eastern shore, he tried to explain it to Adrienne over the phone. He couldn't bear to have any place become his home.

"My home was with Rosalie," he said. One thing Adrienne felt glad about was that even though Don and Mavis had now been together longer than Don and Rosalie, Don did not refer to Mavis as his home. He still loved Adrienne's mother; he would always love her.

Adrienne didn't fault her father for his peripatetic nature; since graduating from high school, Adrienne hadn't stayed anywhere for more than two years. She couldn't count the number of times she had been asked, "Where's your home?" And when she couldn't provide an answer, the well-intentioned soul might ask, "Where does your mother live?" Even at twenty-eight years old, home was where her mother lived. Everywhere. Nowhere.

Adrienne was still in her pajamas, reading and rereading the e-mail from her father and worrying prematurely about a visit from him and Mavis, when the phone rang. Adrienne had heard the growl of the espresso machine a few minutes earlier, and so she knew Caren—and probably Duncan—were awake. The ringing stopped and Caren tapped on the door with her fingernails. She cracked the door and handed in the phone. "It's for you," she said. "It's Thatch."

Adrienne stared at the phone. She had yet to tell Thatcher the truth about her mother. She wanted to tell him but with all that was happening at the restaurant, there was never a good time. He was going to think she was a mental case.

"Hello?" she said.

"Can you come in?" Thatcher asked. "I know it's short notice, but I have reconfirmation calls from ten to noon and I forgot I'm supposed to meet with my priest."

Adrienne might have laughed, but a few nights earlier, a busy Saturday night, Thatcher and Fiona had both been an hour late because they attended five o'clock mass at St. Mary's. His meeting with a priest seemed to follow in this vein.

"I was there until two last night," she said. "And I was hoping to go to the beach today."

"I'll pay you," Thatcher said.

"Obviously."

"I'll have Fee make you lunch."

Adrienne smiled into the phone, thinking: teeth, clothes, her ten-speed bike. "I can be there in fifteen minutes."

According to her sports watch, it only took her twelve minutes to make it to the fork in the road, but that wasn't fast enough. She saw Thatcher driving toward her in his silver pickup on his way into town.

"Good, you're here," he said, though she was still three hundred yards from the restaurant. "I left the book open for you with a list of people to call to reconfirm. It's easy. Just remind them of their time and the number in their party and note any changes, any special requests. Birthdays, that kind of thing. Okay?"

Adrienne was dying to ask him why he was going to see a priest. "What if someone calls for a reservation?"

"Write down the name and number and I'll call back after twelve."

Adrienne saluted and Thatcher drove away.

Adrienne pedaled toward the Bistro. It was another glorious day—bright sunshine, crisp, clean sea air. She had worn her bikini under her clothes; after Thatcher returned, she was going to lie on the beach in front of the restaurant.

Adrienne had expected the restaurant to be deserted but there were five cars and a big Sid Wainer truck in the parking lot. The delivery truck. Adrienne's heart trilled at the thought of JZ, whom she hadn't seen since the first night of bar. A second later she caught a glimpse of him from the back, in uniform, engaged in a heated conversation. Adrienne stopped her bike behind the car she knew to be Fiona's—a navy blue Range Rover with tinted windows. Though she heard JZ's voice, she couldn't make out what he was saying. The back of his delivery truck was open, and in its dim interior she spied crates of lemons and limes, long braids of garlic, cartons of eggs, and a wooden box stamped HAAS AVOCADO—CALIFORNIA. Adrienne dismounted her bike and walked it closer to the front door. As she did, she heard one sentence very clearly. "I love you so much it's making me weak."

And then she heard someone answer. "It's not *enough*, JZ. It will never be enough."

Adrienne knew it was Fiona—of course, it was Fiona—but she had to get a visual. She peeked around the next closest car, Mario's red Durango. From there, she could see them: JZ in his olive drab pants and white uniform shirt, and Fiona in cut-off jean shorts, a pale pink tank top, and pink leather clogs. Both of them looked anguished, close to tears. And then Fiona started to cough, a deep wracking cough that sounded like she was trying to dislodge a piece of concrete from her lungs. It caused her to bend at the waist, one hand bracing her knee, one hand covering her mouth. JZ picked her up under her arms and pressed her tiny body against his. Fiona's clogs dropped from her feet. Adrienne couldn't tear her eyes away—she could sense Fiona's lightness and JZ's strength, their mutual sadness and rage—God, how long had it been since she felt that way about someone? Ever? Fiona continued to cough, her face hidden in JZ's shirt.

Adrienne leaned her bike against the geranium-filled dory and proceeded inside. It was, quite possibly, the most heartbreaking embrace she had ever seen.

The Bistro looked different during the day. It seemed tired and exposed, like a lady of the evening roused from sleep the next morning without her makeup. The tables were bare and the white wicker chairs had been flipped upside down on top of them so that the cleaning crew could do the floors. But the cleaning crew hadn't arrived yet, and the floor was covered with dropped food and sticky puddles.

Since she knew Fiona wasn't in the kitchen, Adrienne poked her head in. Half the crew was at work prepping. Joe was making the mustard in a twelve-quart stockpot. Adrienne watched him for a minute, in awe of the sheer volume of ingredients: a pound of dry mustard, five cups of vinegar, eight cups of sugar, a whole pound of butter, and a dozen eggs. Joe added sixteen grinds of white pepper from a pepper mill that was longer than his arm. Adrienne blew Joe a kiss, then she poked her head around the corner into pastry.

Mario was rolling out dough. She watched him flour the marble counter and work a huge mass of dough with his Walkman on.

When he saw her, he removed his headphones. "What are you doing here?"

"Working," she said. "What are you making?"

"Pies," he said. He checked his watch and wiped his brow on his shoulder. "And I have two kinds of ice cream to make. And a batch of marshmallows. And lemon curd. And I have pineapple to roast. And the rolls, but I save those for last."

"You're in the weeds, then?" she asked.

"Never me, baby," he said.

Adrienne wanted to ask him about Fiona and JZ, but she was afraid that either he wouldn't tell her what she wanted to know or else he would tell Fiona that she'd asked. So instead, Adrienne said, "How's Delilah?" (It came as no surprise to find out that, after the night of the harem pants and finger cymbals, Mario and Delilah were having a fling.)

"Oh, honey," he said. He cut twenty perfect rounds out of the dough and draped them into doll-sized pie pans.

"What?" Adrienne said.

"You want me to tell you about the sex?"

"No," Adrienne said.

"Then what did you ask about Delilah for?"

She was just making conversation. Anything so she could stay and watch Mario work. He moved the pie dough into the freezer and set a timer. Then he began the ice cream. He took a carton of sixty eggs from the walk-in and proceeded to separate the yolks from the whites by sifting the whites through his fingers.

"Some people think sugar is the key to desserts," Mario said. "But I am here to tell you that if you want a good dessert, you have to start with a fresh egg." He held out his palm, displaying a whole, perfect, bright orange yolk, which he slipped into his Hobart mixer.

"What do you do with the whites?" Adrienne asked. "Throw them away?"

"I use them in the marshmallows," he said. "Have you ever tasted one of my marshmallows?"

She shook her head.

"Lighter than air," he said. "I make the best marshmallows in the country, maybe the world."

"Okay, Marshmallow King," she said. "I have to get to work."

Mario replaced his headphones and separated another egg while doing the samba.

Back in the kitchen, Hector was peeling and deveining shrimp with a tool that looked like a plastic dentist's probe. He had a mountain of shrimp on his left and a mountain on his right—uncleaned and cleaned. He tossed the shells into a stockpot.

"That's a lot of shrimp," Adrienne said.

"Shrimp bisque," Hector said without looking up. "Shrimp toast, shrimp for fondue."

The oldest Subiaco, Antonio, a man with a mustache and gray hair around his ears, trimmed lamb. He worked so fast Adrienne feared he would cut himself, especially as he seemed intent on listening to what sounded like a baseball game being broadcast in Spanish on the Bose radio.

The baseball game broke for commercial and Antonio called out, "Where's the steak?"

"It's still on the truck," somebody answered.

"Well, go get it, Louis."

"No fucking way," Louis said. "They're out there fighting."

They're out there fighting. Adrienne hung around for a beat to see if any-one would respond to this, but no one did, and Adrienne took this as her cue to leave. As she stepped into the dining room, she bumped into Fiona. Fiona alone, her eyes pink and watery. She stopped when she saw Adrienne and brushed an imaginary hair from her face.

"Thank you for covering the phones," Fiona said. "I know I'm supposed to make you lunch, but I can't today. I have to get out of here for a while. I'll ask Antonio to do it. You know Antonio? He's my sous."

Adrienne smiled. "Sure. Whatever."

"What would you like?"

"Anything," Adrienne said. "I don't mean to complicate your day."

Fiona coughed—briefly, dryly—into her hand. "Fine," she said. "One anything. I'll have him bring it out to you in an hour or so."

Thatcher had left a list of fifty names and numbers. Eighteen reservations for first seating, thirty-two for second. About half the reservations were people staying at hotels and inns—three reservations from the Beach Club, two from the White Elephant, two from the Pineapple Inn. Next came a bunch of names that Adrienne, after a week of work, recognized: Parrish (six o'clock, of course, it was Tuesday,) Egan, Montero, Kennedy (no rela-tion, though Mr. Kennedy was one of the investors, and Adrienne saw the word "comp" next to his name in the book), Jamieson, Walker, and Lefroy. This last name was underlined and followed by three exclamation points, and Adrienne realized that it was Tyler the busboy's parents—his father the health inspector. That's right, she remembered now: The cleaning crew was coming in late today so that everything had a better chance of staying spic-and-span. The staff was eating family meal out on the beach, picnic-style—sloppy joes, potato salad, and root beer handmade by Henry Subiaco, the sauté cook. If the root beer tasted good, Henry was going to try to market it next year when the restaurant was closed. Next year, when the restaurant was closed, Adrienne might have finally figured out what was going on while the restaurant was open. She glanced up to see Fiona rush out the front door. Through the window, Adrienne watched her climb, climb, climb (Pammy Ipp up the sycamore tree) into the cab of JZ's truck. They were in love. Adrienne felt victorious about this knowledge, despite the fact that she would now have to erase JZ from her shortlist of possible men to date.

The work Thatcher left seemed very straightforward. Taking reservations was another story; that involved the calculus of who fit where and what time and—most crucially—at which table. Apparently some guests got their feelings hurt over where in the restaurant they sat, so this was Thatcher's department. Adrienne called the first name on the list: Devlin. Next to the name Devlin, it said "birthday/dessert-candle/no chocolate."

A woman picked up on the first ring.

"Hello?"

"Good morning," Adrienne said. "Is this Mrs. Devlin?"

"Why, yes it is." The woman sounded both wary and hopeful, like maybe Adrienne was calling from Publishers Clearing House and maybe she'd won something.

"This is Adrienne calling from the Blue Bistro."

"Yes?" More hopeful now than wary.

"Just calling to confirm your reservation tonight for a party of six at six. It's somebody's birthday?"

"It's my birthday," she said. "But I didn't know we had reservations at the bistro. For six at six, you say? I hope we're not bringing the kids. Maybe you'd better talk to my husband, Brian. He's right here."

During the switch of the phone, Adrienne checked the notes after the Devlins' name: "birthday/dessert-candle/no chocolate." Nowhere, *nowhere*, did it say "surprise," and yet that was clearly what it was. Adrienne had single-handedly ruined the woman's birthday surprise.

Mr. Devlin was appropriately gruff. "Thanks a lot," he said.

The next three phone calls were easy—Adrienne left clear, concise messages on voice mail for the guests who were out swimming or golfing or shopping from the Bartlett Farm truck on Main Street. Adrienne called the White Elephant and confirmed for those guests. She called Mack Peterson at the Beach Club, who was also on her shortlist of potential dates, but he showed no special interest in the fact that it was Adrienne calling rather than Thatcher. He was all business. "We have a guest who thinks she may have left her sunglasses there last night," he said. "I guess they're Chanel sunglasses and *très cher*. Last name Cerruci."

Adrienne checked the shelf inside the podium. "I . . . don't . . . see them here," she said. She scanned the book from the night before to see if Thatcher had written a note about sunglasses. "Well," she said, "the Cerrucis sat down last night at nine fifteen. What are the chances that Mrs. Cerruci was wearing her sunglasses at nine fifteen?"

"Oh, Adrienne," Mack said wearily. "You just don't understand the people I deal with all day."

Adrienne glanced at the disheveled dining room. "The cleaning crew hasn't been here yet," she said. "I'll call you if we find them."

"Thank you," Mack said, and he hung up.

Adrienne wrote herself a note—"Sunglasses"—while she dialed the Parrishes' number. Darla picked up.

"Hello?"

"Good morning, Darla. It's Adrienne from the Blue Bistro."

"Oh, you sweetheart!"

"Just calling to confirm two people at six tonight," Adrienne said.

There was a long pause on the other end. *Oh, God,* Adrienne thought. *What now?*

"We have Wolfie," Darla said.

"I'm sorry?"

"We have Wolfie, our grandson, for the next two weeks. I told Thatcher this! To change the next two weeks of reservations to include Wolfie. I told him! Oh, wait, maybe I didn't. Maybe I'm thinking of that darling Mateo at the Boarding House. We eat there every Wednesday. Sorry, sorry. The next four reservations we'll be a party of three because of Wolfie. He's six years old. And here's the thing: He's a picky eater."

"Okay," Adrienne said. Next to the Parrishes' name, she erased "2" and penciled in "3" with an asterisk next to the three that said, "Wolfie—picky eater."

"A very picky eater."

Adrienne remembered babysitting for Mavis's twins. Graham would eat anything she put in front of him, but Coleman, the one who could hear, would eat only mayonnaise sandwiches.

"What does he eat?" Adrienne asked. "I can make a note for the kitchen."

"He likes Froot Loops," Darla said. "And a certain kind of yogurt that is bright pink and has a dinosaur on the package."

"Is that it?" Adrienne asked. She was pretty sure cereal and children's yogurt weren't going to come out of the kitchen, even for the Parrishes. "Does he eat French fries?"

Darla laughed. "Of course! I'm almost certain. Let's just get him French fries, then. Will you write it down?"

"I'm writing it down," Adrienne said.

"It's just . . . well, he lives with his mother."

"Say no more," Adrienne said, as if she understood what that was supposed to mean. Though really, she didn't want to hear it. She liked Darla and wanted to keep it that way. "We'll see you at six."

At eleven thirty Antonio, the sous chef, brought Adrienne her lunch. She was on the phone with Mrs. Lefroy, otherwise she would have kissed the man. The plate looked gorgeous. As soon as Adrienne hung up, she poked her head into the kitchen to say "Thank you, gracias, thank you." Antonio waved. Adrienne sat at a table in the bar and dug in. This was Antonio's interpretation of "anything": succulent black olives, sun-dried tomatoes and marinated artichokes, three kinds of salami, tiny balls of fresh mozzarella, roasted cherry tomatoes, some kind of creamy eggplant dip that made her swoon, and a basket of warm focaccia. Miraculously, the phone stayed quiet while she ate. She had two calls remaining and she was done.

She finished her lunch, took her plate into the kitchen, and returned to the podium to make the phone calls. One to the Wauwinet Inn, one to the message machine of a beauty salon; the woman who cut Thatcher's hair was coming in at nine. Then, just as Adrienne took her first longing look at the beach, Thatcher's truck pulled into the parking lot.

Adrienne greeted him smiling widely. It had been a good morning.

"You have something in your teeth," he said.

She bolted for the ladies' room. Sure enough, tomato skin.

"My worst nightmare," she said when she emerged. "With my father and all."

"How did the calls go?"

"Fine," she said. "I ruined Jennifer Devlin's birthday. You didn't tell me it was a surprise."

"Oops," he said.

"The Parrishes are bringing their grandson."

He winced. "Is it that time of year already?" he said. "What does he eat these days?"

"French fries. Darla said French fries."

Thatcher shook his head. "We served him French fries last year. He fed them to the seagulls. She's forgotten."

"There's a list of people for you to call back. A man named Leon Cross called on the private line to say it was urgent and top secret."

"It's always urgent and top secret with Leon," Thatcher said. "Anything else?"

"I had a delicious lunch."

"Good. Fiona made it for you?"

"Uh, Antonio, I think."

"Okay," Thatcher said. Adrienne thought he looked pale and a little distracted but she was not going to ask him about the priest.

"Can I go?" she asked.

"Wait," he said. "I have something for you." He held up a white shopping bag. "Here."

Now Adrienne was nervous. She peeked in the bag. Clothes? She pulled out a blue dress made of washed silk that was so soft it felt like skin. Size six. There was another dress in a champagne color—the same cut, very simple, a slip dress to just above the knee. There was a third outfit—a tank and skirt in the same silk, bottle green.

"These are for me?"

"Let's see how they look."

She took the bag into the ladies' room and slipped the blue dress on over her bikini. It fell over Adrienne's body like a dress in a dream—and it would look even better when she had the right underwear. So here was her look. She checked the side of the shopping bag. The clothes had come from a store called Dessert, on India Street, and Adrienne recognized the name of the store as the one owned by the chef's wife, the redhead who had been so kind during soft opening. *If you come in, I'd love to dress you, free of charge.* So maybe Thatch didn't pay for these clothes. Still, it was weird. Weird that Thatcher had told her she needed a look, weird that he (or the redhead) had perfectly identified it, and weird that she now had to model it for him, proving him right. She stepped out into the dining room.

He gazed at her. And then he gave a long, low whistle. That did it: Her face heated up, the skin on her arms tingled. She had never felt so desirable in all her life.

"Tomorrow's your night off?" he said.

She nodded. Wednesday was her night off. Last Wednesday, because everyone she knew on the island worked at the restaurant, she stayed home, ate frozen ravioli, and watched a rerun of the *West Wing*.

"I scheduled myself off, too," he said. "I want to take you out for dinner."

This stunned her so much she may have actually gasped. "Who's going to work?" she asked.

"Caren," he said. "She loves to do it. And we only have seventy on the book."

Adrienne ran her hands down the sides of her new dress. The silk was irresistible.

"Will you go out with me?" he asked.

Rule Three: Exercise good judgment about men! Dating her boss did not seem wise. It seemed dangerous, more dangerous than getting entangled with Mario. And yet, she wanted to go. Rules, after all, were made to be . . .

"Sure," she said.

When Adrienne saw Thatcher at work that night, she thought things would be different between them. But Thatcher was preoccupied by the Lefroys' reservation. It wasn't a health inspector *visit*, but he wanted the restaurant to be clean. He wanted it to sparkle. And so, when Adrienne arrived, expecting compliments on the new champagne-colored dress, he set her to work polishing glasses and buffing the silver with the servers. At the menu meeting, he demonstrated the way he wanted the busboys to use the crumbers (and they were short a busboy since Tyler would be eating tonight with his parents). The staff ate family meal on the beach and Thatcher made them brush every grain of sand from their person and wash their feet in a bucket before they were allowed back in the restaurant.

As if that wasn't bad enough, Thatcher assigned Adrienne to the Parrishes during first seating.

"I want you to really watch them," he said. "Anticipate their needs. Especially Wolf's."

"It sounds like you're asking me to babysit," Adrienne said.

"We're going to do what it takes to give Darla and Grayson some peace," Thatcher said. "We want them to enjoy their meal, yes or no?"

The Parrishes arrived fifteen minutes late, which was unheard-of, and what this meant was that instead of getting them squared away early on, they were smushed at the entrance with three other parties who needed to be seated, and two gorgeous blond women who showed up without a reservation. Adrienne directed the Swedish bikini duo to the bar, sat the Devlins at table twenty-five, and led a deuce staying at the White Elephant under the awning. Then she returned to the podium to properly greet the Parrishes.

"Sorry," Adrienne said.

Grayson held up a palm. "It's our fault," he said. "We had a little trouble getting out of the house."

Darla was holding a little boy's hand. "This is Wolfie," Darla said.

Wolf had white-blond hair and eyes that were mottled and puffy. His breathing was hiccupy. Adrienne crouched down. Despite her years of babysitting the twins, she did not consider herself someone who was good with children and yet now she wanted to succeed, if only to impress Thatcher.

"Hi, Wolf," she said. "My name is Adrienne."

He harrumphed and locked his arms over his chest.

Darla smiled at him with all the love in the world, then whispered to Adrienne, "He's not having a good night."

Adrienne led the Parrishes to table twenty, and Bruno appeared seconds later with their drinks.

Adrienne pulled Bruno off to the side. "Order of frites, pronto," she said. "Wolfie's not having a good night and Thatcher wants Mr. and Mrs. P to be able to eat in their accustomed silence."

"Bitchy!" Bruno said. He paused. "Is that a new dress?"

"Yes," Adrienne said. "Thank you for noticing."

Caren approached Adrienne with a stone face. "I'm going to kill you."

"Why?"

"You put those girls at the bar."

"What girls?" Adrienne checked the bar. Ah, yes, the girls. They were laughing, and flashing Duncan with their remarkable cleavage. Adrienne instantly understood the problem, but come on! She was busy and they were all adults here. Well, everyone except for Wolfie.

"They didn't have a reservation," Adrienne said.

"You could have put them at three."

"I guess I could have, but . . ."

"They're all *over* him," Caren said. "And he's just eating it up. Oh, and look. They ordered apple martinis. What an insipid drink."

"Okay, well, I'm sorry. I have to put a . . ."

Thatcher passed by, touching Adrienne's arm. He raised one pale eyebrow.

"I have to put a VIP order in," Adrienne said to Caren.

"Champagne?" Thatcher said.

"I'll get your champagne," Caren said. "Let me get it." She strode toward the bar.

Bruno breezed by with a huge plate of fries. "These are for Dennis the Menace," he said. "You want to deliver?"

"I have to put their VIP order in," Adrienne said.

"Already done," Bruno said. He handed Adrienne the plate of fries. "You go, girl."

The Parrishes were sitting in silence, the elder two focused on their drinks while Wolf lay splayed across the wicker chair, his face sullen.

"Fries!" Adrienne said brightly. She took the seat next to Wolfie, but he couldn't be convinced to eat even one. She tried to lead by example, eating one fry, then another, then another. "You don't know what you're missing," she said.

"Please, Wolfie," Darla said. "Just try one. Just one for Gam. Please."

"I want yogurt," he said.

Grayson finished his Stoli tonic and flagged Bruno for another. "Why don't you take Wolf down to the water, Adrienne?"

"To the water?" Adrienne said. She considered informing Grayson Parrish that she had work to do. The restaurant was buzzing around her. Thatcher sat tables, Elliott and Joe recited specials, Gage and Roy poured water and delivered doughnuts. Rex played "Happy Birthday" as Spillman popped a bottle of champagne for the Devlins. Adrienne wanted to get up and join the adult activity.

Bruno came to her rescue. He eased up alongside Adrienne as he served apps to the adjoining table and whispered, "You're needed at the bar."

"I'm needed at the bar," Adrienne told the Parrishes. "I'll be right back."

At the bar, the blondes were splitting a VIP order, and at the far end, by the cherries and the citrus, Adrienne's champagne beckoned. She took a long swill, appraising the situation. Duncan was MIA. It was much commented upon that Duncan had the world's sturdiest bladder—he never used the restroom during service. Christo swaggered up to Adrienne and said, "I need a vodka grapefruit and a glass of zin."

"Who do I look like?"

"The assistant manager," he said.

"Where's Duncan?" Adrienne asked.

Christo shrugged. "I just work here, lady. You gonna get my drinks?"

One of the blondes whipped around. She was one of the most attractive women Adrienne had ever seen, if judged by the standards that certain American men tended to use. Lots of natural blond, lots of natural tan, lots of natural breast.

"I think his girlfriend's pissed at him," she said. "She snatched him away."

The other blonde, who was wearing a blue sequined halter top, sipped her apple martini. "We were just *talking* to him."

"So he's gone?" Adrienne said. "And where's Delilah?"

"Night off," Christo said. He grinned at the blondes.

"Okay, fine," Adrienne said. She was thinking many things at once: She was the assistant manager, this was—if looked at from a very warped and immature point of view—partially her fault, and it had always seemed like fun to be a bartender. Not to mention it gave her an excuse to blow off the Parrishes. Adrienne slipped behind the bar. She felt like she was about to drive an expensive race car. Look at all the stuff—the sink, the fridge, the rows of mixers, the gun, the fruit, the bottles in the well, the bottles of wine. She picked up a bottle of red and scrutinized the label.

"Zin, you said?"

"Zin."

"Well, this is a Syrah," Adrienne said. She eyed the podium. It was clear. "I wonder where the zin is."

"I'd like it this century," Christo said, then he checked to see if either of the blondes had laughed. No such luck. "Ah, fuck it, I'll be back."

"Adrienne!"

Thatcher's hand smacked the blue granite. She felt like, well, she felt like she'd just been caught in her parents' liquor cabinet. One of her heels snagged on the rubber hex mat and she stumbled backward. Her ass hit the rack of bottles behind her.

"I'm trying to help," she said.

"Table twenty," he hissed. "Take Wolf to the water."

Wolf threw the fries, one by one, to the seagulls. Adrienne found herself surrounded by big rats with wings, cawing and pecking. She glanced longingly back at the restaurant, at Grayson eating his chips and dip, at Duncan, returned to his post, wooing his new lady friends. When the fries were gone, Wolf threw rocks in the water.

"Don't you want to go back up?" Adrienne asked. He didn't answer. She tried another tack. "Where do you live?" He didn't answer. "Cat got your tongue?" she asked. He looked at her quizzically, and she could see his mind working: Was she talking about a real cat? But he wasn't curious enough to ask. He sat in the wet sand, shed his dock shoes, rolled up the pant legs of his khakis, and waded into the water. Adrienne wished she had the words to reel him back in. She was afraid to turn around to face Grayson and Darla. What if Wolf went under? She couldn't very well return him to his grandparents soaking wet. She wandered down the beach, saying, "I hope the sharks aren't out there tonight, Wolf. Or the stinging jellyfish." That got him out, though his pant legs were wrinkled and his seat was damp and sandy.

"Do you want to go back up?" Adrienne asked.

"No."

"Why not?"

"I just don't."

"Don't you want to be with your grandparents?"

"No."

"Why not?"

"I miss my mom."

"I miss my mom, too," Adrienne said.

Wolf tossed another rock. "Where is she?"

"She's dead," Adrienne said. It was easy to tell the truth to a child. Wolf said nothing, but he let her take his hand and lead him back to the restaurant. The footbath they had used after family meal came in handy. Adrienne rinsed Wolf's feet and squidged them back into his dock shoes. Then, with her sitting next to him, he choked down a roll smothered with butter.

Darla was elated. "I've never seen him eat like this before," she said. "Can we bring you home with us?"

At the end of first seating, Grayson tipped Adrienne two hundred dollars. She tucked the bills into her change purse.

"That," she said to Thatcher, "was above and beyond the call of duty."

"Nothing is above and beyond the call of duty," he said. "Not here."

No sooner had the Parrishes walked out the door than Caren yanked Adrienne into the wine cave.

"They're still here," Caren said.

"Who?"

"Those girls. They finished dinner twenty minutes ago and they're still here."

"You need to calm down," Adrienne said.

"I can't handle this," Caren said. She plopped down on an untapped keg of beer. "I cannot handle being the bartender's girlfriend."

"He's not doing anything wrong," Adrienne said.

"He's flirting," Caren said. "You notice he put in a VIP order? When I saw that, I flipped. Two nobodies, never been here before, and he VIPs them? I let him have it."

"What did he say?"

"He admitted he was flirting. He said it was part of his job."

"Well, it is, sort of, isn't it?"

"You're not helping!" Caren said. "You put them at the bar in the first place! You should have put them on three. I would have waited on them myself and they'd be at the Rose and Crown by now."

"Okay," Adrienne said. "Next time there are beautiful unescorted women without a reservation, I will put them at three."

"Do you promise?" Caren said. "Promise me."

"I promise," Adrienne said.

Second seating brought the Lefroys—Mr. and Mrs.—along with Tyler and his younger sister, a girl of about thirteen who had the worst case of adolescence Adrienne had ever seen. She was a chubby girl stuffed into a pink satin dress that would have looked awful on anyone; she wore braces and glasses and had greasy hair of no determinate color forced back in an unforgiving ponytail. Tyler looked mortified to be seen with her, not to mention his parents: Mrs. Lefroy had dyed blond hair and the defined biceps of a woman who spent all her free time at the gym, and Mr. Lefroy was easily six foot five, balding, bespectacled, lurching.

Thatcher slapped Tyler on the back and made some perfunctory (and much exaggerated) comment about what a stellar employee he was. Then he handed four menus to Adrienne and said, "Seat them. Table twenty."

"I never eat out," Mr. Lefroy said on his way through the dining room.

"No?" Adrienne said. "And why is that?"

"Well, when you've seen what I've seen . . ."

"On the job, you mean?"

"The cross-contamination dangers alone," he said.

"Dad," Tyler said. "Please shut up. People are trying to eat."

Adrienne let the family settle, then she handed out menus. "Enjoy your meal," she said.

The Lefroys' table was assigned to Spillman, but within minutes he found Adrienne at the bar, where she was drinking her champagne and trying to eavesdrop on Duncan and the two bombshells.

"Lefroy wants you," Spillman said.

"You're kidding."

"He wants your opinion on the menu," Spillman said. "My opinion apparently doesn't matter."

Adrienne returned to table twenty with her champagne. She complimented the sister, Rochelle, on a rhinestone bracelet she was wearing and she asked Tyler about his finals. He made a flicking motion with his hand. "Aced them."

Mr. Lefroy pointed to Adrienne's glass. "Now, what's that you're drinking?"

"A glass of the Laurent-Perrier brut rosé."

Mr. Lefroy looked to his wife. "You want one of those?"

"Sure," Mrs. Lefroy said. "It's my lucky day."

"One of those," Mr. Lefroy said. "And what is fresh on this menu?"

"It's all fresh," Adrienne said. "The fish is delivered every afternoon, the vegetables are hand-selected by our . . ."

"That's nice," Mr. Lefroy said. "But what is *really* fresh?"

When Adrienne returned to the podium, Thatcher was grinning.

"What?" she said.

"Lefroy can't keep his eyes off you."

"Shut up."

"It's because you're so damn fetching in that dress."

For the first time all night, Adrienne felt the electricity that had buzzed up her spine that morning when Thatcher whistled. She was beginning to think she'd imagined it.

The Lefroy family had a wonderful meal. In the end, they all ordered the steak, which was not fresh, but aged, though Adrienne did not point this out. Adrienne asked Thatcher if he wanted to comp the meal, as it was Tyler's family.

"I can't," Thatcher said. "The man is the health inspector."

The two blondes unstuck themselves from the bar at ten o'clock. Off to the Boarding House, they said.

"Cute bartender," the girl in the blue halter said. "He needs to lose the uptight girlfriend."

"Okay, bye-bye," Adrienne said. She was relieved to see them go. It had been another very, very long night, and it wasn't over yet. At eleven, Thatcher helped her bounce, and this was something new. Adrienne relayed the saga of Caren and Duncan as they watched the headlights pull in.

"The bar is popular for two reasons," he said. "Duncan and our indifference."

"Our indifference?"

"Well, Fiona's indifference. She hates the bar. She think it's all about money."

"Isn't it all about money?"

"Oh, yes," he said. "Yes, it is."

At midnight, the crackers came out of the kitchen: parmesan rosemary. Adrienne took a handful and offered the basket to Thatch. He nodded at the kitchen door. "I'm going to eat," he said. "I'll pick you up tomorrow night at seven."

"Where are we going?" Adrienne asked.

"Where aren't we going?" he said.

5

❧

Night Off

***Notre Dame* magazine,**
Volume LXVII,
September 2004
"GREEN AND GOLD GOES BLUE"

Thatcher Smith (B.A. 1991) believes there are two kinds of people in the world: those who eat to live and those who live to eat. Until he was twenty-two years old, Smith, owner of the Blue Bistro, a highly successful restaurant on Nantucket Island in Massachusetts, categorized himself as the former.

"I grew up in South Bend, a town that is virtually devoid of cuisine. My mother left the family when I was young and my father and brothers and I subsisted on shredded wheat, bologna sandwiches, and pizza. And Burger King, of course. But nothing you would ever call cuisine."

So how did this native of South Bend, and Notre Dame graduate, end up in the restaurant business? He gives credit to the girl next door.

Fiona Kemp (daughter of Hobson Kemp, a professor of

electrical engineering at Notre Dame since 1966) lived four houses down from Smith growing up.

"There's a picture of Fiona and I on our first day of kindergarten," Smith says. "I can't remember not knowing her."

Because of a childhood illness, Ms. Kemp could not participate in sports. So she turned her energies to an indoor activity: cooking.

"She was always making something. I remember when we were about twelve she made a chocolate swirl cheesecake sitting in a puddle of raspberry sauce. She invited some of the boys from the neighborhood over to eat it, but it was so elegant, none of us had the heart."

After graduating from John Adams High School together in 1987, Smith and Kemp went their separate ways. Smith enrolled at Notre Dame, where he majored in economics. He planned to join his father and brothers at what he modestly calls "the family store": Smith Carpets and Flooring, which has five outlets in South Bend and nearby Mishewaka. Meanwhile Kemp enrolled at the prestigious Culinary Institute of America in Hyde Park, New York. She wanted to fulfill her dream of becoming a chef.

Smith and Kemp reunited on Nantucket Island in October 1992.

"Fiona had been working on the island for two years at that point," Smith says. "And she felt ready for her own place. She convinced me to visit, and once I saw the island, I decided to leave South Bend behind. I sold my interest in the business to my brothers and took the money and invested it in Fiona. I knew there was no way she would fail."

Indeed, not. Smith and Kemp bought a run-down restaurant on the beach that had formerly served burgers and fried clams, and they transformed it into the Blue Bistro, with seating for over a hundred facing the Atlantic Ocean. The only seats harder to procure than the seats at the blue granite bar are the four tables out in the sand where the Bistro serves its now-famous version of seafood fondue. (Or, as the kitchen fondly refers to it, the all-you-can-eat fried shrimp special.) Many of Ms. Kemp's offerings are twists on old classics, like the fondue. She serves impeccable steak frites, a lobster club sandwich, and a sushi plate, which features a two-inch-thick slab of locally caught bluefin tuna. Ms. Kemp relies on fresh local produce to keep her plates alive.

Ms. Kemp's cooking has been celebrated in such places as *Bon Appétit* and the *Chicago Tribune*. She was named one of the country's hottest chefs by *Food & Wine* in 1998. All this notoriety comes despite the fact that she is, in Thatcher Smith's words, "a highly private person. Fiona doesn't give interviews. She doesn't allow herself to be photographed. She doesn't believe in the new craze of 'chef as celebrity.' Fiona just wants to feed people. It has never been about the reviews or about the money, even. For Fiona, it's all about love; it's about giving back."

For Thatcher Smith, running the Blue Bistro is a dream come true—a dream he wasn't even aware he harbored. "I love every minute of my work," he says. "The fast pace, the high energy, the personal interaction, the management challenges. And yes, I love the food. Once I tried a plate of Fiona's steak frites, I learned the difference between tasting and eating. I knew I would never hit the drive-through at Burger King again. I became a person who lives to eat."

TO: Ade12177@hotmail.com
FROM: DrDon@toothache.com
DATE: June 7, 2005, 7:33 P.M.
SUBJECT: possible dates

How about the last week in July? Love, love.

Adrienne was so nervous when she woke up on Wednesday morning that her ears were ringing. *Where are we going? Where aren't we going?* The blue dress hung in the closet on a padded hanger that Adrienne had borrowed from Caren without her permission. When Adrienne had gotten home the night before, she went online and looked up the article about Thatcher in *Notre Dame* magazine. Then she lay in bed for nearly an hour thinking about it. It gave her a better sense of Thatcher than the other articles. He came from a family of men who worked in carpet and flooring. His mother had left, maybe for that very reason: too many men, too much carpet. Adrienne wondered about Fiona's "childhood illness," just as she wondered about everything else regarding Fiona. She had liked the story about the cheesecake. She could imagine Thatcher and his grubby twelve-year-old friends staring at the marbled cheesecake sitting in a bright pink raspberry pond as though it were a work of modern art they were being asked to understand.

Adrienne heard the swish of Caren's bare feet against the floorboards of the hall, then the espresso machine. She looked at her clock: It was nine. She had hoped to sleep in, but there was no chance—too much on her mind.

By the time Adrienne made it out to the kitchen, Caren was alone, sipping her short black, flipping through the pages of *Cosmo*.

"Where's Duncan?" Adrienne asked.

"I have no idea."

Adrienne eyed the glossy pages of the magazine. Caren was reading an article entitled: "Is Your Relationship on the Rocks? 10 Early Warning Signs."

"Are you fighting?" Adrienne asked.

"I have no idea," Caren said again.

"Oh," Adrienne said.

"You're off tonight?" Caren asked.

Adrienne poked her head into the fridge for some juice. "Yep."

"You're going out?"

Adrienne got a glass out of the cabinet, steeling herself. What was the first thing Caren had ever told her? *I know the dirt on every person who eats at the Bistro and every person who works there.*

"I am," Adrienne said.

"With Thatch?"

"Yes," Adrienne said. She let out a long exhale; it was a relief, having it spoken. "What do you think?"

"I'm psyched to work the front," Caren said. "It's such a breeze."

Adrienne recognized that as some kind of slight, but she let it go. "What do you think about me and Thatch?"

"I think you should be careful."

Adrienne poured her juice and sat down across the table from Caren. Caren was not exactly her friend, but Adrienne knew she wouldn't lie.

"Why?" Adrienne said. "Has he been with a lot of women?"

"No," Caren said. "He hasn't gone on a date in the twelve years I've known him." She slapped her magazine shut. "And that's why you should be careful."

Thatcher arrived at five to seven bearing a bouquet of red gerbera daisies. He looked like an old-fashioned suitor: He was dressed in a jacket and tie, holding out the flowers, and he had a very clean-shaven look about him. *Haircut,* she realized after studying him for a second. Adrienne was glad Caren was at work—she might have teased this version of Thatcher Smith. Earnest, fresh-faced, with flowers, on his first date in twelve years.

"Look at you," Adrienne said. She carried the flowers into the kitchen, where she hunted for a vase. No vase. She filled one of the unused sunflower canisters with water.

Thatcher followed her in. "Look at *you,*" he said. "That dress. I can't get over it."

"Good," Adrienne said, smiling. She grabbed a gray pashmina (borrowed from Caren, with her permission) and checked her silver-beaded cocktail purse (ditto): lipstick, dental floss, a wad of cash, just in case. "Let's go."

Thatcher took her to 21 Federal, in the heart of town. The building was one of the old whaling houses; inside, it had a lot of dark wood and antique mirrors. The woman working the front wore Janet Russo and had a professional manicure. She smiled when they came in and said in a flirty voice, "Thatcher Smith! The rumors are true!"

Thatcher put a finger to his lips, and the woman said, "You don't want anyone to know you're here? Would you like to sit in the back?"

"Even better," Thatcher said, pointing at the ceiling.

The woman led them up the staircase. "Siberia, it is," she said.

The upstairs of the restaurant was even more charming than downstairs, Adrienne thought. There was a darling little bar and a couple of deuces by the front windows that looked down onto Federal Street. Thatcher pulled out Adrienne's chair then seated himself. The hostess whispered in Thatcher's ear. He nodded. A second later, an elderly bartender appeared with their drinks: Veuve Clicquot for Adrienne and a club soda with lime for Thatcher.

"Our compliments, Mr. Smith," said the bartender.

"Thank you, Frank."

"The hostess forgot our menus," Adrienne whispered.

"No, she didn't," Thatcher said. "I've ordered for us already."

Adrienne tried to relax. She gazed out the window at the cobblestoned street below. "Okay," she said. "You're the boss."

Thatcher lifted his glass to her. "Thank you for coming out with me tonight," he said. "I don't do this enough."

Adrienne clinked his glass and sipped her champagne. "From what I hear, you don't do it at all."

"You've been talking to Caren?"

"Of course."

"She thinks she knows everything about me," Thatcher said. "But she doesn't."

The hostess approached the table again and whispered something else in Thatcher's ear. The whispering was in very bad taste; Adrienne would never do it.

Thatcher said, "Not tonight. Sorry. You'll tell them I'm sorry? But not tonight."

The hostess disappeared. Thatcher turned to Adrienne. "The chef wants to prepare us a tasting menu."

"That's nice," Adrienne said.

"It's a commitment," Thatcher said. "And I have other plans for us."

"Do you now?" Adrienne said.

"Yes, I do."

A few minutes later the bartender, who was keeping a shadowy profile behind the bar, presented two plates. "The portobello mushroom with Parmesan pudding," he announced.

Thatcher lit up. He spun the plates. "This is the best first course on the island," he said.

"If you're not eating at work," Adrienne said.

"Right," Thatcher said.

Adrienne brandished her knife and fork. She was used to eating family meal at five thirty and now, nearly two hours later, she was starving. She tasted a bite of the mushroom, then a little of the creamy, cheesy pudding. The dish was perfect. Thatcher stared at his plate, smiling at the mushroom as though he expected it to smile back. Was he nervous?

"I read an article about you this morning," Adrienne said.

"Which one?"

"*Notre Dame* magazine."

He raised his pale eyebrows. "You must have been doing research," he said. "I gather you're not a subscriber."

"No," she said. "I went to three colleges, but I wouldn't call any of them my alma mater."

"Where is your degree from?"

"Florida State," she said. "Psychology. I did my first two years in Bloomington, then a year at Vanderbilt, and I ended up at Florida State—and that's where I got into hotels. My adviser at FSU got me a job on the front desk at the Mar-a-Lago in Palm Beach."

"Starting your enviable life of resort-hopping."

"Exactly." Adrienne took another bite of her mushroom. "In that article, it said Fiona had a childhood illness."

"Now you know why I don't like journalists," he said. He twirled his glass then looked around the dining room—they were the only people eating upstairs. He hunched his shoulders and said, "Can we not talk about the article?"

Adrienne didn't care for his tone of voice; it was the same tone he used at work when he was telling her what to do. She was about to say something tart when the bartender appeared with a second glass of champagne. Adrienne drank half of it down, questioning her decision to come on this date. This was what had happened in her relationship with Kip Turnbull in Thailand; right before they broke up he was micromanaging her personal life, telling her how to defog her snorkel, insisting she condition her hair with coconut milk, feeding her psychedelic mushrooms without her knowledge. That was the problem with dating the boss; they couldn't get over themselves. Adrienne concentrated on her appetizer. It was pretty damn good, though she now resented the fact that Thatcher had ordered it for her, as though she weren't educated enough to select something on her own. She noticed Thatcher still wasn't eating. He was looking at her with a worried expression.

"I'm sorry," he said. "If you want to know something about me, you can just ask. You don't have to read about me in my alumni magazine. Most of what I tell reporters is baloney anyway."

Adrienne nodded once, but only to let him know she'd heard him. She finished her mushroom and her champagne in silence, and feigned interest in the photographs of sailboats on the walls. Then, when she could avoid conversation no longer, she reached for Caren's purse. "I'm going to the ladies' room," she said. "Where is it?"

"Down the hall," he said. He stood up when she left, just like Adrienne's father used to do for Rosalie. Adrienne gave him points for that.

The hall leading to the bathroom was adjacent to a back corridor that was used as a waiters' station. Adrienne noticed the folded food stands, the stacks of china and linen, the racks for the silver, the bud vases, and a plastic pitcher of white freesia stems. She eyed the computer where the waiters placed orders. Just as she was about to step into the ladies' room to check her teeth, she heard two female waiters talking as they trudged up the back stairs.

"He hasn't been here in, like, five years," one said. "And Fiona, you know, never eats anywhere."

"That's not Fiona he's with tonight?"

"No, it's some other chick. He's not married to Fiona or anything."

"Oh, I know."

Adrienne made sure the waiters got a good look at her before she entered the ladies' room. *Some other chick!*

When she returned to the table, Thatcher stood up again and remained standing. Their plates had been cleared.

"The female waiters were talking about you," Adrienne said.

"I'm not surprised," Thatcher said. "Whenever I leave the Bistro at night, it's news. Are you ready?"

"For what?" Adrienne said. "Where are we going?"

"Across the street," Thatcher said. "We've just begun."

They crossed Federal Street to the Pearl, a restaurant that made Adrienne feel as though she were underwater. There was a waist-to-ceiling fish tank filled with tropical fish and the tables and chairs were very modern and sleek. The dining room had a blue glow that gave it a peaceful, floaty feeling despite the fact that it was packed with people. Young, hip, well-dressed. The people smelled like money.

"This is see and be seen in town," Thatcher said. "Which isn't what we're after, but . . . I would have taken you downstairs to the Boarding House for pot stickers, except the Parrishes eat there every Wednesday and I couldn't risk running into them."

"No," Adrienne said. She would have ended up babysitting Wolfie on her date.

"Danger," Thatcher said. "Danger, danger." He put his hand up to shield his face, as though the paparazzi were after him.

"Who is it? Not the Parrishes?"

"Cat is at the four-top by the window," Thatcher said. "And Leon Cross is at a deuce in the corner with a woman who is not his wife. He asked me yesterday if I would hide them away and I said no. Why he would bring her *here* is beyond me."

"Since you don't want to be seen with me, I could ask you the same thing."

"I'm proud to be seen with you," Thatcher said. "I just don't want to work on my night off."

"Should we leave?" Adrienne asked.

Before he could answer, a woman with straight black hair all the way down to her butt emerged from the crowd and pulled Thatcher and Adrienne forward as though she was granting them entrance to a hot club. "Follow me," she said.

The woman was Red Mare, Spillman's wife. She seated them at a table tucked back in the corner. Within minutes, Red Mare brought their drinks: a passion fruit cosmo for Adrienne and a club soda with lime for Thatcher.

"You're Adrienne," Red Mare said. "John really likes working with you. Much better than with Kevin. Didn't you think Kevin had a pole up his ass, Thatch?"

Thatcher shrugged. "Sure."

"I'm glad you finally got smart and put a woman up front. An attractive woman." She touched Adrienne's shoulder. "Great dress."

"Thanks."

"Anyway, Thatch, I know you called in your request, but the kitchen knows you're here and chef wants to make you his six-course Asian seafood menu."

"Tell chef thanks," Thatcher said. "But we'll stick with our original plan."

Red Mare clapped her hands and held them together in front of her chest like a praying mantis. "You got it."

After she disappeared back into the beautiful crowd, Adrienne said, "Everyone knows you."

"I've been here a long time."

"Twelve years isn't that long."

"It is when you're young. Listen, twelve years ago you were still in high school. Am I right?"

"You're right."

"And it's a small island. The restaurant community is tight. Over the course of the summer we'll have all the chefs in on their night off. We take good care of them. They just want to do the same."

Adrienne saw Red Mare peek at them from her position by the door, checking up on them like Adrienne herself did eighty-two times a night. Now that she worked in a restaurant, she noticed the things that other guests wouldn't. For example, the number of glasses hanging from a rack over the bar was dwindling (a few seconds later, the bar back appeared with clean glasses) and a certain busser, in this case a tiny brunette, kept bumping into one of the male servers. (They were obviously having a fling.) Adrienne might have shared these insights with Thatcher but he, no doubt, had outgrown being amused by the behind-the-scenes of other restaurants.

"What do you do around here all winter?" she asked.

"Catch up on my sleep," he said. "And Fiona and I take a trip back to South Bend at Christmas."

Adrienne had worked the last six Christmases but just the thought brought the face of Doug Riedel to mind. Those damn shearling gloves! She drained her cosmo. At that instant, Red Mare appeared with a second cosmo and their food. "Two tuna martinis—this is seared tuna with wasabi crème fraîche."

Adrienne tasted it as soon as it hit the table. "The best second course on the island," she said.

"If you're not eating at work," Thatcher said. He sipped his club soda.

"I have a question," Adrienne said, a challenge in her voice. Just breathing in the vapors from the second cosmo sent her good judgment through the roof.

"Shoot."

She had many questions, all of them provocative: Why had he been to see the priest? Why was he closing the restaurant? Why no journalists in the kitchen? But the one she chose was: "How did you come to be an alcoholic?"

His laugh was so forceful it startled her. "Ha!" After two weeks, she still wasn't used to that crazy laugh. "You're trying to shock me with a direct hit," he said. "And it's working."

Adrienne speared a piece of tuna. Even the silverware here had a sleek design. "You don't have to answer," she said. "I'm at the mercy of alcohol now myself."

"That was my goal," Thatcher said. "Get you drunk so you forget I'm your boss."

"Why do you want me to forget you're my boss?"

"So you'll like me."

"I do like you."

He stared at her a minute then reached for her hand. She looked at the side of his face, at the clean pink skin around his ear, newly exposed from the haircut. With his other hand, he loosened his tie and undid his top button. He had barely touched his food.

"You're not eating," she said.

"I'm pacing myself," he said. "Remember, I know what's to come."

Adrienne reclaimed her hand to finish her tuna, and if Thatcher wasn't going to eat, she would finish his.

"I became an alcoholic as a result of the business," Thatcher said. "It's an occupational hazard."

"What happened?"

"I don't know that anything happened," he said. "I was just drinking a lot every night. A couple of cocktails, a bottle of wine, a glass of port. And by the time the hand bell chimed, I was sloshed. I did stupid things. Forgave all the tabs at the bar. Doubled the tips for the waitstaff. This made me very popular, mind you, but it was bad for our bottom line. I started AA four years ago. Fiona insisted."

"Did she?"

"My behavior was threatening the business. It had to stop."

"Isn't it hard, though, not drinking? Especially when you're around alcohol all the time?"

"At first, I tried to cut back. Have one cocktail, one glass of wine. But I couldn't do it. One cocktail wasn't an option. Alcoholism is a disease and I have it. But it's not so bad." He held up his drink. "I really love club soda."

Adrienne smiled and stared at Thatcher's tuna, ruby red in the frosted martini glass. She could stay here all night. She wanted to enjoy being waited on for a change. But Thatcher seemed antsy. He checked his Patek Philippe. "Time's up," he said. "We're going."

At a restaurant called Oran Mor, Thatcher and Adrienne hid at a tiny table tucked behind the horseshoe-shaped bar. The table had a view of the harbor and the ferry—the same ferry that Adrienne had arrived on two weeks, and another lifetime, ago. A male waiter brought Adrienne a glass of red wine followed by an enormous porterhouse steak topped with Roquefort butter. Thatcher got a shallow dish of lobster risotto.

"I couldn't decide between the two," he said. "So we got both." He watched Adrienne take a bite of steak. "Now taste your wine."

Adrienne bristled once again at being told what to do, especially since she knew he'd be right. The steak and wine were made for each other.

"How's the wine?" he asked.

"Incredible."

He picked up her glass and inhaled. "Big," he said. "Plummy. Just as they described it."

Adrienne offered her steak to Thatcher but he shook his head. "Go on," she said. "There can't be more after this." He relented, then hand-fed her a bite of his risotto, and all Adrienne could think was that it was a good thing no one could see them. Nothing brought more sarcasm from the waitstaff than a couple feeding each other.

Adrienne drank down her wine and another glass appeared. She was officially drunk; across the table, Thatcher was blurry. He was looking at her so intently that it took the place of conversation. *He's soaking me up,* Adrienne thought. *Whatever* that *meant.* The more Adrienne drank, the more it seemed like Thatcher himself was drunk. When she finished eating, Thatcher took her hand again.

"Who are you, Adrienne Dealey?" he said. "Who are you?"

She didn't have anything resembling a good answer. She couldn't say "I'm a dentist and a father." Or "I'm a restaurant owner." Or "I'm a chef." She couldn't even say "I'm a childhood friend of Fiona's. I've been a friend of hers since kindergarten." She had no identity. She lived in a place for a while, working a desk, skiing bumps, visiting Buddhist temples, sitting on a sugar-sand beach, making poor decisions, fudging the details of her past—and six months or a year later she was somewhere else. Someone else. New friends, new boyfriend, new job, new location. The most important thing in her life had been the money for her Future, the money saved up for . . . what? Some bigger plan that she had yet to identify. Her father was right. One of these days she was going to have to pick a place and stay there.

"I'm a student of human nature," Adrienne said. She was so drunk this didn't even sound corny. "I'm trying to absorb it all before I settle down."

"Do you think you'll ever settle down?" Thatcher said. "Get married?"

Adrienne pushed her plate away; she was absolutely stuffed. She reached for her wine and held the glass with two hands. "I don't know. I've had a lot of boyfriends. There was a guy on the Cape who asked me to marry him and I considered it for about a day and a half. Then I freaked out and flew to Hawaii. It was very immature behavior on my part."

"My mother bailed on us when I was nine," Thatcher said. "My three older brothers were sixteen, fourteen, and eleven at the time. There is no doubt in my mind that we drove her away; we would have driven Mother Teresa away. So I used to have an issue with women who run, but I got over it. I forgave my mother—that's one thing AA really helps with, forgiveness. She lives in Toronto now, but I never see her."

"Yeah," Adrienne said. "My mother died when I was twelve."

"I didn't know your mother died," Thatcher said. "Something you said earlier made me think . . ."

"I'm sorry about that," Adrienne said. "I have a hard time talking about it and sometimes it's just easier . . ."

"You don't have to apologize," Thatcher said.

"Maybe not to you," Adrienne said. "But I've lied to a lot of people about it. I pretend my mother is still alive. I want her to be alive."

"Of course."

Adrienne placed a fingertip at the corner of her eye. "I probably don't need any more wine."

Thatcher looked around the restaurant. "I was going to take you to Languedoc for the Sweet Inspirations sundae."

"It may interest you to know," said Adrienne, "that the key to dessert is not sugar." She bent her head close to the table and whispered, "It's eggs."

Thatcher groaned. "When a woman starts quoting Mario Subiaco, I know she's had too much to drink. No sundae for you. Let's go for a drive."

"I have to use the ladies' room," Adrienne said.

She nearly tripped on the uneven floor on the way to the bathroom and when she got inside, she looked at herself in the mirror. Her cheeks were bright pink. *I am drunk,* she thought. *Schnockered.* She splashed her face and pulled out her dental floss. Who are you, Adrienne Dealey? *I am a person who cares about dental hygiene.*

They climbed into Thatcher's silver pickup. His truck was impeccably clean and smelled like peppermint. Adrienne fell back into the gray leather seat while Thatch fiddled with the CD player. He put on Simon and Garfunkel.

"How old *are* you?" she asked.

"Old. Thirty-five." He rummaged through the console and brought out a tire gauge. "I'm going to take you up the beach," he said. "Do you have any objections to that?"

"None," Adrienne said. The clock in the car said ten thirty. She couldn't help thinking about the restaurant: Had Caren and Duncan made up? Would they be sneaking in gropes and shots of espresso, giddy with their freedom like kids whose parents were away for the weekend? Would they be playing techno on the stereo (which Thatch hated) and hogging all the crackers for themselves? "Do you miss work?" she asked. She noticed his cell phone sitting in the console next to the tire gauge, his ring of Bistro keys, and a tin of Altoids, but he hadn't so much as checked his messages.

"No," he said, starting the engine and pulling out of town. "Not at all."

When Adrienne next opened her eyes, she was alone in the truck. It was dark, and looking out the window she saw nothing but more dark.

"Thatcher?" she said.

She heard a hissing noise outside her window. When she opened her door, she saw Thatcher kneeling by the front tire letting out air. From the dome light she could see sand dunes covered with eelgrass.

"This is the last one," Thatcher said. He checked the tire with the gauge and stood up, wiping his hands on his pants. He had removed his jacket and tie and his shirt was open another button at the neck.

"Where are we?"

"Dionis Beach," he said. "Have you been here?"

Adrienne shook her head.

"Good," he said. "Hang on."

He drove the truck up over the dunes with abandon, bouncing Adrienne out of her seat. Thatcher whooped like a cowboy and Adrienne prayed she didn't vomit. (She had a worrisome flashback from twenty years earlier: the Our Lady of the Assumption carnival, cotton candy, kettle corn, and the tilt-a-whirl. Her mother holding back her hair in a smelly Porta-John.) Then, thankfully, they were on the beach, and the water was before them, one stripe shining from the crescent moon. The beach was deserted. Thatcher parked the truck then opened Adrienne's door for her. He spread a blanket on the sand.

"You came prepared," she said.

"Lie down," he said. "But keep your eyes open."

"Yes, boss," she said.

After getting gracefully to the ground in her dress, Adrienne looked at the stars. Thatcher lay on his side, staring at her. She closed her eyes. She could fall asleep right here. Happily, happily. Listening to the waves lap onto the beach. She heard Thatcher's voice in her ear.

"I'm going to kiss you if that's okay," he said.

"It won't be our first kiss," she said.

"No," he said. "I let one slip at the restaurant. I thought about apologizing to you for that, but I didn't feel sorry." And with that, he kissed her. One very soft, very sweet kiss. The kiss was fleeting but it left a big ache for more in its wake. Adrienne gasped, taking in the cool sea air, and then Thatcher kissed her again. Even softer, even shorter. The third time, he stayed. They were kissing. His mouth opened and Adrienne tasted his tongue, sweet and tangy like the lime in his drink. She felt like she was going to burst apart into eighty-two pieces of desire. Like the best lovers, Thatcher moved slowly—for right now, on the blanket, it was only about the kissing. Not since high school had kissing been this intense. It went on and on. They stopped to look at each other. Adrienne ran her fingertips over his pale eyebrows, she cupped his neck inside the collar of his shirt. He touched her ears and kissed the corners of her eyes, and Adrienne thought about how she had come right out with the truth about her mother at dinner and how unusual that was. And just as she began to worry that there was something different this time, something better, of a finer quality than the other relationships she had found herself in, she and Thatcher started kissing again, and the starting again was even sweeter.

Yes, Adrienne thought. *Something was different this time.*

How much time passed? An hour? Two? Of lying on the blanket kissing Thatcher Smith, the man who had handed her a new life on this island. Adrienne felt herself drifting to sleep, she felt him kiss her eyelids closed— and then suddenly, like a splash of icy water, like a bolt of lightning hitting way too close, like the foul smell that wafted from the restaurant garbage, there came a noise. From the car. Thatcher's cell phone.

He pulled away. Checked his twenty-thousand-dollar watch in the moonlight. And ran for the truck.

He took the call standing in the deep dark a few yards behind his truck. Which was smart, because if he'd been closer, Adrienne would have yelled at whomever was on the other end. *How dare you spoil my night!*

Thatcher snapped the phone closed as he walked back toward Adrienne who was now sitting up on the blanket, headache threatening.

"I don't want to hear it," she said.

"That was Fee."

"Fiona? What did she want?"

"It's twelve thirty. My dinner is ready."

"Your dinner is ready," Adrienne repeated flatly. "Your *dinner* is *ready?*"

"We eat together every night," he said.

"Yes, except tonight you're on a date with me. Tonight you ate with me." As soon as she said the words, she realized he *hadn't* eaten—he had barely touched his food. Because he knew all along that he was going back to the

Bistro. *To eat with Fiona.* "Take me home," Adrienne said. "Take me home right now."

"You're tired anyway," he said. "You were practically asleep." He tried to reach for her but she climbed into the truck and made a point of slamming the door in his face. She fastened her seat belt and when Thatcher got in, she stared out the windshield at the black water of the sound.

"Don't be mad," he said.

"This is weird," Adrienne said. "You going back to have dinner with her. It's *strange.*"

"I realize it must seem that way."

"She loves JZ," Adrienne said.

"What do *you* know about it?" he asked.

"I saw them together yesterday," Adrienne said. "She left with him. She loves him."

"She does love him," Thatcher said. "But what I asked was, what do you know about it?"

"Nothing," Adrienne admitted. "She was coughing and he picked her up and held her."

"Okay," Thatcher said, as if he'd made some very important point. He started the truck and eased them out over the dunes, the truck rocking gently this time, as gently as a cradle.

He pulled into her driveway by quarter to one.

"Don't bother getting out," Adrienne said. "I can see myself in."

"I'm walking you to the door," Thatcher said. He returned to his persona of old-fashioned suitor and took her arm. She had forgotten to leave on any lights and so the cottage was pitch-black. As they stood at the doorway, Thatcher touched the strap of her blue dress. Adrienne knew she should thank him for the date; he'd gone to a lot of trouble. But she was angry, incredulous, defiant. *His dinner was ready!*

He leaned in to kiss her and she let him. She thought maybe she could keep him. Maybe his dinner would go cold and Fiona would have to throw it away. They kissed and kissed; Adrienne had never felt such urgency.

"Stay with me," she said.

He pressed her against the door frame and for the first time she felt his body right up against hers and it was an even better feeling, if that were possible, than the kissing. She could feel herself winning, she could see the future: his shirt coming off, her blue dress dropping into a silk puddle on the floor, the two of them entwined in Adrienne's bed. Caren's shock the following morning at the espresso machine when Thatcher joined her for a short black. But then, just as Adrienne knew he would, he surfaced from the pull of her desire with a gulp of air like a man who had been drowning.

"Go," Adrienne said.

And he went.

6

❧

The Wine Key

How did men do it?

It was ten minutes to six on Thursday night, 101 covers on the book, and Thatcher actually had the gall to knock on the door of the ladies' room where Adrienne was brushing her teeth and deciding whether or not to quit.

"Come on out," he said. "I need to talk to you."

Adrienne shut off the water, tapped her toothbrush angrily against the side of the sink, and flung open the door.

"You have some nerve," she said.

He held up a wine key. "I'm going to show you how to use this. Now. We've waited too long."

How did he manage to look better than ever on the one night (possibly of many) Adrienne had arrived at work prepared to hate him? It looked like he had gotten some sun—his face had that healthy golden glow. *Did you go to the beach?* Adrienne wanted to ask. But no, she wouldn't. Just as she wouldn't ask him, *How was your dinner?* (though she had practiced the exact tone of sarcasm and contempt).

How did he have the presence of mind to stand before her holding up the wine key as innocuously as a door-to-door salesman? Did he not remember pressing his body up against hers the night before? Did he not remember how tenderly he kissed her eyelids closed? How did men find the nerve the next day to act as though nothing had ever happened? (And it wasn't just Thatcher, Adrienne conceded. She'd seen it time and time again.)

Over Thatcher's shoulder, Adrienne saw Joe and Spillman lighting candles. Rex began to play "Old Cape Cod." Adrienne rolled her eyes. She would be a brick wall.

"Fine, the wine key," she said. She followed Thatcher into the wine cave. He closed the door behind them and Adrienne thought, *Okay, here it comes.* The wine key was a ruse. He was going to apologize.

Thatcher removed a bottle of red from the rack. Bin forty-one: Cain Cuvée—they sold it by the glass as well as from the list.

"First," he said, "you have to cut the lead."

She stared at him, trying to make her eyes as hard as the point of an awl.

"Some restaurants have a special tool for this," Thatcher said. "Not us. We use the very inexpensive, very user-friendly Screwpull. Wait until you see how easy this is." He used the sharp end of the key to cut the lead, which was the metal wrapper over the cork. He pulled it off. Then he set the plastic arms of the Screwpull over the cork, inserted the key, and turned the knob at the top. Turned and turned—and like magic, the cork appeared. "A third grader could do it," he said. He set the bottle aside and pulled out their most popular bottle of white—Menetou-Salon, from an area of France near Sancerre. Adrienne had heard Thatcher give the spiel on this wine before—the vintner was also the mayor of the town.

"You try," he said, handing her the bottle and the key.

She cut the lead, peeled it away (a little less seamlessly than Thatch, but she got it), set the Screwpull in place, and turned. Out came the cork. Piece of cake.

"Fine," she said.

"The waiters open their own wine," Thatcher said. "I open for VIPs, and I open when the waitstaff is slammed. Step in when you feel you're needed."

"Fine, fine." She dug her heel into the floor in a way that she hoped conveyed her impatience. She was wearing yet another pair of new shoes—buff-colored Jimmy Choo sling backs—that she'd bought that afternoon in an attempt to make herself feel better.

"And there's one more thing," Thatcher said.

Something in his voice made her look at him and their eyes locked. *I am a brick wall,* she thought. *I am a swan carved from ice.*

"What's that?" she said.

He held her gaze for whole seconds of precious time. Outside the door, Adrienne could hear Spillman's voice: "Has anyone seen the boss man?" Thatcher didn't move. He just held Adrienne captive with his eyes and when Adrienne thought it was inevitable—they were going to kiss—he snapped out of his daze.

"Champagne," he said. He opened the refrigerator and pulled out a bottle of Laurent-Perrier. He unfolded a towel from the Sankaty Head Golf Club. "Up front, you'll use a side towel, or even a dinner napkin," he said. He removed the foil from the cork, wrangled off the cage, and showed Adrienne the bottle with the naked cork. "You could push at the bottom of the cork until it shoots out, but champagne corks are unpredictable. You could take out someone's eye. Best-case scenario, the cork gets lost in the sand and one of our guests with an environmental conscience writes a letter to the *Inquirer and Mirror* about how we here at the Blue Bistro are littering Nantucket's pristine beaches. So." He covered the cork with the golf towel and twisted. "Twist while pulling up." The cork came free with a muted *pop.* Thatcher whipped off the towel. The lip of the bottle showed a wisp of smoky carbon dioxide; he tossed the cork in the trash. "Take this out to Duncan and have him pour you a glass," he said. "It's time to get to work."

So that was it. They were together in the wine cave with the door closed for six whole minutes and all she'd gotten was a deep stare and a lesson on the world's easiest tasks. Adrienne saw her options: quit or work as though nothing had happened. Life wasn't made any easier by the fact that everyone on the staff knew she and Thatcher had been out together—and likewise, everyone knew that Thatcher returned to the restaurant to eat with Fiona. Caren had said it best that morning while she and Duncan (reunited) drank espresso and Adrienne drank ginger lemon tea because, to add insult to injury, Adrienne had a killer hangover, the worst of the summer so far. Caren had said, "How was your date? It couldn't have been too wonderful."

And Adrienne said, "There is something very fucked up going on between Thatcher and Fiona."

Caren and Duncan had stared at her blankly but when they thought she wasn't looking, they exchanged an alarmed glance. Adrienne caught it and said, "And you two pissants know what's going on and you won't tell me."

Caren had nodded very slowly. "They're friends," she said.

And Duncan said, "I have to go. I'm sailing with Holt Millman at ten."

Adrienne tried to lose herself in the service. One hundred and one covers on the books, but first thing there was a walk-in party of four, dressed in workout clothes. They informed Adrienne that they had arrived on their bikes after a long ride to Sconset, and they wanted to know if they could eat dinner and get back into town before dark.

"Sure," Adrienne said. Table three was empty; it was a less desirable table, saved on slower nights for walk-ins. She sat the party, gave them the exact time of sunset along with their menus, and told them she'd have the kitchen on top of their order. The head biker palmed her fifty bucks.

"Thanks," he said. "We're really hungry."

Joe took the table; he was psyched. "Good work," he said. "How was your date last night?"

"What date?" she said.

She was a swan carved from ice.

First seating breezed by. She delivered three orders of chips and dip, and she opened four bottles of wine. She completely ignored Thatcher and, at a couple of points, she was so busy, she forgot him.

In between seatings, Thatcher called her over to the podium. "Can I brief you?"

While he talked, Adrienne stared at the ceiling.

Table eleven was a four-top under the awning, a good table: a local lawyer and her husband and their friends visiting from Anchorage, Alaska. The lawyer was not Thatcher's lawyer but she was a prominent Nantucket citizen—on the board of Hospice and the Boys & Girls Club—and a regular guest. VIP. Adrienne had delivered their chips and dip and opened their wine, the fantastic Leeuwin chardonnay from Western Australia. Now they were eating their entrées and Adrienne saw the lawyer glancing around the dining room in distress. Adrienne hurried over.

"What can I help you with?" she asked.

The lawyer beckoned Adrienne closer. "You won't believe this," she said. "But my friend swears her swordfish is overcooked."

"Overcooked?" Adrienne said.

"And I'll tell you what, it must be true because people from Alaska never complain."

Adrienne moved around the table to the Alaska woman and eyed the swordfish. It was black and shriveled; it looked like one of the pork chops that Doug used to murder in his cast-iron skillet before he doused it with ketchup.

"I'm sorry," the Alaska woman squeaked.

"I'm the one who's sorry," Adrienne said. "Let me bring you another piece. Believe me when I say this almost never happens."

She carried the swordfish to the kitchen, poking it once with her finger. It was completely dry; it had the texture of plaster. Adrienne was thrilled. Two weeks earlier a complaint about the doughnuts had nearly made her weep, but today a complaint about the food was a gift from God. She couldn't wait to confront Fiona with this hideous swordfish.

Adrienne slammed into the kitchen and dropped the plate on the pass with a clatter. No one was expediting.

"Where's Fiona?" she said.

"She's in the office lying down," Hector said.

Adrienne deflated. Her rage was overcooked, shriveled, dry, and yet she couldn't get rid of it.

"Well, where's Antonio, then?" she asked.

"It's his night off," Hector said. "Which reminds me, how was your date?"

"Fuck you," Adrienne said.

This set the platoon of Subiacos laughing. Adrienne picked the swordfish up off the plate and flung it at Hector, who was, conveniently, working grill. It hit him in the shoulder, smudging his white jacket.

"You killed the swordfish for eleven," she said. "The guest complained—in fact, she was practically in tears because it tasted so bad. Fire another one."

"Boo-hoo," Hector said, laying a swordfish steak across the grill.

Adrienne marched back out to table eleven. "Sorry about the swordfish," she said. "We're going to comp your bill this evening and I hope you'll forgive us."

The lawyer touched Adrienne's wrist. "You don't have to comp the meal," she said.

"Oh, yes," Adrienne said. "Yes, I do."

A few moments later, table six, a deuce, guests from the Nantucket Beach Club, called Adrienne over. No lobster on the lobster club. What they showed her was a twenty-nine-dollar BLT.

"Please," Adrienne said, picking up the plate. "Let me get you some lobster meat. And your dinner tonight is on the house."

The third table she comped because the top of the butterscotch crème brûlée was scorched. The guest hadn't even complained but Adrienne saw the desserts go out, and she saw the black spots. She had an infuriating vision of Mario back in his lair doing the bossa nova while he took a welding tool to the custard. The dessert was going to a table of six, which meant a tab of at least a thousand dollars. Adrienne bought their dinner. The revenge was so sweet it made her dizzy.

Later, Thatcher cornered her at the podium. It was eleven fifteen; she had a line of five people. The bar was packed but unusually quiet.

"You comped three meals," he said. "One tab was twelve hundred dollars. Because that six-top was drinking a Chateau Margaux."

Adrienne shrugged. "The food was bad tonight. Fiona wasn't expediting. You should have seen the swordfish at eleven. It was a piece of drywall."

"I understand the swordfish. And that was Leigh Stanford's table and I would have comped it myself. But a piece of lobster missing? A bad crème brûlée?"

"The lobster missing was a table Mack sent us, and the brûlée looked like it had the bubonic plague. At the beginning of the season you told me that close to perfect wasn't going to cut it."

"I did. But to *comp* a twelve-hundred-dollar dinner?"

"During first seating, I took a walk-in four-top that one of your other managers probably would have turned away because they weren't wearing

Armani. They drank two bottles of Cristal and had a thousand-dollar tab themselves. Take the difference out of my salary."

Thatcher sighed. "I'm not going to take it out of your salary," he said. "All three tables left huge tips so the waitstaff loves you. And I know you did what you thought was right." He nodded at the kitchen. "I'm going to eat."

Adrienne didn't answer. She was crushed. He didn't even care enough to fight with her.

TO: DrDon@toothache.com
FROM: Ade12177@hotmail.com
DATE: June 16, 2005 9:14 A.M.
SUBJECT: Surprise!

I sent you the last of the money I owe you—not bad for two weeks of work! And your "interest" should arrive at the office tomorrow morning. Bon appetit—and thanks for always being there for me. Love.

TO: kyracrenshaw@mindspring.com
FROM: Ade12177@hotmail.com
DATE: June 16, 2005 9:37 A.M.
SUBJECT: First date of the summer

I can honestly say I would rather go out with drug abuser and felon Doug Riedel than ever go out with my boss again. Doug may have stuck my life savings up his nose and robbed my place of employment, but at least he didn't leave me stranded for another woman!

Business Notes
The Inquirer and Mirror
Week of June 17, 2005
BLUE BISTRO UP FOR SALE

Harry Henderson of Henderson Realty, Inc. announced late last week that Blue Bistro owners Thatcher Smith and Fiona Kemp have put the popular waterfront restaurant on the market for $8.5 million. Mr. Smith was quoted as saying, "This is a classic case of quitting while we're ahead." Rumors have circulated that

Smith and Kemp are looking for another property on the island, and that they have expressed interest in Sloop's on Steamship Wharf, which they hope to turn into a chic café called Calamari. "While we feel that space is currently underutilized," Smith says, "the rumors are absolutely untrue." The only certain plans Smith and his partner Ms. Kemp have in the works, he says, is a trip to the Galápagos Islands in October.

Ms. Kemp could not be reached for comment.

For Father's Day, Adrienne bought her father a gas grill from the Williams-Sonoma catalog and a box of Omaha steaks. It cost her over seven hundred dollars but money, now, was the least of her worries. The balance in her bank account was steadily growing and she had paid off her thirteen-hundred-dollar debt to her father. If for the money alone, she was going to keep her job.

A week had passed and Thatcher hadn't said a word about their date. Of course, Adrienne hardly gave him a chance—she spoke to him in only the most perfunctory way, in only the most professional capacity, and he returned the favor. With each passing day the evening of their date faded into yesterday's news. Adrienne tried to regard it as a failed experiment. A fallen soufflé. She had broken Rule Three and she was paying the price. So now it was back to the straight and narrow. If she felt bruised—her heart, her ego—she was going to make sure that no one could tell.

She did a crisp, clean job on the floor. She handed out menus, delivered the chips and dip, ran food, opened wine, processed credit cards, and worked the door without compassion. Tyler Lefroy informed her that patrons of the bar called her the Blue Bitch. That made her smile for the first time since Dionis Beach.

What she needed, she told herself, was a life apart from the restaurant, and so she started jogging in the mornings. She ran to Surfside Beach, she ran to Cisco Beach, she ran along Miacomet Pond. She rode her bike to the rotary and ran along the Polpis Road. One day she ran to the restaurant—the Sid Wainer truck was in the parking lot and Adrienne saw Fiona and JZ sitting in the back of the truck talking, their legs dangling over the edge. She ran on Cliff Road past Tupancy Links and the water tower, out to Eel Point where the road turned to dirt.

Every way she went, Nantucket revealed its beauty. The rosa rugosa was blooming pink and white, the ponds were blue, the eelgrass razor sharp. The beaches were clean and still not crowded. The island had a lot more to offer, Adrienne told herself, than just Thatcher Smith.

One morning, Adrienne ran all the way out to Madaket Harbor, which was too far on a hot day. She bought a cold Evian at the Westender before she embarked on her limp home. She was on the bike path by Long Pond when a green Honda Pilot stopped; the tinted passenger window went down.

"Do you need a lift?" the driver asked.

It was a man, in his forties, with dark hair. The exact kind of person one imagined offering candy to an unsuspecting young girl.

"No, thanks," Adrienne said, waving the empty water bottle. "I'm fine."

"You sure?"

"All set."

"It's awfully hot. I can drop you in town. It'll take three minutes."

Adrienne looked at her dusty shoes. The soles of her feet burned. The guy was right: It was hot. She was out of water and she had three, maybe four, miles to go. She noticed a child's car seat in the back of the Pilot. So he probably wasn't a serial killer, and he couldn't exactly abduct her on Nantucket.

"Okay," Adrienne said. "Thanks." She climbed in. The air-conditioning was a blessing.

The man put up her window and hit the gas. "I'll just drop you in town," he said. "I'm headed in to pick up my mail."

"Fine."

He hummed along to a song on the radio. Adrienne sat up very straight to avoid sweating all over his car.

"You don't recognize me, do you?" the man said.

Adrienne fumbled with her Walkman and it fell to the floor. She bent over to retrieve it, trying not to panic. She slid in a sideways look. He looked familiar, but she met so many people on a nightly basis that . . .

"Drew Amman-Keller," he said.

Adrienne glanced up. Drew Amman-Keller? Adrienne studied his face. The lips she recognized, but the rest was different. Hadn't he had a beard? And an awful pair of glasses?

"I'm sorry," she said. "You look different."

"I shaved," he said. "My wife insists that I shave in the summer."

"You're married?" Adrienne asked.

"Three kids," he said.

Adrienne stared out the window. They were passing the landfill. She prayed to see another car, but they seemed to be the only one on the road. She tried to parse her fear. The guy was a freelance journalist, not a criminal. And it wasn't as though he was stalking her; he was on his way to the post office.

"You can just drop me off here, if you want," Adrienne said.

"At the dump?"

"I can walk home. It's not far."

"Did Thatcher tell you not to talk to me?"

A car approached, a red Jeep Wrangler with the top down—two very tan college boys with a couple of surfboards strapped to the roll bars. They were gone before Adrienne could think of how to signal for help. What, she wondered, would Thatcher do if he learned she'd accepted a ride from Drew Amman-Keller? And why did she care what Thatcher thought?

"I know what's going on with Fiona," he said. "I've known for years. What she and Thatcher don't understand is that I want to help. I have an offer on the table from the *Atlantic Monthly* if Fiona ever agrees to talk to me. Sometimes by writing a feature in a big magazine, you can create positive change."

Adrienne squeezed her water bottle in the middle, making a plastic crunch. This was the guy who had sent her to the Bistro in the first place. He'd set her up, maybe, hoping she'd spy on Fiona and report details back to him. But what kind of details was he after, exactly? "I have no idea what you're talking about," she said.

Drew Amman-Keller took his eyes off the road for a split second to look at Adrienne. She noticed something funny about the bottom half of his face. It was pink and raw-looking where he'd shaved, as though he'd stripped off a mask.

He downshifted and signaled to the left. "Here's Cliff Road," he said. "Is it okay if I drop you here?"

"I thought you were going to take me into town," Adrienne said. "Are you trying to get rid of me now?"

He laughed. "I'm happy to take you to town," he said. He pulled back onto the road and turned up the radio.

Adrienne collapsed back in the seat. "You're happy to take me to town, but you won't tell me what's going on in the restaurant where I'm the assistant manager. You must think I'm pretty naïve."

"I think no such thing."

Despite the air-conditioning, Adrienne was hot. And thirsty. And angry.

"I went on a date with Thatcher last week," she said. "But Fiona called at midnight and told Thatcher his dinner was ready and he left me at my front door." Adrienne watched Drew Amman-Keller for a reaction, but he had none. She kicked his glove compartment and left a mark with her filthy shoe. The restaurant was turning her into a lunatic, the kind of person who confided in strangers and disrespected their brand-new cars. "You told me if I ever wanted to talk, I should call you. You gave me your card. I still have it at home."

"Good," he said. "Hold on to it."

"I don't suppose you'll write an article about my date with Thatcher?"

"No," he said.

"No," Adrienne echoed. Girl likes boy, boy likes different girl. He'd heard it a thousand times before. Everyone had.

There were only two people in the restaurant whom Adrienne trusted, and one of those people was Mario. This might have seemed counterintuitive, as Mario's reputation among the staff was for being exactly the opposite—untrustworthy, fickle, a scoundrel. He had dumped Delilah by kissing another woman on the dance floor of the Chicken Box while he was there on a date with Delilah. Delilah had cried for three days, and she begged Duncan to defend her honor. Duncan said, "I told you not to go near the guy in the first place."

Mario was deadly as a lover, but as a friend he had a curiously golden touch. The afternoon of her ride with Drew Amman-Keller, Adrienne marched back into pastry.

"It looks like someone could use a Popsicle," Mario said. He pulled a tray out of the freezer and handed Adrienne a creamy raspberry-banana Popsicle then took one for himself. They licked the Popsicles leaning side by side against the marble counter.

"They're good, yeah?" Mario said.

"Yeah," she said. She bit off a big piece and it gave her an ice-cream headache. She moaned. Mario rubbed the inside of her wrist.

"This is supposed to help," he said.

"You just want to touch me," she said.

"You got that right."

She said, "Do you know what's going on between Fiona and Thatcher?"

He dropped her arm. "There's nothing going on."

Adrienne threw her Popsicle stick into the trash. "You're lying to me."

"No," Mario said. He moved down the counter to where the dough for the Portuguese rolls was proofing. He worked the dough with his hands. "I would not lie to you. There's nothing going on the way you're thinking."

"How do you know what I'm thinking?"

"I always know what the ladies are thinking."

"So if it's not what I'm thinking, then what is it?"

"I wish I could tell you," Mario said.

The other person Adrienne trusted was Caren, but only during certain times of the day: mornings after Duncan left, in the Jetta on the way to work, as they listened to Moby.

"I am not a jealous person," Caren said, one morning after four espressos, which was enough to make even her tremble. "You haven't known me very long, so you'll have to take my word for it. Usually, I eat men for breakfast."

"I can tell," Adrienne said.

"I'm a biting bitch."

"You're strong."

"Right. Except not with Duncan. I've known him twelve years and I've seen him do all kinds of outrageous things with women at the bar, and before it was always funny. But now it's awful. They all want to sleep with him, even the married ones. He says he's in it for the money, but I don't know, it's got to be an ego rush for him, right? This is driving me fucking nuts. But don't tell anyone, okay? Promise you won't tell."

"I promise," Adrienne said. She had sworn to herself that she wasn't going to tell anyone about her ride with Drew Amman-Keller, not even Caren. But at that moment Caren seemed vulnerable—pale, sweating, shaking from her mainline of caffeine—so Adrienne said, "I know I've beaten this subject to death, but I really want to know what's going on between Thatcher and Fiona."

Caren gathered up her hair and tied it into a knot. It stayed perfect like that, without a single pin. Adrienne was both fascinated by her manipulations and driven batty by her silence. Caren was deciding how much, if anything, to divulge. "It's a lot simpler than you think."

"Simpler how?"

"They're friends, like I said before. If you're ever going to have a relationship with Thatcher Smith, you need to accept that."

"I'm not going to have a relationship with Thatcher Smith," Adrienne said. She needed to accept *that*.

On the Sunday before the official start of summer, Caren announced from her post in front of the espresso machine that she and Duncan were going sailing on Holt Millman's yacht and that Adrienne was joining them.

"You're not allowed to say no," Caren said. "Holt is thrilled you're coming. We're leaving in thirty minutes and we'll be back at four."

Adrienne knew damn well that Holt Millman had no clue who she was but Caren seemed resolute and Duncan backed her up, saying, "Yep. Better get ready."

It was something different, a welcome change from running by herself and going to the beach by herself. Once she was heading down the docks of Old North Wharf, Adrienne felt excited. It was another gorgeous day and she liked being among the boats—the sailboats, the power yachts—and the people loading up coolers of beer and bags of sandwiches, getting ready for a day on the water. She hoped Thatcher was cooped up inside, the phone stuck to his ear like a tumor.

Holt Millman's yacht, *Kelsey*, was the biggest boat Adrienne had ever seen in person. It was, Duncan told her, 103 feet long with a ninety-foot main mast. It was modeled after the *Shamrock*, a 1930s era J-class racing yacht, but Holt's boat was made out of Kevlar and honeycombed fiberglass. It had clean lines up top, Duncan said, but below deck it was a mansion—with china in cabinets, a Jacuzzi, a washer and dryer.

Duncan paused. "I'm going to guess that you've never seen anything like this."

Adrienne had sailed on the Chesapeake when she was a child, she'd fished in blue water off the coast of Florida, hung on for dear life to a catamaran in Hawaii, and she island-hopped in an old junk during her year in Thailand. When she lived in Chatham, her boyfriend Sully had use of a seventeen-foot Boston Whaler and he'd even let her take the wheel. But none of that had prepared her for *Kelsey*.

They took their shoes off before they stepped onto the teak deck. Holt was standing in the cockpit talking to a man with broad shoulders who looked like the captain. Holt wore a green polo shirt with KELSEY on the pocket; he was drinking something pink and frosty in a Providence Puritans glass. (The Puritans, Duncan had informed Adrienne in the car, were an NHL expansion team that Holt had purchased the year before.) As soon as Holt saw Duncan and Caren, he raised his glass in greeting. Adrienne wished she knew something about hockey.

"Thanks for coming, thanks for coming," Holt said. He pumped Duncan's hand and kissed Caren on the cheek. "And you brought Adrienne. Good for you. This boat needs more pretty women."

Adrienne smiled. "Thanks for inviting us," she said, but Holt Millman didn't hear. He was calling below deck for "Drinks, more drinks," ushering Duncan forward, and introducing the rest of the guests with a sweep of his arm. There were five other people on the boat, some of whom Adrienne recognized. The woman who cut Thatcher's hair sat on a cushioned bench in the cockpit talking to the hostess from 21 Federal. There were two older bond-trader type men who rose to greet Duncan and ask him about his handicap. And out on the bow of the boat was a stunning blond woman in a red bikini. She sat up and waved at Adrienne; it was Cat, the world's most glamorous electrician.

"Cat is everywhere," Adrienne murmured to Caren.

"She could be a model," Caren said. "If she weren't busy wiring Millman's home theater."

Caren joined Duncan's conversation with the bond traders, leaving Adrienne to either sit alone or talk to the hostess and Thatcher's hairdresser. While the first option was infinitely preferable, the hostess—who must have been the social director for her sorority in college—waved Adrienne over.

"Come sit with us!" she called. She moved her tiny butt a fraction of an inch to indicate that she was making room. Holt popped up the stairs with a tray of pink frosty drinks. He held the tray out to Adrienne.

"This is my own recipe," he said. "It's called a Kelsey. I keep trying to get Duncan to make them at the restaurant."

Duncan lifted his head from his other conversation. "No blender drinks," he said. "Sorry."

Holt Millman laughed with his head thrown back, exposing his tan throat. Adrienne guessed he was nearing seventy, yet she sensed he went to great lengths and expense to keep himself looking younger. Spa treatments to erase the wrinkles from his face and neck and the like.

Adrienne accepted a drink and sat next to the hostess from 21. "Hi," she said. "I'm Adrienne."

The hostess clapped her hands. "We know who you are," she said. "Because remember, I seated you? When you were on your date with Thatcher?"

The hairdresser piped in. "I just love Thatch," she said. "That red-gold hair. I have clients who would sell their souls for hair that color."

"Have you two been dating long?" the hostess asked.

"We're not dating," Adrienne said. "It was a business dinner."

"Oh, stop," the hairdresser said. "I cut his hair that very afternoon and he told me he had a hot date. It didn't sound like business to me."

"Well, it was business," Adrienne said. She sipped her drink. It was delicious—watermelon, strawberry, club soda, and what she thought must be vodka. It went straight to her head. She removed her T-shirt so that she was in her bikini top and shorts. The sun felt terrific. *Hot date?* She was relieved when the motor revved and the captain steered them out of the harbor.

One hour and three Kelsey drinks later, Adrienne was happier. Caren had rescued her and now Adrienne, Caren, and Cat were lying in their bikinis on the teak deck near the bow. Above their heads the sails rumbled, the ropes snapped, and a crew of young men in green shirts like Holt's moved about—tightening, loosening, using jargon like "foredeck" and "power winches." Nantucket was a blur of green and gray in the distance. A young woman with an English accent brought a basket of wraps and refills for their drinks. The sandwiches were beautiful pinwheels of color: avocado, tomato and bacon, goat cheese and roasted red pepper, roast beef, cucumber, and horseradish cream. *Forget Fiona,* Adrienne thought. She was never getting off this boat.

Four drinks, five drinks. Then somehow, Adrienne found herself sitting in the cockpit with the rest of the guests passing around a joint. Adrienne smoked rarely but she was so relaxed that she didn't even blink. Everyone smoked except for Holt Millman, who just beamed as though nothing pleased him more than young people smoking marijuana on his boat. When Adrienne looked at him again, she thought maybe he was closer to sixty.

She went below deck for the first time a while later in search of the bathroom, and since she was the only one underneath (aside from whatever sandwich genius was working in the galley) she took a look around. There was a living room with an overstuffed sofa and chairs and a wall lined with books that were held in place by a brass rail. There was a formal dining room with a bouquet of Asiatic lilies and pink roses on the oval table, and eight Windsor chairs, and the promised china in cabinets. There were a couple of small sleeping quarters, the beds decked out in Frette linens. And then Adrienne peeked quickly—because she was pressing her luck snooping around like this—into the master suite. A queen-size bed with a green silk spread, photographs of Holt Millman with Bill Gates, Holt Millman with Bill Clinton, Holt Millman with Elton John, and a framed article from *Time* about Holt Millman and his myriad companies. The article had been written by Drew Amman-Keller.

"Adrienne."

Adrienne gasped; she'd been caught. Holt Millman himself stood in the doorway. This was, no doubt, the kind of situation that Adrienne's father composed in his mind, the kind that turned his hair silver: Adrienne, wearing only a bikini, standing in the bedroom of Holt Millman's yacht.

The pot made her feel like laughing; she bit her lip. "Sorry," she said. "I was looking for the bathroom."

"Use mine," he said. He opened a door that Adrienne had thought was a closet, but it was the master bath. Marble, of course, with the Jacuzzi.

"Okay," she said. "Thanks."

She closed the door behind her and peed—she really had to go—looking at the stacks of fluffy green towels and at the glassed-in shower. She felt the boat listing from side to side. She washed her hands with one of the cakes of sailboat-shaped soap and checked her teeth, hoping and praying that by the time she opened the door, Holt Millman would be gone. But he was right there, sitting on the edge of the bed, talking to someone on his cell phone. When she emerged, he snapped the phone shut.

"I just made a dinner reservation for two, tonight, eight o'clock, at the Wauwinet," he said. "I hope you'll join me."

Adrienne stared at him, unwillingly imagining a woman smoothing essence of sea cucumber on Holt Millman's neck to keep it taut. She wanted to laugh. She bowed her head. This was the eleventh richest man in the United States, asking her on a date.

"I can't," she said. "I have to work."

"Work?" he said, as though he'd never heard of the word. "Okay, then, what night are you free?"

The answer was Wednesday night, but Adrienne couldn't bring herself to tell him. She wished like hell that she was up on deck lying safely between Caren and Cat, picking at the leftover wraps, maybe indulging in one more cocktail since her mouth was dry and ashy.

"I'm dating someone," she said. And in her alcohol-saturated, drug-induced state, she thought, *I'm dating Thatch.*

Holt Millman didn't get to be so successful by being a jerk or by preying on young women in bikinis whom he found nosing around his personal quarters. He was, at all times, a model of graciousness. "Whoever he is, he is one lucky man," Holt said. He offered Adrienne his arm and escorted her up the stairs, back into the sun.

When Adrienne woke up from her nap, it was four o'clock, and the girl with the English accent was offering her a cold Coca-Cola, which Adrienne immediately recognized as the answer to her prayers. She had fallen asleep on her stomach and she could tell just from sitting up that her back was burned. She knocked back half the Coke and went in search of Caren and Duncan, whom she found standing at the stern on either side of the flapping Rhode Island flag. They were tan and laughing; they looked like models in a Tommy Hilfiger ad. Adrienne caught Caren's eye and pointed to her running watch. It was five after four, they were zero feet above sea level, and Nantucket was still a smudge on the horizon. Caren shrugged. Nonchalance was her middle name. Adrienne, on the other hand, was a realist. If they headed back now they might be in the harbor in half an hour.

Leaving twenty-five minutes to drop Duncan off, get home, change (there would be no time for a shower), and get to work. But who was she kidding? They were going to be late.

Adrienne tapped the captain on the shoulder. "I know I'm going to sound like a Providence Puritan," she said, desperately hoping he got the joke, "but there are three of us on this boat who have to be at work at five."

Even with both motors turned on full-throttle, they didn't reach the mouth of the harbor until ten of five. By this time, the effects of the alcohol and the pot were gone and in their place was the special anxiety that hit when Adrienne knew she was going to be fatally late. Her brain ticked like a clock, she checked her jogging watch eighty-two times, and finally—because everyone on the boat could sense she was about to have a nervous breakdown—Holt Millman pulled out his cell phone and told Thatcher that he had taken three of the Bistro's key employees hostage and that they would be to work by the stroke of six. Adrienne was dying to hear Thatcher's response to this, but Holt snapped his cell phone shut, as if closing the book on the problem of the time, and said, "There. Do you feel better?"

"I don't like to be late," she said.

When they finally docked, Adrienne hugged the eleventh richest man in the country and thanked him for a wonderful day, then she hauled ass to the car with Duncan and Caren trailing reluctantly behind. The next hour was a blur of activity: drive, drop off Duncan, drive, wash face, brush teeth, change into the diaphanous blouse, which hid her sunburn, stuff half an untoasted bagel with light veggie cream cheese into her pie hole since they were going to miss family meal (Caren ate the other half and spent four minutes brewing an espresso—Adrienne drank one also in the interest of staying awake through service), brush teeth again, drive. They walked into the Bistro at five fifty-six, trying to look like it was just another lovely day at the regatta. *Pshew!*

Thatcher was at the podium, going over the book. He seemed unperturbed by their late arrival. "How was the sail?" he asked.

"Fabulous," Adrienne said.

Why had they hurried? There were only sixty-two covers on the book and only twenty people for first seating, though Adrienne did have three parties walk in. Joe and Christo both had the night off, as did Rex, so instead of piano music the stereo played Vivaldi.

"It's dead," Adrienne complained.

"The calm before the storm," Thatcher said. "This is a notoriously slow weekend because people have other things going on—weddings, graduations. But I had a hundred calls today about the Fourth. It's going to be a circus."

This was the longest conversation they'd had since their date. The sail had put Adrienne in a more generous frame of mind. She could talk to Thatcher as though he was just another person.

"What was family meal tonight?"

"Grilled pizzas," Thatcher said. "Are you sorry you missed it?"

"I ate at home," Adrienne said, thinking, *Of course I'm sorry I missed it!* "The boat was fun. Holt Millman asked me out to dinner."

At first it appeared Thatcher hadn't heard her—either that or he was letting it go, like he did the time Adrienne asked if Fiona was his wife. But then he tilted his head and peered at Adrienne out of the corner of his eye. "What did you tell him?" he asked.

There was no mistaking his tone of voice: He cared. He cared! Adrienne did her best to keep the trumpet of victory out of her response.

"I told him no."

At seven o'clock, JZ came in with a little girl who had brown bobbed hair and a mouth full of chewing gum.

"Adrienne," JZ said. "I'd like you to meet my daughter, Shaughnessy. Shaughnessy, this is Adrienne Dealey."

"Big dealey," Shaughnessy said, then she giggled.

"You'll excuse my daughter," JZ said. "She's suffering from a cute case of being eight. We're going to sit at the bar."

Adrienne held out a hand. "Be my guest," she said.

But Shaughnessy remained at the podium, studying Adrienne. "We're going to eat caviar," she said. "And then I'm going into the kitchen to help Fiona make a pizza."

"Is that so?" Adrienne said. "Do you like to cook?"

She shrugged. "Of course."

JZ led Shaughnessy to the bar, where the two of them perched on stools. Since there was absolutely nothing else to do—Thatcher had left her to work the door in case of walk-ins while he romanced the floor—Adrienne watched them. Dad and daughter: The sight made Adrienne miss her own father who at that moment would be relaxing in a house Adrienne had never seen, hopefully enjoying a perfectly grilled Omaha steak and watching *60 Minutes.*

Duncan poured JZ a beer and made Shaughnessy a Shirley Temple with three cherries. Shaughnessy removed the gum from her mouth and parked it on her cocktail napkin. Adrienne decided to check in the kitchen; if the chips and dip were ready, she could run them out.

When she walked through the kitchen door she nearly crashed into Fiona, who was on her tiptoes at the out door, trying to see through the window. Behind the pass, the Subiacos were engrossed in the baseball game on the radio; the White Sox were at Fenway tonight. Adrienne had hardly seen Fiona since her date with Thatcher; Fiona had been hiding out a lot in the office. Adrienne certainly hadn't spoken to her. But she looked so funny trying to see out the window that Adrienne decided to excuse the fact that this was the woman who had sabotaged her date and caused her ten days of date-induced angst.

"You should go say hi," Adrienne said. "There's practically no one sitting down."

Fiona spun on the heels of her kitchen clogs. "The last time I went out during service, Ruth Reichl was sitting at table one. The month following there was a tidbit in *Gourmet* about how Chef Fiona Kemp does occasionally peek out of her shell. So I'm not going out. What do you need?"

"I saw JZ. I thought there might be chips for him. His daughter said she was going to eat caviar and then come in here and help you make a pizza."

Fiona's face softened. "She wants to be a chef," she said. "Isn't that crazy?" And then she yelled out, "Spuds, Paco!"

And Paco said, "Yes, chef."

Pfft, pfft, pfft, hiss.

"They'll be ready in three minutes," Fiona said. "Get back to your post."

Adrienne ran the chips, opened two bottles of wine, changed the CD to Bobby Short at the Carlyle Hotel. She saw JZ and Shaughnessy slip into the kitchen. Suddenly, in that way he had, Thatcher materialized at her side.

"She's a cute kid," Adrienne said. "Seeing her with JZ reminds me of me and my dad."

"Adrienne Dealey waxes sentimental," Thatcher said.

"Where's her mother? Is she alive?"

"I'm afraid so," Thatcher said.

"So JZ's divorced?"

"No."

"He's not divorced?"

"No. He's married."

"He's married?"

"Yes." Thatcher handed Adrienne a pile of menus to return to the podium, meaning: Get back to your post.

"But you said he was a nice guy." Thinking: *He brought his daughter to the restaurant to make pizza with his lover? Not nice.*

"Oh, Adrienne," Thatcher said. "Were the world so easy as you appear to believe it is."

Three women who walked in at quarter to eight asked for rolls and butter, giving Adrienne an excuse to poke her head in the kitchen. She had finally learned where the rolls were kept—in a burlap sack hanging from one of the oven doors so the rolls would keep warm. Adrienne fixed a basket of rolls and arranged the cake of butter on a glass pedestal, all while watching Fiona and Shaughnessy make their pizza. The dough was rolled out and Shaughnessy painted it with sauce, then she gathered up two handfuls of pepperoni.

"I want to make a face," she said.

"Not only a chef," Fiona said, "but an artist."

Shaughnessy laid out the pepperoni. Eyes, nose, mouth.

"Your face is frowning," Fiona said.

"Because I feel sad," Shaughnessy said.

Fiona had a handful of sliced fresh mozzarella poised over the pizza, but when Shaughnessy said this, she lowered her hand to the counter and glanced at JZ. JZ shrugged.

Fiona raised Shaughnessy's chin with her finger. Adrienne's attention was captivated by the look on Fiona's face. She recognized that look.

"Why are you sad?" Fiona said.

"Because I want everything to be different," Shaughnessy said. "I want you to be my mother."

Thatcher let Adrienne go early and she was glad; it had been the world's longest day. When she got home, she showered, then fell into bed in her towel with her hair wet. She thought she might have crazy dreams about Holt Millman or the girl with the English accent who worked on the boat or Shaughnessy and JZ and the absent wife/mother whom they both seemed so eager to replace. But Adrienne slept without dreaming at all. When she heard the knock at her door, that was the one thing she was certain of: She hadn't been dreaming and she wasn't dreaming now. There was someone knocking on her door.

She pulled her comforter up under her chin. Thinking, *Caren. But maybe Duncan—and how weird would* that *be?*

"Hello?" she said.

It was dark, but even so, she could tell that the person in the doorway was Thatch. A light from somewhere caught his hair and she knew the shape of him, his tread, his smell. Thatcher Smith was in her room. She checked her clock—one forty-eight—not so late, really. Not by restaurant standards. His presence was so bizarre that she didn't even know where to begin her thinking. She waited for him to speak.

He eased himself down onto the side of her bed. "Hi," he said. "It's me."

"Hi, me," she said. She worried what she looked like; she wondered if he could see her.

There was a long pause and then he sighed. "I'm sorry, Adrienne."

The words hung in the room in an odd way, as if they required more explanation, but they didn't.

"I know," she said.

"You may wonder why I'm telling you now, in the middle of the night."

"The middle of the night part doesn't bother me," Adrienne said. "Nor the fact that you seem to have broken into my house. But you made me wait ten days."

"There's a lot going on," Thatcher said. "Fiona's sick."

"I know," Adrienne said.

"She's very sick."

"I know," Adrienne said—because she *did* know, somehow. The coughing, the childhood illness Thatcher didn't want to talk about, Fiona's reclusiveness, her embrace with JZ, the last year of the restaurant, Drew Amman-Keller's cryptic words, Thatcher's slavish devotion—they had all added up in Adrienne's mind to an instinct she hadn't been able to acknowledge, even to herself. But then there was earlier that evening, the scene she witnessed; Shaughnessy in the kitchen with Fiona. There had been something in Fiona's face, a longing Adrienne had seen before in her own mother's face when Rosalie lay in the hospital bed, her pale head covered with a Phillies cap. So, yes, Adrienne knew: Fiona was sick.

"Do you want me to leave?" Thatcher said.

"No," Adrienne said. "I want you to stay. Do you want to talk about Fiona?"

"Not tonight," Thatcher said. "Is that okay?"

"Of course."

Thatcher removed his blazer and laid it across Adrienne's computer table. Then he shed his loafers and his watch and his belt and he climbed into bed. Adrienne was nude—her towel had long ago been mixed up with the covers—and when he realized this fact, he inhaled a sharp breath.

"Sorry," she said. "I showered when I got home, and . . ."

He kissed her and Adrienne was filled with awe. How had she survived ten days without his mouth on hers, his tongue, his lips, his body pressed against her body? How had she survived? It felt as though she had gone ten days without food, without water. Because she was hungry for him. She was starved.

7

❧

Old Boyfriends

October 1, 2002

Dear Sully,

The one thing I remember my mother telling me about love was that you couldn't hunt it down or sniff it out. Like all great mysteries in the world, my mother said, it just happened.

This summer was the best summer of my life. But although I wished for it and wanted it, love didn't happen to me the way it happened to you. I can't explain it any better than that. I hope someday you'll forgive me for taking off like this, without warning, without good-bye. I thought this would be easiest—for me, certainly—but also for you.

If there was something else I could say, I would say it. Sorry, sorry, sorry.

Adrienne

CYSTIC FIBROSIS

Cystic fibrosis is a genetic disease affecting approximately thirty thousand children and adults in the United States. CF causes the body to produce an abnormally thick, sticky mucus, due to the faulty transport of sodium chloride within cells lining organs—such as the lungs and pancreas—to their outer surfaces. The thick CF mucus also obstructs the pancreas, preventing enzymes from reaching the intestines to help break down and digest food.

CF has a variety of symptoms. The most common is very salty-tasting skin; persistent coughing, wheezing, or pneumonia; excessive appetite but poor weight gain. The treatment of CF depends on the stage of the disease and which organs are involved. One means of treatment, chest physical therapy, requires vigorous percussion (by using cupped hands) on the back and chest to dislodge the thick mucus from the lungs. Antibiotics are also used to treat lung infections and are administered intravenously, via pills, and/or medicinal vapors, which are inhaled to open up clogged airways.

The median life expectancy for someone with CF is thirty-two, though some patients have lived as long as fifty to sixty years.

Before she met Thatcher, Adrienne had been down the road and around the bend with three and a half other men. The first, chronologically, was her academic adviser during her fifth year of college. Adrienne was twenty-two years old, trying to earn enough credits to graduate from Florida State. Her transcript—with courses from IU Bloomington and Vanderbilt and AP credits from her high school in Iowa, not to mention two semesters at Florida State—looked like a patchwork quilt and smacked (so her father claimed) of a half-baked effort that was draining him of his savings. She had plenty of class hours and good grades but nothing that equaled a major. She had started out as elementary ed at IU, then at Vandy she switched to sociology with a minor in art history. Florida State didn't have a sociology major, though they did have anthropology, which she could qualify for with twenty-six more credits. Or she could go the route of art history, but she felt this wasn't a major that would ever present any career opportunities, and her father agreed.

Thus, the academic adviser.

The first time Adrienne met with Will Kovak, she barely noticed him. She was too agitated about her tattered state of affairs. Her father was right: She wasn't taking college seriously, she was flitting around, unwilling to commit to a major or even a school. Sure, some people transferred once, but twice? She hadn't made a lasting friendship or held on to a single interest since her mother died. She had toyed around with notions of law school (everyone she knew who didn't have long-term concrete goals applied to law school); she considered becoming a personal trainer; she had taken a course called African Drumming and really enjoyed it; she wondered if she should drop out of school and get a job. But where? Doing what? Her father and Mavis pelted her with possible vocations. Mavis thought she should teach the deaf. Her father thought she should take the hygienist's courses and join him in practice. Both of them thought she should see a shrink. With all these disturbing notions flooding her mind, Will Kovak registered only as a body behind a desk. His office was dark; the venetian blinds were pulled against the strong Florida sun. She could hardly see him. All Adrienne cared about was her transcript, which lay on his desk like a trauma patient. Could he save it?

"Psychology," Will said, after reviewing Adrienne's file for fifteen silent minutes, during which he referenced the college manual four times. "I can get you out of here in January with a degree in psychology if you take five classes this semester."

Psychology? Adrienne laughed. She could be her own shrink! But psychology had a scientific, even medical, sound that would please her father. Without stopping to think, Adrienne stepped behind Will Kovak's desk and hugged him around the shoulders. "Thank you," she said. "Thank you. Thank you."

He was stiff; he gave her an embarrassed smile. "You're, uh, welcome," he said.

Adrienne met with Will Kovak a second time to figure out what the five classes would be and then a third time to have him sign her add–drop slip. It was during this third visit that Adrienne began to wonder about him. He was an associate professor of world literature, but he was only twenty-nine. And he was cute, in a bookish way, with longish hair that curled at the neck and rimless glasses. Adrienne had hooked up with a few guys at beer parties, but these guys struck her as young and clueless, and because Florida State was as big as some developing countries, she never had to see them again. She hadn't been on a date since her first junior year at Vanderbilt, when Perry Russell took her out for fried chicken then talked her out of her virginity. She was ready for something different. She asked Will out for coffee, and after a very long, very awkward silence with Adrienne standing there in the near-dark and Will staring at his folded hands, he said yes.

In this way, the first real relationship of Adrienne's life began. She entered the peculiar universe of young academics. It seemed to Adrienne that in these circles the person with the most abstemious lifestyle was the most worthy of admiration. Adrienne and Will attended the free foreign film series sponsored by the university, they went to readings at the bookstore, they went for coffee, and, at Adrienne's insistence, splurged on the occasional beer at Bullwinkles. They studied together at the library and they spent every night making love on Will's futon in the condominium unit that his parents bankrolled. The condo had a tiled bathroom and a gourmet kitchen with an island and granite countertops, but it was as if Will were embarrassed by these amenities and, to make up for them, he kept the rest of the condo as spartan as possible. The living room was dominated by two card tables pushed together and covered with an Indian print tapestry and piled with books and Will's laptop computer (also bankrolled by the parents). The bedroom had just the futon mattress on the floor, a row of votive candles on the windowsill, and a boom box on which Will played his favorite kind of CD—the movie soundtrack.

Adrienne was out of place from the beginning. Amid all the older, unwashed, ramen–noodle eating, Edward Said–reading, quiet smart people, she was a dilettante undergrad who had a steady source of cash from her doting dentist father. She liked to sit by the pool, she liked to watch David Letterman, she had zero interest in grad school. Every so often, Will would drag Adrienne to a "party" thrown by one of his teaching assistant friends. These were usually held in an unair-conditioned studio apartment where graduate students and young professors, many of them foreign, drank very cheap Chianti, smoked clove cigarettes, listened to Balinese gamelan music, and talked about topics so erudite they might as well have been speaking another language. Adrienne hated these parties, and when she complained about them to Will, he confessed that he hated them, too, but the danger in not going was that they might gossip about him.

Will was quiet and shy and extremely concerned about what his older and more established colleagues thought about him, but he excelled at intimacy— at lighting the votive candles and putting on soft music and sharing things about himself. Adrienne knew he was an only child, that his parents lived in a Manhattan brownstone on Seventy-second and Fifth Avenue; she knew he occasionally smoked pot before lecturing because it helped him to relax;

she knew the names and complete histories of his six previous girlfriends (one of whom was his second cousin, who sometimes called late at night from her job as night auditor at Donald Trump's posh resort in Palm Beach); she knew the long and Byzantine road that led Will to his dissertation topic about *War and Peace*. It bothered Will that Adrienne never talked about herself. "Tell me about your childhood," he said.

"There's nothing to tell."

"What about your parents?"

"What about them?"

"What are they like?"

"Why are you asking me so many questions?"

"Because I want to know you," he said. "Tell me about your first kiss, your last boyfriend. Tell me *something*."

"I can't," she said. She was afraid if she opened her mouth, a lie would pop out. That was how it always happened.

"You can," Will said. "You just don't want to."

"I don't want to," she admitted.

"You don't trust me," Will said. He would usually end up leaving the bedroom and falling asleep on the bare wooden floor in front of his computer. These fights bothered Adrienne only slightly. It was a small price to pay for her privacy.

When the semester ended and Adrienne graduated, Dr. Don flew to Tallahassee for the ceremony. On the way to the airport to pick him up, Will asked, "Why isn't your mother coming?"

Adrienne could remember staring out the window at the hot, green Florida hills. She yearned to disappear in them. Adrienne's roommate at Vanderbilt had asked her this very same question when Dr. Don showed up alone for parents' weekend, and Adrienne had told the roommate that Rosalie stayed home because Adrienne's brother, Jonathan, was very sick.

"Well," Adrienne said. "Because she's dead."

"Dead? Your mother's dead?"

"This is your exit," Adrienne said.

Dr. Don took Adrienne and Will to Michelsen's Farm House for dinner, and in those three hours, Will mined Dr. Don for every conceivable detail of Adrienne's childhood—including, after two bottles of wine, the maudlin story of Rosalie's illness. Will gobbled up every word; Adrienne sat in astounded silence. She could not believe her father was emoting like this with a virtual stranger.

Dr. Don kept slapping Will on the back. "Professor at twenty-nine . . . really going places." Later, to Adrienne, he said, "Quiet guy, but he's got a strong handshake and a nice smile. And he is solely responsible for getting you out of this place before your thirtieth birthday."

"Funny, Dad."

"I give him credit. A professor at twenty-nine!"

"Don't get attached," Adrienne said.

"Why not?"

"I'm breaking up with him tomorrow."

"Oh, honey, no. Not because of me? If I said I hated him, would you stay together? I hated him."

Adrienne called Will the next day to tell him it was over, and she could hear the anguish in his voice reverberating through his near-empty apartment. "I thought after last night that our relationship was heading in a new direction," he said. "I feel like I know you so much better now."

"I'm sorry?" Adrienne said.

Ten minutes after she hung up, Adrienne called him back. She wanted his cousin's phone number.

"Why?" he said.

"Because," she said. "I want to work with her."

Once Adrienne crossed the bridge into Palm Beach and was escorted through the gates of Mar-a-Lago, her future became clear. There was a world filled with beautiful places and she wanted to live in them all.

On the twenty-eighth of June there were one hundred and ninety covers on the book, and lobster salad sandwiches for family meal. It was seventy-seven degrees in the dining room at the start of first seating, which was abnormally hot, but Thatcher pointed out that everyone would drink more. Adrienne wore the silk outfit in bottle green that matched her eyes or so she convinced herself in the bathroom while she was brushing her teeth. When she came out to the podium, Thatcher said, "I'm sitting down at table twenty to eat at first seating."

"What?" Adrienne said, in a voice that gave away too much. Dating only a few weeks and already her interest and fear were showing. Her mind scanned possible reasons why Thatcher would eat during first service at the most visible table in the room, instead of later with Fiona. Adrienne decided it must be Harry Henderson, the Realtor, who had been calling a lot lately with people who were interested in buying the property. Harry, she was pretty sure, was on the books tonight.

"Father Ott," Thatcher said. "The priest. And here he is now. So you're going to have to cover."

"Fine," Adrienne said.

"Are you Catholic?" Thatcher asked. It seemed like an oddly personal question to be asking fifteen seconds before work started, but among the things they'd agreed upon was that they were going to get to know each other slowly, bit by bit. Adrienne had told Thatcher the story about Will Kovak and he understood. They weren't going to stay up all night confiding their innermost secrets then wake up and claim they were soul mates.

"Lapsed," Adrienne said. Had they been alone in the dark, though, she might have added that the last time she set foot in a Catholic church was on the afternoon of her mother's funeral. As she followed the casket out of Our Lady of Assumption she crossed herself with holy water and left the Catholics behind. It was Rosalie who had been Catholic—and when Rosalie died, so, in some sense for Adrienne, did God. Dr. Don was a Protestant and whenever he and Adrienne moved to a new place they shopped around for a church—sometimes Presbyterian, sometimes Methodist—it hardly mattered to Adrienne's father as long as they had a place to go on Christmas and Easter. Dr. Don donated twenty hours of free checkups to needy kids and senior citizens in the congregation per year. It was nice, but somehow to Adrienne it never felt like religion. That, maybe, was how the Protestants preferred it.

"Hello, Thatcher Smith!" Father Ott was the tallest priest Adrienne had ever seen—six foot six with a deep, resonant voice and hair the bright silver of a dental filling. He wore khaki pants and a navy blazer. A pair of blue-lensed, titanium-framed sunglasses hung around his neck. Never in eighty-two years would Adrienne have pegged him as a priest; he looked like one of Grayson Parrish's golf partners. Thatcher and Father Ott embraced and Adrienne smiled down at the podium.

"Father Ott, please meet my assistant manager, Adrienne Dealey," Thatcher said.

Adrienne was overcome with shyness and guilt—she could feel the words "lapsed Catholic" emblazoned on her forehead.

"It's lovely to meet you," she said, offering her hand.

Father Ott smiled. "Likewise, likewise. Adrienne, you say? Like Adrienne Rich?"

"The poet," Adrienne said.

Thatcher raised his pale eyebrows. "You're named after a poet?"

"Not after," she said. "Just like."

Father Ott rubbed his hands together. "I'm starving," he said. "But I promised Fiona I would bless the kitchen before the holiday. Shall we get business out of the way?"

Thatcher led Father Ott into the kitchen. Adrienne turned around. Bruno and Elliott were checking over the tables, lighting candles. Rex started up with "Clair de Lune." Adrienne heard Duncan pop the champagne at the bar but since no one else had arrived, she decided to sneak into the kitchen. If a priest who wore Revos and knew about feminist poetry was going to bless the place, Adrienne wanted to see it.

When she walked in, the kitchen was silent. The radio had been shut off and all the Subiacos—including Mario, who had actually removed his headphones—were standing with their hands behind their backs, heads bowed. Fiona and Thatcher stood on either side of Father Ott as he placed his right hand on the pass.

"Oh, Heavenly Father, please bless this kitchen, that it may serve nourishing meals to the patrons of this fine restaurant. May we all serve with love and humility as your son, Jesus Christ, taught us to do. Grant us the strength and the patience to follow in his footsteps in this, and in all things. We ask this in the name of the Father, and of the Son, and of the Holy Spirit. Amen."

"Amen." Behind the pass, the Subiacos crossed themselves. Adrienne crossed herself for the first time in sixteen years. Father Ott kissed Fiona and she said something to him quietly while holding on to both of his forearms. Then Thatcher and Father Ott filed out past Adrienne, who was hiding next to the espresso machine. As soon as they were gone, Fiona tugged on her chef's jacket.

"Okay, people," she said. "You've been blessed. Now let's get to work."

Adrienne kept her eye on Thatcher and Father Ott throughout first seating and even checked on them once to see if they needed anything. Thatcher smiled at her like she was a child intruding on her parents' dinner party. In fact, she had hoped to overhear a bit of their conversation, but from what she picked up, it sounded like they were talking about Notre Dame football.

Father Ott ordered the crab cake; Thatcher the foie gras. Father Ott drank bourbon; Thatcher drank club soda with lime. Thatcher was eating and drinking in the dining room just like a regular guest.

"Is it weird?" Adrienne asked Caren. "Or is it just me?"

"He does it every year," Caren said. "Like sometimes an old girlfriend from South Bend will come in, or one of his brothers. And the padre comes in once a summer."

Old girlfriend? Adrienne thought, panic-stricken. Then she thought, *Oh, shit. It's happening.*

After Father Ott left, Thatcher said to Adrienne, "Can you go into the wine cave and count the bottles of Menetou-Salon? I'm worried we're low."

"Sure," Adrienne said.

No sooner had Adrienne entered the luxuriously cool wine cave and opened the big fridge—there were at least thirty bottles of the Menetou-Salon, she wasn't sure what Thatcher was concerned about—than Thatcher came in and shut the door behind him. He lifted Adrienne's hair and pressed his lips to the side of her neck.

They kissed, with Adrienne's back pressed up against the chilled door of the fridge. Adrienne could hear the bussers carrying their trays into the kitchen. Nice as it was to have Thatcher close, even for a minute, she far preferred having him to herself, away from work, in her bed, in the quiet wee hours.

"This is what you do the second the priest walks out the door?" she said.

"I couldn't help myself," he said.

Adrienne's second relationship was a few years after her escape from Will Novak. It took place on the other side of the world with Kip Turnbull, the British owner of the Smiling Garden Resort in Koh Samui, Thailand. That was the year that Adrienne's father worried about her the most, and for good reason. She was twenty-five years old, halfway across the globe, working in a bikini. She lived in the queen bee bungalow of the forty bungalows at the Smiling Garden Resort, sleeping alongside her boss who had a hash problem and who cheated on her, Adrienne was sure, during his monthly pilgrimages to the full moon parties on Koh Phangan.

Kip's biggest fault was that he was too handsome. Adrienne had been addicted to him physically, to the way he would untie the string of her bikini top at the end of her shift and make love to her on his desk in the back office. He rode a motorcycle and he had taken Adrienne for excursions around Koh Samui—to the hidden temples, to the waterfalls, to the giant gold Buddha on the north coast. He had bargained with a Thai woman at the market in Na Thon for the best papaya for a couple of bhat, then he sliced it open with a machete and fed it to Adrienne with his fingers.

Kip was older, too, ten years older, and he had told Adrienne stories about Eton and Cambridge, Hong Kong, Macao, Saigon, Mandalay. She had nothing to offer that could compare. She was provincially American, with only the gentle and studious Will Novak to claim as a past lover. She was plagued for the first time by jealousy. She wanted Kip to take her to one of the full moon parties on Koh Phangan.

"You won't like it," he said.

"Try me," she said.

Kip gave in, and at the end of the month, he and Adrienne were on an old junk cruising through the Gulf of Thailand toward Koh Phangan.

It was lying on the very soft, very white sand of Haad Rin Beach that Adrienne noticed she was the only woman around, except for four Thai girls who were offering massages for fifty bhat. The beach was packed with men—Israelis, South Africans, Germans, Australians, Danish, Americans. They were all eyeing Adrienne in her bikini, and she felt Kip's attention tighten around her. She wanted to stay in that spot forever. Kip called one of the masseuses over.

"For the lady." And he palmed the girl some bills.

"I don't want a massage," Adrienne said. "Really."

Kip said something to the girl in Thai that made her laugh. The girl knelt next to Adrienne in the sand and started kneading her back. It felt wonderful, and Adrienne closed her eyes, trying not to worry if this was some kind of turn-on for Kip or for the other men on the beach. The girl's hands were as soft as warm water.

Later, Kip took Adrienne to dinner. They hiked down a jungle path to a grass shack that had only three stools at a counter. "The vegetable curry," Kip said. "I order it every time."

Adrienne didn't care for curries, but it would have been useless to say so. The curry she was given was mild and sweet with coconut milk, cilantro, lime. She had left the mushrooms to float in a small amount of broth at the bottom of the bowl, and when Kip noticed, he laughed hysterically.

"Eat the mushrooms," he said.

She ate the mushrooms.

The rest of the night was a stew of paranoia and hallucinations. Kip took Adrienne back to their bungalow and somehow locked her in from the outside, claiming he had to meet some Americans to buy some hash. *When are you coming back?* Adrienne asked the already closed door. *Later, love, a little later.* Adrienne lay down on the embroidered satin bedspread. She was cogent enough to realize that the mushrooms had been drugs, and now the simplest tasks eluded her. She couldn't get the door open. She was freezing, but she couldn't turn down the air-conditioning. She had been dreaming of a hot bath since arriving in Thailand months earlier, and this room had a marble bathroom and a deep Jacuzzi. She turned on the water, and then she lost time. The next thing she knew she was lying on her face on the embroidered bedspread drowning in what felt like wave after wave crashing over her.

Kip returned at three o'clock in the morning, high on six different drugs and drunk on Mekong whiskey, to find Adrienne passed out and their entire bungalow ankle-deep with warm bathwater. They left on the first boat the next morning and neither of them said a word to each other. Adrienne was mortified about the water damage (it ended up costing Kip nearly five hundred pounds) and she was livid about everything from the massage to the mushrooms to being locked up like an animal. She couldn't deny the truth much longer: Kip was a control freak. And yet he was so handsome that when they returned to Koh Samui, and he said he forgave her, it took another month of Kip's obnoxious demands and e-mailed pleas from her father to make Adrienne leave. She wasn't even fully packed when Kip announced he'd hired an Australian girl to replace her.

By his own admission, Thatcher "hadn't exactly been celibate" over the past twelve years, but there had been no one special, he said, and Adrienne decided to believe him. The only other woman Adrienne wanted to talk about as they lay in bed late at night was Fiona.

"Fiona was never my girlfriend," Thatcher said. "I've never even held her hand. I tried to kiss her once when we were fifteen but she pushed me away. She said she didn't want me to kiss her because she was dying and she didn't want to break my heart."

Fiona had cystic fibrosis. It was a genetic disease; Adrienne had looked it up on the Internet. Mucus was sealing Fiona's lungs like a tomb. She was thirty-five years old, and losing lung function every year. Over the winter, she had decided to put herself on the transplant list, and that was why this was the final year of the restaurant. If she got a lung transplant, if she survived the lung transplant—there were too many ifs to worry about running a business. Thatcher had mentioned a doctor at Mass General, the best doctor in the country for this disease. To look at Fiona, Adrienne would never know a thing was wrong. She was a pistol, a short pistol with a braid like the Swiss Miss and freckles across her nose. A pistol wearing diamond stud earrings.

"What was it like being friends with her?" Adrienne asked.

"I'm still friends with her."

"Growing up, I mean. What was it like?"

"It was like growing up," Thatcher said. "She lived in my neighborhood. We went to school together. She cooked a lot and I ate what she cooked. We drove to Chicago for concerts in the summer. She had boyfriends, but they all hated me. One of them siphoned the gas from my car."

"Really?"

"They were jealous because we were friends. Because, you know, I would eat over there during the week and I walked into her house without knocking, that kind of thing. Once a month or so, she would go to the hospital—sometimes just to St. Joe's but sometimes up to Northwestern and I was the only one who she let come visit."

"And what was that like?"

"It was awful. They had her on a vent, and the doctors were always worrying about her O$_2$ sats, the amount of oxygen in her blood."

"Who knows that she's sick?"

"Some of the staff know, obviously—Caren, Joe, Duncan, Spillman, and everyone in the kitchen—but it's the strictest secret. Because if the public hears the word 'disease,' they shun a place, and in that case, everyone loses. You understand that."

"I understand," Adrienne said. She nearly told Thatcher that Drew Amman-Keller knew. He knew and was keeping the secret just like everybody else, but Adrienne was afraid to bring it up. She still had his business card hidden in her dresser drawer. "I won't tell anyone."

"Of course not. I trust you. I wouldn't be here if I didn't trust you."

"Does Fiona know about us?"

"Everybody knows about us," Thatcher said. "Which is fine. When the public hears the word 'romance,' they come in droves. The phone rings off the hook."

"We'll have to beat them back with a stick."

Thatcher tucked her under his chin and buried his face in her hair. "Exactly."

If Will Novak was too soft, and Kip Turnbull too hard, then Michael Sullivan, the third man Adrienne dated, was just right. Sully was the golf pro at the Chatham Bars Inn, where Adrienne worked the front desk. Unlike Will and Kip, Sully was Adrienne's age, he had a degree from Bowdoin College, and he, too, was living the resort life with the reluctant backing of his parents, who lived in Quincy, forty-five minutes away. Sully had valued one thing above all others for his entire life and that thing was golf. Adrienne first noticed him on the driving range smacking balls into the wild blue yonder. He was tall and freckled; he wore cleats and khakis and a visor. Adrienne met him a few nights later at a staff party where she tried to impress him by reciting the names of all the golfers she knew:

Jack Nicklaus, Tom Watson, Greg Norman, Payne Stewart, Seve Ballesteros. "Everyone you named is either dead or on the seniors tour," he said.

Still, he asked her out and they went to the Chatham Squire for drinks after her shift one night. Adrienne found him easy to be with. On days when she was free, he let his tee times go; he cancelled lessons so that he could take Adrienne out to lunch, and eventually, he arranged to have the same day off as she did each week. He told her he loved her after only three weeks—and he had all the symptoms: he lost weight, he lost sleep, and he shunned his friends. He wasn't sure what was happening, he told her one evening as they walked Lighthouse Beach at sunset, but he thought this was "it."

The summer as Sully's girlfriend flew by—days at work, nights eating ice cream at Candy Manor and strolling down to Yellow Umbrella Books where they bought novels they never found time to read, partying on the beach with people from work. Bonfires, fireworks, summer league baseball games, days off cruising around in the Boston Whaler, strolling in Provincetown, whale watching. Adrienne loved the flowers that arrived at the desk, she loved waking up in the middle of the night to find him staring at her, she loved it every time he picked up the phone to cancel a golf lesson. She loved his dark hair, his freckles, the way his strong back twisted in the follow-through of his golf swing. The e-mails to her father that summer were full of exclamation points. "I've met a guy! A guy who treats me the way you are always telling me I DESERVE to be treated! I am having the time of my LIFE in this town!"

At the beginning of August, Sully drove Adrienne to Quincy to meet his parents. His father was a neurosurgeon at Brigham and Women's Hospital and his mother had spent many years working as a nurse before she quit to stay home and raise six boys. His parents had both grown up in south Boston and they had stayed there. They lived in a huge Victorian house that was filled with photographs and crucifixes and needlepointed Irish blessings. Sully's mother, Irene, was a lady of about sixty with red hair and a huge bosom. She hugged Adrienne tightly to her chest the moment Adrienne stepped out of the car and, in essence, never let her go. (Adrienne still sent Irene Sullivan a postcard every few months.) They sat on the sunporch and drank iced tea and ate shortbread and Irene filled Adrienne in on the business of her six sons. "God didn't bless me with a daughter," she said, "but I'm thankful for the boys. They're good boys." Kevin, the oldest, was a priest; Jimmy and Brendan were married with sons of their own; Matthew lived in New York City. "Matthew's a homosexual," Irene said, breaking her shortbread into little pieces. "Not what his father and I wanted, but he has a friend who comes for the holidays. I figure I already have six boys, what's one more?" Then there was Michael, then Felix, the youngest, who was a freshman at Holy Cross. Irene brought out pictures of all the boys at their first communion, then in their Boston Latin football uniforms. She brought out pictures of the grandsons, and a picture of Matthew and his boyfriend in Greenwich Village with their arms wrapped around each other. "And here are some of Mikey." All of the pictures showed Sully golfing—in Scotland, in British Columbia, at Pebble Beach. "He has a gift, no question," Irene said, sighing. "But we wish he would settle down."

Adrienne left the Sullivan house feeling like she could move in and become part of the family. When they got in the car to leave there was waving and blown kisses; Adrienne had Irene's shortbread recipe in her purse.

"What did you think?" Sully asked.

"I wish she was mine," Adrienne said.

As autumn approached, Sully began to talk about "the next round." He received a job offer in Vero Beach, and then, a coup: a job offer in Morocco at a course built for the king. Sully wanted Adrienne to come with him to Morocco, and he wanted to get engaged.

"Engaged?" Adrienne said. They were lying in bed, watching Sunday night football on ESPN. How had "the next round," which Adrienne tolerated as yet another innocuous golf term, become *engaged*?

"I want to marry you," Sully said.

"You do?" Adrienne said. This was the moment every girl waited for—wasn't it?—the perfect guy proposing marriage. And yet, what struck Adrienne most forcefully was her shock followed by her ambivalence. She thought of life married to Michael Sullivan—and she had to admit, she could think of worse lives. They could travel, he could golf, she could work hotels until they had a child. Adrienne could call Irene Mom, and the two of them could enjoy a lifetime of chats at the kitchen table.

Adrienne was twenty-six. She understood that what Sully was suggesting—getting married, having children—was what people *did*. It was how life progressed. Adrienne didn't say anything further to Sully on the topic of marriage, but in his chirpy, good-natured way, he played through as though a decision had been made. In the following twenty-four hours, he called Irene and told her that a big announcement was coming, but first he wanted to ask for Adrienne's hand. He pestered Adrienne for Dr. Don's phone number, then with a shy smile, he said, "I have stuff to talk over with him."

Adrienne felt like someone was wrapping a wool scarf over her nose and mouth. She was hot and prickly; she couldn't breathe properly. She was terrified and, in a mindless panic, she ran: packed her stuff while Sully was at work, wrote him a letter, and had a short, teary conversation with her front desk manager. She cried through the cab ride to Logan, and through the flight from Boston to Honolulu. She was afraid to call her father. She knew he would assault her with the obvious question: *What is wrong with you?*

Within a week, Adrienne had a job on the front desk at the Princeville Resort on Kauai. She had photocopied the letter she wrote to Sully and every time she considered dating a man that winter, she read it. To keep herself from doing any more damage.

Before Thatcher there had been three and a half men, and the half a man was Doug Riedel. But that was just Adrienne being mean. It was more accurate to say that Doug and Adrienne had only had half a relationship, or a half-hearted relationship. Doug Riedel was a mistake, an accident; he was a one-night stand that lasted an entire winter. Adrienne met him right before Christmas while she was skiing on her day off. They skied together, they après-skied together, they après-après-skied together. The next thing Adrienne knew, Doug Riedel was showing up at the front desk of the Little Nell on Christmas morning with a gift-wrapped box from Gorsuch. Adrienne, who had been feeling sorry for herself for working on Christmas (she always worked on Christmas because she had no kids), opened the box that held a pair of shearling gloves and thought: What luck! Doug was darkly handsome, he had a great dog, he worked as one of the ski school managers at Buttermilk. He was a catch. She started meeting him after work to walk

Jax, he took her out for a day of cross-country, he was calling her before he went to the gym, after he got home, before he went out to the Red Onion, after he got home. He was, somehow, becoming her boyfriend.

Right around the busy February holidays, Doug lost his job at Buttermilk Mountain and, subsequently, his housing. *You're probably going to break up with me now,* he'd said. If Adrienne had been half paying attention, then this was exactly what she would have done, but instead she found herself fibbing to management so that he could move in with her and bring Jax. Then, his unevenness began to register. Sometimes he was funny and charming, but sometimes he was disparaging and negative. He hated Kyra (what a slut), he hated the Little Nell (a bastion of phony luxury), he hated Aspen in general. He spent more and more time in Carbondale with a mysterious friend. Adrienne thought he was sleeping with someone else, but she didn't care. He was a houseguest who had overstayed his welcome—he was grouchy, he had a constant head cold, he stayed up all night watching *Junkyard Wars,* and every morning he went to the Ajax Diner for scrambled eggs with ketchup. He did nothing about finding a new job, and yet he never seemed to be short on money.

Well, yeah! Adrienne shuddered with anger every time she thought of her empty Future box, her money gone, her prospects stolen, her master key card swiped. Doug Riedel was the devil himself. But if it hadn't been for Doug and his felonious ways, Adrienne reminded herself, she wouldn't be here on Nantucket, working at the Blue Bistro, with Thatcher.

Adrienne and Thatcher had been dating for less than three weeks and already this relationship was different. *Exercise good judgment about men!* her napkin screamed. Talk about your feelings, but give nothing away. Be careful, but don't act scared. Nothing she told herself helped. With Thatcher, she felt like a person afraid of flying: Was it safe to board the aircraft? Would the plane crash? Would she be left on the open sea with a broken leg and a flimsy flotation device? Would she die? Already her emotional investment was so great that complete devastation of the life she had worked so hard to cultivate seemed possible. This was all brand-new.

On July second, there were two hundred and fifty covers on the book, their first sellout of the year. It was eighty degrees at four o'clock and when

Adrienne sat down for family meal at five, she was uncomfortably warm. Thatcher was at an AA meeting; it was his second meeting that day. He had gone to one at ten that morning while Adrienne covered the phone. Now, as she ate, she worried about Thatcher. Was it normal to go to two AA meetings in one day, or was there something wrong? Then she worried about Mrs. Yannick.

Mrs. Yannick had called that morning with a trick question. "Is your restaurant child-friendly?"

"How old is your child?" Adrienne asked.

"Two."

Adrienne faltered. Thatcher, no doubt, had a smooth answer that would perfectly convey to Mrs. Yannick that while they did have one high chair in the back of the utility closet, it was covered with cobwebs, and seemed to be there only in case of emergency. Would it be grossly inappropriate to suggest Mrs. Yannick get a babysitter?

"We don't have a children's menu," Adrienne said. "And we don't have any crayons. This is fine dining."

"So you're not child-friendly."

"Well . . ."

"You allow children but don't encourage them."

"We do allow children." Adrienne thought of Shaughnessy—and Wolfie. "And I myself am not a parent. But it seems like you'd be asking an awful lot of a two-year-old to have her sit through a meal with wine and so forth. And the other guests . . . I think you might be more comfortable if . . ."

"We tried to get a babysitter," Mrs. Yannick said. "We tried and tried. But we're away from home and I don't want a stranger. I'm afraid I'm out of options."

"Maybe another night?" Adrienne said.

"Not possible," Mrs. Yannick said. There was a long pause. "We're bringing William with us." There was another long pause. "I'm really sorry about this in advance. I'd just cancel the reservation but the number-one reason why we come to Nantucket is to eat at your restaurant."

Ah, flattery! Adrienne still wasn't immune to it. "We'll see you at six," she said.

Adrienne had been too cowardly to mention the Yannicks' reservation at the menu meeting. She tried to tell herself it was no big deal. After family meal, Adrienne pulled the high chair out of the closet and wiped it down with a wet rag. She set it at table four, the least desirable table in the restaurant—the farthest away from the beach, the piano, and the glitz of table twenty. The waitstaff worked on a rotating schedule; Adrienne hoped table four would go to Elliott or Christo, who were too new to complain. But no such luck. Tonight, it was Caren's table.

At six o'clock, Thatcher still wasn't back. Adrienne sat parties, Rex played "You Make Me Feel So Young," and a very slight breeze from the water cooled the dining room down. At ten after six, the Yannicks arrived. They were a handsome, well-dressed couple and the two-year-old, William, was darling. He had strawberry blond hair and freckles that looked like they were painted on. He wore white overalls and little white sneakers. Adrienne congratulated herself for allowing such a cute little boy to come to the restaurant. When he saw her, he held out a plastic fire truck.

Adrienne smiled. "You must be the Yannicks." She snapped up two menus and a wine list. "Follow me." She led them to table four and stood aside as Mr. Yannick buckled William into the high chair. William was angelic. He chewed the top of his fire truck. "Caren will be your server tonight," Adrienne said. "Enjoy your meal."

Five minutes later, Caren stormed the podium. "I hate you."

"I'm sorry. They're sorry. They couldn't find a sitter."

"I don't like babies," Caren said. "Or toddlers. Or children in preschool."

"But he's cute," Adrienne said.

"I don't like anyone who isn't old enough to drink," Caren said.

"At least he's well-behaved," Adrienne said.

"They gave him a sugar packet to play with, which he spilled all over the tablecloth. And he got into the mother's water. They asked for doughnuts 'right away,' but the kitchen isn't making doughnuts tonight. Too hot. They asked for a plastic cup with a top. It seems they forgot his at home. Already it's too much work. Why didn't you refer them to the Sea Grille? It's perfect for families."

"I'm sorry," Adrienne said. "I'll take care of it."

But because Thatcher was gone, Adrienne had to seat fifteen more tables, open wine, run chips and dip, and answer the phone. She went to the bar to pick up her champagne and Duncan was so in the weeds that he couldn't pour it. "Get it yourself," he said. "You know how."

Adrienne didn't have time. She raced over to check on table four. William was gnawing on a piece of pretzel bread and there were little bits of pretzel bread all over the floor. And the floor was wet. Adrienne nearly slipped.

"Whoa," she said.

"Sorry," Mrs. Yannick said. She was valiantly trying to keep William occupied by reading a small, sturdy book called *Jamberry*. Mr. Yannick studied the wine list. Adrienne bent down to pick up the pieces of bread. The floor underneath the high chair was soaked.

"Please don't worry about the mess," Mr. Yannick said. "We'll get it before we go."

"William spilled his water," Mrs. Yannick said. "We're very sorry. Our waitress couldn't find a plastic cup with a top."

"I'll look in the back," Adrienne said. "Have you placed your order?"

Mr. Yannick looked at his wife. "What are you getting, honey?"

Mrs. Yannick slapped *Jamberry* down on the table. "I haven't exactly had a chance to read the menu."

William threw his pretzel bread and it landed in Mr. Yannick's water. Mr. Yannick laughed and fished it out.

"I'll get you fresh water," Adrienne said. She glanced about the dining room. Were people staring? William pushed himself up by the arms in an attempt to launch himself from his high chair.

"All done," he said.

"You are not all done," Mrs. Yannick said. "We haven't even started." She wiped the gummy bread from around William's mouth with her napkin and this made him angrier. "Just order me the steak, Carl. Steak, rare, nothing to start. He won't make it through two courses."

"Honey . . ."

"Honey, what?"

"What was the point of coming if . . ."

"If you can't order the foie gras? Fine, order the foie gras. I'll take William out to the parking lot and you can eat it in peace."

"Honey . . ."

"Let me get you the water," Adrienne said.

"All done!" William said in a more insistent voice. He kicked his feet against the underside of the table and then swept *Jamberry* to the floor where it landed in the puddle.

Adrienne cast around for a busboy. Roy was at table twelve refilling water. Adrienne waved him down. "We need a new glass here."

"The water is the least of our worries," Mrs. Yannick said. "Can you get our waitress so we can place our order?"

"Certainly," Adrienne said. She found Caren coming out of the kitchen with apps for table twenty-eight. Adrienne followed her. "Here, let me help you serve."

Caren eyed her. "Why? What do you want?"

"Table four," Adrienne said. "They'd like to place their order. William is restless."

"They made their bed," Caren said.

"So you won't go over there?"

"When I'm good and ready."

Adrienne heard a shriek. All the way across the dining room, she saw William red in the face, kicking, trying to free himself from his chair. Adrienne hurried over. Mrs. Yannick was trying to read *Jamberry* over William's screaming. Mr. Yannick raised his arm in a sign of distress; his ship was going down.

"Would you take our order, please?" he said.

"Certainly," Adrienne said.

"Foie gras and the duck for me and my wife will have the crab cake and the steak."

"Rare," Mrs. Yannick said.

"And a bottle of the Ponzi pinot noir," Mr. Yannick said.

"Really, Carl, wine?" Mrs. Yannick said.

"You love the Ponzi."

"You think we have time to drink a bottle of wine?"

"We'll just drink what we can," Mr. Yannick said. "The Ponzi."

"Very good," Adrienne said. William was temporarily mesmerized with a lipstick Mrs. Yannick had pulled from her purse. He took off the cap and put the lipstick in his mouth.

"For God's sake," Mr. Yannick said.

"At least he's quiet," Mrs. Yannick said.

William threw the lipstick to the ground and started to cry. Mrs. Yannick dug through her purse. "I thought I had a lollipop in here." Adrienne headed for the kitchen. She didn't have time for this, and yet she felt responsible. *Is your restaurant child-friendly?* No, it's not. The next time, Adrienne would just come right out and say it. No children under six. Why wasn't this a rule already? She tried to think about how to help the Yannicks. Maybe she should comp their dinner and insist they come back another night. *What,* she wondered, *would Thatcher do? Where was he?*

"Ordering table two: one bisque, one crab cake, SOS. Where's the duck for fourteen? Louis? Get your head out of the oven, Louis! Ordering table six: one frites, medium-well, one pasta. That's right, I said pasta, so Henry, you're going to work tonight after all. Ordering table twenty-one . . ." Fiona noticed Adrienne at her elbow. The kitchen was brutally hot even with two standing fans going. "What do you want?"

"I came to put in an order for table four."

"Who's the server?"

"Caren, but she's busy."

"News flash: We're all busy. What is it?"

"What?"

"The order!"

Adrienne thought for a second. If you gave Fiona the food in the wrong sequence, she got pissed. "Foie gras, crab cake, duck, frites rare."

Fiona scribbled out a ticket. "Fine."

"Can you rush it?" Adrienne said. "These people brought their two-year-old and he's *freaking* out."

"Ordering table four: one foie gras, one crab cake, pronto," Fiona said. Then to Adrienne, she said, "What's the kid eating?"

"He's not eating. But they would like a plastic cup with a top. I know Caren already asked, but . . ."

"Sippy cup, Paco," Fiona shouted.

Seconds later, a plastic cup with a bright blue plastic top whizzed through the air. Fiona caught it and handed it to Adrienne. "Go get him."

"Who?"

"The kid. Go get the kid and bring him in here."

Adrienne thought she had heard wrong. The kitchen with the grill and the fryer and four sauté pans going and the fans running was loud.

"You want me to bring William in here?"

"If you think it would help the parents enjoy the meal, then yes," Fiona said. And—surprise!—she smiled. "I keep some toys in the back office. I love kids."

Adrienne popped into the wine cave for a bottle of Ponzi. By the time she reached the podium, she noticed the dining room was not only cooler, but quieter. She looked at table four. Thatcher was standing by the table with William in his arms, William was chewing on the top of his fire truck. Adrienne felt a surge of tenderness and awe and whatever else it was a woman felt when she first saw her lover holding a small child. She hurried to the bar, where her champagne glass was waiting. She took a drink, then she set down the sippy cup.

"Orange juice, please," she said.

Duncan filled it without a word, and Adrienne took the sippy cup and the wine to table four. She handed the sippy cup to Mrs. Yannick who brightened, then Adrienne presented the Ponzi to Mr. Yannick.

"Juice!" William said.

Mr. Yannick nodded at the wine, visibly relaxed. Adrienne uncorked and poured, he tasted.

"Delicious."

"I put a rush on your order," Adrienne said as she poured a glass of wine for Mrs. Yannick. "Your appetizers should be out any second."

"Would it be all right if I took William into the kitchen?" Thatcher said. "I know our chef would love to see him."

"She has some toys in the office," Adrienne said.

"All right," Mrs. Yannick said. "You'll bring him back if he's any problem?"

"This guy, a problem?" Thatcher said. William was resting his head on Thatcher's shoulder, sucking noisily on the cup. Thatcher winked at Adrienne and vanished into the back.

Mrs. Yannick collapsed in her wicker chair. "I love this place," she said.

Fourth of July. Two hundred and fifty covers on the books, the maximum. Prix fixe menu, sixty dollars per person. First seating was at six; the guests were to eat then move out to the rented beach chairs in the sand to watch the fireworks. Second seating was at ten; those guests would watch the fireworks first, then sit down to dinner. Duncan was working the bar outside, and Delilah took over the blue granite, her first solo flight.

Everything was different and Adrienne was anxious. Thatcher asked her to arrive early, and she was there at quarter to four, but the front of the house was deserted. When she poked her head back into the kitchen it was 182 degrees—the deep fryers were going full blast with the chicken, and Fiona had the ribs in enormous pressure cookers. Adrienne checked in pastry to find Mario up to his elbows in fruit. He wasn't listening to music, and he didn't smile when he saw her.

"I have fifty pounds of peaches that need to be skinned. Everybody else gets a prep cook and I get left in the shit. One hundred twenty-five peach pies I have to make. I spent all morning with the blueberries. Look at my hands." He held up his palms. They were, of course, impeccably clean. "My nails are blue. I can tell you one thing. I'm gonna have nightmares tonight. You ever have a nightmare about stone fruit?"

"No," Adrienne said.

"Where you have a bushel of peaches looking as gorgeous as *Playboy* asses and then you break one open and it's brown and rotten inside? And the next one? And the next one? They're all that way?"

"I never had that dream," Adrienne said.

"Yeah, well, lucky you."

In the kitchen, Adrienne heard Fiona yelling about deviled eggs. She wanted five hundred deviled eggs.

Adrienne retreated to the empty dining room just as a man with a clipboard walked in saying, "I got two hundred and fifty folding chairs, sweetheart. Where do you want them?"

Some help would be nice, she thought. She had never done the Fourth of July thing on Nantucket before and she didn't know where on the beach Thatcher wanted the chairs or even which direction they should face. If she told this man the wrong thing then two hundred and fifty chairs would have to be moved. (Adrienne pictured herself slogging through the sand in her Jimmy Choo heels.) So better get it right the first time.

Adrienne called Thatcher's cell phone.

"Where are you?" she said. Then thought: *Try not to sound like a wife.*

"At Marine. I wanted to get flags for the tables."

"The gentleman is here with the chairs. He would like to know where to put them."

"On the beach."

"Right, but where?"

"Let me talk to the guy."

"Happily," Adrienne said. She handed off the phone to the chair man, then surveyed the dining room. What could she do to help? Set the tables? A roll of red, white, and blue bunting sat on top of the piano along with a book of music, *101 Patriotic Songs*. Deviled eggs, bunting, patriotic songs. These people really got into it.

A moment later, Caren walked in. It looked like she'd been crying.

"It's over," she said. "I'm finished with that rat bastard."

"Duncan?"

Caren glared at her. Adrienne tried to think: He had been there that morning. She'd heard them in the kitchen, though as a rule, she and Thatcher didn't fraternize with Caren and Duncan. Too much like work.

"What happened?" Adrienne asked.

"He's been cheating on me during the *day*," Caren said. "This morning? He says he has golf at ten with the bartender from Cinco. Fine. I decide to do something different because of the holiday so I set myself up with a gorgeous Cuban sandwich from Fahey and then I go to the beach at Madequecham. And lo and behold, whose car is there? Who is lying on the beach with the hostess from 21 Federal?"

"The hostess?" Adrienne said. "You mean Phoebe?"

"Phoebe!" Caren spat. "So I saunter up to the happy couple and Duncan doesn't even blink. But I could tell he thought I followed him there or was spying on him or something. However, he pretended like it was no big deal and therefore I had to pretend like it was no big deal. He asked me to put lotion on his back, and I said, 'No way, motherfucker.' So then Phoebe pipes up and says she would love to put lotion on his back—and I have to sit there and *watch*." Her eyes filled up. "What am I going to do?"

Adrienne put her arm around Caren, awkwardly, because Caren was so much taller. Duncan was a woman magnet; Caren had to learn to accept it. Before Adrienne could find a way to say this, Thatcher walked in, clapping his hands.

"Good, good, good," he said. "The two of you can hang the bunting. All the way around and try to make it even, okay? Joe's coming in at four thirty to set the tables—and look! I got flags." He waved a small flag in the air and his smile faded. "Is something wrong?"

Caren tucked in her shirt and sniffed. "I can't work with Duncan," she said. "Either he goes or I go."

Thatcher groaned. He yanked at his red, white, and blue necktie to give himself some air. Then, slowly, he said, "I told you . . ."

"I know what you told me!" Caren snapped, and she burst into tears.

Thatcher's hands hung at his sides. He gazed at Adrienne with longing. But what about Caren? Adrienne tried to make her eyes very round.

"You need to have an espresso and calm down," Thatcher said. "Or, hell, have a drink, I don't care. Just, please, pull yourself together because we have two hundred and fifty people coming and you are working and Duncan is working, and if tomorrow, July fifth, you two want to battle it out to see who stays and who goes, that's fine. It's fine on July fifth. It is not fine tonight. Tonight you have to be a brave soldier."

Caren pouted. She was lovely, really—Adrienne had a hard time believing that Duncan would ever prefer Phoebe. "I'll have an espresso martini," Caren said. "Kill two birds." She stepped behind the bar. "God, I feel like trashing his perfect setup."

"Well, please don't," Thatcher said. "Delilah is working back there tonight anyway. Duncan's on the beach. You'll barely have to see him."

Caren slammed a martini glass on the blue granite then poured generously from the Triple 8 bottle. "Brilliant."

Thatcher put his arm around Adrienne and kissed her ear. "You'll have to hang the bunting by yourself," he said.

"What are you doing?" Adrienne asked.

"Everything else."

By ten to six, the restaurant was ready. The bunting hung evenly all the way around the edge of the restaurant, and the tables were set with a tiny American flag standing in each silver bud vase. On the beach, two hundred and fifty chairs were set up in perfect rows. It was a beautiful night. Adrienne had wolfed down a plate of tangy, falling-apart ribs and three deviled eggs at family meal and then she rushed to brush her teeth. When she went to the bar to get her champagne, Duncan confronted her.

"I'm innocent," he said.

"Delilah, would you pour me a glass of Laurent-Perrier, please?" Adrienne asked.

Delilah, also wearing a red, white, and blue necktie, seemed harried. She studied the bottles in the well. "Where's the champagne?" she asked Duncan.

"In the door of the little fridge," he said. "You'd better learn quick; you only have ten minutes." And then, turning back to Adrienne, he said, "I know she told you."

Adrienne watched Delilah grapple with the champagne bottle. It took her forever just to unwrap the cork. Finally, Duncan wrested the bottle from his sister. He had it open in two seconds and he poured Adrienne's drink.

"Hey," Delilah said. "I'm supposed to learn how to do it myself."

Duncan ignored her. "She talked to you," he said to Adrienne. "So if she asks, you tell her I'm innocent. Golf got cancelled, I bumped into Phoebe in town . . ."

Adrienne picked up her champagne. "Tell her yourself," she said. "I'm not getting involved."

She walked to the podium to await the onslaught with Thatcher: 125 people arriving at once.

"What was your best Fourth of July?" Thatcher asked her.

This sounded like another getting-to-know-you question. Why didn't he ever ask her when she had time to answer?

"I'll have to think about it," she said.

"Tonight is going to be right up there," Thatcher said. "Nobody does this holiday better than we do."

By six thirty, 125 people were sitting down, including the Parrishes; the local author and her entourage; Holt Millman with a party of ten; Senator Kennedy; Mr. Kennedy the investor; Stuart and Phyllis, a couple who dined at the Bistro so often that their college-aged kids referred to the food as "mom's home cooking"; the Mr. Smith for whom the blueberry pie was named, and his wife; Cat, her sister, and their husbands; Leigh Stanford with friends from Idaho; and Leon Cross and his mistress. The place was hopping. Rex played "Yankee Doodle Dandy," followed by "Camptown Races." The busboys brought out the pretzel bread and mustard and when Adrienne poked her head into the kitchen, Paco and Eddie were frantically plating shrimp skewers. Adrienne ran the skewers out. Ten of the thirty tables were drinking champagne; the corks sounded like fireworks.

Adrienne saw Caren out by the beach bar. From the looks of things, Caren was letting Duncan have it, but in a quiet, scary way. Letting him have it while Adrienne ran Caren's apps and Delilah drowned in drink orders.

"Adrienne!" Delilah cried. "I need help."

Rex launched into "American Pie."

Adrienne ran to the wine cave for wine, she refilled Delilah's juice bottles, and went to the kitchen for citrus. It was even hotter in there than before—so hot that Fiona had taken off her chef's jacket. She worked in just a white T-shirt that had a damp spot between her breasts. It seemed like it took forever to get Delilah out of the weeds, yet Rex was still playing "American Pie," and half the restaurant was singing.

Adrienne walked by table fifteen, where Thatcher was chatting with Brian and Jennifer Devlin. She heard the word "Galápagos" and stopped in her tracks. A woman at the table behind had gotten up to use the ladies' room and Adrienne took great, slow pains in folding the woman's napkin so that she could listen to Thatcher.

"We leave on October ninth," he said. "Fly to Quito overnight then to the islands for ten days. We're on a fifty-foot ship. I'm really looking forward to it."

Adrienne returned to the podium. Rex finished "American Pie," and half the restaurant applauded. She thought back to her first breakfast with Thatch: *As soon as we close this place, I'm taking Fee to the Galápagos. She wants to see the funny birds.* He had told Adrienne right from the beginning that he was going away with Fiona. There was no reason for Adrienne to expect that he would change his travel plans just because he and Adrienne were now dating. But she did expect it. She had made peace, sort of, with the dinners. The dinners were business. They talked about the restaurant mostly, he said. The dinners were important.

Fine, Adrienne could live with the dinners. He came to her house afterward and always spent the night. But hearing him talk about ten days in the Galápagos with Fiona physically hurt. And yet what could she say? His best friend was sick and she wanted to see the funny birds. He would take her.

Caren came in off the beach and charged past the podium into the ladies' room. The ladies' room only accommodated one person at a time, so Adrienne knocked. "It's me," she said.

Caren cracked the door. "Men!" she said, leaving Adrienne with nothing to do but agree.

By quarter to nine, most of the tables had finished eating and Adrienne went crazy running credit cards. The guests moved out onto the beach to order more drinks and settle in their chairs. Adrienne ordered a coffee. She was exhausted and her red T-shirt dress was soaked with sweat.

Thatcher rallied the waitstaff. "We have an hour of peace and quiet. Once these tables are stripped and reset, you're free until the finale of the fireworks starts. Then I want you back in here ready for second seating."

The fireworks began at ten after nine. By that time, the guests for second seating had all arrived and the only people working out front were Duncan, who was pouring the drinks, and Bruno and Christo, who were serving them. Thatcher took Adrienne by the hand and led her out of the restaurant. She wanted to say something to him about the Galápagos, but she had yet to come up with the right words. *Please don't go? Take me with you?* Or how about this: *Would you at least not say you're looking forward to it?*

He led her into the sand dunes behind the restaurant. Adrienne took off her shoes and climbed after him. They plopped in the sand, hidden from the crowd by eelgrass. Thatcher held Adrienne in his lap like she was a child, and she pressed her face into his neck. She could feel his pulse against her cheek.

"How are you?" he asked. "Isn't this great?"

There was a bang, and a burst of red exploded in the sky, like a giant poppy losing its petals. The water shimmered with color. Then gold, blue, purple, white.

Adrienne's best Fourth of July, just like the other best moments of her life, had happened Before—before her mother got sick. Adrienne was eleven years old. In the morning, Rosalie and Dr. Don worked together in the kitchen preparing a salad for the potluck dinner while they watched Wimbledon on TV. Then, at four o'clock, they walked across the street.

(Adrienne remembered her old neighborhood in summer—the smell of the grass, the huge, beautiful trees, the grumble of lawn mowers and the whirring of sprinklers.) Seven families gathered at the Fiddlers' pool for swimming and croquet and a cookout. And Popsicles and flashlight tag and sparklers. Adrienne had been part of a family with the other kids, kids she hadn't seen or thought of for years and years: Caroline Fiddler, Jake Clark, Toby and Trey Wiley, Tricia Gilette, Natalie, Blake and David Anola. The girls lined up their Dr. Scholl sandals and lay back in the grass looking up at the stars and searching for any hint of the big fireworks being set off in Philadelphia. They talked, naïvely, about boys; Natalie Anola had a crush on Jake Clark. The world of boys at that point to Adrienne was like a wide, un-explored field and she was standing at the edge. At ten o'clock, Rosalie and Dr. Don, flush with an evening of Mount Gay and tonics, dragged Adri-enne home where she fell asleep in her clothes. Happy, safe, excited about the possibilities of her life.

That one was the best, and Adrienne had spent all the interceding years mourning, not only the loss of her mother, but the loss of that happi-ness. Right this second she felt a glimmer of it—Nantucket Island, in Thatcher's arms, watching the colors soar and burst overhead, feeling a breeze, finally, coming off the water. *Forget the Galápagos,* she told herself. Forget that there were 125 people yet to feed. Forget that Fiona would have twice the amount of time alone with Thatcher that Adrienne had. Forget all that because this moment *was* great, great enough to make it into her mem-ories. Adrienne savored every second, because she feared it wouldn't last.

8

❦

Hydrangeas

July was true summer. It was eighty-five degrees and sunny—beach weather, barbecue weather, Blue Bistro weather. The bar was packed every night, and the phone rang off the hook. Florists came in to change the flowers in the restaurant from irises to hydrangeas. Hydrangeas like bushy heads, bluer than blue.

Adrienne was admiring the bouquet of hydrangeas on the hostess podium when the private line rang. It was a Monday morning and she was covering the phones while Thatcher met with a rep from Classic Wines.

"Good morning, Blue Bistro."

"Adrienne?"

"Yes?"

"Drew Amman-Keller. I'm surprised you're not out jogging. It's a beautiful day."

"Well, you know," Adrienne said, glancing nervously around the dining room, "I have to work."

"I'm calling to confirm a rumor," Drew Amman-Keller said.

Adrienne held the receiver to her forehead. Should she just hang up?

"What rumor is that?"

"Is Tam Vinidin eating at the bistro tomorrow night?"

"Tam Vinidin, the actress?"

"Can you confirm that she has a reservation?" he asked.

Adrienne laughed. *Ha!* "I wish she did. Sorry, Drew." She hung up.

A few minutes later, JZ's truck pulled into the parking lot. He rolled in the door with two boxes of New York strip steaks on a dolly.

"Hey, Adrienne!" he said.

"Hey," she said. "How's everything? How's Shaughnessy?"

"She's fine," he said. "She leaves for camp in two weeks."

"Is that good or bad?"

"It's good," he said. "I'm going to sneak over here for a vacation."

"That'll be nice," Adrienne said. "Fiona will be happy."

JZ backed up the dolly. Before he headed into the kitchen, he said, "I heard Tam Vinidin is eating here tomorrow night."

"You did?"

"Yeah. Guy on the boat told me."

"She hasn't called," Adrienne said. She flipped a page in the reservation book. "I hope she calls soon. We're almost full."

As JZ pushed into the kitchen, Hector popped out. Of all the Subiacos, Hector was Adrienne's least favorite. He used the foulest language and was merciless when he teased his brothers and cousins. Adrienne was not excited to see his tall, lanky frame loping toward her.

"Hey, bitch!" he said.

Adrienne rolled her eyes. "What do you want, Hector?"

"Special delivery," he said. He palmed a fax on top of the reservation book. "It's our lucky day."

Tam Vinidin was coming to eat at the Blue Bistro! She wanted table twenty at seven thirty and she wanted it for the night. She would allow one photographer, a woman almost as famous as she was, to take her picture while she ate. She was on the Atkins diet. She wanted Fiona to make her a plate of avocado wrapped in prosciutto and Medjool dates stuffed with peanut butter. She would drink Dom Pérignon.

Adrienne checked the book. Tuesday nights the Parrishes ate at table twenty first seating, and one of Mario's friends from the CIA was coming in with his wife at nine. Adrienne would have to bump them both for Tam Vinidin. She wondered about the photographer. Would she need a table, too?

And what about the Dom Pérignon? The bistro didn't carry it. Adrienne called Thatcher on his cell phone. Since he was with a wine rep, he could order a case. Her call went to voice mail. "Thatch, it's me," Adrienne said. She was so excited, she could barely keep from screaming. "Tam Vinidin is coming in tomorrow night at seven thirty. We need a case of DP. Call me!"

Adrienne loved Tam Vinidin with a passion. She was sexier than JLo and prettier than Jennifer Aniston. And she was eating at the Bistro! Adrienne would get to meet her, open her champagne, deliver her chips and dip. She reread the fax. She had to e-mail her father.

Adrienne took the fax into the kitchen. Hector was drizzling olive oil over a hotel pan of fresh figs, and Paco was shredding cabbage for the coleslaw.

"Where's Fiona?" Adrienne asked.

Hector nodded at the office. The door was closed. Adrienne knocked.

"Come in!"

Adrienne opened the door. Fiona was sitting at Thatcher's desk filling out order forms. She had plastic tubes up her nose; she was attached to an oxygen tank.

"Oh, sorry," Adrienne said.

Fiona looked up. "What is it?"

Adrienne tried not to stare at the tubes. "Tam Vinidin is coming in tomorrow night."

Fiona blinked. "Who?"

"Tam Vinidin, the actress?"

Fiona shook her head. "Never heard of her."

Never heard of her? She must be kidding. "You must be kidding," Adrienne said.

Fiona took a deep breath, then coughed. "What can I do for you, Adrienne?"

"This is a fax from her manager," Adrienne said. "She wants all this . . . stuff. She wants— Here, you can see." Adrienne let the fax flutter onto the desk.

Fiona read. "She can't have twenty tomorrow night and certainly not at seven thirty. It's Tuesday. She can't have a photographer. She can't have DP and I'm not making that ridiculous food." Fiona handed the fax back to

Adrienne. "If she wants to sit at table eight and drink Laurent-Perrier and eat off the menu like everybody else, then fine. Otherwise, send her to the Summer House."

"Wait a minute," Adrienne said. "This is Tam Vinidin, Fiona. You don't know who this person is."

"That's right," Fiona said. "Thank you, Adrienne."

Adrienne appealed to Thatcher when he returned from his meeting, but he backed up Fiona.

"She's right," he said. "We might be able to slide Mario's buddy to table twenty-one, but we can't move the Parrishes."

"Why not?"

"Because they're the Parrishes."

"But this is Tam Vinidin."

"I didn't order DP and Fiona won't make special dishes." He checked the fax. "Medjool dates? Is she kidding? And as for the photographer— Do I really need to go on?"

"No."

"She'll be happier at the Summer House," Thatcher said. "Sorry. Do you want to call her manager or do you want me to do it?"

"You do it," Adrienne said. "I'm going home."

On Tuesday, Tam Vinidin's visit to Nantucket rated a front-page story in the *Cape Cod Times* and the *Inquirer and Mirror*, and there was a two-column article in *USA Today* written by Drew Amman-Keller describing the house she rented (on Squam Road), naming all the shops where she dropped bundles of cash (Dessert, Gypsy, Hepburn), and disclosing where she ate (the Nantucket Golf Club, 56 Union, the Summer House). Mr. Amman-Keller made a point of noting that Ms. Vinidin's trip to the Blue Bistro had been cancelled because Chef Fiona Kemp "would not accommodate her strict adherence to Dr. Atkins's diet." One of the Subiacos had clipped Drew Amman-Keller's article out of the paper and taped it to the wall next to the reach-in. Under the picture of Tam Vinidin (sitting on the bench outside Congdon & Coleman Insurance in cut-off jean shorts) someone had written: "Feed me fondue."

Wednesday was Adrienne's day off, and she forgot about Tam Vinidin. Wednesday night, Thatcher took Adrienne to Company of the Cauldron for dinner and he ate every bite. After dinner they went back to Thatcher's house—a cottage behind one of the big houses in town. His cottage was only large enough to accommodate a bed and a dresser, and on top of the dresser, a TV for watching college football in the fall. There was a bathroom and a rudimentary kitchen. Not exactly impressive digs, but Adrienne was honored to be in his private space. She studied the pictures of his brothers, she flipped through his high school yearbook. In the back, on the "Best Friends" page, she found a picture of Thatcher, with a bad haircut and acne on his nose, and Fiona, who looked exactly the same as she did now, twenty years later.

Adrienne and Thatcher spent the entire next day together. They drove Thatcher's pickup to Coatue, where they found a deserted cove and fell asleep in the sun. Thatcher skipped rocks and built Adrienne a sand castle. At four o'clock, he'd dropped her at home so she could shower and change. She caught a ride to work with Caren, who informed Adrienne that she and Duncan were back together, though Duncan was on probation.

"One more fuckup and it's over," Caren said.

Adrienne tried to listen seriously, but she couldn't stop smiling. The sand castle Thatcher built had been as beautiful as a wedding cake.

There were 229 covers on the book. Family meal was grilled cheeseburgers and the first corn on the cob of the season. Thatcher was late, but all Adrienne could think of was how happy she was going to be when he came walking through the door.

The phone rang, the private line. It was Thatcher. "Is everyone there?" he said. Adrienne turned around to survey the dining room.

"Everyone except Elliott," she said. "It's his night off."

"Okay," he said. "Listen. I need you to listen. Are you listening?"

She heard the normal sounds of the restaurant—the swinging kitchen door, the chatter of the waitstaff, the first notes of the piano—but none of that could overtake the high-pitched ringing in her ears. She could tell he was about to say something awful.

"Yes," she said.

"Fiona isn't doing well. Her doctor wants her to go to Boston for at least three days. And I'm going with her."

Adrienne stared at the kitchen door. She hadn't realized Fiona wasn't in.

"You'll be in Boston for three days?" she said.

"At least three days," Thatcher said. "Antonio knows, and he's told the kitchen staff. They're used to it, okay? For them, this is no big deal. And you're going to cover for me." He paused. "Adrienne?"

"What?"

"You do a terrific job. On the floor, on the phone. Everything. The wait-staff knows how to tip out, so all you have to do at the end of the night is add up the receipts and make a deposit of the cash in the morning. The restaurant can run itself."

"What about reservations?"

"Just do the best you can."

"Can I call you? You're taking your cell?"

"Absolutely. I have a room at the Boston Harbor Hotel. You should call me there before you lock up at night. And I'll need you in at ten to do reconfirmations and answer the phone."

"Okay."

"I'll pay you."

"You don't have to *pay* me," Adrienne said. She felt like a tidal wave was crashing over the perfect sand castle of her life. Thatcher gone for three days. Fiona sick enough for a hospital. Adrienne left in charge of the restaurant in the height of the season. It was impossible, wasn't it, what he was asking of her? As though he had told her she had to land an airplane or dock an ocean liner. "You can pay me, but I'm not worried about money. I'm worried about you. And Fiona. Is she going to be all right?"

"I'll know more tomorrow," Thatcher said. "She has a lot of anxiety. Father Ott is sitting with her right now."

"Father Ott?"

"She's afraid she's going to hell," Thatcher said. He cleared his throat. "Listen, I have to go. Call me before you close, okay?"

"Okay," Adrienne said.

He hung up.

Some time would have been nice, a few minutes to collect herself, to wrap her mind around what this phone call meant. But it was six o'clock, the waitstaff wanted confirmation that they were perfect—they were—and Rex played the theme from *Romeo and Juliet*. The first table arrived: a male couple who was staying at the Point Breeze. Adrienne sat them at table one, handed them menus, and told them to enjoy their meals, but when she said this, it sounded like a question, and in fact, as she looked at their perplexed tan faces, she was thinking: *Fiona is afraid she's going to hell.* Adrienne headed for the bar; she needed her drink.

"Where's the boss man?" Duncan asked.

How much was she supposed to say? Thatcher hadn't given her any guidelines. "He's not coming in tonight."

"Out last night *and* tonight?" Duncan said. "You need to take it easy on him."

"Funny," Adrienne said. "May I have my champagne, please?"

Duncan nodded at the door. "I'll bring it over to you," he said. "You have work."

Two couples were standing by the podium. Adrienne hurried over. "Good evening," she said. "Name?"

"You don't remember us?" asked a man with red hair and a red goatee. "We were in two nights ago? You talked us into a bottle of that pink champagne? We're from Florida?"

"Boca Raton," one of the women said.

Adrienne stared at the foursome, utterly lost. She would have sworn she had never seen them before in her life.

"You told us you used to work at the Mar-a-Lago," the red-haired man said.

"I did?" Adrienne said. She must have. Okay, she had to get a grip. Shake off this feeling of being stranded in the Sahara without any Evian. She scanned the book, looking for a familiar name. *Cavendish? Xavier?* She smiled. "Please forgive me. I can't remember what name the reservation is under."

"Levy," the man said. "But our feelings are hurt."

Adrienne sat them at table fifteen and made a mental note to send these people, whom she still did not remember, some chips and dip. She saw Leon Cross and his wife waiting by the podium. Leon's wife was a TV producer, a hotshot who recently tried to talk Thatcher into a reality show set at the Bistro. Initially, Adrienne had thought the Bistro would make a great setting for a reality show, but if a camera had filmed the last fifteen minutes no audience would believe it. Anxiety, death, and hell among the hardest-to-get reservations in town? Then there was Leon Cross himself, who sometimes came to the restaurant with his wife when he sat at table twenty (Adrienne led them there now), but just as often came with his mistress (who was older than his wife and a nicer woman) when he sat at table nineteen in a dark corner under the awning.

No one would believe it.

Party of eight from the Wauwinet, party of four waitresses from the Westender celebrating a birthday, party of five that was a single mom out with her two kids and their spouses. Then a series of deuces, then a four-top that was two couples celebrating the fact that they'd been friends for twenty years. The phone rang and rang. Adrienne checked each time to see if it was the private line—no. She didn't answer. Delilah ran her a glass of champagne and Adrienne took half of it in one long gulp.

She hurried into the kitchen to put in two orders of chips. The kitchen seemed the same except that instead of Fiona, Antonio was expediting.

"Ordering sixteen," he called out. "One foie gras, one Caesar."

"Yes, chef," Eddie said.

"Ordering twelve," Antonio said. "Two chowder, one beet, one foie gras killed, Henry baby, okay?"

"Yes, chef," Henry said.

Adrienne held up two fingers to Paco and he started slicing potatoes on his mandolin. Adrienne knew it would take six minutes and she should get back out front, but she lingered in the kitchen for a minute. Everything seemed way too normal. The Subiacos worked as though nothing was wrong. The baseball game was on. She poked her head back into pastry. Mario was pulling a tray of brownies out of the convection oven. Adrienne stared him down. They had never talked about Fiona's illness.

"What?" he said. "You want one?"

"Thatcher and Fiona are in Boston," Adrienne whispered. "They're going to be gone for three days. Fiona is in the *hospital*."

Mario squeezed Adrienne's face to make fish lips. It hurt. "It's okay," he said. "This happens. They put Fiona on a vent and it clears things out. They pump her full of miracle drugs. It makes things better. Trust me. It's no big deal." He let Adrienne's face go.

"Really?" Adrienne said.

"Fifteen years ago, we're in Skills One together and the day before our practical, she goes into the hospital. Big hospital down in the city. So I know something's wrong. As soon as I finish my test, I take the train to see her and she tells me about her thing. And I think maybe I'm gonna cry but then I realize Fee is the toughest person I know. She's gonna survive. And, like I said, that was fifteen years ago. She goes back to school the next week, makes up her practical, scores a ninety-seven out of a hundred. I get a seventy-three. Suddenly, she's the one who's worried about me. And for good reason." Mario cut the crispy edges off the brownies. "She'll outlive us all. You watch."

"Okay," Adrienne said. That was what she wanted to hear. She smacked Mario's butt and walked back to the hot line.

Spillman burst into the kitchen. "Adrienne, can you open wine for table fifteen? I'm slammed, and they say they're friends of yours."

"Sure," Adrienne said. She returned to the dining room. Rex was playing Barry Manilow. She took the Levys' wine order, retrieved the bottle from the wine cave, opened the wine and served it, all in under five minutes, at which point she remembered the chips and dip. Adrienne delivered chips and dip to the Levys, then Leon Cross. She returned to the podium and finished her champagne. *Run the restaurant by herself?* she thought. *Piece of cake!*

Smack in the middle of first seating, two women walked in wearing baseball hats and jeans. Adrienne felt a headache coming on. The Bistro didn't have a dress code, she reminded herself. The best tippers were often the guests who were underdressed. One of the women was wearing giraffe-print Prada mules and Gucci sunglasses. She took the sunglasses off as she approached the podium.

"Is it all right if we eat at the bar?"

Adrienne was caught completely off-guard. She made a gurgling sound. It was Tam Vinidin.

"Sure," Adrienne said finally, her mind ricocheting all over the place. She wanted to shout, but she had to remain cool. She wanted everyone in the restaurant to know Tam Vinidin was there, yet it was imperative that no one found out. Did anyone recognize her? She was beautiful and all the more so because she wore no makeup and had her hair in a ponytail under a hat. Her friend was . . . no one Adrienne recognized. Sister, maybe.

"Follow me," Adrienne said. She plucked two menus and led the women to the bar.

"Duncan!" Tam Vinidin said.

"Hey, Tam," he said. "I heard you were on-island." They kissed. Adrienne stared at Duncan in genuine awe.

"This is my cousin Bindy," Tam said. "We decided to stay through the weekend. It's so relaxing here."

"Cool," Duncan said. "What can I get you ladies to drink?"

"Champagne," Tam Vinidin said.

"Laurent-Perrier?" Duncan asked.

Tam Vinidin took off her hat and let her fabulous black hair free of its elastic. "Sure."

"Adrienne, are you willing to share your bottle with these ladies?" Duncan said.

Adrienne realized she had been gaping. "Okay?" she said, then she beat it into the kitchen.

"Okay," she said to Paco ten seconds later. "Guess who's eating at the bar."

"I don't give a shit," Paco said. He was helping Eddie build club sandwiches. "I'm fucking busy."

"Tam Vinidin."

Paco yelled to Hector, who was grilling off steaks. "She's here. Eating at the bar."

Hector whooped then pleaded with Antonio. "Can I go out and see her, Tony? Please, man?"

Antonio wiped his forehead with a side towel. He was older than Fiona by at least ten years and it showed. He was sweating; he looked exhausted and second seating hadn't even started yet. "Tam Vinidin's here?" he asked Adrienne.

Adrienne nodded. "I came to put in a VIP order."

"Hers is in the reach-in," Antonio said. "Fiona ordered those Medjool dates, just in case."

"You're kidding," Adrienne said. She checked the reach-in and found a plate of dates stuffed with peanut butter.

Caren slammed into the kitchen. "Is Adrienne in here?"

Adrienne turned around, holding the dates. "Did you see who's—"

"You promised me you wouldn't," Caren said. She threw her hands up in the air. Her lovely neck was getting red and splotchy. "You put Tam Vinidin at the bar!"

"She asked to sit at the bar. She knows Duncan from . . ."

"You promised me you wouldn't do it!" Caren said. "You could have put her at table three."

"Put Tam Vinidin at table three?"

"Because now she's out there with Duncan!"

"She's a movie star," Adrienne said. "She's not interested in Duncan."

"He's interested in her."

"No, he's not . . ."

"Shit, yeah, he is," Hector interjected.

"Shut up!" Caren said.

"You're a bitch," Hector said. "You think he wants you instead?"

"You're a bitch, *bitch*," Caren said.

"No fighting in the kitchen!" Antonio said. He clapped his hands and pointed to the door. "I don't want to hear anything else about the movie star. The dates, the organic peanut butter, fine. But not another word. And no more special treatment."

As it turned out, Tam Vinidin didn't want special treatment. She was thrilled about the dates and offered one to her cousin, one to Duncan, one to Adrienne, one to Leon Cross's wife who knew Tam from New York and popped over to say hello, and one to Caren who passed by the bar three times in two minutes to keep an eye on Duncan. Everyone refused.

"You don't know what you're missing," she said.

Rex played "Georgia, on My Mind." Adrienne forced herself to return to the podium. The phone rang and she realized she hadn't thought about

Thatcher for almost half an hour. She wanted to call him and thank him and Fiona.

Thank you for creating a restaurant so wonderful that people like Tam Vinidin want to come even without a reservation, even in their jeans. Thank you for ordering the Medjool dates and the organic peanut butter even though you never go to the movies or read People *magazine. You made someone happy tonight. You make people happy every night.*

You're going to heaven.

That night, Thatcher didn't answer his cell phone. Adrienne tried three times then called the hotel but he didn't answer in his room either. It was nearly two o'clock in the morning. Adrienne left a message in his room then called his cell phone a fourth time and left the same message.

"Hi, it's me. Everything went smoothly tonight. We made twenty-one six on the floor and another nineteen hundred seventy at the bar." Adrienne paused, thinking about how astounding those numbers were. Because she was the only one working, she herself had cleared over six hundred dollars in tips. And yet, under the circumstances, the money seemed very beside the point. "So I'll take it home and make a deposit at the bank on my way in tomorrow morning. Call me . . . I hope everything is okay . . . I'm thinking of you."

The first call that came in the following morning was on the private line. Adrienne punched the button, thinking *Thatcher, Thatcher, Thatcher.* There had been no message from him on the machine.

"Good morning," Adrienne said. "Blue Bistro."

"Harry Henderson for Thatcher, please."

Harry Henderson of Henderson Realty. Adrienne had sat the guy half a dozen times and he still didn't know her name.

"This is Adrienne, Harry," she said. "Thatcher won't be in today."

There was a big noise of annoyance on the other end of the line. "What are you talking about? Forget it! I'll call him at home."

"He's off-island," Adrienne said.

"No!" Harry cried out, as though he'd been shot. "Listen, I have a couple standing in my office this minute who are extremely interested in the property. I'm bringing them over."

"Wait," Adrienne said. She glanced around the dining room. The cleaning crew had been in but the restaurant had that dull daytime look. And Adrienne was in jean shorts and flip-flops. When she'd walked back into the kitchen upon her arrival, Eddie and Hector were having a contest to see who knew more curse words. "I don't think you should come now. Nothing's ready."

"You might not understand real estate, Amanda," Harry Henderson said. "We have to strike while the iron is hot. See you in ten." He hung up.

Adrienne dialed Thatcher's cell; she got his voice mail. Then she called the hotel. Ditto. She called his cell again. What was the point of taking his cell phone if he wasn't going to answer it? Then she pictured the hushed corridors of the hospital, the room where Fiona lay in bed hooked up to a ventilator, worrying about hell. She left a message.

"Harry Henderson is on his way over with some prospective buyers. I told him to wait but he couldn't be dissuaded. He thinks my name is Amanda. Call me at the restaurant."

Adrienne saw the Sid Wainer truck pull into the parking lot. JZ parked diagonally, taking up sixteen spots. He shut off the engine and climbed down from his seat. Instead of going around to open the back, he marched inside.

"JZ," Adrienne said. He stared at her and Adrienne could see he wasn't doing well. Just looking at him made Adrienne feel like a person with her act together.

"Have you heard anything?" he said.

She shook her head.

"You haven't talked to Thatch?"

"He's not answering his cell. And I couldn't reach him at the hotel."

"That's not good news," JZ said. "Either her O$_2$ sats are low or she has another infection."

"I saw her the other day hooked up to oxygen," Adrienne said. "But she seemed okay."

JZ took hold of the podium as though he planned to walk away with it. "I love her," he said. "I really fucking love her."

"I know," Adrienne said.

"I'm married," he said. "My wife and I are in love with other people."

Adrienne met this with silence. As interested as she was, she didn't have time for a confessional this minute.

"You're probably wondering why we don't get divorced," he said. "The reason is eight years old and four feet tall."

"Shaughnessy?"

He nodded. "Jamie says if I file for divorce, she'll take Shaughnessy away. And Jamie is just enough of a bitch that she means it. The guy she's been screwing for the last five years is married and won't leave his wife. And if she can't be happy, she won't let me be, either."

"Oh," Adrienne said.

JZ paced the floor in front of the restrooms. "I love Fiona but I can't lose my daughter."

The phone rang. The private line.

"I have to take this," Adrienne said. "It might be Thatch."

JZ nodded.

"Good morning," Adrienne said. "Blue Bistro."

"What in God's name is going on with this truck?" Harry Henderson asked. "We're in the parking lot and this truck is blocking the front view of the restaurant. Do you hear what I'm saying? We can't see the front."

"It's deliveries," Adrienne said.

"Well, tell him to move." With that, Harry Henderson hung up.

Adrienne smiled at JZ apologetically. Out in the parking lot, she heard Harry Henderson honking his horn.

"They want you to move," she said.

"They can fuck themselves."

"I'd agree," Adrienne said. "Except it's the Realtor with potential buyers. They want to see the front of the restaurant."

JZ ran a hand over his thinning hair. "Do you understand about Shaughnessy?"

"It doesn't matter if *I* understand," she said. "It only matters if . . ."

"I know. And she does understand. Or she claims she does. But she doesn't have kids. It's difficult to comprehend losing a child when you don't have one of your own."

Harry Henderson honked again.

"I'll move," JZ said. He took a Blue Bistro pencil and wrote a phone number on Adrienne's reconfirmation list. "Here's my cell. Will you call me if you hear anything?"

"Of course," Adrienne said.

"They're filthy rich."

This was what Harry Henderson whispered in Adrienne's ear while the prospective buyers wandered through the restaurant. Adrienne had been expecting a couple who *looked* filthy rich—an older couple, distinguished, like the Parrishes. Instead, Harry introduced Scott and Lucy Elpern. Scott Elpern was handsome despite his best efforts. He was tall and had a just-out-of-the-locker-room thing going in jeans, a dirty gray T-shirt, and a Red Sox cap. The wife, Lucy, wore a flowered muumuu that she must have picked up at Goodwill. She was hugely pregnant. Three days past her due date, she told Adrienne when they shook hands, as though she didn't want anyone around her getting too comfortable. Lucy herself could not have looked less comfortable. She was swollen and perspiring, her face was red, her hair oily. She resembled one of the cherry tomatoes the kitchen roasted until the skin split and the seeds oozed out.

"Technology billionaires," Harry Henderson said. "Nobody thinks there are technology billionaires anymore but I found two of them."

Adrienne looked out the window by the podium. JZ had swung the truck around so that it was perpendicular to the restaurant and now he was going about his business of unloading crates of eggs and peaches and figs. He moved sluggishly, plodding like he was being asked to carry gold bullion.

The Elperns stood by table twenty gazing out at the water. Lucy Elpern rested her hands on her belly. Harry Henderson gave them a moment to enjoy the view, then he gently led Lucy Elpern up the two steps and through the bar area.

"This is a blue granite bar," Harry said.

Lucy eyed her husband. "We could keep that."

"Of course!" Harry said. "And there's a state-of-the-art wine room and, naturally, an industrial kitchen."

"Can we see the kitchen?" Lucy asked.

"Of course!" Harry boomed. He looked to Adrienne for confirmation.

"I didn't tell anyone you were coming," Adrienne said.

"We'll just poke our heads in," Harry said. "Is Fiona back there?"

"No," Adrienne said.

"Too bad," Harry said to the Elperns. "You could have gotten a glimpse of the most famous chef on the island." He led Scott Elpern to the kitchen door.

"I have to use the ladies' room," Lucy Elpern said to Adrienne. "This baby is sitting on my bladder."

Adrienne pointed to the bathroom door.

Lucy rubbed her belly. Her fingers were swollen; the diamond wedding band she wore cut into her flesh. Her ankles looked soft and squishy, like water balloons. She had on a pair of turquoise flip-flops, the plastic kind you could buy at the five-and-dime. "I have to go every five minutes," she said.

Once Harry and Scott disappeared into the kitchen and Lucy closed the door of the restroom, Adrienne dialed Thatcher's number. Voice mail. She hung up. She heard water in the bathroom and a second later, Lucy emerged. Instead of heading into the kitchen, she wandered over to the podium, where Adrienne was pretending to review the reconfirmation list.

"You've worked here a long time?" Lucy asked.

"Not really," Adrienne said. "Only about six weeks."

"Harry told us that most of the staff has been here for years."

"Most of the staff has."

"But not you?"

"Not me."

Lucy Elpern inhaled. "This place has good karma."

"Are you in the restaurant business?" Adrienne said.

"No," Lucy said, and she laughed. "We're going to demolish and build a real house. But it would be nice if there were things we could keep. The bar, for example. We could put it in our family room, maybe."

"In your family room?"

"And then we could say this is the bar that used to be in a famous restaurant." She picked a pack of matches out of the bowl. "The Blue Bistro."

"You've never eaten here?" Adrienne asked.

"No. We've only been on Nantucket for a week. But we really want a second home on the beach. We live on Beacon Street in Boston. Nice, but very urban."

Adrienne checked her reservation sheet. There were 232 on the books for tonight, but she did have a couple of deuces left during first seating.

"Why don't you come in tonight on the house?" Adrienne said. "Around six?"

Lucy smiled, then ran a hand through her unwashed hair. "You're a doll to offer. That way we'd know what it might feel like to eat . . . in our new dining room. Let me ask Scott." She waddled to the kitchen door and with great effort, pushed it open.

Adrienne stared at the phone. She wanted to tell Thatcher that some people were here who wanted to demolish his restaurant but salvage the blue granite bar to put on display in their family room like a museum piece from a country they had never visited. She heard a noise and looked out the window. JZ was pulling out of the parking lot. *Don't go!* Adrienne thought. The feeling of abandonment returned and she picked up the phone to call Thatcher, but at that minute, Harry Henderson and the Elperns emerged from the kitchen.

"They weren't very friendly back there," Harry said.

Adrienne tried not to smile. She wondered if Hector had shared his seventeen words for copulation. "You support the wrong baseball team," Adrienne said, nodding at Scott's hat. "They're White Sox fans."

Scott shrugged. "Nice refrigerator," he said.

"We'd like to come to dinner tonight," Lucy said.

"And I'll join them," Harry Henderson said. "Amanda, you're a genius."

At five o'clock, Adrienne still hadn't heard from Thatcher. She led a very brief menu meeting, keeping her voice stern so that no one would be brave enough to mention the elephant in the room: *Thatcher is absent from class again today.*

It was Friday night and the first people in the door were the Parrishes. Earlier that afternoon, Adrienne had done the unthinkable: She had called the Parrishes to ask if they would give up table twenty.

"Just for tonight," Adrienne said. In a stroke of what she thought would be bad luck, she'd gotten Grayson on the phone, and hearing his gruff voice, she'd almost chickened out. "I can't tell you the reason, but believe me, I would never ask you to move if it wasn't critical."

Grayson had chuckled. "Sweetheart, Darla and I don't give a rat's ass where we sit. For the last twelve years we've had everyone thinking we're more important than we are. Put us wherever you want."

"Oh, thank you," Adrienne said. "Thank you, thank you."

Now she led Darla and Grayson to table eleven under the awning. It was a very warm night so she felt they would be happiest here.

Darla took her seat and looked around in amazement. "I feel like I'm in a whole other restaurant. And look! You've changed the flowers!"

Adrienne sent Bruno over and told him to comp the Parrishes' first round of drinks though she doubted they would care. Grayson never checked his bill. Once the Parrishes were squared away, Adrienne relaxed a wee bit. She had called Thatcher's cell phone four times over the course of the afternoon but she hadn't left a message. Too much to say.

Adrienne sat guests, handed out menus, opened the white burgundy for the Parrishes, delivered their chips and dip, and helped Christo rearrange seating to accommodate a hundred-year-old woman in a wheelchair. Then Adrienne spotted Harry Henderson's florid face at the podium and she hurried over. The Elperns stood behind him. Lucy's hair was damp and she had changed into a clean muumuu. Scott had thrown a white dress shirt over his gray T-shirt and traded in his jeans for khakis. Lucy was visibly dazzled.

"Look at this place," she said. "It is glam-or-ous." Rex was playing Frank Sinatra. "Can we keep the piano?" she asked.

Adrienne led the party to table twenty and Harry stopped along the way to shake hands with two gentlemen at table eight.

"Amanda," he said when she handed him his menu, "this was a really smart move on your part."

He sounded absolutely giddy. *And why not?* Adrienne thought. He was sitting down to a free dinner with a potential six-figure commission at the best table in the restaurant.

"My name," she said, "is Adrienne."

Harry smiled. He had no idea what she meant.

"My name is Adrienne, not Amanda."

"Like Adrienne Rich, the poet," Lucy said.

"Yes. Thank you," Adrienne said. "Now what can I get everyone to drink?"

Adrienne did a kamikaze shot at the bar before she delivered the Elperns' drinks. Unprofessional, possibly even unethical, but her stress level was so high that champagne wasn't going to cut through it and she told Duncan so and he put the kamikaze shot in front of her. It tasted like a bad night in college, though once she chased it with the Laurent-Perrier she regained her sense of humor. She went into the kitchen to put in a VIP order for the Elperns.

The restaurant can run itself. Joe walked by carrying two quesadilla specials. They looked delicious. Antonio was expediting with his usual avuncular charm, calling everyone baby. Everything was going to be fine.

Back in the dining room, Caren grabbed Adrienne's forearm. "Table twenty wanted the fondue. I told them no."

Adrienne peeked at twenty. Lucy Elpern had ordered a glass of Laurent-Perrier and from the looks of things, it had gone straight to her head. She was waving her champagne flute in the air, calling out to anyone who looked her way, "This bread is baked!"

"Let them have it," Adrienne said.

"Let them *have* it?" Caren said. "You bumped the Parrishes for Harry Henderson of all people, and now you're going to let them have the fondue first seating?" She gave an incredulous little laugh. "This isn't your restaurant, you know."

"Let them have it," Adrienne said. She walked away before she and Caren moved on to more sensitive topics, like how Caren was still pissed at Adrienne for putting Tam Vinidin at the bar, or how, technically, Adrienne was Caren's boss.

Adrienne thought Antonio might veto her decision about the fondue, but a little while later Caren passed by holding a pot of oil. She wouldn't meet Adrienne's eyes and Adrienne's confidence wavered. She had never even worked at Pizza Hut. What was she doing, breaking all the rules while Thatcher was away? Was it all in the name of selling the restaurant, or was it to exercise power in a situation where she felt utterly helpless?

A couple of minutes later, she checked on the Elperns again. Scott

Elpern lifted a golden brown shrimp from the pot and dragged it lavishly through the green goddess sauce, then the curry. Was it any surprise that the man had no table manners?

"How's everybody doing?" she asked.

"Adrienne," Harry Henderson said before he popped a shrimp into his mouth. It wasn't a response to her question so much as a demonstration that he had learned her name.

Lucy Elpern finished her glass of champagne. "Never better," she said.

Adrienne approached the Parrishes. They were eating in complete silence.

"Is there anything at all I can get you?" Adrienne asked.

"We love the new table," Darla said. "We like it better than the other table."

"You're kidding."

"At the other table, everyone watches you."

"Yes, they do," Adrienne said. She glanced at table twenty. The Elperns were having the time of their lives. There was no doubt in Adrienne's mind that this time next year the floor under her feet would be the Elperns' new living room.

Adrienne stopped at the bar to pick up her champagne.

"Another shot?" Duncan asked.

"Your girlfriend's pissed at me," Adrienne said. "She thinks I put too many pretty women at the bar."

"If you stop, I'll be pissed at you," Duncan said.

Elliott, who never said a word unless spoken to, chose this moment to interrupt. "Where's Thatcher?" he said. "Does he normally take a vacation in the middle of summer?"

Adrienne was saved having to answer when she spied Harry Henderson on his cell phone, which was a Blue Bistro no-no.

"Excuse me," Adrienne said, and she hurried back into the dining room.

Before she could scold Harry for using his phone, she sensed something was wrong. The atmosphere at the Elperns' table had altered. Lucy's face was screwed up and Scott hovered close, squeezing her hand. Darla was right.

Every other table in the restaurant had their attention fixed on the Elperns. The hundred-year-old woman in the wheelchair touched Adrienne's arm.

"I think that woman is having her baby."

Adrienne smiled. "She may have started labor. We'll get her to the hospital." She sounded preternaturally calm, thanks to the kamikaze shot, thanks to the fact that she'd prepared herself for this possibility. You didn't invite a woman three days past her due date to dinner and not consider the worst-case scenario.

Harry snapped his cell phone shut. "I called nine-one-one. An ambulance is coming."

"An ambulance?" Adrienne said, thinking: sirens and lights, the pall of emergency and doom. "The hospital is less than two miles from here. You could drive."

Scott Elpern glanced up. "We're in a rental car." These, Adrienne realized, were the only words she'd heard him speak other than *Nice refrigerator.*

"So?"

Lucy spoke through pursed lips. "My water broke," she said. "I'm sitting in a huge puddle of yuck."

Adrienne nearly laughed. Was this or was this not the theater of the absurd? She caught a whiff of something acrid: Three shrimp burning in the peanut oil. Adrienne fished them out, then she lassoed Spillman. "Let's get guests their checks. This could turn into a circus."

Unfortunately, it was too late. A minute later, Adrienne heard sirens in the distance, then lights flashed through the restaurant and three paramedics stormed in like they were rescuing a hostage. Conversation in the restaurant came to a dead halt; Rex stopped playing. Adrienne led the head paramedic, a woman with a long, scraggly ponytail, through the now-hushed restaurant to the Elperns' table.

"She just started labor. I really don't think there's any reason to panic . . ."

The paramedic knelt down and spoke quietly to Lucy Elpern. Adrienne wondered what to do in the way of damage control. They would need a towel. She retrieved the Sankaty Golf Club towel from the wine cave, and on her way back to the Elperns' table, she passed Darla and Grayson leaving.

"We loved the table," Darla whispered. "But we're going to get out of here before there's any blood."

"There won't be any blood," Adrienne whispered back. Would there? Grayson palmed Adrienne a hundred dollars.

The golf towel was very little help. The back of Lucy Elpern's muumuu was soaked and this seemed to be a cause of concern for her; she didn't want to leave the restaurant.

"Everyone will know," she whispered.

"Everyone already knows," Adrienne said. "And it's no big deal. It's perfectly natural."

"This is so embarrassing," she said.

The head paramedic called one of her guys for a blanket and once they had wrapped Lucy Elpern up, they led her out of the restaurant to the ambulance. The guests at the remaining tables applauded politely, much like they did when the sun set, and the decibel level rose back to normal. Adrienne trailed Lucy and the paramedic to the front door. The phone rang. Adrienne glanced over the top of the podium: It was the private line.

"Good evening," she said. "Blue Bistro."

"Hi," Thatcher said. "It's me."

Tears welled up in Adrienne's eyes so that when she looked out the window, the lights of the ambulance blurred and became a psychedelic soup. She didn't know exactly why she was crying though she imagined it was a combination of anxiety, relief, and the kamikaze shot. *Where the hell have you been?* she wanted to scream, but she held her tongue. She should ask about Fiona, about the hospital. However, there wasn't time to listen to the answers.

"Can I call you back?" she said. "In, say, fifteen minutes? I have to get first seating out of here."

"Sure," Thatcher said.

There was a long pause during which Adrienne tried to think of something else to say, but then she realized that Thatcher had hung up. She replaced the phone as the ambulance pulled out of the parking lot, sirens screeching. Tyler Lefroy was standing at the podium, a put-out expression on his seventeen-year-old face.

"Do I really have to clean that gross shit up?"

"Get a mop," Adrienne said.

Adrienne wanted to call Thatcher back, but she couldn't. Tables had to be turned; there were a hundred and twenty people sitting down at nine, and because of the Elpern spectacle, first seating was running behind. Adrienne monitored the progress of dessert and coffee; her foot was actually tapping. *Turn 'em and burn 'em,* she thought. The busboys were humping. Then Caren had a credit card war. Adrienne had heard about these but never seen one. Two men at table eight (by chance, the very men Harry Henderson had stopped to greet) wanted the bill. They were *fighting* over it. Adrienne's attention was called to the problem when she heard Caren's voice, much louder than it should have been.

"Gentlemen, I'm sure we can work this out! I am happy to split the bill."

The men were on their feet now, tugging at either end of the bill. Thankfully, this was one of the last tables in the dining room. Adrienne approached: The table was another Realtor and his wife and a local lawyer and her husband. The lawyer's husband was the louder of the two men, though the Realtor was physically bigger.

"I thought we agreed . . ." the lawyer's husband said.

"Please, I *insist*," the Realtor growled.

Adrienne felt badly that she hadn't at least asked Thatcher how Fiona was doing; it was a big mistake that needed to be rectified as soon as possible. With a lightning quick movement, Adrienne snatched the bill from both men, then put her palm out.

"We don't have *time* for this," she said. Blue Bitch voice. "Cards."

They handed over their cards and Adrienne spun on her heels. Caren followed her.

"Impressive," Caren murmured.

Adrienne tried to call Thatcher back after everyone from second seating was settled, but just as she felt it was safe to pick up the phone, Hector appeared from the kitchen.

"The exhaust fan is out," he said.

"What does that mean?"

"It means the kitchen is getting smoky."

"Okay," Adrienne said.

"We need it fixed," Hector said.

"Fine."

"Tonight."

"Tonight?" Adrienne said. She checked her watch. "It's a quarter of ten."

"Cat," Hector said. "Call her on her cell phone."

"I will not," Adrienne said. "She's probably *asleep.*"

"If you don't call her, the fire alarms are going to go off and the fire department will show up."

"Take the batteries out," Adrienne said.

Hector readjusted his White Sox hat. "This is an industrial kitchen," he said. "Do you really think our fire alarms run on a couple of double As? You have to call Cat."

"You're kidding me, right? This is a joke?" Adrienne was *certain* it was a joke. A prank to go with Lucy Elpern's labor. A little laugh at her expense while the boss was away.

"I'm serious," Hector said. "Look." He pointed to the window of the kitchen door. Smoke.

"I can't believe this," Adrienne said. *The restaurant can run itself. Ha!* as Thatcher would say. *Ha ha ha!*

She found Cat's cell phone number on a list pasted to the front of the reservation book and Cat answered on the first ring. It sounded like she was in high spirits. Too high.

"Cat? It's Adrienne calling from the Blue Bistro."

"Hey, girlfriend!"

"Hi. Listen, I'm sorry to bother you, but we have an exhaust fan out."

There was a long pause. Adrienne feared she had lost the connection, but then Cat spoke up. "I just needed to step outside," she said. "I'm having dinner at the Chanticleer."

Adrienne groaned. The Chanticleer was in Sconset, on the other side of the island. "So you can't come fix it?"

"And leave behind the duck for two with pomme frites?" Cat said. "The bottle of 1972 Mouton Rothschild . . ."

"We could give you dinner here," Adrienne said. "Hector said if it's not fixed, the alarms will go."

"Well," said Cat. Another pause. "I'm with a party of ten and I know for a fact my husband can eat the duck for two by himself. I'll sneak out now and come back. They're so drunk, they might not even miss me."

Fifteen minutes later, the kitchen was filled with smoke such that Antonio could barely read the tickets. They had opened the back door of the office and the six narrow windows and they pulled the two oscillating fans out of the utility closet and Paco was yanked off his station—his new job was to stand in front of the smoke detector waving a large offset spatula. Adrienne returned to the front. She drank her third glass of champagne and contemplated another kamikaze shot. Every time one of the waitstaff emerged, he smelled like a barbecue.

"Whew! It's getting bad back there," Joe said. "Have you called Cat?"

"She's on her way," Adrienne said, praying that Cat didn't get stopped on Milestone Road for drunk driving. Adrienne considered calling Thatcher and asking quickly about Fiona, but she wouldn't be able to keep the panic out of her voice. As she finished her champagne, Cat walked in the door—black cocktail dress, Manolo Blahniks, tool belt.

"Praise Allah," Adrienne said.

Cat stuck out her lower lip. "The 1972 Mouton Rothschild," she said.

"We'll make it up to you," Adrienne said.

Cat disappeared into the kitchen and Adrienne called Thatcher.

"Hi," he said. "Is everything all right?"

"I was just going to ask you the same thing," Adrienne said.

"Her O$_2$ sats are back up for the time being," Thatcher said. "The doctors are worried, though."

"About what?"

"She's becoming resistant to the antibiotics, and there's a lot of other stuff going on that I don't even pretend to understand. The doctor nixed the trip to the Galápagos, and Fiona was crushed. Can you make a note in the book for me to cancel with the travel agent? We'll be home tomorrow night, Fiona will be back to work on Monday. Would you pass that on to Antonio?"

"Sure," Adrienne said, scribbling a note about the travel agent. No Galápagos, then. She thought she might feel relieved, but instead she just felt sad. "JZ was in this morning. He's worried."

"He should be here," Thatcher said. "She's been asking for him." He sighed. "I got your messages. Sounds like everything is going well there."

"Going well?" Adrienne said.

"Isn't it?"

At that moment, Adrienne heard a muted cheer from the kitchen and Cat stepped out, hoisting her tool belt in victory. Adrienne blew her a kiss as she ran out the door.

"Sure," Adrienne said.

"Good. I'll see you tomorrow night. We'll be on the four o'clock flight so I hope to make the menu meeting. How many covers are on the book?"

"Two thirty-five," Adrienne said.

"Whoa," Thatcher said. "It's July. Hey, would you call Jack at the flower shop in the morning and have him deliver fresh hydrangeas on Monday? I want it to look nice when Fee comes back."

"No problem," Adrienne said.

"I miss you," Thatcher said. "Do you miss me?"

"I do," she said.

She hung up the phone. She felt better, like she was the one whose exhaust fan had been broken, and now she sucked in clean, fresh air. The phone rang again, private line. Adrienne had to do rounds through the dining room, but she picked up the phone in case it was Thatcher with one last thing.

It wasn't Thatcher, but Adrienne was glad she took the call anyway. Harry Henderson informed her, in a voice both jubilant and humbled, of the birth of Sebastian Robert Elpern, nine pounds, twelve ounces, perfect in every way, and of an official offer on the Blue Bistro for eight and a half million dollars.

9

❦

Phosphorescence

The Inquirer and Mirror, Week of July 15, 2005
"Here and There" column

There have been several reports of phosphorescence in the water at beaches along the north shore this week. Phosphorescence is caused by a type of algae called dinoflagellates, which are capable of bioluminescence when the water they reside in is disturbed.

Sports Illustrated cover story:
**"The Heroes of America's Heartland:
Can the White Sox Win the Pennant?"**

TO: Ade12177@hotmail.com
FROM: kyracrenshaw@mindspring.com
DATE: July 13, 2005, 9:02 A.M.
SUBJECT: Things I can't believe

I can't believe you've traded in the cushy life of the hotel front desk for the restaurant business. I can't believe you're dating your boss. I can't believe you're living with my dreamboat Duncan. You should thank me for recommending Nantucket. You should remember me in your will.

TO: kyracrenshaw@mindspring.com
FROM: Ade12177@hotmail.com
DATE: July 13, 2005, 10:35 A.M.
SUBJECT: Thank you

Thank you for recommending Nantucket. I am in a much better place, following my new rules, feeling good about myself. I paid off both Mr. Visa and Ms. MasterCard and I have a positive bank balance. I am in a relationship with a real, live, grown-up man. I sing in the shower.

It is amazing, Kyra, the way that happiness changes a person.

TO: Ade12177@hotmail.com
FROM: kyracrenshaw@mindspring.com
DATE: July 14, 2005, 8:41 A.M.
SUBJECT: the way that happiness changes a person

Is happiness contagious? Can you send me some spores in the mail?

When Fiona returned from Boston, Adrienne studied her for signs of illness, but Fiona had never looked better. One very busy Thursday night, the kitchen was waist-deep in the weeds. The kitchen had so many tickets, there wasn't enough room for them above the pass. The Subiacos were sweating and cursing and busting their humps to keep up. Fiona slid behind the line to plate soups, sauce pasta, and sauté foie gras while singing "The Sun Will Come Out Tomorrow." Every time Adrienne peeked her head in, she found Fiona in soaring good spirits.

"One plate at a time," Fiona called out. She even helped Jojo, the youngest Subiaco, load the dishwasher. She was a general in the foxhole with her men, but singing, gleeful. It was strange. Adrienne thought maybe the hospital had given Fiona a personality transplant.

It didn't take Adrienne long to figure out that Fiona's improvement in attitude had nothing to do with the hospital or facing her own mortality. It had, very simply, to do with love. Right after first seating, JZ walked in.

Shaughnessy was away at camp and he had rented a house on Liberty Street. Today was Day One of a week's vacation.

Fiona and JZ were inseparable. By Day Three they had established a routine: They did yoga together on the beach in the mornings, and then JZ helped Fiona in the kitchen. One morning Adrienne found him pitting Bing cherries and joking with the Subiacos. (The Subiacos were in a collective good mood because the White Sox had won eleven straight and held first place by a game and a half.) Fiona and JZ escaped from the kitchen by noon with a picnic basket and off they would go in Fiona's Range Rover to secret, out-of-the-way beaches where no one would ever find them. JZ ate dinner at the bar and spent the hour after second seating in the kitchen— and Adrienne knew that after eating with Thatch, Fiona drove her Range Rover to the house on Liberty Street and spent the night.

Was happiness contagious? By Day Four, it was safe to say that the food at the Bistro had never been better and Adrienne wasn't sure how to explain that. How did the best get better? It just did. Every single guest raved about the food. *Perfectly seasoned, perfectly cooked, the freshest, the creamiest, the most succulent. The best I've ever had.* Adrienne noticed it, too, at family meal: the Asian shrimp noodles, the Croque monsieurs, the steak sandwiches with creamy horseradish sauce and crispy Vidalia onion rings. *Are you kidding me?* Adrienne thought as she stuffed her face. She thought: *JZ, never leave.*

On Day Five, Adrienne was working reservations when the private line rang. By this time, Adrienne realized the private line could be anybody: Thatcher (who was at an AA meeting), Cat, Dottie Shore, Harry Henderson, Ernie Otemeyer, Leon Cross, Father Ott.

"Good morning, Blue Bistro," Adrienne said.

A woman's voice said, "This is Jamie Zodl. I'm looking for my husband. Have you seen him?"

Adrienne found herself at a loss. "I'm sorry? Your husband?"

"Jasper Zodl. JZ. There's no need to play games. I know you know who he is and I know he's there. Or if he's not there now, he'll be there at some point and I want to speak to him."

Adrienne wrote JZ's name at the top of her reconfirmation sheet. She thought of Shaughnessy at summer camp and all the things that might have gone wrong: sunburn, mosquito bites, sprained ankle, homesickness. "He normally delivers here at ten," Adrienne said. "But he's on vacation this week."

"You can cut the crap," Jamie said. "I'm not stupid. Have him call me. His wife. At his house. He knows the number."

"Okay, if I see him—"

Jamie Zodl hung up.

Adrienne passed on the message that evening when JZ came into the bar for dinner. He was wearing a dolphin-blue button-down shirt and his face and forearms were very tan. He and Fiona had rented a Sunfish that afternoon and sailed on Coskata Pond. Adrienne delivered the bad news with his chips and dip.

"Your wife called this morning," she said.

"Here?"

Adrienne nodded. "She wants you to call her at home."

"It can't be important," he said. "Or she would have called me on my cell. I had it on all day. She probably just called to make a point. To let everyone know she knows I'm here."

"Okay, well," Adrienne said. "That was the message."

Later that night as they lay in bed, Adrienne asked Thatcher what he knew about Jamie Zodl.

"She's unhappy," he said. "She's one of those people who thinks the next thing is going to save her. When I first met her twelve years ago, she was desperate to marry JZ. They used to come into the restaurant all the time. He proposed to her at table twenty."

"Oh, you're kidding," Adrienne said.

"After they got married, Jamie wanted to be pregnant. That didn't happen right away and they went to Boston for fertility help and it worked, obviously, because they had Shaughnessy. But then Jamie realized how hard it was to be a mother. So to afford a live-in, she and JZ sold their house here and moved to Sandwich. Jamie had an affair with the guy who owned the gym that she joined, and JZ found out. Jamie promised to break it off, they went into counseling for a while, and JZ took a job driving for another company so he wouldn't have to be gone every day. We didn't see him here for two whole summers. But then he found out Jamie was back with the guy from the gym and he gave up. Got his old job back and he's been trying to file for divorce, but Jamie won't let him. She threatens to take Shaughnessy away and she disappears to her mother's in Charlottesville, and once she and Shaughnessy flew to London for the weekend. The only way JZ was able to find them was by calling his credit card company. Jamie has run them into mountains of debt on top of it all. Pretty woman, gorgeous, but what a disaster." Thatcher rubbed his eyes. "JZ used to talk to Fiona about the whole thing. It was strange because Fiona and I and the staff had watched the relationship from the beginning—the courtship, the proposal, the wedding, the child, the breakup, and the next thing I knew Fiona and JZ were in love."

"When was that?"

"Two years ago."

"So what do you think will happen, then?"

"What do I think will happen?" Thatcher repeated. He was lying on his back, arms folded over his chest like someone resting in a coffin. "Nothing will happen."

"What does that mean?"

"JZ won't leave Jamie. He's too cowardly."

"He's worried about his daughter."

"That's what he says."

"You don't believe him?"

"JZ is a good guy," Thatcher said. "But he's not going to risk anything for Fiona. Leave his wife and lose his daughter for someone who's going to die?" Thatcher rolled onto his side, away from Adrienne. "That would take a hero. JZ is nobody's hero."

Happiness might be contagious, but it was also fleeting, delicate, mercurial. On Day Six, Jamie called again, in the middle of second seating. The restaurant was loud, but Adrienne picked up a new tone in Jamie's voice.

She sounded manic and untethered, like someone who had pounded six shots of espresso.

"This is Jamie Zodl," she said. "ISJZTHERE?"

"Yes," Adrienne said. "Please hold on one minute."

"You hold on one minute," Jamie said.

"Excuse me?"

"I know Fiona's sick," Jamie said. "I know all about it."

Adrienne said nothing. Across the room, a table burst out laughing. Rex played, "In the Mood."

"Let me get JZ," Adrienne said.

"I have a phone number," Jamie said. "For a journalist who wants to write about her. He wants to talk to me about Fiona and JZ. The question is, do I want to talk to him?"

"Let me get JZ," Adrienne said again, though she was afraid to put Jamie on hold. Bruno swung by the podium.

"I need your help on ten," he said. "Can you pull a bottle of the Cakebread?"

Adrienne's ears were buzzing; she felt like she had a bomb threat on the phone.

"Get JZ," Adrienne whispered to Bruno. "His *wife* is on the phone."

Bruno wasn't listening closely—what he heard was Adrienne asking him for something in response to his asking her for something. He wagged a finger. "Honey, I'm slammed. Can you get the wine for me, please?"

Adrienne searched the dining room for Thatcher. Her eyes snagged on table ten, a deuce, a middle-aged couple, fidgeting, glancing around. They wanted their wine. Adrienne snapped back to her senses. This was a restaurant! She put Jamie Zodl on hold, zipped into the wine cave for the Cakebread, then she shouted into the kitchen, "JZ, call for you on line three!" By the time Adrienne opened the wine for table ten and made it back to the podium, the phones were quiet. Jamie had hung up.

Adrienne didn't see JZ on Day Seven, but she gathered he had packed up and left. Fiona took a day off; when she returned, she was back to her old sarcastic, scowling self. The White Sox lost a double-header to the Mariners. Adrienne stayed out of the kitchen.

TO: kyracrenshaw@mindspring.com
FROM: Ade12177@hotmail.com
DATE: July 21, 2005, 10:35 A.M.
SUBJECT: happiness

Not sending spores. You don't want them. Happiness is fickle. Plays favorites.

A couple of days later, Adrienne was working the phone when a man walked in dressed entirely in black. Black jeans, black shoes, black dress shirt open at the neck. Bulky black duffel bag. He was a young guy who had shaved his head to hide his baldness, so all Adrienne could see was something like a five o'clock shadow where his hair used to be. *New York*, Adrienne thought, and immediately her guard went up. The press. Who else dressed in black on a hot July day at the beach?

"Can I help you?" Adrienne said.

He offered her his pale hand. "Lyle Hardaway," he said. *"Vanity Fair* magazine."

Yep. Adrienne eyed her phone. If he didn't leave when she asked, she would call the police.

"I'm sorry," Adrienne said. "You don't have an appointment and our owner isn't here."

He held up his palm. "I have a meeting scheduled with Mario Subiaco. He said he'd be working. He said I should come here."

"He did?"

"Yeah. Mario, the pastry chef. This is the Blue Bistro?"

"It is." Blue Bitch voice. She pointed a finger at his raised hand. "You wait right here. Don't move. Is there a camera in that bag?"

"Yes," he said.

"No photographs," she said. "Understand?"

"Okay," he said, and he smiled like maybe this tough act of hers was supposed to be funny.

Adrienne marched into the kitchen. She heard Fiona's voice in the walk-in; she was making an order list with Antonio. Adrienne slipped into pastry. Mario was all gussied up in his houndstooth pants, washed and pressed, and his dress whites—the jacket with black piping and his name over the chest pocket. He was rolling out dough.

"You have a visitor," Adrienne said.

He didn't look up. "Do I?"

"Lyle somebody. From *Vanity Fair*."

"Okay," Mario said.

"He's not coming back here," Adrienne said.

"Yeah, he is," Mario said. "He wants to watch me work. I'm making my own pretzels today. For chocolate-covered pretzels. It's a special on the candy plate."

"I thought there was no press allowed in the kitchen," Adrienne said. "I thought that was a law."

"This isn't the kitchen," Mario said. "It's pastry."

"Does Fiona know this guy is coming?" Adrienne asked.

"Not yet."

Adrienne watched Mario fiddle with the pretzel dough, twisting it into nifty shapes. "What's going on?" she said.

"They're doing an article about me," he said.

"Just about you?"

"Just about me. I hired a publicist."

"You did *what*?"

"I hired a publicist and she sent out my picture and my CV and *Vanity Fair* called. They're doing some article about sex and the kitchen. You know, sexy chefs. Rocco DiSpirito, Todd English, and me." He raised his face from his work and mugged for her.

"Now I've heard it all," Adrienne said. "You hired a publicist and you have a writer from a huge New York magazine in the bistro with a camera to take pictures of you making chocolate-covered pretzels because you're sexy."

"King of the Sweet Ending," he said. "They loved the name."

"Yeah, well, Fiona doesn't know. And guess what? I'm not telling her."

"No one was asking you to."

"So you'll tell her yourself?"

"Tell her why? It's my business."

"It's not your business," Adrienne said. "It's her business."

"Just send the guy back, please, Adrienne."

As Adrienne returned to the dining room—Lyle Hardaway was right where she'd left him—the phone rang. Darla Parrish, bumping her reservation to three people. Adrienne asked cautiously, hoping, praying, "Not Wolfie?"

"No, it's our youngest son, Luke. I can't wait to introduce you. Oh, and Adrienne, dear, will you put us at that new table?"

"Sure thing," Adrienne said. She made a note on her reconfirmation list. The writer was watching her every move. She hung up the phone, then said, "Follow me."

Adrienne and Lyle Hardaway made it three steps into the kitchen before Fiona stopped them.

"Whoa," she said. "Whoa. Who's this? Not a wine rep back here?"

"His name is Lyle Hardaway." Adrienne was afraid to say more.

"Is he a friend of yours?" Fiona asked.

"No," Adrienne said.

Suddenly, Mario appeared from the back. "He's here for me."

"What is he, your new dance instructor?" Fiona said. She glared at Lyle Hardaway. "Who are you?"

"I'm a writer for *Vanity Fair*," he said. He offered Fiona his hand. "You're Fiona Kemp? It's an honor to meet you."

Fiona pointed to the door. Her cheeks were starting to splotch and she bent her head and coughed a little into her hand. Antonio spoke up from behind the pass.

"Get him out of here, Adrienne," he said. And Adrienne thought, *Yes, get him out before he sees Fiona cough.*

"Fuck off, Tony," Mario said. "He's here for me."

Antonio said, "What are you, crazy?"

Fiona spoke to the floor. "I have to ask you to leave," she said. "I don't allow press in the kitchen."

"Come on, Fee," Mario said in a voice that normally got him whatever he wanted. "He's here to take pictures of my pretzels."

"No," Fiona said.

Lyle Hardaway held his arms in front of his face, like the words were being hurled at him. "Maybe I should wait out front while you work this out."

"Wait outside," Fiona said. "In the parking lot."

Lyle Hardaway disappeared through the door.

Fiona slammed her hand on the pass. "And now there will be a line in *Vanity Fair* or one of the other magazines they're sleeping with—you can bet on it—about what a bitch I am." She glared at Mario. "What were you thinking? You *invited* him into our kitchen?"

"He wants to write an article about me," Mario said.

"No," Fiona said.

"You can't tell me no," Mario said. "The article is about me. It's not about you, it's not about the Bistro."

"That's where you're wrong," Fiona said. "He told you the article is about you. But that was just so he could get through the door. Did you hear him a second ago? 'You're Fiona Kemp? It's an honor to meet you'? He's using you to get to me."

Mario laughed and looked around the kitchen at his cousins, and his brother Louis, who was filling ravioli and pretending not to listen. Only Adrienne was captive, rooted in the kitchen, afraid to leave lest she attract attention to herself, or worse, miss something.

"I cannot believe how self-centered you are," Mario said. "You think the world revolves around your tiny ass? It does not. You think people care so much about you? They do not. That man came here to interview *me*. And I'm going to let him. Because my career isn't over in September, Fee. I have to move on, I have to build my prospects, increase the value of my stock. So maybe I get investors and open my own place. Maybe my cousin Henry gets investors for his root beer. We have to move on, Fee. Move forward. We aren't quitting at the end of the summer."

"I'm not quitting, either," Fiona whispered.

"The Bistro is closing," Mario said. "That's a fact. The building is sold, it's torn down, it's rebuilt as somebody's fat mansion. There is no more Bistro. So what do you expect us to do, lie down and die with you?"

"Mario!" Antonio said.

"Get out!" Fiona shouted. She whipped around and caught Adrienne standing there, but she didn't seem to care. Her eyes were ready to spill over with tears. Was Adrienne going to see Fiona *cry*? "Get out! Get out of my kitchen!"

Mario ripped off his chef's jacket and threw it to the floor. "Fine," he said. "I'm finished with you."

He stormed out the door, leaving the kitchen in a stunned silence. Adrienne felt a strong desire to run after him. She liked Mario and she saw his point—once the Bistro closed, everyone had to fend for himself. Fiona would be four million dollars richer, but where would the rest of them be?

Fiona retreated to the office and slammed the door.

Adrienne heard the faint ringing of the phone. She went out front to answer it. That was her job.

That night, there were 244 covers on the book. Family meal was pulled pork, corn muffins, grilled zucchini, and summer squash. At the menu meeting, Thatcher announced that there would be no desserts. All Antonio had been able to find back in pastry were a few gallons of peanut butter ice cream, a tray of Popsicles, and the unfinished pretzels.

"I'll say one thing for my cousin," Antonio said. "He works fresh."

No one knew where Mario was; at last report, he hadn't checked in at the Subiaco compound. Adrienne wondered if he had flown off-island in search of another job. She wondered if she would ever see him again.

"What do you think?" Adrienne asked Thatcher at the podium as they awaited first seating.

"I stay out of the kitchen's business."

"Yeah, but what do you think?"

"Fee's afraid," he said quietly. "And fear does strange things to people."

"It's too bad," Adrienne said. "They've been friends a long time."

"They're still friends," Thatcher said. "This is just a fight."

"So you think he'll come back?"

"Where's he going to go?" Thatcher said.

"I don't know. Chicago?"

"Ha!" Thatcher gave her the laugh, and Adrienne felt better. She was smiling when the Parrishes walked in.

"Halloo," Darla called out. She was holding a young man by the hand, pulling him along like he was Wolfie's age. "Adrienne, this is my son, Luke Parrish. Thatcher, you remember Luke."

Thatcher shook hands with Luke and patted him on the back. Luke smiled shyly at the floor. He was the exact opposite of what Adrienne expected a Parrish son to look like: He wore tiny frameless glasses and had long brown hair that spilled over his shoulders and down his back. He wore a blue blazer over a white T-shirt, jeans, and sandals. Between the lapels of his jacket, Adrienne could only read a single word printed on the front of his shirt: CASTRO.

"It's nice to meet you, Luke," Adrienne said. "Let me show you to your table."

As she walked the Parrishes out to the awning, Rex launched into "Hello, Dolly!" Adrienne heard Darla behind her. "Isn't she just lovely? Isn't she exquisite? She used to live in Aspen. And Hawaii. Adrienne's a real adventure girl, aren't you, Adrienne?"

Adrienne pulled out a chair for Darla. She handed Luke and Grayson their menus. "Just to let you know, there aren't any desserts tonight. Our pastry chef is on vacation."

"On vacation in the middle of July?" Grayson said. He leaned closer to Luke. "That must mean they fired him."

"So I'll get your drinks, then," Adrienne said. "Stoli tonic and Southern Comfort old-fashioned. Luke, what can I bring you?"

"A beer, please," he said.

"We have Cisco Summer Brew on tap. Is that okay?"

"Perfect," he said. "And a shot of tequila, please."

"A beer and a shot of tequila," Adrienne said. "I'll be right back."

She put in the drink order with Duncan and went back to the kitchen to give Paco the VIP order. Antonio was expediting.

"Where's Fiona?" Adrienne asked Paco.

"Lying down," he said. "She's upset."

"About Mario?"

"No," Paco said. "Something about JZ. Eddie got the story."

"Have you heard from Mario?" Adrienne asked.

Paco scoffed. "He's out getting drunk somewhere. Getting drunk and looking for ladies."

"You think?" Adrienne said. She seemed to be the only one who was worried about him. She couldn't bear to peek around the corner and see the abandoned pastry station.

Back in the dining room, she sat tables: the local author was in; Mr. Kennedy; a real jackass named Doyle Chambers; and one of the local contractors with a party of twelve. Adrienne opened a bottle of champagne for Kennedy—his wife, Mitzi, was now a devotee of the Laurent-Perrier—and then she swung back into the kitchen to pick up the chips for Parrish and put in two more VIP orders. She headed for the Parrishes' table. From behind, Luke looked like a girl in men's clothing. But that wasn't quite right; his hair wasn't feminine so much as biblical. He looked like the original Luke, the one who wrote the Gospel. But this Luke had inherited the Parrish demeanor. Adrienne found the three of them sitting in silence, sipping their drinks. The shot of tequila had been drained and pushed to the edge of the table. Adrienne scooped it up as she set down the chips and dip.

"Another?" she asked Luke.

"Please," he said.

This seemed to startle Darla from her reverie. "Oh, Adrienne, honey, won't you please stay and chat with us for a second?"

"I'd love to."

"I told Darla that arranged marriages have been out of fashion for over a hundred years," Grayson said. "She refuses to believe me."

Darla laughed and threw her hand in the air. "I just thought they might have something in common. Luke loves to travel. After Amherst, he spent a year in Egypt."

"Egypt?" Adrienne said. "I've always wanted to see that part of the world. I had a boyfriend once who offered to take me to Morocco, and at times I regret not going."

Luke tented his fingers. He was looking at Adrienne longingly, she thought, but then she realized that he was eyeing the empty shot glass in her hands. He wanted his tequila.

"How old are you, Adrienne?" Darla asked.

"Twenty-eight."

"And Luke is twenty-nine!" Darla said. "He's our youngest."

"And our nuttiest," Grayson piped in. "It was a hard lesson but I finally learned that our three boys were not mined from the same quarry. This guy"—and here he pounded Luke on the shoulder—"is a free spirit."

"Josh and Timmy are more traditional," Darla said.

"They're into wearing suits and paying alimony," Luke said.

"Okay, well," Adrienne said. "I'll get you another tequila. Darla, Grayson, can I bring you anything else right now?"

"Just yourself, when you have a minute," Darla said.

Adrienne stopped at the bar to order another tequila and then met Thatcher at the podium. Everyone from first was down.

"I think Darla is trying to set me up with her son," Adrienne said.

"Oh, I know she is," Thatcher said. "For years she's been wondering if he's gay. She told me on Tuesday that it was her intention to introduce him to you."

"And what did you say?"

"I said, 'Good luck. I hear she's very picky.'"

Adrienne swatted him. "Not picky enough."

"I want to have a meeting after closing tonight," Thatcher said.

"A meeting?"

"On the beach outside my office."

"Because of Mario?"

"Morale booster," he said. "It's mandatory. Please spread the word."

No one on the staff expressed enthusiasm about a mandatory meeting at one o'clock in the morning. Joe looked at Adrienne cross-eyed; Spillman claimed he had a date with his wife at Cioppino's.

"Morale booster?" he said. "What are we going to do—have a sing-along around the campfire?"

Caren, who was standing right there, said, "Thatch likes to give a little speech when the first person burns out." She nudged Spillman. "Last year, remember, when Bruno lost his shit on that woman with the alligator shoes, Thatch gave us the talk and we all got a raise?"

"True," Spillman said.

Tyler Lefroy asked if there would be beer. Adrienne was too afraid to tell anyone in the kitchen about the meeting; she would make Thatcher handle that.

Between their appetizer and entrée, Adrienne visited the Parrishes again. She had to admit, Luke Parrish fascinated her, not because of anything he said or did, but because he was so different from Darla and Grayson. He was a revolutionary. He'd ordered the mixed green salad with beets, and the ravioli; he was a vegetarian. And now, after two beers and three shots of tequila, Adrienne could tell he was getting drunk. His posture was falling apart. He was slumped in his seat.

"How's everyone doing here?" Adrienne asked. Again, the empty glass of tequila had been pushed to the edge of the table, and Adrienne picked it up and held it discreetly at her side. "Would you like another?" she asked Luke.

"No more tequila," Grayson said.

Luke sank a little lower in his chair. Adrienne was afraid he might slip under the table. Darla, for the first time ever, seemed distressed. She looked at Luke imploringly, as though she wanted him to speak. He was not picking up whatever signal she was trying to send. She laughed.

"Well, I suppose I might as well say it. Adrienne, Luke would like to take you out to dinner on your night off. He'd like to take you to Cinco."

Luke put both his hands on the table and Adrienne noticed he was wearing a silver pinkie ring. What to say? That she didn't normally go out with men who had their mothers ask? Luke pushed himself out of the chair. "I have to piss," he said, and he propelled himself toward the men's room.

Darla pretended not to have heard this last declaration. She smiled at Adrienne. "I hear Cinco has wonderful tapas."

Adrienne glanced around the dining room. There were no emergencies calling her name, and there was no one available to save her. She lowered herself into Luke's vacant seat.

"Thank you for thinking of me," she said. "But I'm already seeing someone."

Darla put her hand to her throat. She looked stunned. "Who?"

Adrienne took another look around. She felt the way a criminal must feel just before breaking the law. She was going to tell Darla and Grayson the truth—tell them because she wanted to—even though she could feel indiscretion coating her tongue like a film.

"Thatcher."

"No!" This came from Grayson.

"Thatcher?" Darla said. "You and Thatcher?"

"That's a dead-end street, my girl," Grayson said. "A dead . . . end . . . street." He picked up his wineglass and swirled his white burgundy aggressively. "Let me ask you a question. Why would someone as beautiful and smart and *charming* as yourself pick someone like Thatcher? Don't you want stability? A house? Children? Don't you want, someday, to be one of these soccer moms with everything in its place?"

"I thought you liked Thatcher," Adrienne said. "I thought you loved him."

Darla put her hand on top of Adrienne's hand. "Thatcher is a dear, sweet fellow and one of our very favorites. But he's a restaurant person."

Adrienne felt her temper rear up, though she knew they had arrived at this place in the conversation because of her own stupidity. "So am I."

"Why, one of the first things you told us is that you've never worked in restaurants. You said this was just another adventure. You aren't like the other people who work here. You aren't like them at all."

"Restaurants are as risky as the theater," Grayson said. "They're as derelict as television. It's a volatile and transient life. It's goddamned make-believe."

"Honey, now you're being dramatic," Darla said.

"Am I?" Grayson pitched forward in his chair. "What do your parents think of this?"

"My parents?" Adrienne panicked. She didn't want to answer a question about her parents. She wanted to defend restaurant people and restaurant life and all the exciting, diverse, and enriching aspects of it. She wanted to tell them that she was as happy as she'd ever been in her life because of this restaurant. But instead, Adrienne did what any good restaurant person would have done. She salvaged the moment.

"I really love you two," she said. She flashed them her biggest, toothiest smile. "Thank you for the vote of confidence. And if I ever come across a good prospect for Luke, I'll let you know." She stood up and touched Darla's shoulder. "Your dinners will be out shortly."

Adrienne dropped off the empty glass at the bar, picked up her flute of Laurent-Perrier, and returned to the podium. The podium was her home.

At twelve thirty that night, Thatcher slipped through the throng at the bar holding the cash box and wad of receipts close to his chest.

"I'm going to eat," he said.

Adrienne had just finished a stack of crackers. Hector had brought them out to her, along with the news that Mario was still MIA.

"No news is good news," Hector said. "They find him in his Durango at the bottom of Gibbs Pond, that's bad news."

■

Forty minutes later, Duncan rang the hand bell. The decibel level in the bar increased; the frenzy for one more drink looked like the scenes shown on TV of the floor of the New York Stock Exchange. Guests' hands shot in the air, waving money. In her change purse, Adrienne had four hundred dollars in tips. Two hundred of it had been palmed to her by Grayson Parrish, possibly as an apology for his tirade, but more likely an apology for Luke's bizarre and ultimately miserable behavior. He hadn't returned from the men's room for a long time and Grayson was forced to check on him. Luke had vomited and was trying to clean up the mess with toilet paper. Adrienne sent Tyler Lefroy into the men's room with the mop (why did he get all the foul jobs, he wanted to know) and Grayson led Luke back to the table, where he stared down his ravioli but didn't eat a bite. *This is who you want me to go out with?* Adrienne thought. *This is your idea of stability?*

After last call, the bar crowd thinned and eventually disappeared. Duncan cashed out, tipped his sister, and poured drinks for the waitstaff and Eddie and Hector, who were waiting around for the meeting to begin. Eddie filled Adrienne in on the story circulating about JZ and Jamie: Jamie had found out from a Realtor friend on the island that the house JZ rented on Liberty Street went for three thousand dollars a week. In furious revenge, Jamie had bought a hot tub from Sears. Meanwhile, the director of Shaughnessy's summer camp called threatening to send Shaughnessy home because her tuition had yet to be paid. JZ was, in Eddie's words, "wickedly screwed" because Fiona had paid for the house on Liberty Street but JZ didn't want to admit that to Jamie, and Jamie had spent Shaughnessy's camp money on the hot tub. JZ had gone home to straighten out the mess and in the end, Fiona had paid the summer camp.

"Because she's cool like that," Eddie said. "She's the coolest."

Adrienne checked her watch. It was twenty of two. Her feet hurt. "Okay, people, let's go," she said. "Beach outside Thatcher's office."

They exited through the dining room and walked around the restaurant to the back door of the office. There they found Thatcher and Fiona eating Popsicles at a plastic resin picnic table. Fiona was wearing jean shorts and her chef's jacket. Her hair was down—it was lovely and wavy released from its braid—but her face looked drawn.

Adrienne and the rest of the staff plopped down in the sand and Thatcher called for the remaining kitchen staff—Antonio, Henry, Paco,

Jojo. When everyone was seated in the sand, he did a strange thing. He lifted Fiona up out of her chair and carried her toward the water.

"Follow me," he said.

The staff followed, including Adrienne, who couldn't help feeling stupidly jealous that Thatcher was carrying Fiona. Fiona screamed in protest, her head thrown back, her hair streaming in the breeze. It was a beautiful night, moonless, still. The staff trudged to the water's edge but Thatcher plunged right in until he was up past his knees. He let Fiona go and she splashed into the water and the water lit up around her like a force field.

"Whoa-ho," said Paco. (Adrienne knew he and Louis had been smoking dope back in pastry.) "That's cool."

Delilah was the next one in because she was young and unabashed about swimming in her clothes. She dove under, and again, the water illuminated around her.

Soon the whole staff, including Adrienne, was in the ocean, marveling at the way the water sparkled and glowed around their arms and legs.

"Phosphorescence," Adrienne heard Thatcher say. In the dark, she couldn't tell which body was his. "I didn't want any of you to miss it."

Thatcher had called this a morale booster, but Adrienne's heart was aching, for reasons unknown. She put her head under and opened her eyes as she waved her hands to light up the water around her. For weeks, she had been so happy she felt like her life was phosphorescent, like the space she moved about in glowed and sparkled around her. But now, this minute, that notion seemed silly and wrong. *You're not like the other people who work here. You're not like them at all.* The Parrishes were right, though Adrienne didn't know how she was different or why that bothered her. Her eyes stung from the salt water. She wanted to be swimming next to Thatcher, and what she really wanted was for it to be her and Thatcher out here alone. Just the two of them, floating in the sea of light. But Thatcher had brought them all out here for Fiona's sake. Fiona came first, and she should come first. She was a good person, better than anyone knew, paying for Shaughnessy's camp, tolerating JZ's manipulative wife. She was good. And she was sick.

The staff horsed around. Adrienne saw Duncan and Caren kissing. Paco grabbed Adrienne's ankle and tried to tip her over but she squirmed from his grip and dove under, feeling the material of her red T-shirt dress swirling around her. There was something about being underwater that made her feel lonely, even amid a group of people. When she surfaced, it was quiet, and Adrienne checked to see who was nearby. A man she didn't recognize was treading water next to her, and Adrienne became confused until she realized it was Bruno without his glasses. Bruno pointed at the shore and then Adrienne heard some of the Subiacos murmuring in Spanish.

A man stood on the beach, silhouetted by the light of the office. He just stood there at first, hands on his hips, menacing. *Police?* Adrienne thought. *JZ? Drew Amman-Keller?* But then, very slowly, the figure started to sway and the swaying became dancing. The figure was dancing in the sand and the Subiacos laughed and catcalled and Adrienne heard Fiona shout, "Get in here, Romeo!"

He came running toward the water, and Adrienne caught a glimpse of his face before he dove into the light.

Mario.

10

Dr. Don

TO: Ade12177@hotmail.com
FROM: kyracrenshaw@mindspring.com
DATE: July 24, 2005, 9:01 A.M.
SUBJECT: To Hell You Ride

The spores you didn't send me worked! I have officially Met a Man. Thirty-six, divorced, two kids. Sounds like my worst nightmare except I am falling, head over heels. Even worse, he is a landscape painter—but his work sells—some people pay more for his paintings than I paid for my last car. So although my mother is crying out about No Steady Income, he does just fine. In the winters he goes to Telluride and paints there and skis, and he's asked me to go with him. And I, in turn, will ask you (because I miss you, but also because I think you'd like it). Do you want to join us?

TO: kyracrenshaw@mindspring.com
FROM: Ade12177@hotmail.com
DATE: July 24, 2005, 11:22 A.M.
SUBJECT: It's July!

Since when do you plan more than one day in advance? You *must* be in love! I hate to admit it but I am not far from that pitiable state myself—this thing with

217

Thatcher is getting serious. Tomorrow he will meet the other man in my life—that's right, the good doctor. I'll let you know how it goes. As for this winter, I can't bear to think about it, but I'll keep Telluride in mind.

TO: Ade12177@hotmail.com
FROM: DrDon@toothache.com
DATE: July 24, 2005, 11:37 A.M.
SUBJECT: A quick (don't) pick-me-up

We fly in tomorrow—US Air flight 307, BWI to Philadelphia, US Air flight 5990 Philly to Nantucket arriving around three. We'll take a cab from the airport to the Beach Club and we'll meet you at the restaurant at six o'clock sharp. You'll eat with us? And what about this Thatcher person? Can't wait to see you, honey. Love, love, love.

TO: DrDon@toothache.com
FROM: Ade12177@hotmail.com
DATE: July 24, 2005, 11:40 A.M.
SUBJECT: Breakfast and lunch

Dad, I will *not* be able to have dinner with you. I have to work dinner—get it? As does Thatcher. So reorganize your expectations to include breakfast and lunch. Those are the meals for which I am available. Breakfast and lunch.

You guys are going to love the Beach Club. It's the best. Please tip generously as they know you're my father! Love.

"I shouldn't have invited them," Adrienne said to Caren on the morning of her father and Mavis's arrival. She and Caren were at the kitchen table, which, now that the weather was consistently nice, they had moved out into the backyard. They drank tea and espresso in the sun together on mornings like this one—when Duncan went sailing with Holt Millman and Thatcher left for the restaurant to give Fiona extra help. "No one else's parents come to visit."

"Mine certainly don't," Caren said. She had informed Adrienne early on that she was a casualty of the nastiest divorce in history.

Duncan and Delilah's parents lived in California and were too old to travel. Fiona's parents didn't like to fly. Thatcher's father was too busy with the stores. Spillman's parents were divorced like Caren's and remarried to other people with whom they had had more children (Spillman had a brother in kindergarten). Joe's mother, Mrs. Peeke, had come once years earlier and spent the whole time back in the kitchen teaching Fiona how to make the corn spoon bread that now was on the menu with the swordfish.

"In general, though," Caren said, "I think the restaurant business attracts people who, you know, want to escape their families."

"My father sort of invited himself," Adrienne said. "I couldn't tell him not to come."

"I thought you loved your father," Caren said.

"I do," Adrienne said. "More than anyone in the world."

"So you should be happy," Caren said. "Does he know about Thatch?"

"I told him we were dating," Adrienne said. "But there's a lot I didn't explain. He's going to ask why the restaurant is closing. He'll ask about Thatcher and Fiona. He'll ask about next year."

"Thatcher will be rich next year," Caren said. "That's an answer any father would love to hear."

"But what will happen between Thatcher and me?" Adrienne said. "My father will ask."

"Have you asked?"

"No," Adrienne admitted. "I'm too afraid." With Fiona's illness it seemed fruitless, not to mention unfair, to ask about the future of their relationship.

"Does he tell you he loves you?"

"No," Adrienne said. This was another thing she tried not to dwell on. "What about Duncan?"

Caren fired off a laugh that sounded like a shrill machine gun. "As far as Himself is concerned, I've resorted to desperate measures."

One desperate measure was this: At three o'clock that afternoon Caren was flying to Boston to meet her friend Tate for the second night of the Rolling Stones concert (they were playing three nights at the Fleet Center). Caren and Tate were then sharing a room at the Ritz Carlton. Tate was gay but Caren had not disclosed this fact to Duncan. Duncan, she said, was seething with jealousy—not only about Tate but about the sixth-row seats that Tate had procured from his very wealthy and influential friends. Duncan did not like being outdone in the wealthy and influential friends department, hence that morning's sail with Holt.

"It better work," Caren said. "I'm betting all my chips on this one." True enough—she had basically sold herself in slavery to Bruno to get him to switch nights off with her.

"Well, you're going to miss my father," Adrienne said. "Tonight's the only night he's eating at the Bistro." And that only because he insisted. The other two nights Adrienne had booked him at the Pearl and the Club Car. Thatcher had set Don and Mavis up in a hotel room at the Beach Club, where reservations in July and August had been booked for six months. Thatcher talked to Mack and Mack had a last-minute cancellation and so Dr. Don and Mavis were staying in a room on the Gold Coast. Adrienne had worried about the price, but her father seemed excited about paying six hundred dollars a night for a room. This was a very special vacation, he said, and there would be no skimping.

By the time she got to work, Adrienne's stomach was churning like Mario's Hobart mixer. There were 247 covers on the book. Family meal was shrimp curry over jasmine rice and a cucumber salad, but Adrienne couldn't eat. She begged Mario to make her some of his banana French toast with chocolate syrup—what she needed was some comfort food—and Mario bitched about the two hundred and fifty other people he had to feed that night. Since he had put the writer from *Vanity Fair* on a plane back to New York without a story, and since he had lost five hundred dollars for breaking his contract with his publicist, Mario had gotten good at bitching. He worked too many hours, he made too little money, he wasn't treated like the genius he knew himself to be. Still, Adrienne knew that he liked her.

"My father is coming in tonight with his . . . friend," Adrienne told him.

"Your father's gay?" Mario said.

"No," Adrienne said. "Why do you ask?"

"The way you said 'friend' sounded funny."

"It is funny," Adrienne said. "But he's not gay. The woman he's coming with is his . . . hygienist. She's his employee. Just please don't think it's my mother. Mavis is not my mother. My mother died when I was twelve."

Mario crossed himself then held up his palms. "I'll make the toast," he said.

But Adrienne couldn't eat the French toast either—her anxiety level rose to her eyebrows every time she reviewed the reservation book. The circle that stood for table twenty said "Don Dealey." Her father was coming to the restaurant tonight, stepping into her life for the first time since he'd flown to Tallahassee for her college graduation. Always she went to him. She liked it that way; it gave her control. This feeling she had now was a distinctly out-of-control feeling.

Thatcher joined her at the podium. "I missed you today," he said. "What did you do?"

"Sat on the beach and stressed."

"About what?"

"Do I really need to say it?"

"Your father?"

Adrienne nodded. She didn't want Thatcher to know how nervous she was because she wasn't sure she could explain why. Her father meeting Thatcher, Thatcher meeting her father. The disastrous dinner with Will Kovak years earlier festered in her mind. Why was her father coming to see her this year of all years? Why hadn't he come to see her in Hawaii when she was low on friends and spent most of her evenings wallowing in misery over her breakup with Sully? It seemed so much sager to follow the example of her fellow employees and keep family members out of the restaurant. She thought of how morose Tyler Lefroy had looked at the table with his parents and his sister. Tonight, that would be her.

"You haven't noticed my haircut," Thatcher said. "I had Pam squeeze me in because your father was coming."

Adrienne looked at him blankly. "You're right," she said. "I didn't notice." She checked her watch. "Five minutes until post time." She wandered over to the bar and Duncan slid her drink across the blue granite.

"So what do you think about Caren going to see the Stones with this Tate guy?" Duncan said.

Adrienne shrugged. "She's psyched about the concert."

"Yeah, but what about the guy?"

"He's loaded, I guess. He owns a villa on St. Bart's."

"She says they're just friends."

"Of course, they're just friends," Adrienne said. "You're not worried about Caren?"

"They're sharing a hotel room," he said.

"It has two beds," Adrienne said. "I'm sure that since the two of you are so happy together, nothing will happen with this Tate person, even if he is rich. And handsome."

"Handsome?"

Adrienne tried not to smile. "I saw his picture. The guy looks like George Clooney." She pointed to the row of bottles behind Duncan. "But I'll bet he can't make a lemon meringue pie martini."

"Thanks," Duncan said. "You're a pal. Hey, your parents are coming in tonight?"

Adrienne took a long sip of her champagne. "My father," she said. "And his hygienist."

Duncan looked at her strangely.

"My father's a dentist," Adrienne said. "He's coming with a woman who works for him. His hygienist."

Duncan smiled. "Sure."

Adrienne took another drink. This was more than half the problem—explaining about Mavis. There was no easy way to do it, and yet Adrienne had vowed that she was going to be honest. She would not pretend Mavis was her mother.

She heard Thatcher say, "You must be . . ."

Adrienne slowly turned around to see her father and Mavis standing by the podium. Dr. Don was a good six foot two, and he looked tan and handsome. He'd lost weight and he was wearing new clothes—a lizard green silk shirt and a linen blazer. Adrienne was suddenly overwhelmed with love for him. It was a love that had lasted twenty-eight years and had solely sustained her for the last sixteen. It was a love that was the ruling order of her life; she was able to exist only because this man loved her.

"Dad," she said.

He hugged her tight and kissed the top of her head, rocking her back and forth. "Oh, honey," he said. Adrienne hid her face in the soft material of his shirt. "I forget just how much I miss you." He held her apart. "Smile."

She had brushed and flossed when she first got to work because she knew he would ask. He always did. She smiled, but when she smiled she felt like she might cry. She took a deep breath and regarded Mavis, who was beaming at her. No, this was not her mother, but Mavis was, at least, familiar. She had the same haircut, the same frosted coral lipstick, the same minty smell as Adrienne kissed the side of her mouth. She wore a red dress with gold buttons—that was new.

"Mavis, hi."

"Hi, doll." The same vaguely annoying nickname: doll. Mavis called everyone by diminutives: doll, baby doll, sweetie, sugar, honey pie. Except for Adrienne's father whom she called "the doctor," when she was speaking about him, and "Donald," when she was speaking to him.

Adrienne felt a light hand on her lower back and she remembered Thatcher. Thatcher, the restaurant, her job.

"Daddy, Mavis, this is Thatcher Smith, owner of the Blue Bistro. Thatcher, my father, Don Dealey, and Mavis Laroux."

"We just met," Thatcher said. He glanced from Adrienne to Don and back again. "I wish I could say I saw a family resemblance."

Don laughed. "Adrienne looks like my late wife," he said. He turned to Mavis. "Doesn't she?"

Mavis nodded solemnly. "Spitting image."

Adrienne plucked two menus from the podium. "Okay, well," she said. "Since you're here, you might as well sit. Follow me." She walked through the dining room to table twenty, wobbling a little in her heels. Something felt off. She tried to think: Her father was definitely at table twenty. She would seat him, give him a menu, and have Spillman get him a drink. Thatcher would put in the VIP order. Fine. The restaurant was sparkling and elegant. Rex played "What a Wonderful World."

"This place is not to be believed," Mavis said. "And our hotel room! Adrienne, doll, you are a marvel. It's the nicest room I have ever stayed in."

"Good," Adrienne said. "I'm glad you like it."

"We don't like it," Don said. "We love it." He pulled a chair out for Mavis, then he sat. Adrienne stood behind them with the menus. Something still was not right; she felt artificial, like she was playacting. But no—this was her job. She was the assistant manager of this restaurant and had been for two months.

When she handed Mavis a menu, she saw the ring. One emerald-cut diamond on a gold band. Immediately, Adrienne thought: *Mavis is engaged.*

And then she nearly cried out. She closed her eyes. *Okay,* she thought. *It's okay.* She pictured her mother's face—one eyebrow raised suspiciously, the face Adrienne got when she had asked for permission to wear eye shadow. When Adrienne opened her eyes, her vision was splotchy and she was glad she hadn't eaten anything because suddenly it felt like someone was holding her upside down under water. She wavered a little and her father took her by the wrist.

"Are you okay, sweetheart?"

"Sorry," Adrienne said. In her peripheral vision, she saw Spillman approaching. "I haven't eaten anything all day."

"Good evening," Spillman said. "You're Adrienne's parents?"

Dr. Don stood up to shake Spillman's hand while Mavis smiled at her Limoges charger. Adrienne had lost language. *This is my father and his friend Mavis. His hygienist, Mavis. His fiancée, Mavis.*

"We'll have champagne," Adrienne heard her father say. "You'll sit and have a glass with us, Ade?"

"Actually . . . no," she said. They wanted to tell her. They had come all the way to Nantucket to tell her in person. Meanwhile, Adrienne wished her father had simply sent an e-mail. That way she could have digested the news privately. But no—they were going to make her sit through it here, in front of them, while she was supposed to be *working.* She turned around—there was a cluster of people at the podium. "I have to go," she said. "Because remember, Dad, I told you . . ."

Dr. Don smiled and shooed her off. "Go. I want to watch you."

Suddenly it was like Adrienne was twelve years old again, in the school play. Peppermint Patty in *You're a Good Man, Charlie Brown.* Adrienne's mother had been in the hospital so Dr. Don came to the play with—yes—Mavis. As if to make up for Rosalie's absence, the two of them had paid extra close attention. After the play was over, they commented on Adrienne's every gesture; they remembered each of her eight stiff lines.

Act natural, Adrienne had thought then, and now. Leigh Stanford and her husband were in with friends from Guam—where did they find these far-flung friends?—and Thatcher's hairdresser, Pam, was in with a date. Adrienne sat a party of six women, then a couple celebrating their twenty-fifth wedding anniversary. When Adrienne glanced over at her father and Mavis, they were sipping Laurent-Perrier, studying their menus. Her father caught her eye and waved. Adrienne went to the bar and reclaimed her second glass of champagne.

Charlie, Duncan's friend, owner of the gold marijuana leaf necklace, was seated at the bar drinking a Whale's Tale Ale. He gave Adrienne the up-down, as he did every time he came in. It was one of a dozen things about the man that made Adrienne shiver with dislike. He smelled like very strong soap.

"This is her roommate?" Charlie asked Duncan.

"Yes," Duncan said. He smirked at Adrienne. "I was just telling Charlie about the stunt Caren pulled."

"It's not a *stunt*," Adrienne said. "She went to a concert."

"With another guy," Charlie said.

"A friend of hers," Adrienne said. She glanced back over her shoulder at her father. He waved. Scene where Adrienne defends her roommate's decision to share a hotel room with another man. "You have women in here every night throwing themselves at you. You hardly have a right to get angry."

"I'm not angry," Duncan said. "But I'm onto her."

"What's the guy's name again?" Charlie asked.

"Tate something," Duncan said.

"Tate," Charlie said. "Goddamned prep school name if I ever heard one."

"What I don't understand," Duncan said, "is why they're sharing a room. If he's so *rich* and well-connected, he should be able to afford two rooms."

"He didn't want two rooms," Charlie said. "He wants to be in the same room with your bitch."

Adrienne glanced at Duncan to see how he would react to Caren's being so designated, and Duncan looked at her, possibly for the same reason. Adrienne shrugged.

"You eating tonight?" she asked Charlie.

"I need a menu."

"Do you want something other than the steak?"

"Maybe," he said. "Why don't you bring me a menu."

Duncan pulled a menu out from behind the bar. Charlie pretended to study it, his brow wrinkled and threatening.

Joe set a highball glass on the bar. "The woman who ordered this asked for Finlandia on the rocks."

"That is Finlandia," Duncan said.

"She swore it was Grey Goose," Joe said.

"It is Grey Goose," Duncan admitted. His neck started to redden around the collar of his shirt. "We're out of Finlandia. I can't believe she could tell the difference."

"She could tell the difference," Joe said. "She's a serious vodka drinker."

"Tell her we're out of Finlandia," Duncan said. "We have the Grey Goose or Triple 8."

"You're making me look bad," Joe said.

Duncan threw his hands in the air. "What is this? Beat-up-the-bartender night?"

"Yeah," Charlie said to Joe. "Lay off my friend here. His woman skipped town."

Thatcher came up behind Adrienne. "The VIP order is up for your dad. Would you let Paco know we need three more?"

"Sure," Adrienne said. She turned to Charlie and eyed his necklace. It was the dog tag of his stupidity. "Do you know what you'd like?" she asked. "I'm headed for the kitchen. I could put your order in."

"I'll have the steak," he said. "Well-done. If there's even a little bit of pink, I'll be sick. I swear."

"Well, we don't want that," Adrienne said. She checked, one more time, on her father. He waved.

The kitchen was ridiculously hot. Fiona was drenched in sweat. "We're short our dishwasher," she said. "Jojo went to see the Rolling Stones last night in the big city and hasn't managed to find his way home. I don't know why one of these clowns didn't go with him, but they'll pay. Paco, when you're done with the chips, you're dish bitch. And Eddie, I don't want to hear one word about the weeds from you."

Paco and Eddie groaned.

"Save the whining for your cousin," Fiona said. "Maybe next time you'll clue him in on how to find the bus station." She glanced over at Adrienne, who was scribbling out a ticket for the bar: one steak, killed. "How are you doing?"

"I'm okay," Adrienne lied. She held up three fingers for Paco, who started slicing potatoes, muttering curses about Jojo. There was one order of chips and dip up. Adrienne took it.

"That's for your parents?" Fiona asked.

"My father," Adrienne said. The explaining was becoming tedious. "And his girlfriend."

"His girlfriend," Fiona said.

"Yes." There, she'd said it, and it sounded a lot less bizarre than hygienist. Girlfriend, fiancée, did it really matter? Adrienne's mother had been dead for sixteen years; her father deserved to be happy. Getting upset about this was as adolescent as partying too hard at the Rolling Stones concert and missing work.

"I'll cook for them myself," Fiona said. "They're on twenty, right?"

Adrienne was confused. "Right. But . . . you don't have to do that. You have other stuff. The expediting."

Fiona took a swig from an enormous Evian bottle. "When it's family, I like to do the cooking myself."

"Even my family?" Adrienne said.

"Of course," Fiona said. "Your family is our family."

Adrienne reentered the dining room slightly cheered. She liked the idea of her father as a shared responsibility. Maybe she could send Fiona to her father's wedding in her place. Adrienne delivered the chips and dip to her father's table.

"Hand-cut potato chips with crème fraîche and beluga caviar," she announced.

"Honey, this is too much," Dr. Don said.

"No, it isn't, Daddy," she said. "We do it for people a lot less special than you."

"Well, okay, then," he said, digging in. "Thank you."

Thatcher materialized at the table. "Everyone's down," he said to Adrienne. "You can have a drink with your dad and Mavis here. You can even order if you'd like."

"I ate already," Adrienne said tightly.

"You told me you haven't eaten anything all day," Dr. Don said.

"Sit and eat," Thatcher said. He put his hands on Adrienne's shoulders and pushed her into a chair. "I'm going to order you the foie gras and the club."

"Please don't," Adrienne said. "I want to work."

"You can work second," Thatcher said. "Right now you should enjoy your family."

Enjoy your family: For so many people this phrase was a paradox, as tonight it was for Adrienne. Still, she didn't want to throw a tantrum or make a scene in the middle of a very full restaurant so she sank into the wicker chair next to her father and Spillman brought over her drink.

"We should have a toast," Dr. Don said, raising his glass. "To you, sweetheart. You've done it again. This island is beautiful."

"And the restaurant," Mavis said. "I always thought restaurants were, you know . . . a seedy place to work."

"Risky, derelict, volatile, transient, goddamned make-believe," Adrienne said. "I've heard it all."

"But this place is special," Mavis said. "As anyone can see."

"Thank you," Adrienne said.

They clinked glasses. Adrienne helped herself to caviar. Across the dining room, she caught Leigh Stanford's curious eye. The curse of table twenty. Adrienne wished she had a big sign: THIS IS NOT MY MOTHER!

"Thatcher is so charming," Mavis whispered. "He really seems to like you."

"He does like me," Adrienne said.

"Do you have any long-term plans?" Dr. Don asked.

"Long term? No. Right now I'm celebrating my solvency. I paid you back, I paid my credit cards off, and I have money in the bank. You should be happy about that. I am."

"Oh, honey," Dr. Don said. "If you only knew how much I worried about you."

"You don't have to worry," Adrienne said. "I'm self-sufficient. Now."

"Of course you are," Mavis said.

"I keep your picture in my examining room," he said. "Everyone asks about you. And I tell them all about my beautiful daughter who lives in . . . Hawaii, Thailand, Aspen, Nantucket. They always ask if you're married or if you have children . . ."

"And you tell them no."

"And I tell them no."

"But you want to tell them yes. You want me to be a soccer mom with everything in its place."

"No, honey."

"Well, what then?"

"I want you to be happy," he said.

"I am happy," Adrienne snarled.

"Good," Mavis said, and Adrienne saw her hand land on Dr. Don's arm. As if to say, *Enough already, Donald!* This was a sad state of affairs. There was no one to come to Adrienne's defense except for Mavis.

"Anyway, how's Maryland?" Adrienne asked. "You like it?"

"Oh, yes!" Mavis said, clearly relieved at the shift in topic. "You're a doll to ask."

"Business is good," Dr. Don said. "And the eastern shore is something else, especially now that it's summer. A few weeks ago we went to Chincoteague to see the wild horses."

"We didn't actually see any," Mavis said.

"I think we might stay in Maryland awhile," Dr. Don said. "Settle in. I'm too old to keep moving around so much."

These words had the same effect on Adrienne as a drum roll. *Just say it!* she thought. She wanted it over with. Spillman approached with the appetizers. Foie gras for Adrienne, corn chowder for Dr. Don, the Caesar, no anchovies, for Mavis. Spillman twisted the pepper mill over everyone's plates.

"Can I bring you anything else right now?" he asked.

"Kamikaze shot," Adrienne said. She stared at him, thinking: *Get me out of here!* Then, finally, she smiled. "Only kidding."

Spillman's facade never cracked. The man was a professional. "Enjoy your food," he said.

The sun was a juicy pink as it sank toward the water. Rex played "As Time Goes By." The foie gras was good enough to shift Adrienne's mood from despondent to merely poor. It was deliciously fatty, a heavenly richness balanced by the sweet roasted figs. Who wanted to be married and have children when she could be eating foie gras like this with a front-row seat for the sunset? Adrienne forgot her manners. She devoured her appetizer in five lusty bites, and then she helped herself to more caviar. She was *starving*.

Dr. Don took soup into his spoon back-to-front, the way Adrienne's mother had taught her eighty-two years earlier. Adrienne tried to imagine what her mother would think about her father and Mavis getting married. It was impossible to imagine Rosalie feeling betrayed or hurt. *Sixteen years,* she would say. *What took you so long?* Adrienne couldn't stage a protest to the marriage on her mother's behalf. She would have to claim responsibility herself. She didn't want her father to get married because then he wouldn't belong to her anymore. By marrying Mavis, he would be calling an end to their sixteen-year mourning period. Rapping the gavel. *Time to move on!* Easy enough when it was your wife, but there was no way to replace your mother. Had he bothered to think of that? There was no way to replace your mother. The hole was there forever.

"How are the boys?" Adrienne asked.

Mavis dabbed her coral lips with a napkin. "Good, good. Graham is at Galludet getting his master's in education. Cole is in California working for Sun Microsystems."

"Girlfriends?"

"Graham is dating a girl named Charlotte who goes to Galludet with him."

"She's deaf?"

Mavis nodded, eyes wide. "And with Cole, I can't keep track of the girls from one week to the next."

Adrienne pressed the soles of her fabulous shoes to the floor. "Do they know that you're engaged?"

Mavis put down her fork slowly as though Adrienne were holding a gun to her head and had forbidden any sudden movements. "Yes," she said. "They do. We called them last week."

"Honey," Dr. Don said.

A few tears fell on to Adrienne's appetizer plate. Here it was, then: the scene where Adrienne cried at her father's happy news.

"Congratulations," she said. She couldn't look at either of them because she was afraid she'd break down, and so she studied the band of bright pink sky hovering above the ocean.

"Honey," Dr. Don said. He reached into her lap and squeezed her wrist. "Both Mavis and I have the utmost respect for the memory of your mother. And we have respect for you. We wanted to tell you in person."

Adrienne could feel the gazes of a hundred and twenty interested guests at her back. She took a deep breath and said, "When's the wedding?"

"In the fall," Dr. Don said. "Just Mavis and myself, the boys, and you, if you'll come. Small church, a nice dinner out afterward . . ."

Adrienne didn't have to answer because Roy appeared to clear their plates and crumb the table, and although Adrienne knew she should introduce him, she was silent until he left.

"We're sorry to spring this on you," Mavis said. "I told Donald we should give you the news in private."

"That's okay," Adrienne said. "I noticed your ring. It's beautiful."

"Thank you." Mavis held out her hand to admire the ring, then she fidgeted with one of the gold buttons on the front of her dress. "I think I'll go to the ladies' room."

"It's by the front door," Adrienne said.

Mavis left and Dr. Don tightened his grip on Adrienne's wrist.

"Don't say anything, Dad," she said. "Please. You'll make me cry."

"Even if I tell you how much I love you?"

"Yes. Please stop."

"And your mother loved you. She loved you, Adrienne, and she was so afraid you would grow up not remembering that."

Tears splashed onto Adrienne's charger. She held her napkin to her face. For two months she had watched guests eat dinner at these tables. She had seen guests laugh, cry, argue, declare their love, tell stories, hold hands, kiss, and in the case of Lucy Elpern, go into labor. From the safe distance of the podium, this all seemed well and fine. However, sitting at table twenty was turning out to be a keenly painful experience.

"I remember," Adrienne said. To avoid her father's gaze, she turned around. Charlie was waving at her from the bar. He pointed to his steak and gave her the thumbs-up. Out of the corner of her eye, Adrienne saw the red of Mavis's dress coming closer and behind her, Spillman with their dinner. Adrienne waited for the table to settle. Mavis sat, and a minute later Spillman served. Did they need anything else? *Nothing he could bring them,* Adrienne thought. The plates were gorgeous. Mavis had ordered the lamb lollipops.

"They're adorable," she said. "Donald, will you take a picture of my dinner?"

Adrienne shifted ever so slightly in her chair.

"We can't embarrass Adrienne like that," Dr. Don said.

Adrienne took a huge bite of her sandwich. Guests took pictures of the food all the time, but somehow Adrienne felt victorious about robbing Mavis of this one pleasure. There would be no toast celebrating the marriage and no pictures taken at the table. Adrienne licked a glob of mayonnaise from her lip and thought about Fiona constructing her sandwich. *Your family is our family. Yeah, right.* Adrienne couldn't wait to get back to work.

It wasn't until two o'clock in the morning when she and Thatcher were safely in bed that she told him the news. By that time, she had cultivated the offhand tone she wished she'd had access to at dinner.

"My father and Mavis are getting married," she said.

Thatcher lay on his back, and Adrienne was sprawled across his chest. Sometimes they fell asleep like this.

"Is this good news or bad news?"

"Bad."

"Yeah," he said. "I thought so."

They lay there in the dark and Adrienne cried, free at last, and freer than ever because Caren wasn't home. She could make as much noise as she wanted, she could scream and yell, but she just sobbed quietly, wallowing in the childish sadness she felt. Sad, sad, sad—and not even really about the marriage. It was all the old stuff, too. Thatcher rubbed Adrienne's back and touched her hair and when she quieted and her eyes were burning and her throat ached, he kissed her and her need for him was so deep and overwhelming that when they made love, she batted herself against him furiously. She grabbed his red-gold hair and clung to him, thinking, *Can you make this longing go away? Can you fill up the empty spot? Can you help me, Thatcher Smith? You who do so much for so many people night after night, granting wishes, fulfilling dreams, can you help me?* She put her hands around his neck while they thrust together and then Thatcher groaned and fell back against the mattress with a soft thud but Adrienne remained upright, even as he softened and slipped from her.

"I love you," she whispered.

As soon as the words were out, she hoped and prayed that he was asleep—he did that after sex, fell hard and immediately to sleep. But she didn't hear him breathing; if anything she heard him *not* breathing. She wondered what had made her say those words, words she had never said to anyone before, except, of course, her parents. Then she thought, stupidly, of a Norma Klein book she had once begged her mother for, a book called *It's OK If You Don't Love Me,* whose plot Adrienne had long forgotten though it certainly had a moment in its pages just like this one. *I'm sorry,* she almost said, *I'm sorry I said that.* Except she wasn't sorry. She did love him and she didn't feel like playing games to make him say it first. She was being honest with her feelings; no one would catch her in a room at the Ritz-Carlton with a sham lover. She was brave, like Kyra in Carmel, making plans four months in advance to move halfway across the country with her landscape painter.

And yet, she listened for the catch of his breath. The room was completely dark; they always pulled the shades against the morning sun, which rose at five. So she couldn't even tell if his eyes were open.

"I . . ." he said.

Her skin prickled, her sweat drying in the cool night air. *Shit!* she thought. *Shit, shit, shit!*

"I love you, too," he said. "I've loved you since the first second I saw you."

Adrienne tried to speak but the noise she made sounded like water trying to pass through a clogged drain. What was he saying?

Finally, she managed a whisper. "You mean, in the *parking lot?*"

"My heart fell on its knees in front of you. *I thought maybe I could wait tables. Someone told me it was a piece of cake.* Your purple jacket. Your rosy cheeks. And then you inhaled that breakfast like you hadn't eaten in three days. My heart was prostrate at your feet."

"You're kidding."

"I've loved you since that very first morning."

"I don't believe you."

"You can ask Fiona," Thatcher said. "After you left I went back into the kitchen and told Fiona that I had fallen in love with a woman named Adrienne Dealey and that everyone else would fall in love with her, too."

"You said that to Fiona?"

"I did."

Adrienne thought back to her first conversation with Fiona when Adrienne told her the Parrishes wanted her to bring their bread.

Thatcher was right about you, then.

Right about me how? I mean, what did he say . . .

"Caren loves you. The Parrishes. Mario. Mario wanted to ask you out and I told him if he did, I would fire him. He didn't speak to me for three days."

"Stop it," Adrienne said.

"You think I'm making it up," Thatcher said. "I am not making it up. I love you . . ." His voice trailed off and Adrienne sensed the other shoe about to drop.

"But?" she said.

"But," he said. He rolled onto his side so that he could look down on her. "The reason why I haven't had a relationship in twelve years is because of Fee. There hasn't been time to think about anyone else."

Adrienne was silent.

"And I never met the right person," he said, quickly. "You, Adrienne Dealey, are the right person. I love you. But I love Fee, too. Differently. She's my best friend and has been for a *long time.*"

"I know that," Adrienne said, trying not to let impatience creep into her voice.

"And sometimes, I don't know how to handle things. I don't know who to put first."

That's clear, Adrienne thought. She could tell Thatch was at a loss, like a teenager trying to figure it all out for the first time.

"I don't have to be first," Adrienne said, then she checked herself. Was she lying? Was she just trying to be brave? What had she learned earlier that night? That being first or second had nothing to do with love, really. Her father loved her, Thatcher loved her. Her father also loved Mavis, Thatcher also loved Fiona. That was okay, wasn't it? It would have to be okay. "I understand."

"You do?" Thatcher said. He sounded unconvinced, but hopeful. "Do you really?"

"I do really," Adrienne said. She lifted her head to kiss him, and then, deciding she didn't want to talk anymore lest she ruin the moment or change her mind, she closed her eyes, pretending to sleep.

The next morning at nine, Thatcher and Dr. Don went fishing on the *Just Do It, Too*. Dr. Don had offered the fishing trip up to Thatcher the night before and Adrienne was sure that Thatcher would decline, but instead he'd looked beseechingly to Adrienne. He could only go if Adrienne covered the phone in the morning.

"Go," she'd said, though, really, the last thing she wanted was her father and Thatcher alone for three hours on a boat when the only topic they had in common was her.

She dropped them off at the docks in the morning. Pulling out of the A&P parking lot in Thatcher's enormous truck, she almost ran over a family of four. Lack of sleep. Nerves.

She drove out to the airport to pick up Caren, who had called very early on a sketchy cell phone line and begged a ride. *I don't have a dime left for a taxi*, she'd said. Adrienne found her standing on the curb in front of the terminal. Caren was wearing the same outfit she'd left in—her white jeans and black halter top. Her hair was down but tangled and messy and her clothes were rumpled. She looked like a half-smoked cigarette. And when she climbed into the cab of Thatcher's truck, there was a horrible smell: spoiled wine, rotten meat, a bad fart. Adrienne cracked her window.

"So," she said. "How was it?"

"I drank too much. Smoked weed. Did a line of cocaine. Took X."

"Does that mean it was good or bad?" Adrienne said.

"The concert was good. Are you kidding me? Sixth row for Mick Jagger? But that was the great beginning of something bad. I never even saw the inside of the Ritz. We left the concert and went to Radius. I had three martinis for dinner. Then we went to Mistral. Then a party somewhere in Back Bay where we all did coke. Haven't been that stupid in many, many years. Then to Saint." She eyed the dashboard. "I left Saint at six."

"This morning?"

"Choked down a ricotta cannoli in the North End. I feel lousy."

"So you haven't slept."

"Half an hour on the plane. I need a shower and a Percocet. My bed. Room-darkening shades. Six cups of espresso before I go to work."

"That would be a start," Adrienne said.

"Did you talk to Duncan? Was he upset? He didn't call my cell."

Adrienne gnawed her lower lip. Before she'd left the restaurant the night before, she had one more conversation with Duncan as he cleaned up the bar.

"I guess I won't be seeing you at our house tonight," Adrienne had said. "It'll probably feel weird to sleep in your own bed."

"Who said I'm sleeping in my own bed?" Duncan said.

"Where else would you sleep?" Adrienne asked.

"We're going *out*," Duncan said. He nodded toward Charlie who, after seventeen beers, was staggering near the front door. "Last call at the Chicken Box. For *starters*. And when you talk to Caren, feel free to tell her so."

But Adrienne had no desire to tell Caren so. Adrienne had too much emotional work of her own.

"Well," Adrienne said, "he asked a lot of questions about Tate."

"What kind of questions?"

"Just about who he was."

"You didn't tell Duncan that Tate was gay?"

"Of course not." Adrienne glanced at Caren. It was a hundred degrees out and the woman was shivering in her seat. "What do you expect from Duncan, anyway?"

"The same thing every woman expects," Caren said.

"Which is what?" Adrienne was asking because she really wanted to know. Thatcher had said he loved her, but now what happened? Where did they go? What did they do?

"Which is this," Caren said. She pointed to a white van from Flowers on Chestnut idling in their driveway.

Adrienne parked alongside the van while Caren bolted for the house. By the time Adrienne got inside, Caren had her face buried in what must have been three dozen long-stemmed red roses.

For me, Adrienne thought. *Thatcher? Dad?*

But the card was addressed to Caren. She held it in the air like a winning lottery ticket.

"He loves me," she said.

By the time Adrienne was ready to leave for work fifteen minutes later, Duncan was carrying Caren down the hall toward the bedroom.

"Don't ever take off on me like that again," Duncan said. "You made me crazy. Wasn't I crazy, Adrienne?"

"You were crazy," Adrienne said. She inhaled the deep perfume of the roses. Proof that there was more than one way to skin a cat. Adrienne wondered if her father and Thatcher were talking about her. Two hours left.

At work, the phone rang off the hook. Now that summer was more than half over, she heard a new desperation in everyone's voice. Or maybe everyone else was the same and it was Adrienne with the desperation.

Jennifer Devlin: I heard you're *closing*. For *good*? How many nights can I get in this week? And what about next week? The week after that? Just book me for any night you have open between now and Labor Day. Party of four. No, six.

Mrs. Langley: Hello, honey. You don't know me but I am a very good customer even though I haven't managed to get in once all summer. I'd like a table for ten Saturday night at seven thirty. What do you mean you don't seat at seven thirty? You always used to before. Well, at six I'm just starting to think about cocktails and by nine I'm half asleep. Can't you make an exception just this once? We'll pay double.

Harry Henderson: We need Fiona to come in and sign the purchase and sale agreement. She's holding the whole deal up, and you know these new parent–types. They're so sleep-deprived, they're likely to back out without warning! I don't suppose Fiona will come to the phone?

Darla Parrish: Sorry, honey, about the scene with Luke. He's normally such a good boy. And sadly, we have to cancel our reservation for tonight. Grayson has business back in Short Hills. And just so you know, Grayson won't be coming in on Friday, either. I'll be in with my sister.

Mr. Mascaro: Five people at nine on Saturday night. Heard my secretary wasn't allowed to make the reservation, which is the dumbest thing I've ever heard. Do you people want to lose all your business?

Kevin Kahla: Hi, hi, hi! I used to be the manager there? Now I work at Craft in the city? I have two *very good customers* coming to Nantucket this week and I told them I'd get them a reservation for Saturday night, first seating. Last name Gibson. Can you put them at table twenty and VIP them? Thanks, you're a superstar. Love to Thatch and Fiona, and please, please tell Caren there isn't a woman in New York as bitchy as she is—and that's a compliment. Ta!

Lana, personal assistant to Dustin Hoffman: Mr. Hoffman would like a table where he won't be bothered. Is there a back entrance? And he'd like to chat with the chef after dinner. He's been trying to do this for three years and since we hear you're closing forever on Labor Day, it becomes imperative that we get it done this Saturday. Tell me I have your help on this.

Cat: My sister and her husband are coming in for their anniversary on Friday. Would you send them a bottle of Cristal from me? I'll drop off some cash later. Thanks, girlfriend!

Mack: I need a party of two at six o'clock for Saturday. Name Chang. A party of six for nine on Saturday—name, O'Leary—and a party of two at six on Sunday. Name Walker. Do you want me to repeat that?

Mr. Kennedy: I have to have Saturday and I have to have table twenty. Party of four. Very big clients. Book us for six but we'll probably be late because we'll be playing at the golf club all afternoon.

Red Mare: You want to send your father and his fiancée a bottle of Cristal? I see them here—Dealey at six thirty. Consider it done. What's your credit card number?

Mr. Lefroy: Please tell Thatcher I'll be in for an official visit one morning next week. This is standard operating procedure—he doesn't have to tell me it's stupid. I already know that. In twelve years I've never cited him for an infraction and if I did, what would I do? Shut him down? Ha!

Mme. Colverre: I'm calling from Paris, France. Table for six for Saturday at six, *s'il vous plait?*

Leigh Stanford: Rumor on the cobblestones has it that Thatcher isn't happy with his attorney on this real estate transaction. Would you, delicately, mention that I'd be happy to take it on in exchange for credit at the restaurant. Speaking of which, we have friends coming in from the Ozarks on Saturday. Can we do an early table of four?

Ms. Cantele: Do you have vegetarian dishes on your menu? What about vegan dishes? Can you just read me the whole menu? That's right, the whole menu.

Mack: It's me again. I have to change Simon O'Leary's party from Saturday to Sunday the thirty-first.

"The thirty-first is Saturday," Adrienne said. Her brain was a swarm of names, dates, and times, as pesky as gnats.

"No, the thirty-first is Sunday."

"No," Adrienne said, checking her reservation sheet. "The thirty-first is Saturday."

"Reference your calendar," Mack said. "I'll wait."

Adrienne flipped to the front of the book where the calendar was pasted inside the front cover. The hair on her arms stood up. She felt like she was the one on a boat, a boat precariously keeled to one side, threatening to dump her in with the sharks. Her book was all wrong. She had been booking reservations for Friday on Saturday's page. She flipped to Saturday and was horrified to find it was full—and so all the people who had called that morning asking for Saturday had to be called back. There was no room! Adrienne scrambled with her eraser. This was awful. A hideous mess. How many reservations had she made today? How many really were for Sunday? This was her worst fuckup so far. This was worse than skipping a line on her SATs and not realizing it until the end of the section when she had one more answer than space. Now she had to call back nearly everyone she had spoken to in the past hour to tell them, *Sorry, Saturday is booked.*

Adrienne hung up with Mack and tried to channel her thoughts. Paris, France. Kevin in New York. Kennedy could eat on Saturday night but not at table twenty, unless Thatcher wanted to move him. Who else? Dustin Hoffman? Adrienne walked away from the podium. The phone rang but she didn't answer. She went into the ladies' room and, out of habit, checked her teeth.

The two of them were out on the water, talking about her.

When Adrienne next saw her father and Thatcher, they were walking down the dock like lovers. Adrienne was quaking. She had managed to staunch the bleeding of her massive trauma that morning, but it wasn't pretty. In the end she gave the three tables she had left on Saturday night to Kennedy, Hoffman, and Leigh Stanford and she called everyone else back to renege with enormous apologies. Mrs. Langley screamed so loudly Adrienne had to set the receiver down. Kevin changed his party's reservation to Sunday but at the end of their conversation he said, "This kind of thing never happened when I worked there." Mascaro threatened to call the chamber of commerce.

"It was a *mistake*," Adrienne said.

Just as she thought she might fill her pockets with tablecloth weights and walk out into the ocean, Henry Subiaco emerged from the kitchen with a mug of his homemade root beer.

"This is the best root beer I've ever tasted," Adrienne said.

"Next year," he said, "you work for me."

Now Adrienne was confronted with her father's hand on the back of Thatcher's neck as they strolled toward her. Grinning, faces red from the sun. With his free hand, her father waved.

"Did you catch anything?" she asked.

"Thatch caught a thirty-nine-inch striper," Dr. Don said. "It was a thing of beauty."

"Family meal tonight," Thatcher said.

"Where's the fish?"

"First mate's cleaning it for me. How was work?"

"I quit," she said. "I'm going to work for Henry Subiaco."

"That bad?"

"Worse than bad." She looked at her father. "We're taking you back to the hotel?"

"Can you join Mavis and I on the beach?" Dr. Don asked.

Adrienne checked her running watch. Twelve fifteen, one foot above sea level, and sinking by the minute. "I can. After I go over some work stuff with Thatcher. Say two o'clock?"

"Thank you, sweetie."

"You don't have to thank me for spending time with you," she said.

They waited on the dock until the first mate delivered a huge plastic bag of filleted fish. Dr. Don clapped Thatcher on the shoulder. "This is a great guy, Adrienne."

Three hours on the water and they were best friends.

"You're the great guy," Thatcher said. "I haven't been fishing in years. Thank you for taking me."

Adrienne stifled a yawn. Nerves. Lack of sleep.

Thatcher and Adrienne dropped Dr. Don off at the Beach Club and headed back to the restaurant. Adrienne tried to explain the train wreck that was her morning, but Thatcher seemed distracted.

"What's wrong?" she said. "Did my father say something inappropriate? He's famous for that."

Thatcher took her hand. "He wants your blessing. With Mavis."

"He has my blessing. I sent him and Mavis a bottle of Cristal at the Pearl tonight."

"That's my girl," Thatcher said.

"What else did you talk about?" Adrienne asked.

"Baseball. Football. Notre Dame. My family's business. I think your dad wanted to get a sense of me. I tried to give it to him."

"Did my name come up?"

"From time to time. Like I said, he wants you to feel okay about Mavis."

"Did you talk about . . . us? You and me?"

"A little."

Adrienne banged her head against the window. *What a morning!* "I need you to tell me word for word what was said."

Thatcher smiled. "That's not my style and you know it." He grabbed her knee. "Hey, it's fine. I had a really nice time. Your father is a quality person."

They pulled up in front of the restaurant. Fiona was sitting on the edge of the dory, crying into her hands. Thatcher hopped out and went to her. Adrienne stayed in the truck, wishing she could vaporize. Should she walk into the Bistro as though nothing were wrong, or approach them and make herself the most egregious of intruders? Sitting in the car, gaping, wasn't an option. She got out.

"Harry brought down the purchase and sale agreement," Fiona wailed. "And I *signed* it."

Thatcher sat next to her. "That's what you were supposed to do."

"So we're really going to sell?"

"It was your idea."

"Yes, but . . ." She let out a staccato breath. "Mario was right. They're going to tear it down. Next year it will be a fat mansion."

"It's better that way," Thatcher said. "Think how awful it would be if it were still a restaurant but not *our* restaurant."

Fiona nodded with her lips pressed together in an ugly line. She raised her eyes and noticed Adrienne standing there.

"What do you think?" Fiona asked. "Are we making a mistake?"

"That's not for me to say."

"If it were your restaurant, would you sell it?"

"If you had asked me a few hours ago . . ." But now Adrienne regarded the Bistro: the dory filled with geraniums; the menu hanging in a glass box; the smells of the kitchen wafting through the front door; the way the guests' faces glowed when they walked in and saw candlelit tables and heard piano music; the sound of a champagne flute sliding across the blue granite; the crackers—God, the crackers.

"No," she said. "I wouldn't."

"Thatcher is one great guy."

"So you've said."

Adrienne and her father were sitting under a canary yellow umbrella at the Beach Club eating sandwiches from Something Natural. Mavis was having a massage in the room.

"Your mother would have loved him."

"She loved everybody."

"True." Dr. Don popped open a bottle of Nantucket Nectars and studied the label. "These things are just filled with sugar." He took a long swill.

"So what did you and Thatcher talk about on the boat?"

Dr. Don leaned back in his beach chair. "Oh, you know. The Fighting Irish. His father's business. His decision to sell to his brothers. And the restaurant. It sounds like he has quite a friendship with this Fiona person."

There was an understatement. "He does," Adrienne said.

"She's sick?"

"He told you that?"

Dr. Don took a bite of his smoked turkey and cheddar.

"So that's why they're closing the restaurant," Adrienne said. "She's on the list for a transplant."

"Thatch seemed uncertain about his next step," Dr. Don said. "It hinges, I guess, on the girl."

"Girl?"

"Fiona."

"Yeah," Adrienne said.

"Which leaves you in a funny position."

"I've been in a funny position all summer," Adrienne said.

"In what way?"

"I don't know," Adrienne said, though she did know. She thought about it all the time. "Thatcher and Fiona have been friends since they were born. And Duncan has his sister Delilah. And the Subiacos, who work in the kitchen, are all brothers or cousins. And Spillman and Caren and Bruno and Joe have all been at the Bistro since it opened. I was worried when you and Mavis showed up because nobody on the staff seems to have a family. But that's because they're each other's family. And what I realized is that I don't have any relationships like that. Because we moved." She looked up to see her father swallow. "We moved and moved and then I moved and moved and so there's nothing in my life that's lasted relationship-wise. And that's strange, isn't it? I'm twenty-eight years old and there's no one in my life, you know, permanently."

"This may be pointing out the obvious," Dr. Don said, "but you have me."

"Yes," Adrienne said. "I have you."

Two days later when it was time for Dr. Don and Mavis to go to the airport, Thatcher insisted on driving them in Fiona's Range Rover. Mavis sat up front with Fiona's oxygen tank at her feet, and Adrienne sat in the back holding hands with her father. She didn't want him to leave. The Cristal had been a big hit—it brought Mavis to tears—and Adrienne felt saintly, bestowing her blessing.

At the airport, Thatcher stayed in the car while Adrienne walked into the terminal with her father. Mavis hurried ahead to get in line at the US Air counter. Adrienne's nose tingled. It was the school play again: teary good-bye scene.

"October?" her father said. Dr. Don and Mavis had chosen October sixteenth as their wedding day. Even though it was only two and a half months away, Adrienne wondered what she'd be doing. Would she be staying on this island or leaving?

"I'll be there," she said.

Her father put down his suitcase and hugged her. "I probably don't have to say this, but I will anyway because I'm your father. I want you to be careful."

"I will."

"He told me he loves you."

"Did he?"

"He did. And I took him at his word. But that doesn't mean . . ."

"I know."

Her father scanned his eyes over the scene in the terminal: the people on cell phones, the Louis Vuitton luggage, the golden retrievers. "I wanted you to get married first," he said. "I wanted you to be settled before I married Mavis. Do you forgive me for wanting that?"

"Yes," Adrienne said. "But I'm glad you didn't wait for me. I may never be settled."

"You will someday." He kissed her forehead. "I'm proud of you, honey. And so is your mother. You know that?"

"Yes," she said.

He picked up his suitcase and kissed her again. "Love."

"Love," Adrienne said. She watched her father join Mavis in line. Then he turned around and waved one last time, and only then did she let herself cry.

11

❦

The Sturgeon Moon

Sign hanging next to the walk-in refrigerator:

35 DAYS UNTIL THE END OF THE WORLD

Adrienne had been hearing about August since her first day of work. When the bar was busy, Caren might say, "It's busy, but not as busy as August." When the dining room was slow back in mid-June, Thatcher had said, "You'll be longing for this once it's August." What was it about August? *Everyone* was on Nantucket in August—the celebrities, the big money, the old families. It was America's summer vacation. Thirty-one days of sun, beach, boating, outdoor showers, fireflies, garden parties, linen sheets, coffee on the deck in the morning, a gin and tonic on the patio in the evening.

In the restaurant business, August meant every table was booked every night. Thatcher and Adrienne were forced to start a waiting list. If a guest didn't reconfirm by noon, he lost his reservation. There was no mercy; it was simply too busy. It was too busy for anyone to take a night off; the staff was to work straight through the next thirty-five days until the Saturday of Labor Day weekend when the bistro would close its doors forever.

"You want a break," Thatcher said one night during the menu meeting, "take it then."

In the restaurant kitchen, August meant lobsters, blackberries, silver queen corn, and tomatoes, tomatoes, tomatoes. In honor of the last year of the restaurant, Fiona was creating a different tomato special for each day of the month. The first of August (two hundred and fifty covers on the book, eleven reservation wait list) was a roasted yellow tomato soup. The second of August (two hundred and fifty covers, seven reservation wait list) was tomato pie with a Gruyère crust. On the third of August, Ernie Otemeyer came in with his wife to celebrate his birthday and since Ernie liked food that went with his Bud Light, Fiona made a Sicilian pizza—a thick, doughy crust, a layer of fresh buffalo mozzarella, topped with a voluptuous tomato-basil sauce. One morning when she was working the phone, Adrienne stepped into the kitchen hoping to get a few minutes with Mario, and she found Fiona taking a bite out of a red ripe tomato like it was an apple. Fiona held the tomato out.

"I'd put this on the menu," she said. "But few would understand."

In August, it felt like someone had turned up the heat, bringing life to a rolling boil. It wasn't unusual to have nineteen or twenty VIP tables per seating; it wasn't unheard-of to have thirty-five people waiting in line for the bar. The Subiacos had never done a better job—they cranked out beautiful plates, they made a double order of crackers at the end of the night, and they kept a sense of humor. The staff in the front of the house, on the other hand, started to resemble prisoners of war. Adrienne actually heard Duncan say to Caren, "I can't have sex with you tonight. I'm too tired." For Adrienne, work started at five fifty-nine when she checked her teeth, and after a blur of Beluga caviar, Menetou-Salon, foie gras, steak frites, requests for Patsy Cline, compliments on her shoes, and the never-ending question, "So what's going to happen to this place next year?" it would end with six or seven hundred dollars in her pocket and Thatcher leading her at two o'clock in the morning out to his truck where she invariably fell asleep with her head against the window.

And it was in August that Adrienne's nightmares started, nightmares much worse than a bushel of rotten peaches. She forgot coffee for table ten. She threw the contents of her champagne glass in Duncan's face and only when his face started to melt did she realize she'd thrown boiling oil. She sat down at the piano to fill in for Rex, then panicked because every guest in the restaurant was silent, waiting for her to begin. It was a *recital*, but she didn't know how to play. She crammed ten two-year-olds in high chairs at table twenty. She sent Holt Millman to the end of the bar line. She went into the back office to find Thatcher and Fiona having sex on Thatcher's desk. She got locked, somehow, in the walk-in refrigerator and when she pounded on the door with the heel of her Jimmy Choo sling back, nobody answered. The restaurant was closed. She was alone. She was going to die.

When strange things started to happen at the restaurant, Adrienne thought she was suffering from sleep deprivation. Garden-variety fatigue.

August ninth: two hundred and fifty covers and an unprecedented twenty-six reservations on the wait list. Special: whole tomatoes stuffed with a crab, smoked corn, and Thai basil salad, dressed with a lime-shallot beurre blanc.

At the end of first seating, Adrienne had a complaint from Tyler Lefroy. On the Tuesday after Labor Day, Tyler was headed to the Citadel for four years of military college—his father's idea. Tyler was dreading the end of summer. He loved this job, he told Adrienne. She knew he loved it because of the money and the crackers and because he partied after work with Eddie, Paco, and Jojo at the Subiaco compound. The actual work left him cold, though, and he was forever complaining.

"The guests have been stealing the silverware," he said. "And the plates."

"Stealing?"

"Yeah." He held out his rubber bin. "This, for example, is what I just cleared from table twenty-seven. A four-top. And, as you see, I only have three chargers. I only have three dessert forks. And there was a cappuccino at that table, but I don't see the cup or the saucer. Seem strange?"

"Maybe Roy or Gage cleared them," Adrienne said.

"They never help me out," Tyler said. "Nev-er."

This was true. Roy and Gage didn't like Tyler. They thought he was a smart-ass. They thought he *deserved* four years of military college.

"Maybe they did it as a joke, then," Adrienne said.

"Okay," Tyler said. "Except it's not funny."

"So you're telling me you think someone at table twenty-seven stole dishes."

"Yes."

Adrienne checked the reservation book. Table twenty-seven had been two couples from Sconset with houses on Baxter Road, the oldest money on the island. What was the likelihood that they had *stolen* dishes?

"The one lady had a big purse," Tyler added.

"Okay, Nancy Drew," Adrienne said. "Let me know if you notice anything else."

The next evening after second seating, Gage approached the podium. "I saw a woman hide a wineglass under her blouse," he said. "She walked out with it."

Adrienne stared at him in disbelief. She didn't know exactly what to make of Gage. Sometimes she thought he was a wasted life and other times she thought he was a good, though unlucky, man trying to make the best of bad circumstances by taking a job suited for teenagers. "Why didn't you stop her?"

He shrugged. "I just bus."

The following night there was a third incident. A well-dressed, middle-aged couple who had languished on the waiting list three nights running agreed to come in and have their meal at the bar. When they were through, they left money for their bill and a good tip, but absconded with the leather folder that the bill came in. Duncan was sure of it, because—*Hello, Adrienne, it's missing and where the hell did it go?*

"We're all tired," Adrienne said. But that didn't explain it. At the podium, her bowl of matches had to be refilled every two days and her Blue Bistro pencils kept disappearing. A count showed that she was short five menus. Five! She confronted Thatcher.

"The guests are taking things," she said. "Silverware, plates, wineglasses. The matches, my pencils, the menus. They're stealing."

Thatcher looked upon her with weary eyes. Of everybody up front, Thatcher seemed the most exhausted. And not only exhausted but sad. The sign that hung in the kitchen seemed to speak straight from his heart. His world was ending in twenty-five days. "Can you blame them?" he said. "We close in three and a half weeks. Whatever they took, that's all they'll be left with."

August thirteenth: two hundred and fifty covers, twenty-one reservations on the wait list. Special: oven-roasted tomatoes with garlic and thyme, served with grilled peasant bread.

Thatcher and Fiona went to mass at St. Mary's and were not expected in the restaurant until after first service started.

"Is everything okay?" Adrienne asked Thatcher when he told her he was going to church.

"She wants to see Father Ott," he said. "She wants to take communion."

"Could you go tomorrow morning?" It was bold of Adrienne to ask, but the restaurant business did not lend itself to five o'clock mass on Saturday.

"She wants to go tonight," Thatcher said.

After family meal but before service, Adrienne snuck into pastry. Mario had the ice cream machine running (special tonight: blackberry sherbet); he was melting Valrhona chocolate over a very low flame and reading *Sports Illustrated*. He had a garish red-purple mark on his neck the size of a quarter.

"Really," Adrienne said. "A hickey?"

"Girl I met last night at the Muse," Mario said without lifting his eyes from his magazine. "She was crazy about me. Said I looked like Antonio Banderas."

"Well, you don't."

"Okay, thanks," he said. He stirred the chocolate with a wooden spoon. "What do you want?"

"They're at church."

"Who?"

"Thatch and Fiona."

"So?"

"So, do you think that's bad?"

"No."

"Do you think it means she's getting worse?"

"Hospital means she's getting worse," he said. "Church just means . . ." He looked up for the first time, slapping the magazine down on the marble counter. "It means she wants religion. It's August, for God's sake."

"Twenty-two days until the end of the world," Adrienne said, and suddenly she felt like she was going to cry. Even if they were the longest three weeks of her life, it wouldn't be long enough. "What are you going to do when it's over?" she asked Mario. "Will you and your cousins try to open your own place?"

"We're talking about it," he said.

This answer saddened her even more. They were making plans without her. Everyone was: That morning, Adrienne had heard Caren on the phone with a Realtor in Providence, Rhode Island.

"Providence?" Adrienne had said when Caren hung up, only slightly cowed by the fact that she'd been eavesdropping. "What happened to St. Bart's?"

"That part of my life is over," Caren said. "It's time to move on. I have to get a real job. I have a degree in biology, you know. I could work in a lab."

"You're a scientist? I thought you did ballet."

"I'm too old for ballet now. I'm almost thirty-three. I have to get some structure in place. Some health insurance."

"What about Duncan?" Adrienne said.

"He'll be in Providence, too," Caren said. "Providence is not a place I would have chosen on my own."

"What's he going to do in Providence?"

"Work for Holt Millman," Caren said.

"As a bartender?"

Caren laughed. "You're kidding, right?"

So Caren and Duncan were off to Providence and the Subiacos were talking about opening their own place. Henry Subiaco had his root beer. Spillman and Red Mare were moving to Brooklyn; they were going to work for Kevin Kahla at Craft and start trying to have a baby. To avoid being stranded out in the cold, Adrienne told herself she could always go to Telluride with Kyra and the painter—or she could put her finger on the map and pick a new place. But what Adrienne really wanted was to go where Thatcher went and do what he did. He had cancelled the trip to the Galápagos, but no plans appeared in its place. Adrienne was left to speculate: He would ride it out with Fiona, whatever that entailed.

While Adrienne was lost in this train of thought, Mario picked up his magazine and started reading again.

"I should get back to work . . ." Adrienne said, but he didn't answer. He wasn't listening.

Adrienne returned to the front to find Doyle Chambers pacing by the podium. Adrienne steeled her resolve, then breezed around him as if he weren't there. She checked her running watch, which she kept inside the podium: five fifty-five, three feet above sea level. She rechecked the reservation book.

"Adrienne," Doyle Chambers said.

She held up a finger—*One minute*—with the authority (she hoped) of the conductor of an orchestra. Doyle Chambers worked on Wall Street. He was intense, he was fastidious, he was busy. He and his mousy wife, Gloria, rented a house in Quaise, and flew to Nantucket on their jet every weekend. Doyle never requested reservations so much as demanded them. Adrienne had sat him at least six times over the course of the summer and each time he had made her feel increasingly menial. The world was Doyle Chambers's servant. But not tonight.

"I called you three times and left three messages on your cell phone," Adrienne said. She glanced up to see Gloria, wearing a fringed shawl like a rock diva of a certain era, slinking around by the front door. "I made myself clear. Call back to reconfirm or I give away your table."

"Adrienne."

"It wasn't like you," Adrienne said. "But you didn't call me back."

"A reservation is a reservation," he said. "Do you understand the meaning of the word? I *reserved* a table."

"It's the middle of August, Mr. Chambers," Adrienne said. She breathed in through her nose and if she could have breathed out fire, she would have. "I gave away your table."

"No!" he said. His voice reverberated through the restaurant. Adrienne turned around. It was empty except for the servers who looked up from their polishing and straightening, startled. When they saw it was just Doyle Chambers releasing testosterone, they resumed work.

In response to his raised voice, Adrienne lowered hers. "Yes," she said. "Those, I'm afraid, are our rules. However, since you're here early, you're more than welcome to sit at the bar."

"Sit at the bar?" he said. "Sit at the bar like I'm someone who doesn't have enough *pull* to get a real table?"

Adrienne wished she could blink herself back into pastry with Mario, love bite, indifference, and all. She could watch the ice cream machine churn liquid into solid. She peeked out the window, hoping that Thatcher and Fiona had skipped the last hymn and Thatcher's silver truck would be pulling into the parking lot any second. Doyle Chambers never spoke like this to Thatcher; he only bullied women. Caren had refused to serve him years ago.

"*Pull* has nothing to do with it," Adrienne said, her voice practically a whisper. "If you'd like a table, you have to make a reservation, then reconfirm. It's a Saturday night in August. I have a twenty-one-reservation wait list. I called your cell phone three times. You did not call me back. I waited until two o'clock, which is, incidentally, two hours past the deadline, then I gave away your table."

Doyle Chambers snatched a pack of matches out of the bowl and whipped them sidearm at the wall behind Adrienne's head. Gloria Chambers slipped out to the parking lot. Adrienne felt someone by her side: Joe.

"I can't believe this!" Doyle Chambers shouted. "What is the point of making a reservation if it doesn't reserve you shit!"

"Hey, man," Joe said. "Lower your voice. Please. And stop throwing things at the lady. She's just doing her job."

Doyle Chambers glared at Joe and took a step toward him. *Fight,* Adrienne thought. Duncan rushed over from the bar and grabbed Doyle Chambers's arm in a good-natured, break-it-up way.

"Doyle," he said. "Dude, you have to chill. I'd be happy to set you up at the bar."

Doyle Chambers shrugged Duncan off. "I'm not eating at the bar," he said. "I'm eating in the dining room. I have a reservation."

"You *had* a reservation," Adrienne said. She was shaking, but it felt good to be enforcing the rules, especially with a cretin like this. He beat his wife; there wasn't a doubt in Adrienne's mind.

Doyle Chambers looked at the ground and said nothing. His face and neck were red, the part in his sandy blond hair was red. Adrienne thought he was collecting himself. She thought maybe he would apologize and maybe he would agree to sit at the bar. Duncan, who prided himself on being a man's man, would buy him a round of drinks and put in a VIP order. But when Doyle Chambers raised his head, Adrienne could see nothing of the sort would happen. He lifted his hand and Adrienne thought he was going to strike her, but what he did was more devastating. He grabbed Adrienne's reservation book and ripped out the page for that night, crumpling it in his fist. "No!" Adrienne cried. But before she or Joe or Duncan could comprehend the full meaning of his action, Doyle Chambers was out the door, pushing past a party of eight that was on their way in. Adrienne darted out from behind the podium and made it to the doorway in time to see Doyle and Gloria Chambers tear out of the parking lot in their convertible Jaguar.

"There goes my night," Adrienne said. "Literally. *There goes my night.*" One of the men in the party of eight looked at her expectantly; she didn't know who he was or where he belonged. Joe and Duncan stared at Adrienne with dumb, shell-shocked expressions. "What am I going to do?" Adrienne asked them. Joe retreated to the dining room to pass the bad news on to the other servers.

Duncan repaired to the bar. "Let me get your drink," he said.

Adrienne returned to her post behind the podium. Her book was destroyed. In addition to Saturday, Doyle Chambers had ripped out half of Sunday. Adrienne tasted the grilled sausage she'd had for family meal in the back of her throat.

"I'm sorry?" said the man with the party of eight. "We have a reservation at six o'clock. The name is Banino. The Banino family from Oklahoma."

A glass of Laurent-Perrier materialized at the podium and Adrienne felt Delilah give her arm a squeeze. She could do this. She remembered that there were three eight-tops first seating and Adrienne sat Mr. Banino at the best of the three, handed out menus, and said, "Someone will be your server tonight. Enjoy your meal." On the way back to the podium she wondered if she could call the police and press charges against Doyle Chambers. Attempted assault with a pack of matches. First-degree rudeness.

Adrienne sat the restaurant as best she could on the fly. The local author and her entourage were one of the other parties of eight and the author told Adrienne, a bit impatiently, that Thatcher had promised her a table under the awning, the table that she had already given to the Oklahoma contingency. Adrienne was flummoxed; she nearly launched into the whole long story because an author would appreciate the drama. You couldn't even put a character like Doyle Chambers into fiction. He was too awful; no one would believe him. But as Adrienne was short on time she offered to put the author out in the sand at two of the fondue tables pushed together. This solved the problem temporarily. Adrienne just waited for those tables to show up and complain about being stuck inside on such a lovely night. Call Doyle Chambers, she would say.

Thatcher didn't show up until everyone from first was down. When Adrienne saw his truck pull in, she checked her watch: six forty-five. What a night to be late. She tried to summon words poisonous enough to describe what had happened. She had quelled some of her rage by writing across the top of Sunday's ripped page: "Doyle Chambers never allowed back." Never in the next twenty-one days. *So there,* Adrienne thought. Take that. She would throw the remainder of her fury against Thatcher the second he walked in. He should have a computer like every other restaurant! He should make a backup copy of the book! But most of all, he should have been here where he was needed and not at church.

When he stepped through the door, he looked somber, verging on mournful. Fiona and Father Ott trailed him in. Fiona gave Adrienne a weary glance then vanished into the kitchen with Father Ott in her wake. Adrienne dropped her load. There was no one like Thatcher and Fiona to make her feel like the restaurant business really was not all that important.

"How was mass?" she said.

"Good," he said dully. "Everything okay here?"

"Sure," Adrienne said. "Doyle Chambers absconded with tonight's page from the reservation book, but I got everybody down. It's not perfect, but . . ."

"Looks fine," he said, scanning the dining room with disinterested eyes. "Father Ott is going to sit with Fiona in the back office for a while. Her O_2 sats are low and she's afraid she's getting another infection. She's lost seven pounds since we got back from Boston. The doctors want her in the hospital."

"When?"

"Tomorrow."

"Tomorrow?"

He flashed Adrienne a look she had never seen before. He was angry. "Well, she can't breathe."

This was enough to push Adrienne over the edge into hysteria. Doyle Chambers, the precarious state of her future: job, relationship, and all. And she was premenstrual. But Adrienne simply nodded. "Okay, I understand."

Thatcher backed down. "Sorry," he said. "It's just . . ."

"It's all right," she said.

"So let me see the book," he said. He regarded Doyle Chambers's damage, then whistled. "In twelve years, this has never happened to me."

"He isn't allowed back," Adrienne said. "If you let him in, I'll quit."

"You'll quit?"

"Yep."

"Don't want that," Thatcher said. He squeezed Adrienne's hand. "Let's get out of here."

"What do you mean?"

"We were invited to a party."

"A party?'

"At Holt Millman's house."

Holt Millman's house. Duncan had told Adrienne about this party a few mornings earlier over espresso. Holt Millman threw a legendary cocktail party every August. Two hundred guests, vintage Dom Pérignon, flowers flown in from Hawaii, a full-blown feast by Nantucket Catering Company, and a band from New York City. Every year people got so drunk that they jumped in the pool with their clothes on.

"Are you going?" Adrienne had asked Duncan.

"No," Duncan said. "I never get to go anywhere."

Now Adrienne stole a glance at Duncan. He had four people eating at the bar and he was shaking up martinis.

"We can't go," Adrienne said. "Who's going to work?"

"Caren," Thatcher said.

"You've asked her?"

"I'll ask her right now."

"And who's going to take her tables?"

"The other waitstaff can cover. Heck, I'll give Tyler and Roy a table or two. They've been begging me for one all summer."

"They have?" Adrienne said. This didn't sound right. Tyler, especially, would not want more work. Adrienne looked around the dining room. The waitstaff was humping—it wasn't even seven o'clock and Christo was sweating. Every single table was packed, food was just starting to come out from the kitchen. Caren was at table seventeen opening champagne, Joe was delivering appetizers. Spillman was at the Baninos' table taking their order. Adrienne wondered if Thatcher saw what she saw. "I think it's too busy for us to just disappear."

"I'm the boss," he said. "I have to get out of this place for a little while."

"You go, then," Adrienne said. She could sense he was about to lose his cool. "I'll stay here and cover."

"I will not go without you," he said.

"Thatch."

"We're going," he said. "It's just down the road. We'll stay an hour. We'll be back before second seating. They won't even notice we're gone."

He sounded so irresponsible, Adrienne thought he must be joking. He grabbed her by the wrist.

"Wait," she said. "You have to tell Caren, at least."

He took a deep breath, then made a face like a judge deliberating.

"Okay, I'll tell her. Be right back."

He pulled Caren away from a four-top and whispered in her ear. Caren did not seem pleased. She glanced at Adrienne at the podium. Adrienne stared down at her ruined reservation book. Why did there have to be nights like these?

Thatcher dragged Caren back to the podium. Adrienne chose not to meet her gaze.

"I'll just stay here," Adrienne said.

"No," Thatcher said. "You won't. You're coming with me or you're fired."

Adrienne rolled her eyes for Caren's benefit, but Caren would have none of it. She was pissed. The first thing she did was march to the bar to tell Duncan. *They're going to the party.* Adrienne said, "Okay, let's get out of here, then." And they left.

Holt Millman's house was located on the harbor side of Hulbert Avenue. It was a thirty-second drive from the bistro.

"See?" Thatcher said as he pulled up to the white gates. A valet came out to take his keys. "We could have walked."

Adrienne tried to exude nonchalance. She had come to terms with Holt Millman's wealth during her sail on *Kelsey*. But she had never seen a house or grounds—or a *bash*—like this one. She and Thatcher walked through the white gates onto a expansive lawn bordered by lush flower gardens. A tent was set up in the middle and there were people everywhere—people and tables of food and waiters in white jackets with silver trays of hors d'oeuvres and champagne. Adrienne took a glass and Thatch said, "I'm going to get a club soda."

"I'll come with you," Adrienne said.

She and Thatcher weaved between the clumps of laughing, chatting guests. The house loomed in front of Adrienne; it was the biggest house she had ever seen at this proximity. It had classic Nantucket features: gray shingles, climbing New Dawn roses on trellises, huge windows, and five brick chimneys. Adrienne snatched an hors d'oeuvre from a passing tray. She had eaten a sausage grinder for family meal but this food was too gorgeous to pass up. She stopped at the buffet table and dipped a crab claw in a lemony mayonnaise. Her champagne was ice cold; it was crisp, like an apple. Across the tent, she saw Darla Parrish and her sister Eleanor standing in front of a table where a man was slicing gravlax. Adrienne turned away; she wasn't in the right mood for Darla. She saw Brian and Jennifer Devlin talking to the manager of the Nantucket Golf Club and his pregnant wife. Everywhere Adrienne turned—guests! She looked for Thatcher but he was gone. She moved through the crowd to the bar hunting for his blue blazer. Nearly every man at the party wore a blue blazer, so she cast her eyes at the ground hoping to pick out his Gucci loafers.

Where was he? Adrienne experienced a twinge of panic, like when she had gotten lost as a child (the Christmas light show at Wanamaker's—her mother had been hysterical with worry). The panic gave way to guilt; she should leave now, escape, run down the road back to work. But mostly what Adrienne felt was curiosity, a pressure behind her eyes, urging her to see, to soak it in. Tomorrow, she would e-mail the details to her father.

Behind the tent, a slate walkway led to a tall privet hedge and through an archway was the pool area. The pool was a simple rectangle, dark and exotic-looking. There was a waterfall at one end. There were people surrounding the pool, another bar, more tables of food. Adrienne saw Mr. and Mrs. Kennedy talking to another couple and when Mrs. Kennedy saw her, Adrienne felt like she had no choice: She had to go over and say hello.

She positioned herself at Mrs. Kennedy's elbow. "Hello," she said.

The man Adrienne didn't know was telling a story. He paused when Adrienne spoke and looked at her briefly, then went back to telling his story. Something about a flight he had recently been on, an aggressive passenger, a pilot who had been sent back from the cockpit with pepper spray.

Adrienne was trapped at Mitzi Kennedy's elbow—it would be too awkward to walk away and yet no one in the circle had acknowledged her presence. So walk away. But then the man finished his story and there were *ohs* and *ahs* and then a brief silence. Adrienne touched Mrs. Kennedy's arm.

"Mrs. Kennedy, hello."

Mitzi Kennedy stepped back; it seemed Adrienne had caught her off-guard. She regarded Adrienne with a blank expression, and Adrienne thought, *I have sat you every week since the first of June, I have opened your champagne and chatted with you about your son's college applications, and I have bent over backward to give you a better table. Don't tell me you don't recognize me.* But sometimes, if you saw someone out of context . . . so Adrienne identified herself. "Adrienne," she said, "from the Blue Bistro."

"I know who you are," Mrs. Kennedy said. "I'm just trying to figure out what you're doing here."

"I . . ." Adrienne was at a loss for words. She smoothed the material of her dress and wished she was wearing something new. "We were invited. Thatcher and I. He's around here somewhere."

Mrs. Kennedy looked nonplussed. Adrienne considered drowning herself in the pool. She tried to catch Mr. Kennedy's eye—he was always friendly, friendlier than his wife. But he was deep in conversation with the man who had been telling the story about the airplane and he didn't notice Adrienne.

She drifted away in what she hoped was a graceful fashion, like a flower petal being carried off by the breeze. Who was she kidding? She qualified as staff to 99 percent of the people at this party and no one wanted to be caught chatting with the staff.

Her main objective now was to find Thatcher and convince him to return to the restaurant. She wasn't wearing a watch but it was nearly dark and she guessed it must be almost eight. They would have to be back by nine: thanks to Doyle Chambers, Caren didn't even have a book to work from to get second seating down. So Adrienne decided to return to the tent to track down Thatcher. Problem was, the Kennedys were standing on the slate path that led back to the tent and now, worse than almost anything Adrienne could imagine, they were talking to Drew Amman-Keller. Adrienne spun around and headed in the opposite direction, praying Drew hadn't seen her. She followed a path that led around the right side of the house—over a white shell driveway, through an arbor hung with grapevines, toward the ocean. This was the front lawn, which had a stunning view of the harbor: sailboats, Brant Point lighthouse, the jetty. Adrienne wished she could enjoy the party instead of negotiating it like a live minefield.

There were fewer people on the front lawn: several couples who, like herself it seemed, had strayed from the heart of the party and wanted to get a look at the water. Then Adrienne heard a burst of joyous laughter and she knew a group of people was approaching behind her but she was afraid to turn around.

Someone took her arm at the elbow. "Adrienne? My God, it's you, it's really you."

A wave of relief and salvation rolled over Adrienne. She wished Mitzi Kennedy was nearby to see the look of delight on Holt Millman's face.

"You must meet my friends," he said. "Frank and Sue Cunningham. Jerry and Ann Longerot. And certainly you know Catherine."

Catherine. For the first time since she walked through the white gates, Adrienne smiled. It was Cat. Conservative tonight in a blue seersucker sundress and flats.

"I can't believe you're here," Holt said. "I'm honored. I'm thrilled. I want to give you a tour of my house. Would you like more bubbly?" He took Adrienne's glass and handed it to one of his friends. "Jerry, your job is to get that filled, pronto. And bring Adrienne one of those shrimp puffs. Those are good."

"I'm fine," Adrienne protested. "Actually, I have to find Thatcher. We just stopped in for a minute. We have to get back to work."

"Work?" Holt Millman said. "No, no, no, sweetie. I'm not willing to let you leave."

Adrienne turned her eyes to the house. They were now standing on a gorgeous semicircular deck—another bar, more food. Jerry Longerot handed Adrienne a filled champagne glass and a shrimp puff. A tour of the house would take forever. It was not an option.

"I must find the ladies' room," Adrienne said. She grabbed Cat's forearm. "Do you know where there's a ladies' room?"

"Follow me, girlfriend," Cat said. "I wired every inch of this house."

They left Holt Millman standing on the deck. "We'll be back," Adrienne said.

"Because I want to give you a tour!" he called out.

Adrienne followed Cat to the pool house. Adrienne was feeling happier. The eleventh richest man in the country—the owner of all *this* and more—loved her. And she had found Cat, who was ten times more glamorous than Mitzi Kennedy.

"Where's your husband?" Adrienne asked. "Is he out back?"

"He's in Montana," Cat said. "Fly-fishing."

"Oh," Adrienne said. "I have to find Thatcher. You haven't seen him?"

"I've never seen Thatcher at a party before in my life," Cat said. "I didn't think he went to parties."

"He doesn't," Adrienne said. "This is an aberration."

They opened the door to the pool house. Adrienne heard a strange noise; it sounded like a hurt kitten. Cat disappeared into the powder room and Adrienne poked her head into the changing room. A woman sat at an old-fashioned dressing table, crying into her hands. Adrienne said, "Oh, I'm sorry," and the woman looked up. Adrienne saw her face in the mirror. Darla Parrish.

Again, Adrienne wondered why there had to be nights like this. Why had she agreed to come to this party? And why, oh why, had she strayed from Thatcher's side?

"Darla," she said. "Is everything all right?"

"Adrienne, honey," Darla said. She held her arms out. "Give me a hug."

Adrienne bent down and embraced her. She watched herself in the mirror. From the back, she thought, Darla could have been her mother. They could have been mother and daughter hugging. Gently, Adrienne released her hold. She heard the toilet flush, then water, then Cat's face appeared in the mirror. Cat pointed at the door. Adrienne nodded and Cat left.

"Is everything okay?" Adrienne asked. She felt herself slipping back into restaurant mode. "Is there anything I can get you?"

"I need another drink," Darla said, though Adrienne could smell the Southern Comfort on Darla along with her Shalimar. She eyed the glass of melting ice on the dressing table. Did Darla expect Adrienne to fetch her another drink? Maybe she did. Adrienne considered it, but instead she said, "Let's go out. I'm trying to find Thatcher and we can look for your husband."

"Grayson isn't here," Darla said, and she started to weep again.

"Oh, right," Adrienne said. "You came with Eleanor?"

Darla nodded, face in her hands. Adrienne plucked a tissue from a box on a nearby table and held it out to Darla. It was getting later and later; it might be as late as eight thirty. Adrienne started to panic. She had to get back to the tent and find Thatcher—if she couldn't find him, she was leaving anyway. Either way, Caren was going to be bitter and with good reason.

Darla dabbed her eyes with the tissue. "He's having an affair," she said. "He's been having an affair for twelve years."

"Oh," Adrienne said.

Darla nodded firmly as though Adrienne had just said something she very much agreed with. "One of my bridge partners back home."

Back home was Short Hills, New Jersey. Darla had cancelled once, and another time come to the Bistro with Eleanor, because Grayson had business back in Short Hills.

"I'm sorry, Darla. That's awful. Shall we try to find your sister?"

Darla gripped Adrienne's arm in a way that made it clear she wasn't going anywhere.

"Promise me you won't marry Thatcher," Darla said.

"Excuse me?"

"You're as free as a bird," Darla said. "That's always what I think of when I see you. Drinking champagne, in your beautiful silks, flitting here, flying there—you're a bird. Free, free. I wouldn't want to see Thatcher or anyone else clip your wings. Promise me you won't marry Thatcher."

"I can't promise anything," Adrienne said. "Life has too many surprises."

"Oh, honey," Darla said. She had a smudge of lipstick on the bottom of her front tooth. Adrienne nearly pointed it out, but she didn't have the heart. She excused herself for the powder room. When she peeked back in a minute later, Darla was gone.

At ten minutes to nine, Adrienne found Thatcher standing at the main buffet table eating stuffed mushrooms. She took his arm. "Let's get out of here," she said. "How do we get the car from the valet?"

Thatcher smiled at her. Something was funny about him. Funny peculiar.

"What?" she said.

"I love you," he said. "I was just standing here thinking of you and how much I love you. And I was also thinking about Fiona. Fiona is really fucking sick."

Discreetly, Adrienne surveyed their surroundings. There was a man replenishing the buffet and a couple of guests lingering at the end of the table by the crab claws. "I wouldn't say that too loudly," Adrienne said.

"It's true," he said. "She's sick. She can't breathe. Her lungs are polluted. They're a junkyard."

"Thatcher?"

He grinned, then pulled her in close. "This is a great party. You know how many years I've been invited to this party? Twelve. And I've never come. You know, I heard the band warming up. They start playing at nine."

"That's nice," Adrienne said. "But we have to go back. Second seating. Caren has no book."

"I'm not leaving."

"What?"

"And you're not leaving, either. We're going to dance. I've been dying to dance with you all summer."

Adrienne picked up Thatcher's glass. She took a sip. It looked like club soda with lime but it was the tail end of a gin and tonic.

"You've been drinking," she said.

"Yep."

"How many of these have you had?"

"Several."

"Several?"

"Yep." Thatcher took the glass from her hand and emptied it into his mouth in one gulp. "Come on, let's find the dance floor."

"No, Thatcher."

"Yes." He kissed her. As angry and agitated as she was, she succumbed. She'd had two glasses of champagne herself, three including the one she drank at work to calm her Doyle Chambers–induced stress, and she had a little buzz. For the second that Thatcher kissed her, she let her mind wander. How bad would it be if she just went along with this reckless course of action? Allowing Thatcher to get drunk and dancing to this band from New York instead of heading back to the Bistro to work second seating.

Caren could get everyone down with a little creativity; she knew the guests as well as Thatcher and better than Adrienne. How bad would it be to blow off a little steam?

Bad, she decided. The bar would be packed. They still had the stealing problem. Fiona was sick and the priest was there. As for Thatcher's drinking, Adrienne didn't know what to think. He once told her that drinking, for an alcoholic, was like falling into a river filled with raging rapids. It was easy to get swept away, to drown. So should she stop him? Yes. Get him a Coke. Or a coffee.

"We're leaving," Adrienne said. At that minute, she heard Thatcher's cell phone ringing. She removed it from his blazer pocket. She didn't check the number; the only place that ever called him was the restaurant.

"We're on our way back," Adrienne said.

"Don't bother." It was Caren. "I'm calling to tell you that Chambers's wife came in with the page from the book. Is it me or does that woman look like Stevie Nicks? Anyway, she apologized and I can get second down. Fiona and the padre left—she went home to sleep and Antonio said everything was fine. The kitchen is cranking the plates. We're all set. You stay and enjoy yourself."

"No, we can't," Adrienne said.

"Sure you can." And Caren hung up.

Adrienne slipped the phone back into Thatcher's blazer. Now what to do? Thatcher didn't ask about the phone call. He was too busy attacking the buffet table—tenderloin, crab claws, gravlax, mushrooms, cherrystones on the half shell. He held one out to Adrienne.

"Eat this," he said.

"No, thanks."

"Come on."

"I'm not hungry."

"Not hungry?" he said. He piled his plate with Chinese spare ribs. "This food is incredible."

"Okay," Adrienne said. "We can stay. But you have to promise me you'll stop drinking. You have to promise, Thatch."

He gave her big eyes as he gnawed on a spare rib. "I don't need to stop drinking," he said. "Because I feel fine. I feel better than I have all summer.

When the restaurant is closed, this is what I'm going to do. Party like this."

Adrienne surveyed the tent. Across the lawn, she saw Eleanor leading Darla Parrish out of the party. Home for ice water, aspirin, and bed. Adrienne was relieved. Darla's news was still ticking in her brain like a bomb that had yet to go off.

"If you feel good now," Adrienne said, "you should stop drinking."

"What are you drinking?" Thatcher asked.

"I was drinking champagne," Adrienne said. "But I'm ready for coffee. Do you want coffee?"

"No."

"Okay. We don't have to drink anything. We can dance. There's the band over there. Come on."

"I have to use the bathroom," Thatcher said.

Adrienne regarded him. She had no idea if he was going to sneak another drink and she was too worn down to care. She remembered back to a time in high school, her senior year in Solon, Iowa, when she snuck out of her house to go to a party in one of the cornfields. She drank beer and smoked a cigarette and after the party she sat in the back of one of the kid's vans and played strip poker and drank more beer. To recall the events in this way made them sound like fun, but they hadn't been fun at all because the entire time, Adrienne experienced fear like a cold hand gripping the back of her neck. She was afraid that her father would find out, that he would call the police and start a manhunt. At five o'clock in the morning, the kids she was with wanted to go to the Egg and I for breakfast and at that point Adrienne finally relaxed. Sure enough, when her friends dropped her off at six thirty and Adrienne slipped back into the house, her father was asleep. He hadn't realized she'd been gone.

She convinced herself that this was a similar moment. It was a Saturday night in August, it had been weeks since she'd had a night off. And here she was at the fanciest party she could ever hope to attend with a man she loved. If she got swept away in the spirit of things, who would ever know— and who would blame her?

Adrienne drank and Thatcher drank.

They danced. Thatcher spun and dipped her, and through the crowd, Adrienne caught sight of Cat dancing with Holt Millman, and a few minutes later, Cat dancing with one of the handsome male waiters. Only Cat.

The band slowed down. They played "Wonderful Tonight." Adrienne clung to Thatcher; they were holding each other up.

Someone tapped Adrienne's shoulder. She turned, a flash went off. Drew Amman-Keller had snapped their picture.

Thatcher recoiled. "Hey," he said. He blinked. "Hey, fuck you, Drew."

Drew Amman-Keller smirked. "It's good to see you out, man." He held out his hand. Thatcher and Adrienne stared at it. "Hey, come on. Adrienne?"

"Don't talk to her," Thatcher said. "Don't talk to either of us, you fucking parasite."

"Thatcher," Adrienne said. Her mind was fuzzy, buzzing television snow. "Don't give him anything to write about. That's what he wants."

Drew Amman-Keller bowed and shuffled backward off the dance floor. "I'm still waiting for you to call me," he said to Adrienne. "Callmecallmecallme." He was drunk, too. Adrienne looked around. Everyone at the party was drunk.

"Let's get out of here," Adrienne said. "Let's go look at the water." They stumbled through the tent (where coffee and dessert were set up), past the pool (where people were indeed swimming with their clothes on), and out onto the small beach in front of Holt Millman's house. They fell over into the sand, Adrienne first and Thatcher on top of her. Adrienne felt a shell behind her ear, some damp seaweed under her left leg. Was anyone watching them? Was Drew Amman-Keller going to take a picture of them in this compromising position? Thatcher started to kiss Adrienne in a sloppy way. She struggled to sit up but Thatch pressed her down.

"We're not," she said. She lifted her knee between Thatcher's legs. "Thatch, I mean it."

She had sand in her hair and inside her dress. Thatcher fiddled with her bra; it came unhooked. "We're not going to do this," Adrienne said. She pushed him off her and he fell heavily to the side with a grunt. His eyes were closed, his features were blurry. He didn't even look like himself. Adrienne poked him in the ribs harder than she meant to. She reached inside her dress to shake out the sand and rehook her bra.

"I want to ask you something," she said. She was feeling so confrontational, she scared herself. Off to the right she saw the red light of Brant Point, warning, warning. She had read somewhere that the definition of elegance was restraint. Adrienne wanted to be elegant—what woman didn't?—but it was hard to be elegant when her skirt was hitched up and her bra was left of center and she had sand in her ears and under her fingernails. It was hard to be elegant when she was drunk. Restraint was a good idea, noble, but at that moment it was too flimsy to hold back the urgency of her question. "Are you and I going to make it past the summer?"

Thatcher opened his eyes for a second, then closed them again. "I don't know," he said.

Later, Adrienne would call a cab and have the driver take them to her cottage, where Thatcher would vomit until sunrise and then fall into a comatose sleep. Over espresso the next morning, Caren and Duncan would berate Adrienne for letting him drink. "Couldn't you see he was in a dangerous state when you went to that party?" Caren would ask. And Adrienne would counter that Caren had granted them permission to stay and that was when things had gotten out of hand. Duncan would concede that Thatcher was an adult and not Adrienne's responsibility. He and Caren would pump her for details of the party and various images passed through Adrienne's mind—the crab claws, the dark-tiled pool, the smell of the powder room, the distaste on Mitzi Kennedy's face, the smudge of lipstick on Darla Parrish's tooth, the semicircular deck—but all Adrienne would really retain, the only part of the night that had any meaning for her, were those three words spoken as she buried her feet in the cold sand and gazed out across Nantucket Sound. *I don't know.*

The next morning, Fiona was at work as usual. Adrienne went in early to answer the phones and generally atone for her many sins of the night before. The only two cars in the parking lot belonged to Fiona and Hector. Through the window of the kitchen door, Adrienne saw Fiona behind the pass portioning swordfish. The restaurant had a Sunday hush, which was a good thing since Adrienne was suffering from a dreadful hangover. She poured herself a Coke at the bar and sat down with the phone and the reservation book. There were two hundred and fifty covers and a fourteen reservation wait list. The two halves of Sunday's page had been smoothed out and carefully repaired with Scotch tape.

Adrienne jumped when the door to the kitchen opened and Fiona came out. Adrienne wanted to ask how she was feeling, but she was too afraid.

Fiona set down a plate of toast, a cake of butter, a Ball jar of apricot jam. The same toast that Adrienne had eaten at her first breakfast.

"You didn't have to . . ." Adrienne said. "I mean, how did you know I was here?"

"I heard the brakes of your bike. You should have those oiled."

"Oh." Adrienne looked at the toast. "Thank you for this. I really need it."

"Yeah." Fiona stared at her and Adrienne attempted a smile. Fiona didn't look sick. She was wearing white cotton drawstring pants, a white tank, clogs. She was tan, she wore lipstick.

"I want you to have dinner with me tonight," Fiona said.

"Tonight?"

"At the table out back. Around midnight. Thatcher can take the bar while we eat. I want to talk to you."

"About what?" Adrienne said.

"Stuff," Fiona said. "I'm tired of Thatcher. I'm tired of him worrying about me. He worries so much that I start to worry and I made a decision this morning that I'm done worrying. Whatever happens, happens. To think that I can control it, or the doctors, or the priest . . . no, it doesn't work like that."

Adrienne sat, speechless.

"So midnight?" Fiona said.

"Yes," Adrienne said. "Of course."

The special was a tomato salad with bacon, basil, and blue cheese. It was a work of art. Fiona had found a rainbow of heirloom tomatoes—red, orange, yellow, green, purple, yellow with green stripes—and she stacked them on the plate in a tower as colorful as children's blocks. It flew out of the kitchen; by the end of first seating, it was eighty-sixed.

Adrienne didn't see Thatcher until five, though he'd called her at noon to say he'd woken up and, first thing, cleaned the bathroom. Then he'd gone to an AA meeting.

"I'm sorry about last night," he said.

"I'm sorry, too," Adrienne said. There was no denying the regret she felt about letting Thatcher stay at the party and drink. It was monstrous of her. The worst thing was, she had *wanted* him to drink. She had wanted to see what he was like and she had hoped that with his guard down she might wheedle some promises out of him about the future. But all she had gotten was the truth: He didn't know.

At menu meeting, Thatcher looked and smelled chastened. He was clean-shaven, his red-gold hair held teeth marks from his comb. He wore his stone white pants and a new shirt from Thomas Pink with cuff links. He had shined his loafers. He was professional, in charge, sober. It was time to move on.

At family meal, Adrienne ate only a salad.

Caren said, "On a diet?"

"No. I'm eating tonight with Fiona."

Caren's eyebrows arched. She said nothing, though Adrienne knew she was curious. Adrienne was not only curious but worried. She expected to be chastised for running out of the restaurant and allowing Thatcher to drink. Adrienne had no words to offer in her own defense; she was going to take her punishment. She had to admit, though, that Fiona hadn't seemed angry or perturbed that morning when she invited Adrienne to dinner, and so what really worried Adrienne was that Fiona might not even know that Thatch had been drinking, but she was sure to find out over the course of the night. Every time Adrienne went back into the kitchen for chips and dip, she expected Fiona to cancel. But Fiona treated Adrienne normally, which was to say, with complete indifference. She was expediting, the kitchen was brutally hot—so hot they had the oscillating fans going—and they were too busy to gossip.

"Ordering table four," Fiona called out. "Two Caesars, one crab cake SOS. Ordering table twenty-three, three bisques, one foie gras, killed. Another person who doesn't know how to eat. Jojo, baby, I need more of those square plates. Stop the cycle now and finish them by hand, please."

Adrienne inhaled the smells of grilling and sautéing and frying. Three weeks until the end of the world.

Between seatings, Adrienne stood with Thatch at the podium. His hands were shaking.

"Are you okay?" she said.

"Fine."

"Fiona seems better."

"I just hope she isn't wearing herself down."

"She thinks you worry too much."

"Ha!"

"I'm eating with her tonight," Adrienne said.

"Yes. She told me."

Adrienne wished the news had come as a surprise to him. But Thatcher and Fiona were like an old married couple; they shared everything with each other first.

"What do you think she wants?"

"A woman's perspective."

"Why not Caren?"

"Do I really have to answer that?"

"I guess not." Caren wasn't exactly the girlfriend type. "I just wonder what she wants to talk about."

"She didn't tell me and I didn't pry. I assume it's something that I, as a man, wouldn't understand."

Christo approached the podium with a pepper mill. "This thing's empty. I twisted it over a Caesar at table fifteen for, like, five minutes until we figured there wasn't anything coming out. Unless it's white pepper. It's not white pepper, is it? Because if it is, that old guy eating the Caesar is going to croak."

"Your former boss told me you were smart, Christo," Thatcher said. "That's why I hired you."

"Yeah, I know."

"There are peppercorns in the pantry," Adrienne said. "They're black."

"I don't have time. I thought the busboys were supposed to do it. I thought they filled them every night."

Thatcher nodded at the kitchen door. Christo went, huffing.

"Are you angry?" Adrienne asked.

"You mean because it's August and one of my servers hasn't deciphered the pepper mill?"

"No, because I'm eating with Fiona."

"No."

"You're sure?"

"Yes."

By midnight, Adrienne was starving. The crackers came out and she could have eaten the whole basket. But she held herself to two, then two more the next time Louis passed by. She longingly contemplated two more, but then she saw Thatcher coming toward her with the cash box and receipts. He was smiling.

"Lots of expensive wine tonight. Table twenty-six ordered two bottles of the Chateau Margaux. I don't even know who those people are, do you?"

Adrienne checked the book. "Beach Club. Mack sent them."

"Guy knew his wine."

"Mack said he was a doctor in Aspen."

"You know him?"

"No. Duncan knows him. Can I go?"

"You can go."

"And what will you eat? Are they sending something out?"

"I'll be fine," he said. "Go."

"Are you sure, because . . ."

"Adrienne," Thatcher said. "Go."

It felt awkward, like a first date. Fiona was in the walk-in checking inventory, telling Antonio what she needed to get up at the farm and what they should order from Sid Wainer. Adrienne poked her head in and said, "I'm here."

Fiona looked confused, sweaty, and pale. Then, it seemed, she remembered. "What do you want to eat?" she said.

Adrienne was so hungry she would have eaten straight from the industrial-sized container of sour cream on the shelf in her line of vision. "I don't know," Adrienne said. "What are you having?"

"What I'm having is neither here nor there. You should order what you want. You know the menu?"

"Yes." Already, Adrienne felt like this was a test she was failing. *Think,* she implored her brain. *What did she want for dinner?* "Steak frites. Actually, no, the crab cake."

"Start with the crab cake. Then you can have the steak. What temp?"

"Rare."

Fiona looked sideways at Antonio. "Got that?"

"Yes, chef," he said. "You feel okay?"

"I'll just have some bisque," Fiona said. She wiped her forehead with a side towel. "I may not come in tomorrow."

"I'm making you a sandwich, too," Antonio said. "You have to eat."

Fiona shooed Antonio out of the walk-in. "All these men telling me what to do," she said. "Did you bring a drink from the front?" she asked Adrienne.

Adrienne held up her champagne. "Would you like anything?"

"I drink water," Fiona said. "Wait for me outside. I'll be just a minute."

Adrienne got a glass of ice water with lemon and carried it out to the plastic picnic table. It was another lovely night. The full moon lit up the whole beach; Adrienne could see her shadow in the sand. She sat in one of the plastic chairs. It was peaceful here. The noise from the bar was reduced to a faint bass line.

Adrienne waited for what seemed like an eternity—she was nervous and hungry—but then Fiona appeared holding two plates and two sets of silverware. She had taken off her chef's jacket to show a white tank top underneath and had let her hair down. Adrienne rose to help her.

"The crab cakes," Fiona said. "Go ahead and sit. I sent Jojo to the bar to get us a bottle of champagne."

"You did?"

"I decided I want some. I haven't had a drink in forever."

Adrienne sat down, staring at the two plump, golden brown crab cakes floating in a pool of Dijon cream. She restrained herself until Fiona sat, then she took a bite, and another. Then, she felt, she had to confess.

"Thatcher was drinking last night," Adrienne said.

"He told me."

"He started while I wasn't looking. I was . . . off somewhere."

"But once you got back, you asked him to stop?"

"I asked him. He didn't stop."

"Of course he didn't," Fiona said. "He's an alcoholic."

"I know."

"Do you know? It's a disease. Thatcher has a disease just like I have a disease."

"I wasn't sure what to do," Adrienne said. "I didn't know anybody at the party except for guests and I didn't feel like I could ask a guest for help."

"It's okay," Fiona said. "I don't mean to scold you."

"But I feel awful . . ."

"Don't," Fiona said. "It's not your fault. It's my fault. I'm the reason why he drinks. I'm the albatross around his neck."

"No, you're not," Adrienne said.

"Yes, I am," Fiona said, in a voice that ended the topic.

Adrienne took another bite of her crab cake and gazed at the water. Next to her, Fiona spooned soup in tiny bites. Adrienne looked at Fiona's hands. There was something funny about her fingers. They were clubbed on the ends and her nails were bluish. Fiona caught Adrienne staring, and Adrienne looked at the sky.

"Full moon," she noted.

"The Native Americans call it the sturgeon moon in August," Fiona said. "That's one of the useless things I happen to know."

Fiona was sweating despite the breeze; she looked sick for the first time to Adrienne, but sick like a normal person, like she might vomit or faint. She took a huge breath and Adrienne could hear the struggle it took to get air in. Then Fiona coughed. She coughed and coughed until her eyes were watering and it looked like her face was falling apart. Adrienne didn't know what to do. Was this the time to call the ambulance? Just then Jojo came out with a bottle of Laurent-Perrier. He set the bottle down and walloped Fiona on the back, like it was the most normal action in the world.

"You okay, chef?" he said.

She coughed a bit more then stood up, moved into the shadows, and spat. When she came back, her face was dark red. "Sorry," she said.

"Please don't worry," Adrienne said. "Would you like some water?"

Fiona chugged the whole glass of water. "Thanks for the bubbly," she said.

"No prob," Jojo said. He was the only Subiaco who was still boyish. Adrienne loved his long eyelashes and his slow smile. He was what a Subiaco looked like before he became smooth like Mario or capable like Antonio or gross like Hector. "I'm going to call it a night."

"Okay," Fiona said. "See you tomorrow."

Jojo left and Fiona reached for the champagne. Gently, Adrienne took the bottle from her, opened it with the softest pop, and poured two glasses.

It might be worse for Adrienne to drink with Fiona than it had been for her to drink with Thatcher. She had no idea. But Fiona seemed eager—she raised her glass in Adrienne's direction and took a long sip.

"How's JZ?" Adrienne asked.

"Married."

"Married," Adrienne agreed. "But you can't doubt that he loves you."

"Sure I can."

"He loves you."

"Yes. But it's not enough. I want him to marry me."

"Oh."

Fiona took another drink and pushed her soup bowl away; she'd barely eaten anything. "You will, no doubt, find this surprising, but I am a big believer in marriage."

"Are you?"

"My whole life that's all I've ever wanted—to be married and have kids. Probably because I've been told since I was young that those two things would never happen. No kids, certainly. My body couldn't handle it. And probably no marriage. No one wants damaged goods."

"Fiona . . ."

"It's true," she said flatly. "If JZ really wanted to, he would have gotten a divorce. He would have taken Shaughnessy and left that awful woman. *Jamie.* She's manipulative and dishonest. But she's not damaged. He doesn't make love to her like she might break."

"Fiona."

"Even if I get off the damn transplant list, there's no guarantee that I'll survive the operation, and if I do survive, they give me another five years. Five years is hardly worth leaving your wife over."

Antonio appeared at the table with their entrées. He set down the steak frites for Adrienne and a grilled cheese and tomato sandwich with frites and a dill pickle for Fiona.

"I'm going home, Fee," he said. "Take tomorrow off, if you want. I can do the special."

"What would you do?" she asked.

"Those tomato flans," he said. "With a red pepper coulis."

"Okay," Fiona said. "Thanks for dinner."

"Yes, thank you," Adrienne said.

Antonio kissed the top of Fiona's head like she was indeed someone who might break. He nodded at Adrienne and disappeared back into the kitchen.

"I don't want you to feel sorry for me," Fiona said. "Because I have things in my life other than JZ. I'm a damn good chef. I have a devoted staff. I've had my own restaurant since I've been twenty-four years old and I'm a woman, okay? It's unheard-of."

"You're the best," Adrienne said.

"You're trying to flatter me," Fiona said. "But I *am* the best. I never wanted to be famous. I never wanted to have my own TV show or my own cookbook or a line of salad dressings. I just wanted to be the best, pure and simple. Next year, when this restaurant is closed there won't be anyone on this island or anywhere else who does things the way we do them. It ends with us."

"You're right," Adrienne said.

"You're still trying to flatter me," Fiona said. "But I *am* right. And that's what I've always wanted, too. Immortality. When I die, I want people to say, 'Nobody cooks like Fiona Kemp anymore. Nobody makes foie gras like Fiona. Nobody makes shrimp bisque like Fiona.'" She slammed back the remainder of her champagne and narrowed her blue eyes. "All these years I've been claiming I cook out of love. But I don't. I've been cooking out of ambition."

"That's okay," Adrienne said. "Ambition is okay."

"Love would have been better," Fiona said.

Somehow they made it to the bottom of the champagne bottle. Adrienne couldn't believe her eyes when she saw Fiona empty the last drops into her glass. Suddenly, Adrienne became aware of certain things: she had finished her steak frites, though she barely remembered eating them. Behind her, the restaurant was quiet and dark, though she didn't recall seeing the lights go off and no one had come out to check on them. According to Adrienne's running watch, it was five past two. Everyone had gone home, including, Adrienne presumed, Thatcher. For the last who-knew-how-long, Adrienne had been talking about herself in a way that used to make her shudder. She was giving herself up, turning herself over. She wanted Fiona to know her.

On the subject of her mother, Adrienne said: *She was a lovely person. The loveliest. Gracious, kind, funny. She died when I was twelve of ovarian cancer.*

I'm sorry, Fiona said. *Do you worry that you'll get it?*

Get what?

Cancer.

No.

On the subject of her father: *He's getting married again after sixteen years. To the woman he brought here, Mavis.*

Will you go to the wedding?

Yes.

When will that be?

October sixteenth.

Oh, Fiona said. *That's my birthday. I'll be thirty-six.*

This was followed by a space of silence.

On the subject of her travels: *My favorite place aside from Nantucket has been Thailand.*

Never been, Fiona said. *Never been anywhere. Not going anywhere.*

Right before Adrienne became aware of the time, she had been regaling Fiona with the story of Doug, the cocaine, the theft of Adrienne's Future, the arrest. Fiona was shaking her head, coughing. She drank some water, then she poured the last of the champagne, and watching it dribble out of the bottle snapped Adrienne out of her reverie. And Fiona, too, because she said, "I think we should talk about Thatcher."

"Should we?" Adrienne said. She was drunk now—*again*—and talking about Thatcher sounded like a bad idea. And yet, the tone of Fiona's voice made it seem like this had been the point of the whole dinner: to talk about Thatcher.

"We should," Fiona said. Her long hair hung over the back of her chair and her face had regained its color—lightly suntanned with freckles across her nose. Adrienne felt her eyes drooping, but Fiona seemed as alert as ever. Alert, intense, focused. What was the first thing Thatch had ever said about her? *My partner, Fiona. She never sleeps.*

"Go ahead," Adrienne said with a grand sweep of her hand. "Talk."

Fiona fidgeted with the crusts of bread on her plate. She'd eaten nearly the whole sandwich and half the pickle. "I've never talked to one of Thatcher's girlfriends like this before," she said.

"He told me he didn't have girlfriends."

"He had a girlfriend in high school. Carrie Tolbert. She hated me," Fiona said. "And he had a girlfriend in college, Bridget, her name was. Hated me. And since he's been on Nantucket . . . the occasional one-night stand he never wanted me to find out about." She took a huge breath, like she was planning on going underwater. "Anyway, here's what I want to tell you, because I think it's only fair you should know. Thatcher and I have a special bond."

For whatever reason, these words incensed Adrienne. They made her as mad as a bee sting, or a glass of ice water in her face, or lemon juice in her eye. Something clicked in her, or unclicked.

"Why don't you tell me about it?" Adrienne said. "You can start by telling me how you've known each other since you were in diapers. Then you can tell me about how you walked together on the first day of kindergarten and about how he tried to kiss you on top of the slide the night before tenth grade started when you were out drinking on the elementary school playground. I've heard it. You pushed him away. But you never let him go. You invited him to Nantucket because you knew he would sell everything he had and hand it over to you. Now it's twelve years later and the man is as devoted to you as ever. You wonder why he never has girlfriends, and why the ones he did have resented you. You *wonder*!" Adrienne paused. She felt like a bottle of Laurent-Perrier that had been violently shaken and then opened, spewing everywhere. Restraint was a mountaintop on a faraway continent. She couldn't stop herself. "I can't believe you have the nerve to tell me you have a special bond like I am too *stupid* to have figured it out on my own. Where do you think I've been the last three months, Fiona? He's my boyfriend. I sleep with him every night. But you think I don't know that you're in bed with us, too? That you never leave his mind? I get it, Fiona. Your relationship is special. It is more special than my relationship with Thatcher. It is the most special."

Fiona was quiet, staring out at the moonlit water like she hadn't even heard. "I was afraid this would happen."

"What?"

"You're upset."

"I'm not upset," Adrienne shouted. "I'd just like some credit for understanding how things are. My first date with the man he ate exactly nothing and left me cold as soon as you called. The night he first told me he loved me he made sure he mentioned that he loved you, too. 'Differently,' he said, whatever that means."

"It means we're friends," Fiona said. "Nothing but friends."

"Nothing but friends!" Adrienne said incredulously. "Thatcher is yours and he's been yours all along."

"I've never seen him like he is this summer," Fiona said. "You changed him. He's different. He's happy."

"That may be," Adrienne said. "But it won't mean much in the end. You know it and I know it." She threw her napkin onto her empty plate and moved her chair back from the table. "This was a nice dinner. I enjoyed myself. But just now I can't figure out why you invited me here. Did you want to *gloat*?"

"No," Fiona said. In the moonlight, her tank top and pants looked very white, like she was an angel. Or a ghost. "I wanted to say I was sorry."

TO: DrDon@toothache.com
FROM: Ade12177@hotmail.com
DATE: August 16, 2005, 9:33 A.M.
SUBJECT: the sturgeon moon

The full moon in August is called the sturgeon moon by the Native Americans. There's a piece of useless trivia to share with your patients.

Did you know that the summer you sent me to Camp Hideaway I lied to all the girls in my cabin? I told them my brother was dying. Jonathan. I tried to tell myself that it wasn't exactly a lie because I did have a brother Jonathan who died. But for years I wondered what it was that made me say that. Why not just say Mom was sick? I wasn't okay saying she was sick and I've never been okay saying that she's dead. I never learned to deal with it, Dad. I never learned how to make it okay in my own mind.

I know the girls in my cabin had a reunion later that summer. Pammy Ipp told me about it in a letter. They all met at the Cherry Hill Mall and ate at the food court. She wrote to let me know I hadn't been invited.

Love.

TO: Ade12177@hotmail.com
FROM: DrDon@toothache.com
DATE: August 16, 2005, 10:27 A.M.
SUBJECT: none

Honey, are you all right? Love, love, love.

TO: kyracrenshaw@mindspring.com
FROM: Ade12177@hotmail.com
DATE: August 16, 2005, 9:42 A.M.
SUBJECT: Another season

I don't know how things got so messed up. I came here for money and money
I now have. I thought that was what I wanted—money saved up for my Future.
Then I fell in love and now my wanting is ten-fold but the problem is that what
I want doesn't have a price. It's this big, important, shapeless thing—I want to
be loved in return, I want my situation to be different, somehow, but I don't
even know how. I thought I had problems in Aspen. Ha! I did not. In compari-
son, I did not.

TO: Ade12177@hotmail.com
FROM: kyracrenshaw@mindspring.com
DATE: August 16, 2005, 12:02 P.M.
SUBJECT: Another season

Adrienne, are you all right?

12

❀

It's Okay if You Don't Love Me

Darla and Grayson Parrish were getting divorced. They had been married forty-two years, but twelve of those years were tainted by Grayson's adulterous relationship with Nonnie Sizemore from Darla's bridge group. Nonnie Sizemore was six months older than Darla and fifty pounds heavier. She was a clownish woman, Darla told Adrienne, jolly, she talked a lot, laughed a lot, ate and drank a lot. She smoked. Darla wouldn't say she had always pitied Nonnie Sizemore, who had been divorced from her husband since 1973, but she would say she had never envied her. And she certainly never believed Nonnie was capable of betrayal—but, in fact, Nonnie had been sleeping with Grayson for a dozen years. They had even snuck off for a week together some years earlier to Istanbul. Grayson had claimed business—the hunt for tile and stone—in Europe. But Istanbul! It was a place that held zero appeal for Darla, and she had to admit it was possible that she'd lost touch of how different her predilections were from those of her husband. They had practically nothing to talk about.

"I did notice your dinners this summer were a little . . . quiet," Adrienne said. She and Darla were sitting at table nineteen in the most secluded corner of the restaurant. It was occupied every night, but Adrienne always thought of it as the table where Leon Cross sat when he ate with his mistress. She thought of it as the table where Thatcher did the bills each night.

Now it was the table where Darla Parrish had bravely decided to eat alone. She wouldn't give up the standing Tuesday and Friday night reservations, not when the restaurant was less than two weeks away from closing. She could have invited other people to dine with her—her sister Eleanor, her best friend Sandy Beyrer—but that felt like denial somehow. She was to be a single woman; she would eat alone, with Adrienne as occasional company. Ten minutes here or there; Darla appreciated whatever time Adrienne could spare.

"Watching you gives me hope," Darla said. "When you leave this island for the next fabulous place, you call me. I'm going with you."

For three nights running, Thatcher had spent the night at Fiona's house. Fiona slept hooked up to an oximeter, and when her O$_2$ sats dropped, an alarm sounded. Thatcher was there to respond to the alarm, call an ambulance, get Fiona to the hospital, and although this hadn't happened, he wasn't sleeping. He showed up at work with his hair parted on the wrong side and his cuffs buttoned incorrectly. He misplaced his watch for twenty-four hours. In the days since Holt Millman's party, the only real conversation that Adrienne had had with Thatcher was about the lost watch. He bought it for himself with his profits from the Bistro the first year. The watch and the Bistro were linked in his mind. He received compliments on the watch every night; once, Charlie Sheen had tried to buy it right off his wrist.

Adrienne understood how certain objects could hold real value, though she didn't have anything herself that was worth anything—except now, a couple of great pairs of shoes. She offered to help Thatcher search Fiona's place, but when she suggested this, he backed up.

"Whatever," he said. "It's just a watch."

The following morning, however, when Fiona's cleaning lady found the watch on the windowsill of Fiona's bathroom, Thatcher's mood improved. He led Adrienne from the podium into the wine cave, where they made love standing up with Adrienne's back against the cooling unit. It seemed sneaky and cheap, and Adrienne thought miserably of the one-night stands Fiona had mentioned.

"I love you," Adrienne said.

Thatcher kissed her neck in response, then he laughed. "Ha!"

She could tell he was thinking about the watch, and sure enough, once Adrienne was back at the phone, Thatcher asked her to clear a table for Consuela, Fiona's cleaning lady—dinner for two, on him.

Three nights without Thatcher turned into five, six, seven.

"It's been a whole week," Adrienne said to Caren. It was another hot, sunny morning. They sat at the sawed-off table in the shade of the back-yard, Adrienne drinking tea, Caren drinking espresso and poring over the Pottery Barn catalog. She needed furniture for her new apartment.

Caren looked up from a page of leather sofas. "Are you worried?"

"I'm furious," Adrienne said. She was in her running clothes, ready to put on her shoes and go. But now that she had Caren's attention, she wanted to keep it. "I know I should feel sorry for Fiona, but I can't."

Caren bit her thumbnail. "That's tricky."

"You think I'm horrible," Adrienne said. "I am horrible." She stared at her bare feet. They were tan with white lines from the straps of her flip-flops; her toenails were painted "ripe raspberry." These were the feet of a woman who had learned to stand for eight-hour stretches, and who had learned to walk in slides and sling backs with a four-inch heel. These were the feet of a woman who had kicked the bad habit of lying about her past and who had learned to trust a man and love him. The summer had been so brilliant. What was happening to her sense of peace, her happiness? What was happening to her?

Since her dinner with Fiona, Adrienne had tried to stay out of the kitchen, but she couldn't avoid the normal course of her job. She had to pick up the chips and dip; she had to help the waitstaff. The previous evening, when Adrienne walked into the kitchen to put in a VIP order for the owner of American Seasons, she found Fiona whipping a side towel against the pass like she was a jockey in the Kentucky Derby. The sweat streamed down her face, her hair was matted to her head.

"Ordering table one: one chowder, one bisque. Who are these people eating soup when it's so hot?" She glanced over at Adrienne. "And you, my dear, look as fresh as a fucking daisy."

Adrienne could not get past her fury. It was a boulder blocking her path.

Adrienne left Caren to her armchairs and ottomans. Caren couldn't handle Adrienne's anger. There was, perhaps, only one person who could.

Adrienne pulled Drew Amman-Keller's card out of the top drawer of her desk.

She thought he might sound smug, or victorious, but when Drew Amman-Keller answered the phone and learned it was Adrienne calling, he treated her like a friend.

"Adrienne, how's the summer going? I mean to come in one more time before you close, but, as you know, I'm at the mercy of Mr. Millman. That was some party last week, wasn't it?"

"Yeah," Adrienne said. She closed the door to her bedroom even though Caren was still outside. And Duncan—was he lurking around somewhere, or was he golfing? Adrienne hadn't even thought to ask. She was discombobulated. She had mustered the guts to call, but now what?

"So . . ." Drew said. "Is there something I can do for you or did you just call to chat?"

She pictured him licking his womanish lips.

"I called to talk to you about Fiona."

Drew Amman-Keller cleared his throat. "Would you like to talk in person? You could come here or I could come to you."

His voice was low and smooth, like a lover suggesting a rendezvous. Adrienne moved into the doorway of her closet.

"No," she said.

"Okay, then, the phone."

"The phone."

There was silence. Drew Amman-Keller was either feeling as awkward as she was or else his silence was a tactic to get her to talk. And what, exactly, was she going to tell him? Did she tell him about the concealed illness, the transplant list, the affair with the married delivery driver, the smothering friendship with Thatcher? What Adrienne needed was a friend—someone to take her side, someone to sympathize with her. She had shown up on this island with an empty Future box. Now she had plenty of money but she had nowhere to go and no plans. Her life was so devoid of people who cared that she was forced to talk to a reporter.

Drew Amman-Keller took a breath. "I can pay you," he said.

Adrienne hung up.

She spent the rest of the day feeling both proud of herself for shutting the lid on Drew Amman-Keller and ashamed of herself for calling him in the first place. She went to Dionis Beach and lay in the hot sun at low tide. She felt her anger wilting. On the way to work that night, she stopped at Pam's salon and bought Thatcher a gift certificate for a massage. She gave it to him before menu meeting.

"Ha! When am I supposed to use this?"

"I don't know," Adrienne said. "It only takes an hour."

"Ha!"

"What is wrong with you?" Adrienne said. She felt blood rise to the surface of her face; the hair on her arms stood up. They were going to fight, and she was glad. She wanted a fight. The phone rang, the private line. Tempting, but she ignored it.

Thatcher didn't even seem to hear the phone. "I'm tired," he said.

"That's a cop-out," Adrienne said. "We're all tired. I'm just trying to figure out what's going on. You don't . . ."

He pointed a Blue Bistro pencil at her nose. "I don't what?"

"You don't say you love me anymore."

"I love you."

"That wasn't very convincing."

"Why do I have to convince you?"

"Because!" she said. "Our sex life . . . you don't stay over . . ."

"I've been up for seven straight nights at Fiona's, hoping and praying that she doesn't stop *breathing*!" He snapped the pencil in half across the back of his hand, and the pieces sailed through the air, bounced off the wooden floor, and rolled under the podium.

"Father Ott said he'd spell you. Let him take a night or two."

"So I can focus on our sex life?"

"No," Adrienne said.

"No, my ass. That's what you want."

"I want you to get some sleep," Adrienne said.

"I thought you said my being tired was a cop-out."

The phone rang again. Private line. Adrienne watched the blinking light. *Pick it up?* She was getting nowhere with Thatcher.

"You've stopped caring about me," Adrienne said.

"You know that's not true."

"Do I?"

"I told you it was going to be like this," Thatcher said. "I told you I was limited in what I could give and you said that was okay. You said you understood. However, it sounds very much like you don't understand. Now, answer the phone, please."

Adrienne snatched up the private line, glaring at him. "Good evening, Blue Bistro."

"Harry Henderson calling for Thatcher, please."

Thatcher disappeared into the kitchen.

"He's not available right now, Harry."

"Not available? He and Fiona are supposed to sign the closing documents tomorrow morning. We have ten days to put this deal to bed. I expect them at noon, and I don't want to hear that they're too busy making bouillabaisse. Not *available*? Really, Adrienne, I expected more from you."

August twenty-fourth: two hundred and fifty covers on the book, thirty-two reservation wait list, and then Adrienne disconnected both of the public phone lines. The special was lobster ravioli with a charred tomato cream sauce. They served it at family meal and Adrienne ate until she felt heavy and lethargic.

The Elperns arrived at six o'clock with their new baby, Sebastian. Adrienne tried to exude enthusiasm when she gazed at Sebastian's chubby cheeks, but she contradictorily felt both stuffed and deflated. Scott held the baby in the infant car seat, and Lucy held out the blueprints for their fat mansion. They had been to Harry Henderson's office to sign the closing documents that morning and tonight was a celebration of that. In ten days, the restaurant would be theirs. Adrienne was the only person they knew at the Bistro; she had somehow become intimately involved in this new phase of their lives. They thought of her as a friend, and while she was flattered, it took all of her strength just to smile and coo at the baby appropriately. She envied them—not because they were technology billionaires and not because they were buying the building that Adrienne now loved better than any building on earth—but because of their family-ness: Mama, Papa, baby. They were smug without meaning to be, smug about the simplest and yet most enduring things in life—their love for each other, their love for their child.

Adrienne was amazed at the transformation in Lucy Elpern; only four weeks after giving birth, every part of her previously swollen body was now slender and tight, except for her breasts, which were alluringly large. Tyler Lefroy ogled Lucy when he walked past with a sweating water pitcher.

"You're under the awning tonight," Adrienne told the Elperns. She led them to the far edge of the awning, table twenty-two, where nobody would be bothered by a crying baby, or startled by the sight of Lucy Elpern's enormous, exposed breast as she nursed Sebastian.

"I just love this restaurant," Lucy Elpern said. "It seems such a shame to tear it down."

Scott Elpern locked eyes with Adrienne. He grinned. "But wait until you see the plans for our indoor pool!"

"Indoor pool!" Adrienne said to Duncan five minutes later at the bar. He slid her a flute of champagne that she was too full to drink. "They're building an indoor pool."

Duncan shrugged. "It's their house," he said. "They can do whatever they want."

"Indoor pool!" Adrienne said to Caren as they walked to the kitchen. Adrienne had to put in a VIP order for the Elperns.

Caren said, "Can you run apps for me? Table five?"

"Did you hear what I said? About the indoor pool?"

"I heard you. Did you hear me?"

"Indoor pool!" Adrienne said to Mario between seatings. The Elperns had further regaled her with details of their new house and had asked her if she wanted to hold the baby. She declined, claiming an oncoming cold. "They're building a six-thousand-square-foot house with an indoor pool. The HDC didn't bat an eye. They break ground September fifteenth."

"These people are loaded, right?" Mario said. "You think they want to invest in our new restaurant? You know them. It couldn't hurt to ask."

Adrienne thought she tasted blood in her mouth. Her eyes stung and she bowed her head. Only ten days left and nobody seemed to care. Everybody was already gone.

At midnight, Adrienne had a line forty people long and the bar was hopping. Duncan blared the CD player—no need to comply with the noise ordinance at this late date—he was convinced that the louder the music, the more people drank. Thatcher emerged from the dancing crowd with the cash box and receipts clutched to his chest. For the first time in days, he was smiling. On his way into the kitchen, he stopped and kissed Adrienne in a slow, searching way. Someone from the back of the line yelled, "Get a room!"

Adrienne felt a surge of hope. "What did I do to deserve that?" she asked.

Thatcher answered, but the music was so loud, she didn't hear what he said.

The kiss changed her channel. She let two people into the bar just for the heck of it, she sang along to the music. The questions in her brain melted away: *Are you okay? Am I okay? It's okay if you don't love me. Do you love me?*

When Thatcher ran out of the kitchen and grabbed both her wrists and shook her—he was shaking her and yelling, yelling! but she couldn't hear what he was saying—she knew that this was the beginning of the end. Bruce Springsteen was assaulting the room at ninety decibels and it took Adrienne several seconds to make out the words coming from Thatcher's mouth. *It's Fee. It's Fee. Get everybody out! Everybody out!*

Adrienne didn't know what to do. She picked up the phone. 911? Thatcher slammed the receiver back down. He raced to the bar and turned off the music; the crowd booed. Duncan whipped around. "Hey!"

"The bar is closing," Thatcher announced. "Right now. Tabs are forgiven, but I have to ask you all to leave immediately. We'll reopen tomorrow night at six."

There was a din of chatter. Adrienne could sense the guests' confusion, their resistance. Thatcher grabbed the hand bell and swung it through the air like a madman swinging a hatchet. Adrienne eyed the kitchen door. *It's Fee.*

People filed past her. "Sorry about this," she said, as calmly as she could. "We'll see you tomorrow." The stench of emergency was in the air—this was even before Adrienne heard the approaching sirens—and someone said the word "fire." There was pushing. One woman stumbled; the heel broke off her shoe and the people behind her piled up, yelling, "Get up! Get out!"

"There's no fire," Adrienne said loudly. "But you have to go. No fire. Please go. See you tomorrow."

Because there was still a crowd in the parking lot—guests lingering, trying to figure out what was going *on*—the paramedics took Fiona out through the back door. Adrienne saw her on the stretcher, and she rallied the staff to act as a barrier to the public. Adrienne stood shoulder to shoulder with Caren and Joe and next to Joe was Spillman and next to Caren was Duncan and Elliott and Christo and Louis and Hector and young Jojo on the end, crying. And Delilah was crying. Fiona was unconscious, her face ashen, her lips blue. The paramedics slapped an oxygen mask on her face and they did a lot of shouting, numbers, a code. Thatcher climbed into the back of the ambulance and the doors slammed shut behind him. Adrienne felt an arm around her—Mario. The ambulance cut a path through the crowd and sped off, sirens wailing.

Adrienne turned to Mario. "Now what?" she said. "What do we do?" She wanted to hitch a ride to the hospital. She wanted to be with Thatcher, but Mario steered her back toward the Bistro.

"Close out the bar," he said. "Get the money. Go home."

"Go home? But what about . . ."

"They'll medevac her to Boston," Mario said. "She'll be at Mass General in less than an hour. It's okay."

"I don't know how you can say that," Adrienne said, and she went inside.

August twenty-fifth: two hundred and fifty covers on the book, twenty reservation wait list. There was no tomato special; Antonio was too distraught to put one together. Adrienne had received a phone call from Thatcher at five o'clock that morning. He talked, Adrienne listened.

"Keep the restaurant open. No matter what happens, keep it open. She's in and out of consciousness. She wants the restaurant open. That's all she asks, *Is the restaurant open?* I tell her yes. The answer has to be yes."

Adrienne swallowed. Her voice was thick with sleep. "Should I call JZ?"

"I already called him."

"Is he coming?"

"No."

"Why not?"

"She says she doesn't want to see him."

"She's lying."

"That's not for you to say." Thatcher paused. "It's really not."

"Okay," Adrienne said. "Sorry."

"You don't know what this is like for me," he said.

"Sure I do," Adrienne said. "I watched my mother die."

"How is that the same thing?"

"Because . . ."

"Because Fiona is dying. Is that what you mean? It just so happens, they're trying another drug today, okay? Another drug!"

"Why are you fighting with me?" Adrienne said. "Thatcher, I love you."

"I have to go," he said. "I'll call you later." And he hung up.

At ten o'clock, Adrienne fielded phone calls, including a call from the *Inquirer and Mirror* with a reporter asking about the emergency vehicle the night before. Adrienne offered no comment. She was edgy, distracted. After she'd hung up with Thatcher she'd lain awake until the sun rose. Adrienne felt like she had just thrown something of enormous value into the ocean and watched it sink. Lost forever.

When the Sid Wainer truck pulled into the parking lot, she went to the door, her heart knocked around. She would talk to JZ. But the driver wasn't JZ; it was some young kid, blond, tan, too good-looking.

"Where's JZ?" Adrienne asked.

"He's out," the kid said. "Sick."

That night, family meal was ten pizzas from the Muse. Adrienne wanted to say something at menu meeting, but what to say? Fiona's left lung had collapsed, she was coughing up blood, her O_2 sats were very low. The lung infection she'd been battling all summer was back, but they were trying a new drug. That, and praying for a lung donor. Thatcher had given Adrienne these stark details but had asked her not to share them. And so, Adrienne sat quietly at the twelve-top while the staff ate pizza. She watched Tyler stuff half a piece in his mouth like a healthy eighteen-year-old boy who was ten days away from having every freedom of his young life rescinded at military college. She watched Caren, who was eating a bowl of lettuce that she had swiped from the reach-in. She watched Joe, who ate his pizza neatly, with a knife and fork. The staff looked tired, worried, uninspired. Adrienne lifted a slice of pepperoni off the greasy paper plate, but she couldn't eat. She was starving, ravenous, but food wasn't going to help. She was hungry for something else: the phone ringing, Thatcher's voice, good news, love.

And yet, the restaurant opened at six and service began: the pretzel bread, the mustard, the doughnuts, the VIP orders, the crab cakes, the steak frites, the fondue. Antonio expedited, the kitchen sent out impeccable plates, Rex played the piano, Duncan poured drinks, Tyler Lefroy complained that he was working twice as hard as Gage who, he informed Adrienne, had gotten *stoned* before work. The guests laughed, talked, paid their bills, left tips, raved about the food. No one could tell there was a single thing wrong.

Holt Millman was in, table twenty, party of four. *Better than ever,* he said. *Tell Fiona I said so.*

Thatcher didn't call. Adrienne left him a message with the totals from the floor and the bar. She said nothing else.

August twenty-sixth: two hundred and fifty covers, thirty-six reservation wait list. The special was an inside-out BLT: mâche, crispy pancetta, and a round garlic crouton sandwiched between two slices of tomato, drizzled with basil aioli. Adrienne's stomach growled at the sight of it, but she couldn't eat.

Cat was in, having fondue at one of the four-tops in the sand. They polished off a magnum of Laurent-Perrier, then ordered port. So Cat was tipsy and then some when, at the end of the night, she pulled Adrienne aside.

"There are rumors going around," Cat said.

"Really?" Adrienne said. "What's the word?"

"The word is that Fiona is dead."

Adrienne laughed; it was a strange sound, even to her own ears. "No," Adrienne said. "She's not dead."

The next morning, Adrienne called her father at work. She got Mavis on the phone, who said, "Adrienne, doll, he's with a patient. Can I have him call you?"

"I have to speak with him now," Adrienne said.

Mavis put Adrienne on hold to some awful Muzak and Adrienne stared at the calendar in the front of the reservation book. One week left. That was it. She took a deep breath. Well, there was always Darla Parrish, who kept insisting she was going to accompany Adrienne into the next chapter. Adrienne couldn't decide if that made her feel better or worse.

Her father came on the phone. "Honey, is everything all right?"

When Adrienne took a breath to answer, a sob escaped. She cried into the phone and imagined herself facedown on a childhood bed she had long forgotten—her father and her mother, too, smoothing her hair, patting her back, telling her not to worry, telling her everything was going to be just fine.

August twenty-seventh: two hundred and fifty covers, twenty-three reservation wait list. Special: whole ripe tomatoes cut into quarters and served with salt and pepper. Antonio decided on this simple preparation as a tribute to Fiona. A man at table two complained that it wasn't fancy enough. "I've been hearing all about these tomato specials," he said. "And this is what you give me?"

Adrienne removed his plate. "Don't you get it?" she said. "The tomato is perfect as it is."

He didn't get it. He ordered the foie gras cooked through.

That night, at quarter to three, the phone rang. Adrienne had just gotten home. Caren and Duncan were opening a bottle of Failla pinot noir that they had stolen from the wine cave.

Caren said, "Who calls at this hour?"

Adrienne had a funny feeling and she snapped up the phone.

"Hello?" she said.

"Adrienne?" It was Thatcher, but something was wrong with his voice. Then she realized he was crying.

"Thatcher?" she said.

The line clicked. She held a dial tone. She called Thatch back on his cell phone but it went to his voice mail. "It's me," she said. "Call me back."

Caren glanced up from the Pottery Barn catalog. She and Duncan were talking drapes.

"Thatch?" she said.

Adrienne managed a nod.

"Did he say anything?"

"Nothing."

"Want a glass of wine?" Caren said.

"Yes," Adrienne said.

She didn't sleep. She finished the bottle of wine and opened another, then she sat at the kitchen table and listened to the muted sounds of Caren and Duncan's lovemaking. She called Thatcher three more times—all three calls went to his voice mail, but she didn't leave a message. Caren came out to use the bathroom and when she saw Adrienne sitting at the table, she offered her a Percocet. Adrienne took it. It made her loopy and vague, but it didn't put her to sleep. At five thirty, the sun rose. Adrienne watched the light through the leaves of the trees in the backyard, and when she couldn't wait another second, she hopped on her bike and rode to the restaurant.

The red Durango was in the parking lot. Mario was in way too early for work. The door to the Bistro was swinging open; when Adrienne stepped through, she saw him sitting at the bar with a drink, a Scotch. He looked at her.

"She's dead?" Adrienne said.

He tossed back the last of his drink, then brought the glass down so hard that it cracked in his hand. He left the damaged glass on the bar and walked toward Adrienne. Adrienne was numb; she had no thoughts.

"There's something else you have to know," Mario said. He hugged her.

"What's that?" Adrienne asked. Her fingers and toes were tingling. She pressed her tongue into the fibers of Mario's cotton shirt. She wanted to taste something.

"Thatcher married her yesterday afternoon. Father Ott was there. He married them in the hospital chapel at two o'clock. Fiona slipped into a coma at nine. She died at two this morning."

"Thatcher married her?"

"He married her."

Adrienne waited to feel something. She thought of Thatcher carrying Fiona toward the phosphorescent ocean, carrying her the same way a groom carries a bride over the threshold. Adrienne had been so jealous then, so typically sorry for herself, as she wondered, *Who is going to carry me?* But now she didn't feel jealous or sad or lonely. She didn't feel anything.

She sat next to Mario on a bar stool and rested her cheek on the cool blue granite. Her eyes fell closed. She felt her mind drifting away.

When she awoke, with a crick in her neck and a flat spot on her face, it was because the phone was ringing. She went to the podium. Line one. Adrienne checked her watch: nine o'clock. *Reporter,* she thought. *Drew Amman-Keller.* She hadn't told him anything. In the end, she hadn't told him a thing.

She pushed open the kitchen door. It was quiet except for the hum of the refrigerators, and it was clean. The floors had been mopped the night before, the pass buffed to a shine, the trash had been emptied, there was a stack of clean side towels on the counter. Adrienne picked one up and pressed it to her face. This was Fiona's kitchen without Fiona. Fiona was dead.

Adrienne found Mario in pastry, surrounded by his usual tools: the mixing cups, the measuring spoons, the stainless-steel bowl that was as big as a wagon wheel. He had flour out, baking powder, butter, and a brick of Gruyère cheese. "Good, you're awake," he said. "You can help me."

"You're cooking?"

"I want to make crackers."

"Crackers."

"We have to call the staff in at eleven," he said. "We have to tell them the restaurant is closing. I want to have the crackers. You know, as something nice."

"The restaurant is closing?" This, somehow, pierced her. No more restaurant. Dead, like Fiona.

"Oh, honey," Mario said. He patted a high stool where she sat like a child to watch Mario work. He measured flour, grated the Gruyère with his microplane rasp until the brick was a fluffy mound, cut in the butter, mixed up a dough. He rolled the dough into three logs, wrapped them in plastic, and put them in the reach-in to chill. He made Adrienne an espresso, which she threw back joylessly. That, she vowed, would be the last espresso of her life.

"How do you make yourself do it?" she asked him. "Cook at a time like this. Aren't you sad?"

"Sad?" he said. "My compadre, my mentor, my *friend,* she's dead. I'm more than sad, honey. I'm something else, something I don't even have a word for. But cooking saves me. It's what I do, it's who I am. I stop cooking, I'm the one who dies."

"I want something like that," Adrienne said. "I want something to do, someone to be. I don't have that. I've never had that."

"You're good at being beautiful."

She knew he meant this as a compliment, but it only proved her point. She was nothing. She had nobody.

Mario retrieved the dough from the walk-in and sliced the logs into thin discs, then laid them out on three cookie sheets. He handed Adrienne a jar of dried thyme and showed her how to lightly dust the crackers, then he put the cookie sheets in the oven.

"I'm going to have a cigarette," he said.

"You don't smoke," she said.

"I do today. You want to come?"

"I'll stay here," she said. She sat on the stool and felt the heat rise from the oven; minutes later, pastry was filled with the smell of the cheese and the thyme. Mario reappeared. He pulled the cookie sheets out of the oven.

The crackers were crispy and fragrant. *Ninety-nine percent of the world think that crackers only come out of a box . . .*

Mario offered her one and Adrienne let him place it on her tongue like a Communion wafer.

"This," he said, "was the easy part."

As Adrienne returned to the dining room, the Sid Wainer truck pulled into the parking lot. She hoped and prayed for the blond kid, but no such luck. JZ walked in. The phone rang, Adrienne ignored it. She was frightened when she looked at JZ. He was filled with something and about to burst from too much of it. Grief, rage, and the something else that nobody had a word for. She stepped out from behind the podium and hugged him.

"I'm so sorry, JZ."

"No one is as sorry as I am." Adrienne let him go. His eyes were watering and Adrienne held out the side towel, but he just stared at it. "You're closing?" he said.

"Yes."

He picked up the bowl of matches and Adrienne feared he might smash it against the wall, but he just held it for a few seconds, then put it back down. "I bought that bowl for her in Boston two years ago," he said. "She was at Mass General then and I went to visit her. We'd just started dating."

"I can't imagine how awful this must be for you," Adrienne said.

"She wouldn't let me come this time," he said. "I didn't get to see her."

"JZ . . ."

JZ stared into the bowl. "Thatcher married her."

"I know."

"She really wanted to be married. I should have done it a long time ago."

"I would have liked that better," Adrienne said.

"But I couldn't. My hands were tied."

"So you've said."

"She never believed that."

"I'm sure she understood."

"She said she did, but she didn't. And now she's dead."

Adrienne nodded.

"I wanted to see her. But Thatch is taking her body . . ." Here, JZ paused, put his hands over his eyes. His left leg was shaking. "He's taking her body back to South Bend. Her parents want a family-only service at their church." He looked at Adrienne, tears falling down his face. "I can't even go to her funeral."

Adrienne held out the side towel again, but JZ didn't take it. The phone rang. Line one. Adrienne wanted to smash the phone against the wall. She still had to call everyone on the staff and have them in here in an hour. The ringing phone seemed to keep JZ from careening into the abyss of his own sadness. He straightened, cleared his throat.

"I should go. I'm making deliveries today. Today's my last day."

"You're quitting?"

"I need to be closer to my family. Shaughnessy."

"That makes sense," Adrienne said. Suddenly, she felt angry at JZ. She guessed being "closer to my family" meant that he would get back together with his wife. So Thatcher had been right. JZ had never risked anything for Fiona at all, not really. He was nobody's hero. Sorrow flooded Adrienne's stomach; she couldn't even fake a smile. "I guess I'll see you later?"

"No," he said. "I'm never coming back."

At eleven, the staff sat around table nine much as they had at the very first menu meeting of the summer: Delilah next to Duncan, Joe, Spillman, Elliott, Christo, Caren, Gage, Roy, Tyler. The Subiacos sat at the adjoining table—Antonio, Hector, Louis, Henry, Eddie, Paco, Jojo. Bruno was in the kitchen brewing espressos and Adrienne stood with Mario holding the baskets of crackers. The place was silent. Everyone knew Fiona was dead, and yet Mario took it upon himself to announce it.

"Fiona died at two o'clock this morning at Mass General. Thatcher was with her."

There was crying. The loudest crying was from Delilah, but the men cried, too—Spillman and Antonio and Joe. Adrienne didn't cry and neither did Caren. Adrienne squinted at the ocean. It was an exquisite day, which seemed so wrong. Everything was wrong.

"Are we staying open?" Paco asked.

"No," Mario said. "We're closing."

"So that's it, then?" Eddie said. "It's over?"

"It's over."

Mario had a sheaf of envelopes and he handed one to each staff member.

Checks. Five thousand dollars for each year employed at the Blue Bistro. Caren's check was for sixty thousand dollars; Adrienne's was for five. Adrienne studied her name typed on the light blue bank check: *Adrienne Dealey*. She remembered back to her first morning, the breakfast. She had taken a gamble, and she had lost. *It's okay if you don't love me,* she thought. But it wasn't okay.

There was still work to do. Adrienne had to call every guest who was on the books for the next five days. It took several hours and she was worried her voice would falter, but it didn't. *The restaurant is closing early. All reservations are cancelled. We're sorry for the inconvenience. I'm sorry . . . that's all I can tell you.* Mario brought her a pile of crackers on a napkin. The rest of the staff was getting drunk at the bar—Duncan was pouring—though some, like Tyler, Elliott, and Christo, had left right away. Adrienne cancelled with Holt Millman's secretary, Dottie Shore, she cancelled with Darla, she cancelled with Cat, the Devlins, the Kennedys, Leon Cross, and the local author.

What happened? Darla asked, Dottie Shore asked, the local author asked.

I'm sorry, Adrienne said. She felt badly because she liked these people, she felt she knew them though she probably didn't and they certainly didn't know her. They would never understand the blow she'd been dealt: *Thatcher married Fiona before she died.* They would never know how her heart felt stripped and exposed, like the yolk of an egg separated from its whole, like a child without a mother.

I'm sorry, she said. *That's all I can tell you.*

The last person Adrienne called was Mack Peterson. Guests from the Beach Club held thirty-seven reservations in the last five nights. Thatcher had been right about Mack: He was good for business.

"We're closing early," Adrienne said. "Please convey to your guests how sorry we are for the inconvenience."

"They'll get over it," Mack said. "The important thing is that everyone there is all right. Is everyone all right?"

"I'm sorry," Adrienne said. "All I can tell you is that we're closing. But thank you, Mack, for all the business you sent us."

"Half my staff leaves on Labor Day and we're open another six weeks," Mack said. "If you're looking for a job, call me. I would love to hire you."

"That's very kind," Adrienne said. "Thank you."

She crossed the last names from the reservation sheet and double-checked her list to make sure she hadn't forgotten anyone. She called Bartlett Farm to cancel their vegetable order, she called East Coast Seafood, she called Caviarteria in New York, she called the mushroom company in Kennett Square, she called Classic Wines, she called Flowers on Chestnut, she called the cleaning crew. Closing, closing, closing. And then it was done.

Mario walked out of the back carrying two steaming plates: omelets.

"You want?"

"No," she said.

"Come on, you have to eat something."

"Something," she said. "But not that."

"I'll tell you a secret," Mario said. "Me and Louis and the cousins are looking to buy Sloop's down on Steamship Wharf. Maybe this fall if we can get the money. Open it up next summer as Calamari Café, Italian with Cuban accents. Antonio as chef. We want you to work the front."

Adrienne shut her eyes. She was shocked that Mario would mention his new restaurant on the very morning that Fiona had died. And yet, wasn't that human nature—the desire to move forward, to move away from the bad, sad news? Wasn't that what Adrienne and Dr. Don had been doing their whole lives? Hadn't they always hoped that grief was something they could run away from? Adrienne imagined the Italian-Cuban café that the Subiacos would open next June. It would be a great place. Another great place.

"Sorry," Adrienne said.

Mario cocked his head. "Come on, you think about it."

"Thank you," she said. "But no."

"Okay," Mario said, holding out the omelets. "I'll give these away to somebody else."

Caren, Bruno, and Spillman sat at the bar, drinking, and eating omelets.

"Fiona was like my sister," Caren said. "I didn't always like her, but I always loved her."

"She knew we loved her," Bruno said.

Spillman set his beer down on top of his check. "I don't even want this money," he said.

"You could give it to charity," Duncan said.

"Red would kill me," Spillman said.

Caren glanced at Adrienne then reached out for her hand. "Are you all done?"

"Yeah."

"So have a drink. Champagne?"

"I can't," Adrienne said. "I don't care if I ever drink champagne again."

"How about something else?" Caren asked. "Martini?"

"No," Adrienne said.

"You look awful. Sit down. How about a Coke?" Duncan pulled out a glass and hit the gun. He slid the Coke across the bar.

"I don't feel like it," Adrienne said. "I'm tired."

"You can sleep for the rest of the week," Caren said. "This is going to be the last time to sit with all of us."

Joe came out of the kitchen. He put his arm around Adrienne and kissed her temple.

"Thatcher married her," Adrienne said. She gazed at the surprised faces of Spillman and Bruno, the downcast eyes of Duncan and Caren who had probably suspected as much all along. Joe tightened his grip on Adrienne's shoulder.

"It was the right thing to do," Adrienne said. This was the only way she could bear to think of it: as a generous gesture on Thatcher's part. A good deed. But she knew it was just as likely that Fiona did it as a favor to Thatcher, that he'd begged her. He loved Fiona more than any woman in the world. Not romantically, maybe, but he loved her just the same. "I don't feel much like hanging out."

"No," Caren whispered.

"I'm going home to get some sleep," Adrienne said.

Caren passed her the keys to the Jetta. "Take my car," she said.

"And take this," Duncan said. He held aloft the brass hand bell that he used each night to announce last call.

"No, I can't," Adrienne said.

"Take it," Duncan said. "You earned it."

"You earned it," Bruno said.

"You earned it," Joe said.

"Take the bell, Adrienne," Spillman said.

She took the bell. It was heavier than she expected. Her eyes filled with tears and she couldn't bring herself to look at anyone, or worse yet, utter words of good-bye, so instead she rang the bell and listened to its deep metallic thrum. The Bistro was quiet then except for the distant sound of the ocean, and the resonant note of the bell.

Adrienne rang the bell again, then again, as she walked out of the restaurant. Its tone was pure and holy, a benediction.

The New York Times, Sunday, August 28, 2005
Chef Dies at 35; Landmark Restaurant Closes
by Drew Amman-Keller

Nantucket, Mass.

Fiona Kemp, 35, chef/owner of the popular beachfront restaurant the Blue Bistro, died at Massachusetts General Hospital early yesterday morning from complications arising from cystic fibrosis. Ms. Kemp was frequently portrayed in the food press as quiet and reclusive. She did not give interviews, she did not allow her photo to be taken, and she rarely set foot in the dining room of her own restaurant. Still, she was widely acknowledged to be a talent without peer in New England kitchens. Her focus on simple, fresh, "fun" foods (such as sandwiches, fondue, and whimsically named entrées like "lamb lollipops") earned her top accolades from the critics and loyal devotion from the restaurant's customers.

In a conversation via cell phone from Logan Airport, Ms. Kemp's partner, Thatcher Smith, denied that Ms. Kemp kept a low profile intentionally to conceal her illness. "Fiona's illness was genetic," Smith said. "She battled symptoms since she was a child. But the illness never took center stage—her career did. Fiona stayed in the kitchen because she didn't want to draw attention away from her food." Mr. Smith did acknowledge that their plans to close the restaurant at the end of the month were, in part, due to Ms. Kemp's health. She was on the list for a lung transplant. "We decided in the spring that this would be our last year. Fiona needed a rest. So, quite frankly, do I." Mr. Smith declined to talk about his plans for the future. "Right now I want to mourn Fiona—an excellent chef, a beautiful person, my best friend."

The Blue Bistro closed its doors yesterday, nearly a week earlier than planned. News of Ms. Kemp's death broke yesterday afternoon in a press release sent to the AP, and since then, according to Mario Subiaco, pastry chef, the restaurant has been deluged with phone calls and over a hundred bouquets of flowers have been left outside the now-locked front entrance.

"She had a lot of fans," Mr. Subiaco said. "She will be missed, most keenly by those of us who worked alongside of her."

Inquirer and Mirror, Week of August 26, 2005
PROPERTY TRANSFERS

Fiona C. Kemp and Thatcher E. Smith to the Sebastian Robert Elpern Nominee Trust: 27 North Beach Extension, $8,500,000.

South Bend Tribune, Monday, August 29, 2005
OBITUARIES

Fiona Clarice Kemp of Nantucket, Massachusetts, and formerly of South Bend, died on Sunday at Massachusetts General Hospital in Boston. She was 35.

Ms. Kemp was born at St. Joseph's Hospital in South Bend to Clarice Mayor Kemp and Dr. Hobson Kemp, a professor of engineering at the University of Notre Dame. She graduated from John Adams High school in 1987 and attended the Culinary

Institute of America in Hyde Park, New York. In 1991, she moved to Nantucket, where she worked for two years as a line cook at the Wauwinet Inn before opening her own restaurant, the Blue Bistro, in 1993.

Ms. Kemp collected many accolades as a chef. Her cuisine was featured in such publications as *Bon Appétit, Travel & Leisure,* and *The Chicago Tribune.* She was named one of America's Hottest Chefs 1998 by *Food & Wine* magazine.

She is survived by her parents and her husband, Thatcher Smith.

A private memorial service will be held at Sacred Heart Chapel, the University of Notre Dame. Memorial contributions may be made in Fiona's name to the Cystic Fibrosis Foundation, 6931 Arlington Road, Bethesda, Maryland 20814.

13

❧

Last Call

Because he is twelve, and in middle school, and because Fiona is a girl, Thatcher always takes friends along when he stops by Fiona's house, and most of the time these friends are Jimmy Sosnowski and Philip St. Clair. This particular day in May, Fiona has slipped Thatch a note in the hallway between history and music class, a scrap of paper that says, simply, "cheesecake." Last week, she passed him notes that said "quiche" and "meatballs," and the week before it was "bread pudding" and "veal parmigiana." Most of the time the word is enticing enough to get him over right after school—for example, the veal parmigiana. Thatcher and Jimmy and Phil sat at Fiona's kitchen table throwing apples from the fruit bowl at one another and teasing the Kemps' Yorkshire terrier, Sharky, while Fiona, in her mother's frilly, flowered, and very queer-looking apron, dredged the veal cutlets in flour, dipped them in egg, dressed them with breadcrumbs, and then sautéed them in hot oil in her mother's electric frying pan. The boys really liked the frying part—there was something cool about meat in hot, splattering oil. But they lost interest during the sauce and cheese steps, and by the time Fiona slid the baking pan into the oven, Jimmy and Phil were ready to go home. Not Thatcher—he stayed until Fiona pulled the cheesy, bubbling dish from the oven and ate with Fiona and Dr. and Mrs. Kemp. His father worked late and his brothers were scattered throughout the neighborhood (his two older brothers could drive and

302

many times they ate at the Burger King on Grape Road). Thatcher liked it when Fiona cooked; he liked it more than he would ever admit.

So cheesecake. Thatcher figures it will be easy to get Jimmy and Phil to come along for a dessert, but Phil has gotten a new skateboard and so, after school, two hours are spent in the parking lot of the Notre Dame football stadium with the three of them trying stunts (none of them particularly impressive). Every twenty minutes or so, Thatcher reminds Jimmy and Phil about the cheesecake. He knows Fiona will be, at these very minutes, making it. Her cooking fascinates him. She is the only twelve-year-old Thatcher knows who has her own subscription to Gourmet magazine. Cooking is something Fiona does, Mrs. Kemp told him once, because Fiona is sick. Really sick, the kind of sick that puts her in the hospital in Chicago for weeks at a time. Fiona's illness makes Jimmy and Phil uncomfortable, on top of the fact that she's a girl. They don't want to catch anything. How many times has Thatcher told them? "She doesn't have anything you can catch. She was born sick."

"You know," Phil says, front wheels of his skateboard in the air. "I think you like Fiona. Really like her."

"I think so, too," Jimmy says.

"Shut up," Thatcher says. He is sweating. It's a true spring day, where even the air in the asphalt parking lot smells like cut grass and forsythia. "I'm just hungry."

They reach the Kemps' house at five o'clock, dangerously close to dinner time, and making the situation more precarious is Dr. Kemp's brown Crown Victoria in the driveway.

"I don't know about this," Phil says.

"Come on," Thatcher says.

When they walk into the side door of the Kemps' kitchen, Sharky's bark announces their arrival. Much to Thatcher's relief, Fiona is alone in the kitchen, wearing her apron, drying dishes. Thatcher is looking at her, but Phil, with his skateboard tucked under his arm, and Jimmy, with his hair sticking up in sixteen permanent cowlicks, are looking at the kitchen table. In the center, where the fruit bowl usually is, the cheesecake rests on a pedestal. It's beautiful—perfectly round and smoothed, creamy white with chocolate swirls on a chocolate cookie crust, sitting in a pool of something bright pink.

"You didn't make that," Phil challenges.

"Sure I did," Fiona says.

"What is it?" Jimmy asks.

"Chocolate swirl cheesecake with raspberry coulis." She holds up the June issue of Gourmet; *the very same cake is pictured on the cover.*

The three of them stare at the cake like it's an alien spaceship landed on the table. Thatcher feels enormously proud of Fiona. He wants to hug her, but then he remembers Phil's words in the parking lot and he tightens his expression.

Dr. Kemp saunters into the kitchen in his professor's clothes—brown suit, bow tie, half-lensed reading glasses, South Bend Tribune *tucked under one arm. He has an imposing academic look, but really, he's very friendly.*

"What do you think of that cake, boys?" he says. *"Isn't it something else?"*

Phil and Jimmy nod nervously. Thatcher thinks how "something else" is exactly the right phrase. He can't believe that someone he knows has made such a cake.

"Um, I have to go," Phil says.

"Me, too," Jimmy says.

They are frightened by the cake, maybe, or by Dr. Kemp, or by Fiona. They leave abruptly, the screen door banging behind them.

"Do you want a slice, Thatch?" Fiona asks.

Dr. Kemp rinses out a coffee mug in the sink. Thatcher does want a slice, and in the years since his mother left, there has been no one to stop him from eating dessert before dinner. And yet, he hesitates. He's worried by how much he wants to taste the cheesecake, by how he craves it, craves Fiona's eyes on him as he brings the first bite to his lips; he's worried that what he really craves is Fiona. He feels himself reddening as Fiona gazes at him expectantly, awaiting an answer, and then Dr. Kemp looks at him from the sink. Suddenly the pressure of the question— Does he want a slice?—is more than he can bear.

Thatcher turns toward the door. "I have to go, too," he lies.

Labor Day, 1984. They are fifteen now, about to be sophomores in high school. Fiona left home by herself for the first time over the summer, to a culinary camp in Indianapolis, but Thatcher knows she's also interested in the things other fifteen-year-old girls are interested in. She spends whole days sunning herself on the roof of her house; she has rigged the telephone so that the cord reaches her perch.

Sometimes, if the wind is right, Thatcher can hear her from his front porch four doors down: Fiona, deep in conversation with her friend Alison.

Thatcher has spent the summer working at his father's carpet store—mostly moving the big-ass Persian rugs off the trucks into the showroom. As his father says, the Persians sell like winter coats on the day hell freezes over, and so there are always rugs to move. His father also has him steam-cleaning the two-by-three-foot samples of wall-to-wall, deep pile, and shag, because nothing ruins sales like a dirty sample. Thatcher moves Persians and steam-cleans samples and makes coffee and runs errands and stands around smiling so that his father can drape an arm over Thatcher's shoulder and say to his customers, "This is my youngest son, Thatcher. Big help to his old man." Thatcher hates carpet, hates wood flooring and linoleum and tile, and he really hates Persian rugs. His brothers hate it, too. His two oldest brothers, Monroe and Cal, work as lifeguards at the community swim club and his brother Hudson, just two years older, is a musical genius (drums) and has spent all summer at a music camp in Michigan. For Thatcher, Labor Day comes as a huge relief; school starts the next morning.

It's Phil St. Clair's idea to sneak out that night and meet at the playground of the elementary school, and it's Thatcher's idea to invite Fiona and convince his brother Monroe, now a junior at IUSB and still living at home, to buy them a six-pack of beer. Thatcher calls Fiona from the carpet store; he pictures her sitting on her roof in her powder-blue bikini. She's all for the plan. Thatcher's next call is to Jimmy Sosnowski, who suggests Thatcher ask for two six-packs. He does, Monroe extorts a price of thirty dollars, which Thatcher pays from his savings of the summer, and at ten o'clock that night, Thatcher walks out the front door of his house with twelve beers in his backpack. Thatcher wishes it could have been more like sneaking, but his father isn't home yet and when he does get home, he won't check on Thatcher; he never does.

Phil is already at the playground when Thatcher arrives. Phil sits on one of the swings. His whisper cuts through the darkness.

"Hey, did you get it?"

"Yeah." Thatcher shifts the backpack; there's a promising clink.

"Jimmy can't get out," Phil says. "His parents are having a barbecue and they're staying up late."

"That sucks."

"Truly," Phil says. "Give me a beer."

Thatcher's experience with beer is limited, and he panics because he hasn't thought to bring an opener, but the beer Monroe bought, Budweiser, are twist-offs. Thatcher gives one to Phil, then opens one for himself and drinks. The beer is lukewarm (after Monroe brought it home, Thatcher hid it from his other brothers in the closet) but it tastes good anyway. It tastes adult.

"Sophomores tomorrow," he says.

Fiona's voice catches him so by surprise that he chokes on his second swallow, sending a spray of beer down the front of his shirt.

"Hey, you guys!" she says. She laughs at Thatch. "Amateurs." *She plucks a Budweiser from Thatcher's backpack, flips the top off, and chugs half the bottle. Thatcher is impressed; Phil just shakes his head.*

"Fiona, what are you doing here?"

"Thatch invited me."

Phil glares at Thatcher. Thatcher shrugs.

Fiona says, "Get over it."

"It was supposed to be a guy thing," *Phil says.*

"We didn't decide on that," *Thatcher says.*

"We didn't decide on it, but . . . I mean, when you're sneaking out to drink beer the night before school starts, that's a guy thing."

Fiona expertly polishes off the rest of her beer and belches. "Excuse me."

"Do you want another one?" *Thatcher asks.*

"In a minute." *She climbs to the top of the slide and comes flying down. She's wearing some kind of one-piece terry-cloth sun suit. Next to Thatcher, Phil huffs.*

"Dude . . ."

"Relax," *Thatcher says.* "She's lots of fun."

"Whatever," *Phil says. He stands up from the swing and sets his nearly full beer down on the asphalt.* "I'm going home. This beer isn't even cold."

"Come on," *Thatcher says.* "Don't be a dope."

"You're the dope," *Phil says, nodding his head toward Fiona.* "I'll see you to-morrow." *He strolls away.*

Fiona climbs back up to the top of the slide. "Where's he going?" *she says.*

"Home."

Fiona coughs. Thatcher holds his breath; he hates it when she coughs. He drinks down his beer, then he's overcome with a loose, tingly feeling. He's happy that Phil's gone.

"I'm coming up after you," *he says.*

"Do what you want."

He climbs the ladder of the slide, hands over feet. When he's almost at the top, Fiona slides down and runs back to the ladder. Thatcher slides down. By the time he's made it to the bottom of the slide, she's at the top of the ladder. They chase each other like this for a while. Fiona's breath is labored; Thatcher can hear it, and he slows down on purpose. Then he climbs the ladder and she doesn't slide down. She sits at the top and he sidles in next to her. It's cramped, their thighs are touching but Fiona doesn't move.

"Go ahead," she says.

"You go ahead."

"I don't want to go ahead."

"Me, either."

Fiona turns her face, carefully it seems, to look at him. Is she thinking what he's thinking? The beer emboldens him. He leans in to kiss her.

She puts her palm on his face and pushes him away.

"Don't you dare."

"Why not?"

"Because I can't have you falling in love with me."

"I won't fall in love with you."

"You will so," Fiona says. "And I don't want to break your heart."

This, he realizes, is what she and Alison spend all day talking about: falling in love, breaking hearts. "You're nuts," he says.

"I'm going to die," she says.

He sits with this for a second. Even when he first learned about her illness, it was never phrased this way. No one has ever said anything about dying.

"We're all going to die," he says.

"Yes," she says. "But I'm going to die first." And then, with a great big breath, she pushes off and swoops down the slide. She disappears into the dark.

Adrienne doesn't cry about Fiona and she doesn't cry about Thatcher. One day, a gust of wind catches the screen door of her cottage and it whacks her in the side of the face, surprising her, stinging her. A different day, she orders a BLT from Something Natural and after a fifteen-minute wait in the pickup line, a college-age Irish girl tells Adrienne they've lost her order. The Irish girl flips to a fresh page on her pad. "What was it you wanted again, love?" These things make her cry.

Adrienne throws away the Amtrak napkin with her three rules on it. They didn't protect her. Her bank account has five digits in it for the first time in her life, but she doesn't care. It is almost impossible to believe that when she got here money was her only objective. Now money is nothing. It's less than nothing.

She gets a new job working at the front desk of the Nantucket Beach Club and Hotel. She can't believe she ever enjoyed hotel work. It's ho-hum eight-to-five stuff: check the guests in, check the guests out, run American Express cards, send the bellmen to the rooms with more towels, an ironing board, a crib. Adrienne works alone, while Mack pops in and out of an office behind the desk. There are hours when it is just her, the opera music, the wicker furniture, the quilts, and the antique children's toys in the lobby. She starts bringing a book so she won't think about Thatcher or Fiona. She tells herself that her mind is a room, and Thatcher and Fiona aren't allowed in.

Caren pays her rent through the fifteenth of October, but she and Duncan leave a week after the restaurant closes and so Adrienne lives alone in the cottage. Caren is kind upon leaving, offering to hook Adrienne up with her connections in St. Bart's: *You could rent my villa,* she says. *You could get a job. My friend Tate, you know, owns a spa, you could work for him maybe . . .* But Adrienne isn't ready to commit to winter plans, not when it's still so hot and sunny and heartbreakingly beautiful on Nantucket.

Adrienne goes out at night, though not to any of the places she went with Thatch. She favors the Brant Point Grill at the White Elephant because it's spacious and on certain nights has a jazz combo, and because she found it herself and she likes the bartender. He's older than Duncan and more seasoned, more refined. He doesn't act like he's doing her a favor to pour her a drink. She orders Triple 8 and tonics because they pack a quiet punch—three, four, five of those and something light off the bar menu, and for hours she floats around in a state of near-oblivion. She loses the haunting pain where she feels as though the best time of her life has come and gone in three short months.

One night she sees Doyle Chambers at the end of the bar, but he pretends not to recognize her. Ditto Grayson Parrish who comes in with a rotund, florid-faced woman whom Adrienne guesses is Nonnie Sizemore. But one awful night, she feels a hand on her shoulder, which shocks her. She realizes at that moment that she has gone weeks without anyone touching her. She turns around to see Charlie, Duncan's friend, wearing the marijuana leaf necklace. His face is stripped of his usual smugness. He looks as lonely as she feels.

"Hey," he says, and that one word conveys a sense that they are the two lone survivors from some kind of fallout.

"Hey."

"Have you seen Caren?" he asks. "Or Duncan?"

"They moved," Adrienne says, surprised that Charlie isn't aware of this fact, as chummy as he was with Duncan. "They live in Providence now. Duncan works for Holt."

Charlie takes a sip of beer and looks Adrienne over. "And what are you doing?"

"Working," she says. "At the Beach Club."

"Oh." Charlie reaches for his gold marijuana leaf and moves it along its chain wistfully, like a teenage girl. "Do you miss the restaurant?"

"Not really," she says.

"No," he says. "Me neither."

The next day on her way to work, Adrienne stops by the Bistro. An excavator is out on the beach tearing down the awning skeleton; it is as awful as watching somebody break bones. A Dumpster sits in the parking lot, filled with boards from the deck. Adrienne runs her hand over one and imagines she feels divots from her spike heels. Then she peeks in the front door. The restaurant is empty. The tables and chairs have been taken to the dump; Thatcher donated the dishes and silverware and glasses to a charity auction. The piano and the slab of blue granite have been moved to storage until the Elperns are ready for them. Someone has dragged the dory away, but its ghost remains: a boat-shaped patch of dry brown dirt.

Mack never asks personal questions. Compared to life at the Bistro, where everyone's business polluted the air like smoke, working at the hotel is bloodless, boring. It's just a job. But one day, shortly after Adrienne watched the bulldozers demolishing the bistro, Mack calls her into his office.

"The Harrisons said they saw you last night at the Brant Point Grill," he says.

"Did they?"

"They said you didn't recognize them."

"I try not to fraternize with guests outside of work," she says. "That was your suggestion."

"It was," Mack says. "They told me you were drunk. They were worried."

The Harrisons are an older couple from Quebec. Mrs. Harrison is another woman who wants to be Adrienne's mother; she fusses and clucks and makes a big deal about her every time they set foot in the lobby. Adrienne really liked the Harrisons until this very second.

"There's no reason for anyone to worry about me," she says. "I'm fine."

It takes fifteen late-night phone calls, several long letters, and Fiona's weak but charming attempt to write up a business plan for Thatcher to agree to come to Nantucket to look at this restaurant she's been talking about. He's hesitant on several fronts: Fiona is young and relatively inexperienced; he, Thatcher, knows nothing about the restaurant business or the business of living on an island. He fears Fiona is asking him to be her partner because he's the only person she knows who has access to real money. He can, with ease, sell his fifth of the carpet business. His brothers are greedy for it; Smith's Carpet and Flooring has become an empire.

He expresses his concerns to Fiona. She, repeatedly, expresses her concerns to him: She hates cooking on the line, the male cooks harass her, they won't stop talking about blow jobs, she has to get her own place, she has to be the boss.

"You're not talking to a normal person," she finally says over the phone late one night after her shift. "I can't put in eight or nine years before I strike out on my own. I don't have that kind of time."

She has never, in the long history of their friendship, invoked her illness as an excuse or a reason for special treatment and the fact that she does so now makes Thatcher see that she is serious. He agrees to come out to the island, sleep on the floor of Fiona's spartan cottage, and meet with the Realtor at the ungodly hour of six in the morning to see the place she's found. It's a burger shack, plain and simple: picnic tables in the sand sheltered by half-walls and an awning. The only things properly inside are the kitchen, the bathrooms, and a meager counter where one places an order, and yet the young, exhausted-looking real estate agent tells them the current owners want seven hundred thousand dollars for it. Fiona loves the place; she loves the way it sits on a beach all by itself like a restaurant on a deserted island. Thatcher remains skeptical; it's still too dark for him to even see the water.

"It's not close to anything," Thatcher says. "It's not in town. How will people know to come here?"

"It will be a destination restaurant," Fiona says. "Ever heard of the Michelin guide?"

"It doesn't even have floors," Thatcher says. How will he explain to his father that he's investing nearly three quarters of a million dollars in a building without floors?

"Let's look at the kitchen," Fiona says. She's skipping, giddy, as happy as he's ever seen her, already dressed in her whites for her other job. She is so small she looks like a child dressed up as a chef for Halloween. The kitchen is, at least, clean, and the appliances are impressively large and modern. Fiona opens the walk-in: it's stocked with burger patties and bags of French fries and tubs of mayonnaise.

"Have you ever eaten here?" Thatcher asks.

"Of course not," Fiona says.

They return to the dining room, where the real estate agent sits forlornly at one of the picnic tables, fiddling with a packet of ketchup. She has, she informed them on the drive out, shown the restaurant almost sixty times between the hours of six and seven A.M. or after eleven at night. In her opinion, it's overpriced.

"Don't you see it?" Fiona says.

"See what?"

"We'll get a piano player, and one of those zinc bars like they have at the bistros in Paris. We'll have white linen tablecloths, candlelight. We'll have new lives, Thatch. Me in the kitchen with a civilized crew, you up front greeting the guests. I can make crackers."

"You can make crackers?" He has no idea what she's talking about. She wants to spend all of his inheritance and then some on a fancy restaurant and make crackers? Still, he feels himself succumbing. If she makes crackers, they will be the best crackers on earth, he knows it.

She smiles at him. She has a burn mark on her cheek from a sauce that bubbled up the night before at work; the burn is round, the size of a dime. "This will be a great place."

"It has no floors," Thatcher says in a last ditch effort to escape his fate.

"The doctors gave me ten years," Fiona says. "Maybe fifteen."

"Maybe fifty," Thatcher says. He sighs, digs a toe in the sand, and nods toward the glum Realtor. Outside, the sky is lightening. "Let's do it, then. Let's make this lady's day."

TO: Ade12177@hotmail.com
FROM: DrDon@toothache.com
DATE: September 26, 2005, 7:01 P.M.
SUBJECT: wedding and worries

I will start by telling you what you already know which is that I am sick with worry about you. I wish you would call. I try you every night at the number you gave me for the cottage but you never answer and you are the last person in America without an answering machine. Please call me soon or I will mortify you by calling you at the hotel. You don't have to pretend to be happy. I just want to make sure you're breathing, eating, brushing.

The wedding has ballooned to include a few of the friends we've made here and some of Mavis's family from Louisiana, so now it's sixty people for sure with the possibility of seventy-five so we've gone and booked a banquet room at this wonderful restaurant in St. Michael's. You will love St. Mike's, and in fact, I think you should consider staying here in Maryland for a while, through the holidays at least. You can get a job if you want, though I would be happy to bankroll my little girl again for a few months so that you can simply relax and reflect and have some quiet time. That way I will see for myself that you're breathing, eating, and brushing.

I'm not sure, Adrienne, what you're still doing there. I worry.

Love love love.

Autumn arrives at the end of September. The weather grows cool and misty, the trees in town turn yellow and orange and red; at the end of her shift each afternoon, Adrienne lights a fire in the lobby's fireplace. Adrienne takes comfort in all this; it's been a long time since she experienced fall. On a rare excursion into town on her day off, she ventures into Dessert to buy herself a sweater. The woman with the red hair isn't in, and Adrienne feels both sorry and relieved. Part of her wants to be recognized as the hostess from the Blue Bistro, Thatcher's girlfriend, and part of her wishes the three months of summer never happened.

She spends a lot of time thinking about the summer before her mother died, her summer at Camp Hideaway. She had grown to love the smell of her cabin, and the soft flannel lining of her sleeping bag. She loved the certainty of flag raising and oatmeal with just-picked raspberries and Pammy Ipp who was her partner in everything from canoeing to late-night trips to the bathhouse. The summer at Hideaway was an escape to a place where the rules for the real world didn't apply. Her mother wasn't sick—her mythical brother was. But Adrienne had realized even then that it wouldn't last forever. The bubble would pop: She would leave behind the days of swimming in the cold green water of Lake Sherwood and sitting around the campfire singing "Red River Valley" as the very cute Nick Boccio strummed his guitar. She would confess the truth to Pammy Ipp and return home to spend August watching *General Hospital* in the air-conditioned dens of her regular, at-home friends, and visiting her mother in the hospital. In many ways it was as though Camp Hideaway had never happened, except it had, and now, so many years later, she was still thinking about it with longing and regret.

One night at the Brant Point Grill, a very quiet Monday night, Adrienne drinks too much. She received an e-mail from her father about his wedding, less than three weeks away, and she realizes she has to make a decision. Her lease at the cottage ends the day after Columbus Day. What *is* she still doing here? She's passing the time, filling up hours, waiting. The thought of not waiting, of going to Maryland or St. Bart's or some other place panics her. So she drinks her vodkas steadily and evenly, with purpose. She forgets to order food. It's the regular bartender's night off, and there's a young brunette woman in his stead. This girl pours with a smile so fake that Adrienne orders more often just to study her insincerity.

Next thing she knows, she's in the bartender's arms, inhaling the wholesome Aveda scent of her hair.

"Here we go," the bartender directs. "Toward the door."

Adrienne stares down at her feet (she is wearing a pair of red suede driving moccasins, a holdover from Aspen). She's doing some kind of dance step—stumbling, weaving, buckling.

"We're almost there," the bartender says. "I called you a cab, though you might need an ambulance." This is said with concern, probably more for her job than for Adrienne's well-being, though maybe not. The bartender's arms are strong and she handles Adrienne firmly but carefully, like she's a child.

"Do you have children?" Adrienne hears herself ask.

The bartender nods. "Three."

Adrienne tries to say something about how she hardly looks old enough but her words come out slurred and mangled and there isn't time to start the thought over because a cab whips into the circular driveway. The cabbie, who looks familiar somehow, accepts Adrienne from the bartender and pours her into the backseat of the cab.

She wakes up at four in the morning with her face stuck to the linoleum floor of the kitchen, but she's powerless to move. At seven thirty, when the sun comes up, she crawls to the phone and calls Mack.

Not coming in today, she says. *Too sick to work.*

Two days later, she agrees to work a double as penance. Tiny, the night desk person, wants a break, and Adrienne volunteers to cover for her. In addition to getting Adrienne out of the doghouse with Mack, it will keep her away from the bars. She has promised herself she will never drink again, and she wonders how long it will be until she wants to.

Adrienne has never worked the night desk before and she finds that she likes it. Between six and seven o'clock, the hotel guests meet cabs out front or walk into town for dinner. All the other great places are still open: Club Car, Boarding House, 21 Federal, American Seasons, Company of the Cauldron, Le Languedoc, Blue Fin, 56 Union, the Pearl, Cinco. Then, when most of the guests have wandered out, Adrienne puts on some opera and makes herself a cup of tea and enjoys the fire.

She is a person with a broken heart. That hardly makes her special. It happens to everyone. She herself broke Michael Sullivan's heart less than three years earlier. How does she think he felt banging around Chatham after she fled for Hawaii? He probably felt like she does now. Adrienne considers calling him up to apologize. Then she thinks about calling Pammy Ipp.

St. Michael's might not be so bad, she thinks. It's another charming resort town that probably needs help through Christmas. She can attend her father's wedding and simply stay with him and Mavis in their new home. In January, she can try St. Bart's, maybe, if she feels up to it. Then in the spring she might join Kyra and the landscape painter in Carmel. So there it is: An entire year of possibility. Adrienne feels better than she has since Fiona's collapse. She feels clean and right-headed and warm, in her new sweater in front of the fire. Her heart is broken, but it will heal. That's what hearts do.

And then, she feels a blast of cold air. The door opens and Mario walks in.

At first, Adrienne mistakes him for a late check-in: a handsome, dark-haired man in a black silk shirt, jeans, tweed blazer. Her newfound optimism blooms, because maybe what she needs is a mild flirtation to carry her even farther from her sadness. But as the man approaches, Adrienne's mind whispers, *Mario. Is it him? No. Yes, it is. No. It is so. It's him.*

She stands perfectly still, her left hand wrapped around the now-cold mug of tea. She wonders if he's heard about her poor showing at the Brant Point Grill. (She finally figured out that the cabbie who drove her home that night was the same one who had picked her up from the Subiacos' first party, because she didn't remember giving him her address, and yet she arrived home safely.) Maybe Mario is here to suggest AA. Or maybe he's come to declare his love for her, and how will Adrienne feel about that? Will she be able, in the face of all her pain and rejection, to turn him down? She takes a shallow breath. Maybe he's here to ask her again about working at his new restaurant, or to show her the piece that has finally been run in *Vanity Fair* (Adrienne has the issue at home but can't bring herself to read it). Or maybe he's just here to catch up because they had, after all, been friends. But his stride is purposeful and his black eyes are intent and Adrienne is petrified. She clenches the mug. He doesn't try to kiss her or hug her; he doesn't even greet her. But he does, with two swift words, cut the rope that ties Adrienne to the heavy load of her uncertainty. She's finished waiting.

Mario's voice is low and husky, barely audible over the crackling fire and the Andrea Bocelli.

"Thatcher's back," he says.

Fiona hasn't been off the vent for more than an hour at a time since they got to the hospital, and when she does come off, the nurses have warned her not to talk— talking uses up too much oxygen. The corners of Fiona's mouth are cracked and bleeding from all the times she's been intubated. Her O₂ sats are very low, the new drug has failed; Fiona won't be getting any better. The doctors suggested Thatcher call Fiona's parents. They're on their way. This is it—Thatcher knows it and Fiona knows it and yet neither of them can speak.

All along, Thatcher has had a plan: Marry her. He's talked about it with Father Ott. For months, they've gone over the sticky emotional territory. Fiona yearns to be married, and what she really wanted was to marry JZ. But JZ is already married; he had a chance to make things right with Fiona and he blew it. So that leaves Thatcher, who wants to make a pledge of his devotion to this person—his friend, his partner, his first love. She is more his family than his own family. He has planned to marry her all along and she agreed to it only by saying, "At the very end. If nobody else wants us."

How ironic, and awful, that this was the summer Thatcher fell in love. He didn't think it was possible—at age thirty-five, as solitary as he liked to be, as devoted to his business and Fiona, as impermeable to romance—and yet, one morning, just as he was wondering where he was going to find the kind of help that would enable him to make it through the summer, there she was. Adrienne Dealey. Beautiful, yes, but he loves Adrienne not because she is beautiful but because she is different. He has never known a woman so free from conceit, vanity, ambition, and pretense. He has never known a woman so willing to show the world that she is a human being. He has never known a woman with such an appetite—a literal appetite, but also an appetite for adventure—the places she's been, unafraid, all by herself. Thatcher loves her in a huge, mature, adult way. He loves her the right way. Now he has to hope that God grants her patience and understanding and faith. Whenever he prays these days, he prays for Adrienne, too.

He calls the hospital chapel and reserves it for two hours. He orders flowers from the gift shop near Admitting. They aren't prepared to outfit a wedding, but they can put together a bouquet. One of the nurses in oncology plays the piano; Thatcher discovers her lunch hour is from one thirty to two thirty. He phones Father Ott who is staying at the rectory of St. Ann's, then he takes Fiona's hand. Her hands are so important to her for chopping and dicing and mixing and blending and stirring and rolling and sprinkling, and yet she's always been so self-conscious about her swollen fingers and her discolored fingernails that he's never been allowed to touch them. There's a scar across her left palm from the day she picked up a hot sauté pan without a side towel. She went to the emergency room for that burn, and for the stitches she got when she cut herself while boning a duck breast—fifteen stitches across the tips of her second and third fingers. There are other marks and scars that Thatcher can't identify; if he could, he'd ask her about each one.

She's off the vent but her eyes are closed.

"Fiona," he says.

She opens her eyes.

"We're getting married at two o'clock."

The words terrify him, because he knows that she'll know what they signify. At the very end. If nobody else wants us.

Fiona's lips are cracked and bleeding, and although it must hurt, she smiles.

In this ward of the hospital there isn't much in the way of good news, but everyone is excited about a wedding. Thatcher goes back to his room at the hotel to shower, shave, and change, and he spends a full, precious five minutes considering the telephone.

Call Adrienne? And say what?

When he returns, the nurses have put Fiona back on the vent—just until she's ready to go—and they have changed her into a fresh white johnny and brushed her hair so that it flows down over the top of the sheet. The gift shop has done a beautiful job with the bouquet of roses and Fiona holds it as they unhook her from the ventilator and wheel her down the corridor toward the chapel. Thatcher tries to be present in the moment, he tries not to peer behind the half-open doors they pass, he tries not to listen to the dialogue of the soap operas on TV. The attending nurse, a woman named Ella, chatters about her own wedding twenty-eight years earlier at the steepled Congregational Church in Acton.

"Do you have rings?" Ella whispers to Thatcher.

He has rings, expensive rings purchased that morning from Shreve, Crump & Low. As Ella and Thatcher wheel Fiona's gurney into the chapel, he checks his shirt pocket for their delicate presence—two circles wrapped in tissue paper. The chapel is a brown room, dimly lit, with sturdy, functional-looking wooden benches and a large plain wooden cross hanging over the carpeted stairs of the altar. Father Ott waits there, all six foot six of him, in his flowing white robe. Oncology nurse, Teri Lee, a diminutive Korean woman, waits for Thatcher's signal, and then she starts to play Pachelbel's Canon in D. On this piano, in this chapel, under these circumstances, the music is plaintive. A third nurse named Kristin Benedict is sitting in the first row; she has spent a great many hours caring for Fiona, and what makes her even more special is that she's eaten at the Bistro (in the summer of 1996, while she was on vacation with her husband). Thatcher has

317

asked her to be a witness. Kristin is a crier; she sobs quietly as Teri plays the piano, as the gurney moves down the aisle, Thatcher on one side, Ella on the other. Once they reach the altar, the music subsides, Thatcher takes Fiona's scarred hand and Father Ott raises his arms and proclaims in his resonant voice: "We gather here today in the name of the Father, and of the Son, and of the Holy Spirit."

Thatcher crosses himself and out of the corner of his eye, he sees Fiona lift her hand and cross herself. She is smiling.

Father Ott leads them, briskly, through the age-old wedding vows. He is hurrying, Thatcher suspects, because no one knows how long Fiona will last without oxygen. Thatcher tries, tries, to stay present in the moment, and not to think of how Father Ott will, at some point, give Fiona the sacrament of Last Rites, he will anoint her with oil, he will whisper Psalm 23 into her deaf ear. Fiona's parents are to land at Logan at six o'clock. Thatcher offered to pick them up but Mrs. Kemp doesn't want Fiona to be alone, even for a second. Thatcher is shaking. Fiona will die, she will be cold to the touch, gone from Thatcher in every human sense, even though she is alive now—she is alive and he is marrying her and she is marrying him. They are getting married, honoring the thirty years that they've been best friends—through the chocolate swirl cheesecake, and the beer on the playground, and the day they bought the restaurant, and every moment in between and since.

Fiona is smiling. She takes a deep breath and whispers, "I do." *Thatcher slips a ring on her finger. It's way too big and he's crushed because he wants her to take the ring with her when she goes. She holds it in place with her thumb. Thatcher puts on his own ring; he swears he will never take it off. Father Ott bestows a blessing and they cross themselves again, but not Fiona; her eyes are glazing over, she's checking out. But not yet! Not yet!*

"You may kiss the bride," *Father Ott says. Teri Lee starts in with the piano and Kristin Benedict sobs and Thatcher kisses Fiona, his new wife, on her cracked lips. For the first time ever, he kisses her.*

Adrienne doesn't sleep.

She was able to wheedle only the most basic information out of Mario before he checked his watch and claimed he was late meeting Louis and Hector at the Rope Walk and left. The basic information was this: Thatcher was back, Mario had bumped into him at the airport, Thatcher asked if Mario had seen Adrienne and Mario said no. Thatcher asked Mario to find Adrienne and let her know that he, Thatcher, wanted to talk to her.

Talk to me about what? Adrienne asked.

He didn't say.

This is not something she bargained for: Thatcher, here, on Nantucket, looking for her. The restaurant is gone, Fiona is dead, and Adrienne is most comfortable placing Thatcher in a similar category: disappeared, vanished, nonexistent. Easier that way to banish him from her mind. Not so easy now that she knows he is asleep (or not) on this tiny island.

She gets home from work at eleven thirty and sits in her kitchen with all the lights off contemplating a glass of wine. But no, she's promised herself, no. She tries to read, she tries turning off the light and closing her eyes. She gets up and looks out into her backyard—the one big tree is swaying. It's windy, but not particularly cold. She throws on a fleece and goes outside. She feels better being outside.

She rides her bike to Thatcher's cottage, the cottage behind the big house in town. There is a light on. She feels like if she opens her mouth, something awful will come out. He's right there, ten feet away, in that cottage, and she panics because she can't face him, she can't deal with closure; it will kill her, and those words are so wrong, so harsh in light of what he's just been through, but they will kill her in a sense. Closure will destroy her fragile sense of okay-for-now. Seeing him will ruin every step toward healing that she's made in the last month.

She rides her bike home and makes a decision. She has to leave. Tomorrow.

She spends the rest of the night packing up her clothes, her new pairs of beautiful shoes, the hand bell. Mack will not be happy that she's leaving him with two weeks until the hotel closes for the season, but what else can she do? At first light, she writes out a note of apology and hops back on her bike. Cowardly girl, she thinks, quitting by note. She will never be able to use Mack or Thatcher as a reference. This is a summer that will be missing from her résumé. The summer that didn't count. The summer that was a mistake.

Nantucket is too beautiful to be a mistake, however, especially this morning. The sun comes up and the sky is pale at first with the promise of that brilliant blue; the air is crisp and rich with smells of the water. She pedals down the road toward the Beach Club, trying to correct her thinking. Nantucket was not a mistake. She learned so much about food, about wine, about people, about herself. Because it is so early and she still has lots of time, she takes the turn in the road that she made the first day here—the stretch that leads to the spot where the Bistro used to be. From a hundred yards away, she sees the frame of the Elperns' new house. It's impressively large, as large as Holt Millman's house. She is so amazed that something so tall and grandiose could be built in two short weeks that she doesn't notice the silver truck in the parking lot until it's too late. But then, once she does see the truck, right there, his truck, a strange thing happens: She keeps going, propelling herself closer to the very thing she's running away from.

Thatcher stands in the parking lot wearing his red fleece jacket, his hands in his pockets, staring at the house. Adrienne has plenty of time to turn around, a more than good chance of leaving undetected. But she is drawn to him. She wonders what it feels like to be looking at the thing that is standing in the place where your life used to be. Is it awful? Is it a relief?

"Thatcher," she says.

He whips around; she's scared him. Good. She wanted to scare him. He stares at her a second, and she dismounts her bike. He squeezes her so tightly she cries out and then, before she knows it, they're kissing. They're kissing and Adrienne starts to cry.

"I'm sorry," Adrienne says. "About Fee. I'm so sorry."

He holds her face in his hands. She can feel his wedding band against her cheek.

"I love you," he says. "I know you don't believe it, but I do."

She does believe it, but she's afraid to say so.

"I wanted to call, but . . . it's been so . . . I was in South Bend for three weeks . . . I wasn't sure if you'd understand . . . I felt like, God, if I got back and you were still here . . ."

"I was going to leave today," she says. She holds up the note, which she has been crushing in her palm since she left her house. "I was about to tell Mack and go."

"Because of me?"

She nods; there are more tears. She can't predict what's going to happen: Is it good, is it bad? Will he come with her to her father's wedding? And what on earth will they do after that? Another restaurant? Another business? Will he marry her and be a man who wears two wedding rings? Maybe he will. And since when is she the kind of person who needs so many answers?

While she was packing her bags she took a minute and inspected the hand bell that Duncan bequeathed to her, the one he rang each night for last call. Inside the bottom rim, she found an inscription: "To Thatcher Smith with appreciation from the Parish of St. Joseph's, South Bend, Indiana." It had alarmed her that she was taking Thatcher's bell, but at the same time she felt she had a right to it; she felt she had earned that small piece of Thatcher. She is not sure she deserves more than that small piece; she is not at all sure she deserves what she has now: his whole self in her arms, declaring his love.

"I want to talk to you," Thatcher says. "So I can tell you I love you. What time do you have to be at work?"

She crumples the note to Mack in her hand. "Eight thirty."

"That's in two hours," he says, checking his beautiful watch.

"What should we do?" she asks.

Thatcher turns her so that she is facing the Elpern house; it will be a lovely house when it is finished. He takes her hand and leads her to his truck and he picks up her bike with one hand and lays it down in the back.

Adrienne doesn't ask where they are going; she already knows.

They are going to breakfast.

Acknowledgments

This one, especially, took a village.

I could never have written this book without the support of the restaurant community on Nantucket.

Robert Sarkisian, H.H. at 21 Federal, talked with me for hours, fed me, allowed me to "work" during Christmas Stroll 2002, and gave me access to his staff, all of whom were honest and charming. Special thanks to Chris Passerati, Dan Sabauda, Russell Jaehnig, and Johnny Bresette, bartender extraordinaire, who very much wanted me to change the name of the bartender in this book from Duncan to "Johnny B."

Al and Andrea Kovalencik, of the exquisite jewel-box restaurant, Company of the Cauldron, shared hours of stories with me from their rich and varied experience in the "resort life."

Joanna Polowy, pastry chef, taught me about the sweeter side of the restaurant business.

Angela and Seth Raynor, owner and chef/owner of The Boarding House and the Pearl, told me more stories than I could possibly include in one book. Angela also inadvertently gave me the idea for this book. In the summer of 2000, when my novel *The Beach Club* was released, Angela said to me, "We decided in the back [of the house] that you could never write a restaurant book. Too scandalous." Thank you, Angela!

Finally, I am indebted to Geoffrey, David, and Jane Silva of The Galley, who for the twelve years as my friends have demonstrated how to gracefully run a successful beachfront restaurant.

I read comprehensively about restaurants, culinary schools, and food and wine. The following publications were especially helpful: *The Art of Eating* by M. F. K. Fisher, *Becoming a Chef* by Andrew Dornenburg and Karen Page, *Cosmopolitan: A Bartender's Life* by Toby Cecchini, *The Fourth Star* by Leslie Brenner, *The Making of a Pastry Chef* by Andrew MacLauchlan, *Waiting: The True Confessions of a Waitress* by Debra Ginsberg, *The Making of a Chef* and *The Soul of a Chef* by Michael Ruhlman, *If You Can Stand the Heat* by Dawn Davis, *Kitchen Confidential* by Anthony Bourdain, *The Last Days of Haute Cuisine* by Patric Kuh, and what felt like hundreds of issues of *Bon Appétit* and *Gourmet*.

Thank you to my early readers: Mrs. Pat van Ryn, Tom and Leslie Bresette, Amanda Congdon, Debbie Bennett, and, as ever, Heather Osteen Thorpe. Thank you to Wendy Hudson of Bookworks and Mimi Beman of Mitchell's Book Corner. It is a lucky writer who has two stellar independent bookstores on her home island. In New York, as always, thanks to Michael Carlisle, Jennifer Weis, and Stefanie Lindskog.

Finally, thank you to the people who gave me the time, space, and support to write. My sitters (who are also friends): Becca Evans, Julia Chumak, Kristen Jurgensen, Jennifer Chadwick, and Dan Bowling. My friends (who are also, occasionally, sitters): Amanda Congdon, Anne Gifford, Sally Bates Hall, Margie Holahan, Susan Storey Johnsen, and Wendy Rouillard. My sons' school: The Children's House of Nantucket. The sanest hour of my week: the Thursday morning parenting group. My mother, Sally Hilderbrand, and my husband, Chip Cunningham.

Chip shines his light on my every page. In this instance, I am especially grateful to him for sharing the details of his beautiful and unique friendship with Katie van Ryn, who died from complications of cystic fibrosis in 1995 at the age of thirty.

Sun-drenched reading with soul from
Elin Hilderbrand

"Simply a great read."
—Kathleen Hughes

"Things get more twisted
at every turn." —*Publishers Weekly*

"A work of fiction you're likely to
think about long after you've
put it down." —*People*

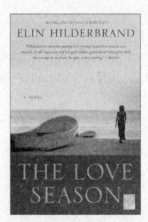

"Eminently readable results . . .
so gratifying." —*Entertainment Weekly*
(Grade: A-)

St. Martin's Griffin
www.stmartins.com